whistle

A NEW GOTHAM CITY HERO

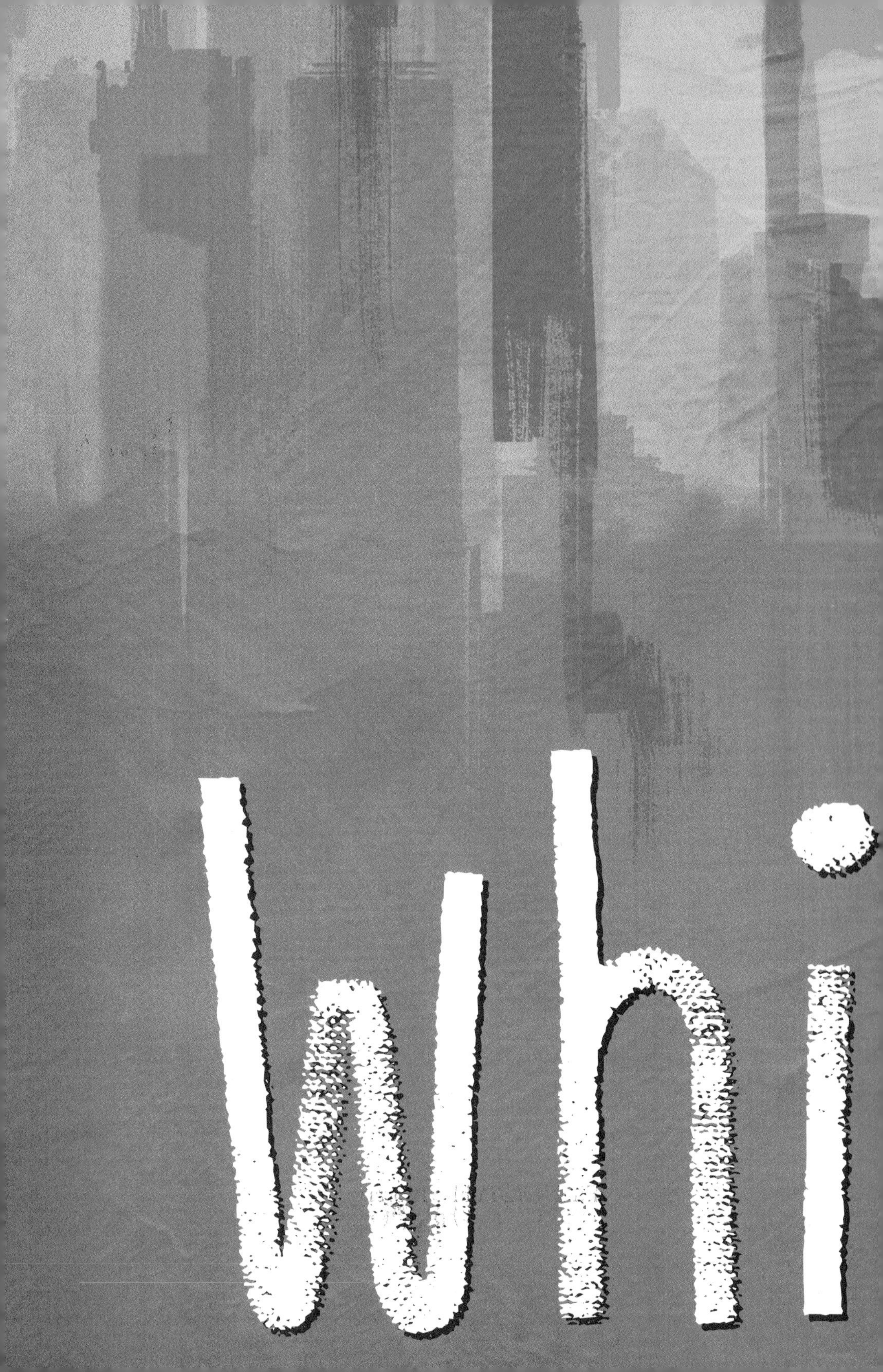
whi

written by
E. LOCKHART

illustrated by
MANUEL PREITANO

colors by
GABBY METZLER

letters by
ALW's TROY PETERI

A NEW
GOTHAM
CITY HERO

st:le

Diego Lopez Editor **Steve Cook** Design Director – Books
Amie Brockway-Metcalf Publication Design **Sandy Alonzo** Publication Production

Marie Javins Editor-in-Chief, DC Comics

Daniel Cherry III Senior VP – General Manager **Jim Lee** Publisher & Chief Creative Officer
Joen Choe VP – Global Brand & Creative Services **Don Falletti** VP – Manufacturing Operations & Workflow Management
Lawrence Ganem VP – Talent Services **Alison Gill** Senior VP – Manufacturing & Operations
Nick J. Napolitano VP – Manufacturing Administration & Design **Nancy Spears** VP – Revenue

WHISTLE: A NEW GOTHAM CITY HERO
Published by DC Comics. Copyright © 2021 DC Comics.
All Rights Reserved. All characters, their distinctive
likenesses, and related elements featured in this
publication are trademarks of DC Comics. The stories,
characters, and incidents featured in this publication are
entirely fictional. DC Comics does not read or accept
unsolicited submissions of ideas, stories, or artwork.
DC – a WarnerMedia Company.

DC Comics, 2900 West Alameda Ave.,
Burbank, CA 91505
Printed by LSC Communications, Crawfordsville, IN, USA.
7/30/21. First Printing.
ISBN: 978-1-4012-9322-2

Library of Congress Cataloging-in-Publication Data

Names: Lockhart, E., writer. | Preitano, Manuel, illustrator. | Metzler,
   Gabby, colourist. | Peteri, Troy, letterer.
Title: Whistle : a new Gotham City hero / written by E. Lockhart ;
   illustrated by Manuel Preitano ; colors by Gabby Metzler ; letters by
   ILW's Troy Peteri.
Description: Burbank, CA : DC Comics, [2021] | Audience: Ages 13+ |
   Audience: Grades 10-12 | Summary: Sixteen-year-old Willow Zimmerman
   reconnects with estranged family friend and real estate tycoon E. Nigma,
   but after he helps her earn enough for medical treatments for her mom
   she is attacked by the monstrous Killer Croc and upon waking after the
   fight she gains powers and insight she will need to make the right
   choices.
Identifiers: LCCN 2021003172 (print) | LCCN 2021003173 (ebook) | ISBN
   9781401293222 (paperback) | ISBN 9781779508737 (ebook)
Subjects: LCSH: Graphic novels. | CYAC: Graphic novels. | Ability--Fiction.
Classification: LCC PZ7.7.L63 Wh 2021 (print) | LCC PZ7.7.L63 (ebook) |
   DDC 741.5/973--dc23
LC record available at https://lccn.loc.gov/2021003172
LC ebook record available at https://lccn.loc.gov/2021003173

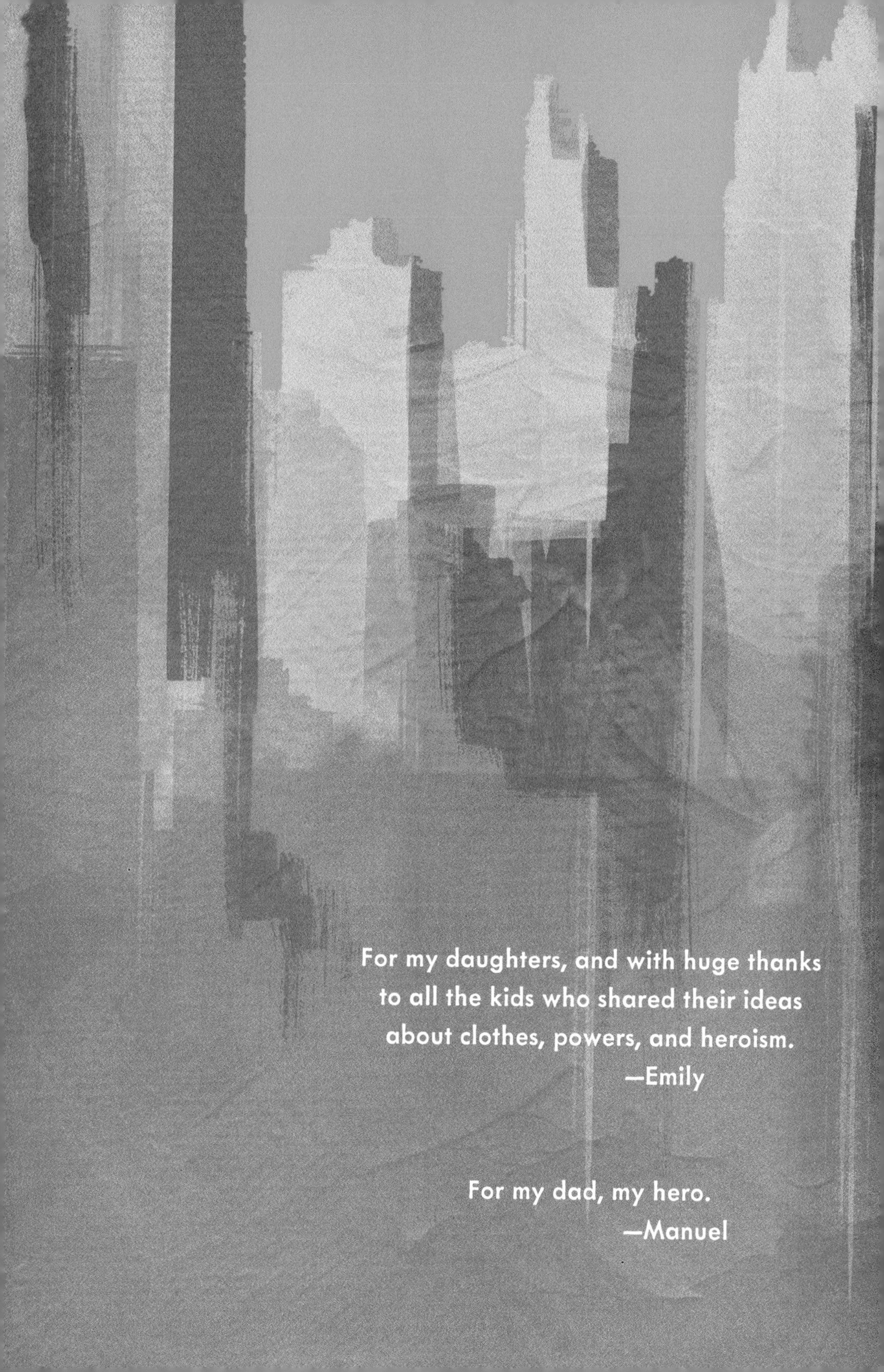

For my daughters, and with huge thanks
to all the kids who shared their ideas
about clothes, powers, and heroism.
—Emily

For my dad, my hero.
—Manuel

part one: **concrete jungle**

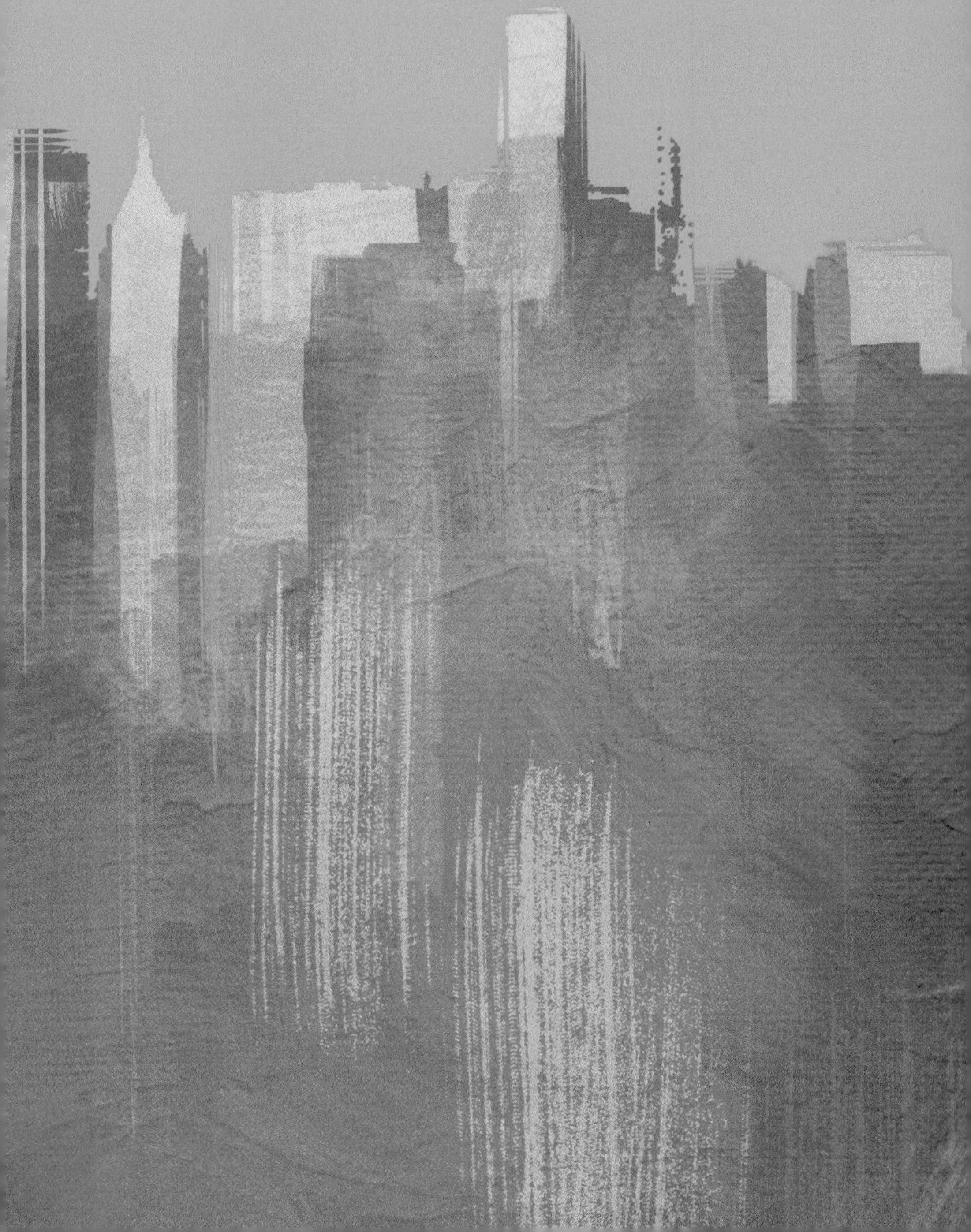

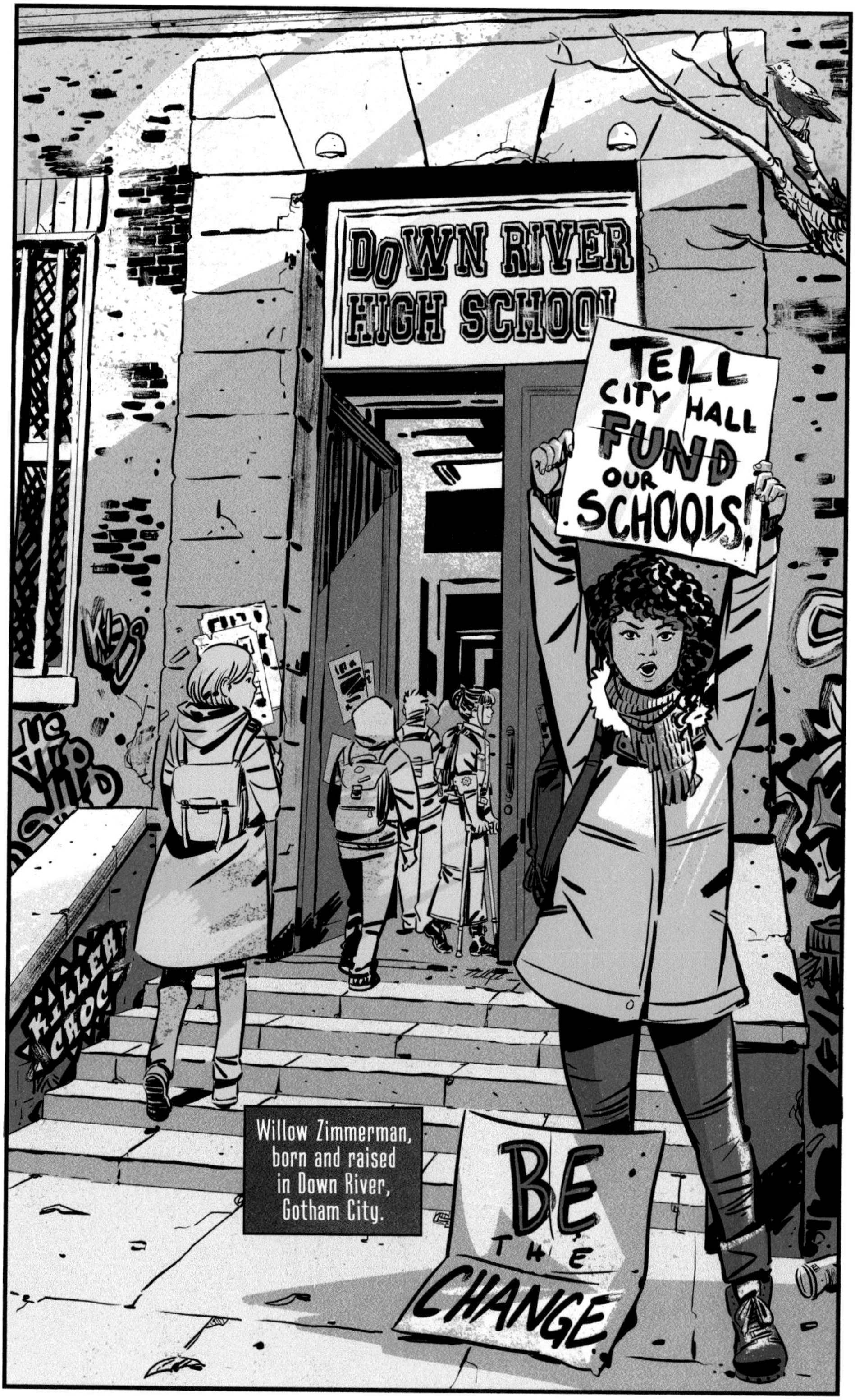
DOWN RIVER HIGH SCHOOL
TELL CITY HALL FUND OUR SCHOOLS!
KILLER CROC
Willow Zimmerman, born and raised in Down River, Gotham City.
BE THE CHANGE

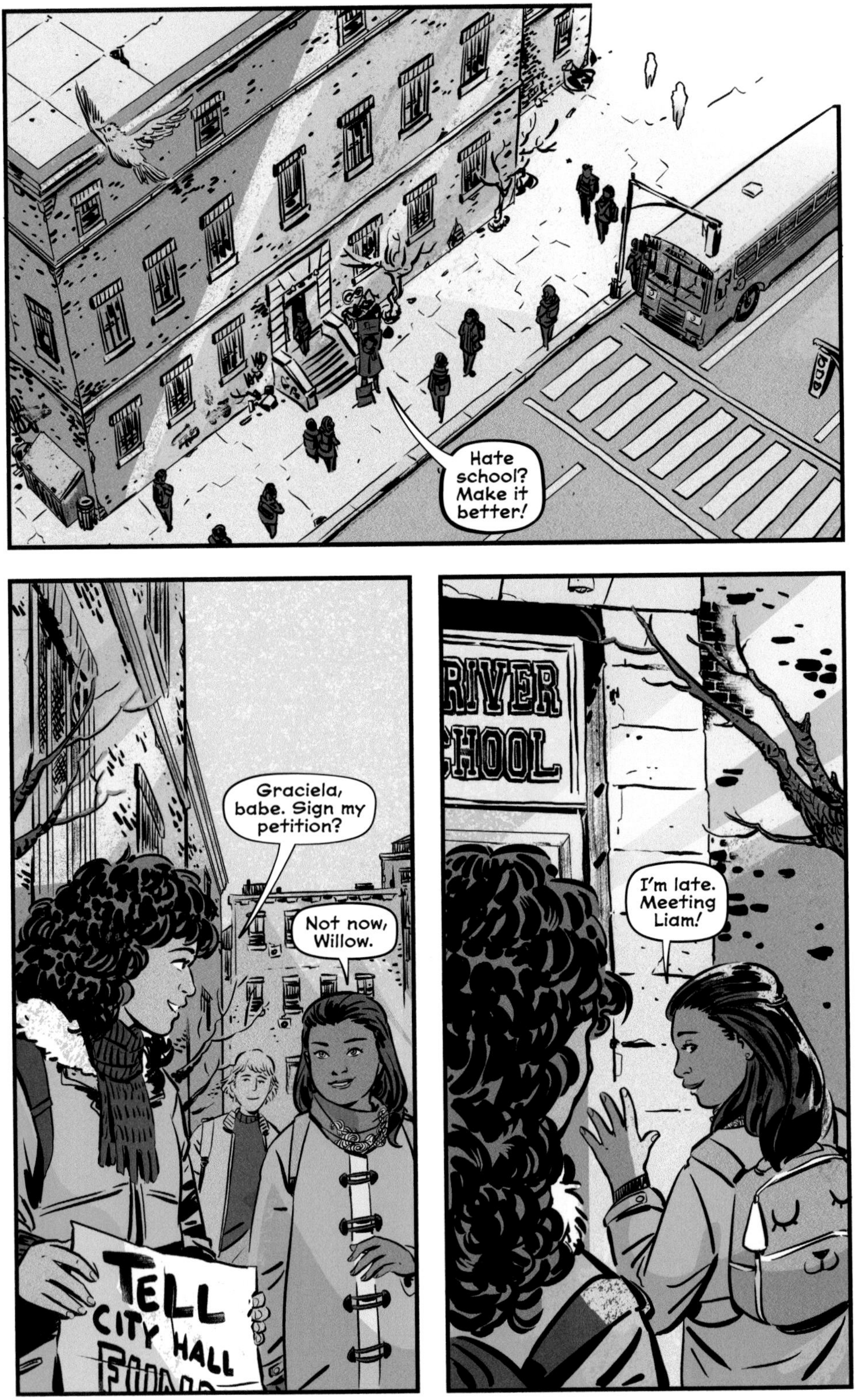
Hate school? Make it better!
Graciela, babe. Sign my petition?
Not now, Willow.
TELL
CITY HALL
I'm late. Meeting Liam!

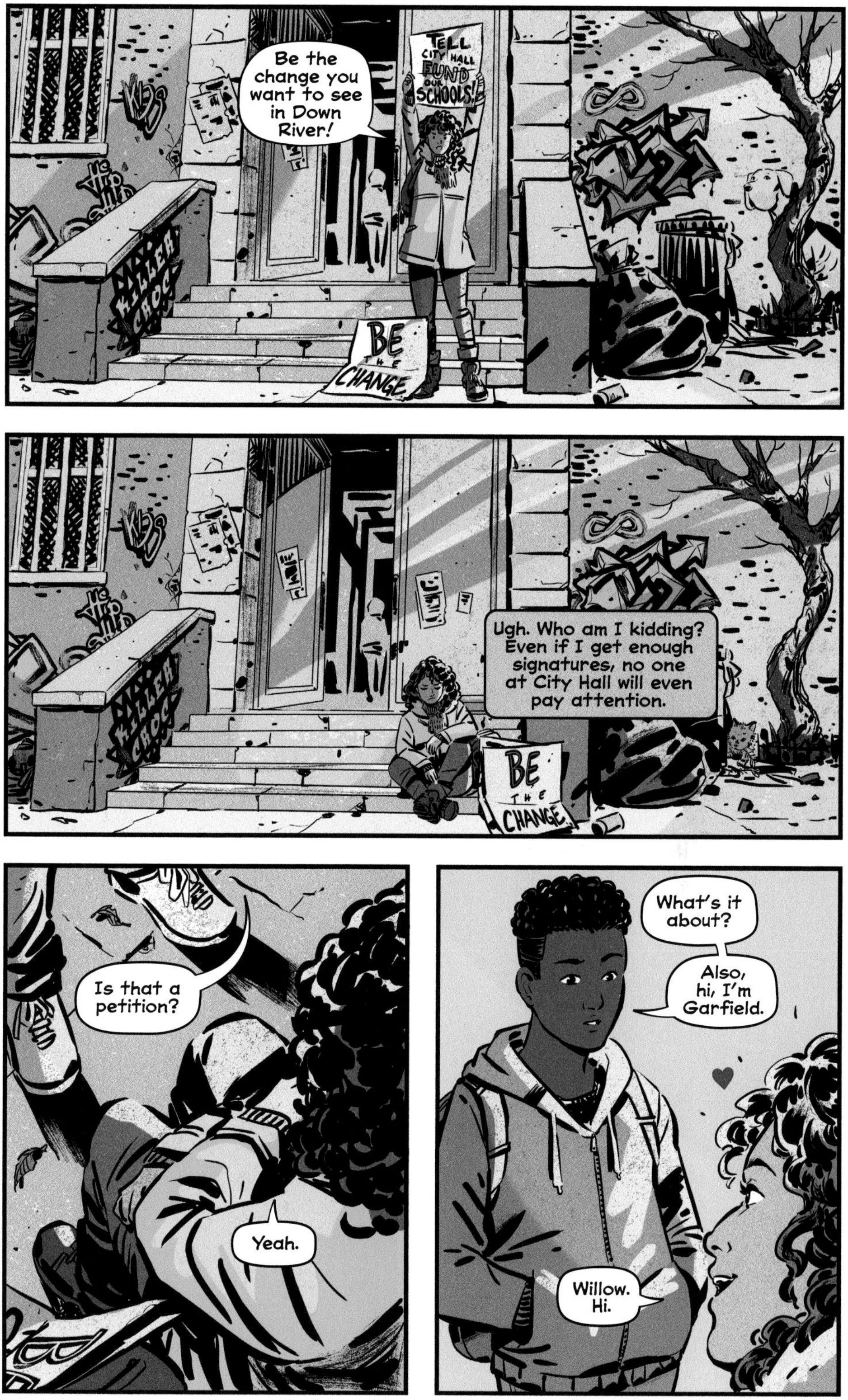
Be the change you want to see in Down River!
TELL CITY HALL FUND OUR SCHOOLS!
BE THE CHANGE
Ugh. Who am I kidding? Even if I get enough signatures, no one at City Hall will even pay attention.
BE THE CHANGE
Is that a petition?
Yeah.
What's it about?
Also, hi, I'm Garfield.
Willow. Hi.

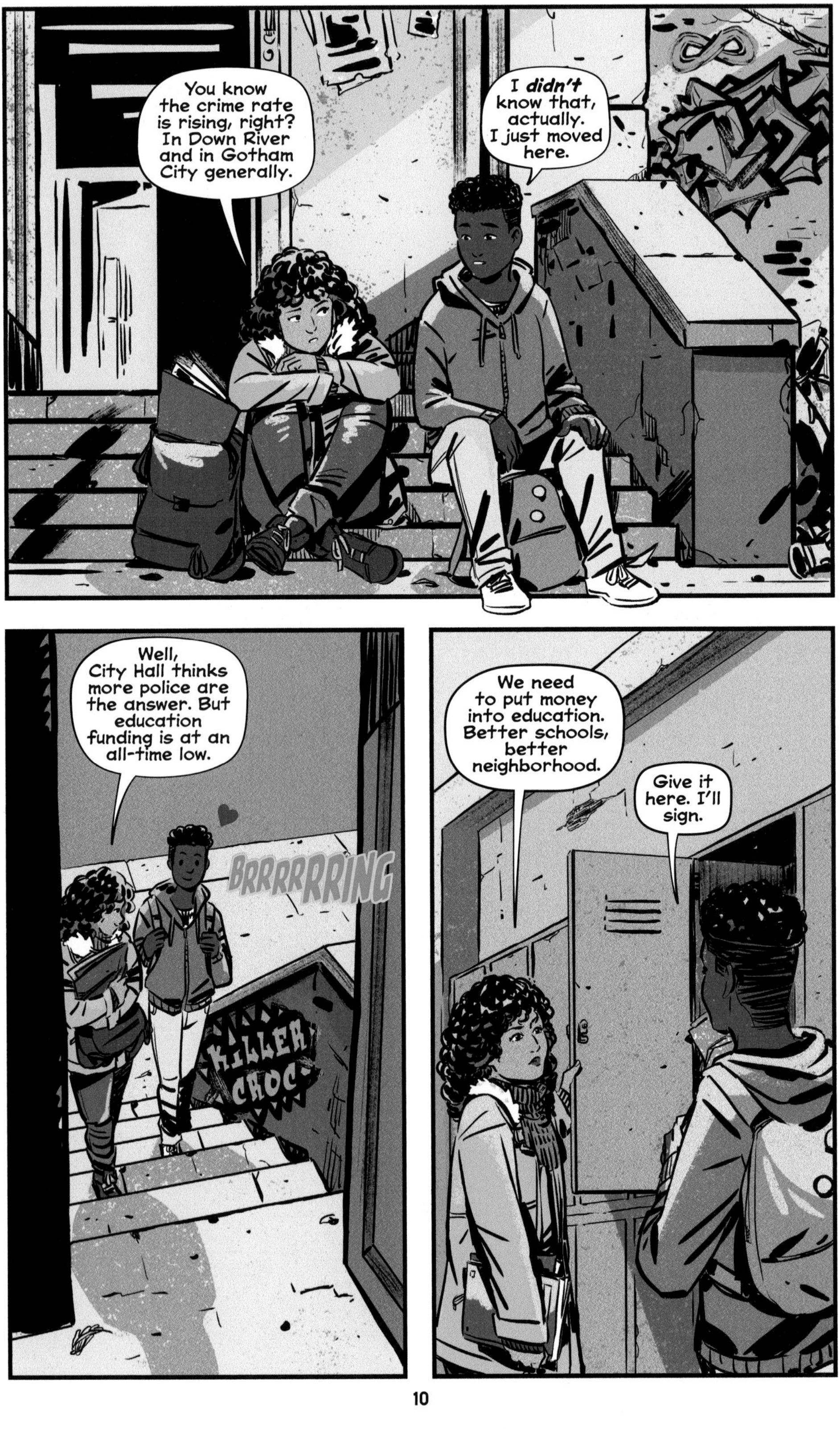
You know the crime rate is rising, right? In Down River and in Gotham City generally.
I *didn't* know that, actually. I just moved here.
Well, City Hall thinks more police are the answer. But education funding is at an all-time low.
BRRRRRRING
KILLER CROC
We need to put money into education. Better schools, better neighborhood.
Give it here. I'll sign.

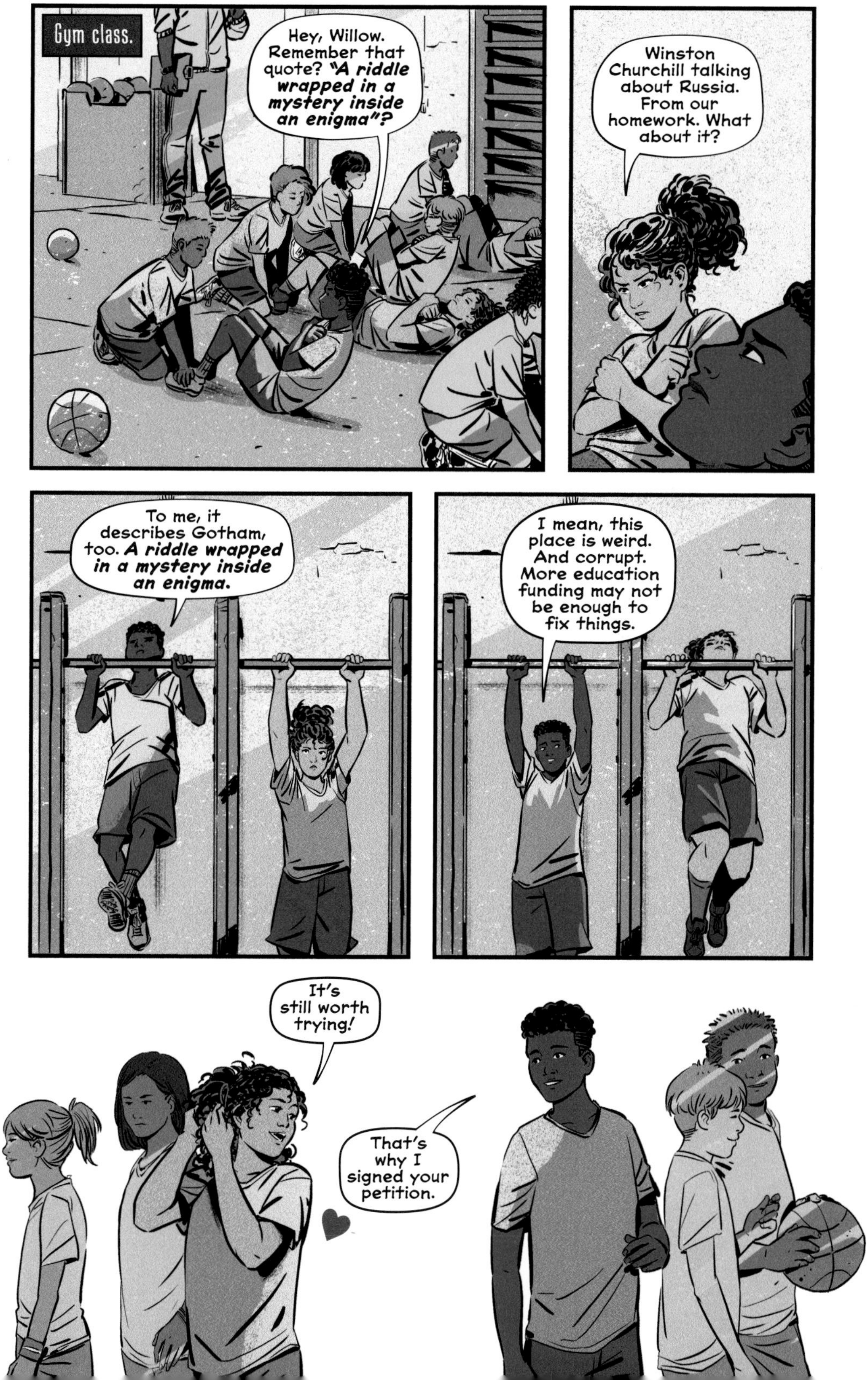
Gym class.
Hey, Willow. Remember that quote? *"A riddle wrapped in a mystery inside an enigma"?*
Winston Churchill talking about Russia. From our homework. What about it?
To me, it describes Gotham, too. ***A riddle wrapped in a mystery inside an enigma.***
I mean, this place is weird. And corrupt. More education funding may not be enough to fix things.
It's still worth trying!
That's why I signed your petition.

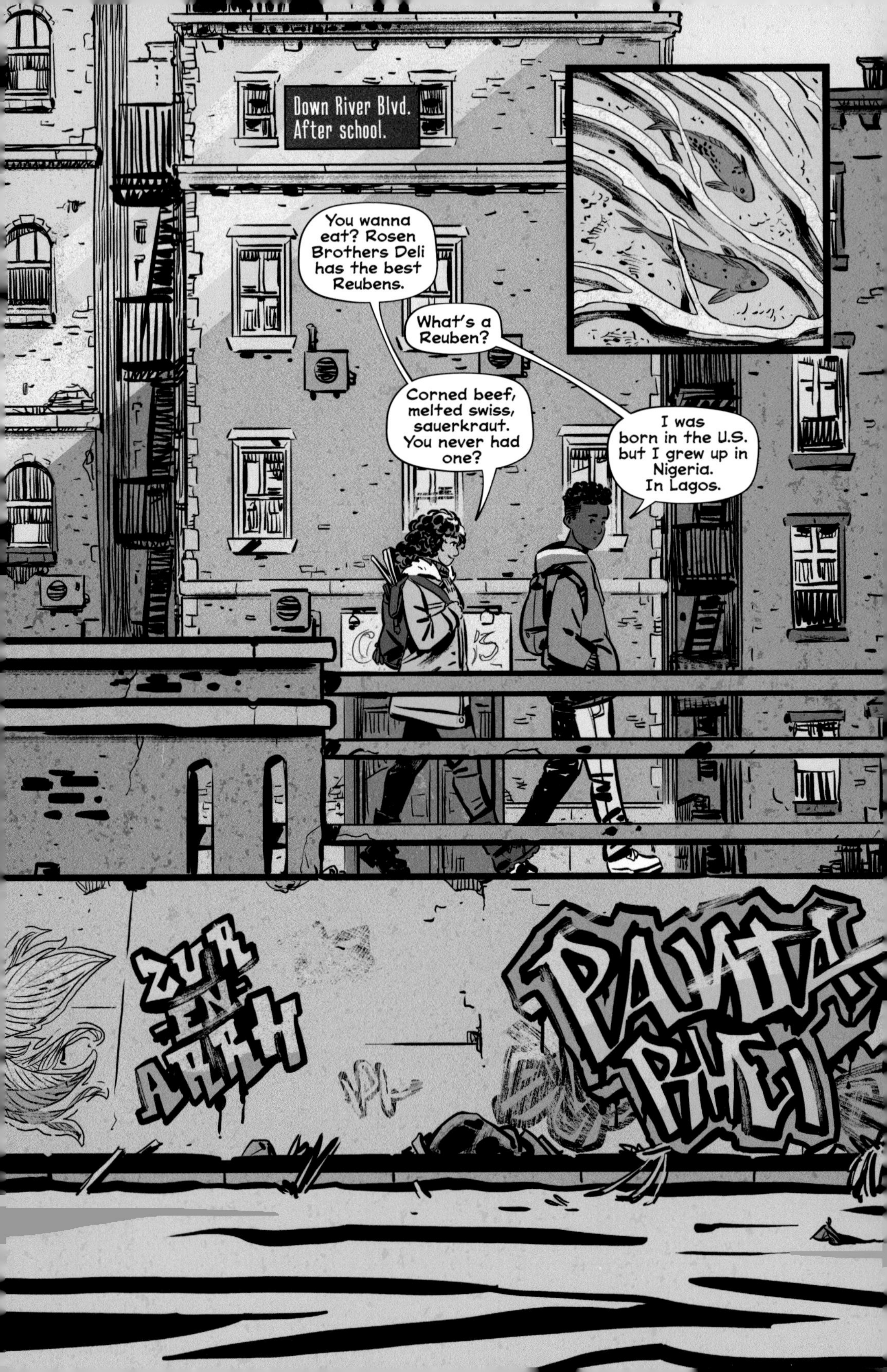

Down River Blvd.
After school.
You wanna eat? Rosen Brothers Deli has the best Reubens.
What's a Reuben?
Corned beef, melted swiss, sauerkraut. You never had one?
I was born in the U.S. but I grew up in Nigeria. In Lagos.

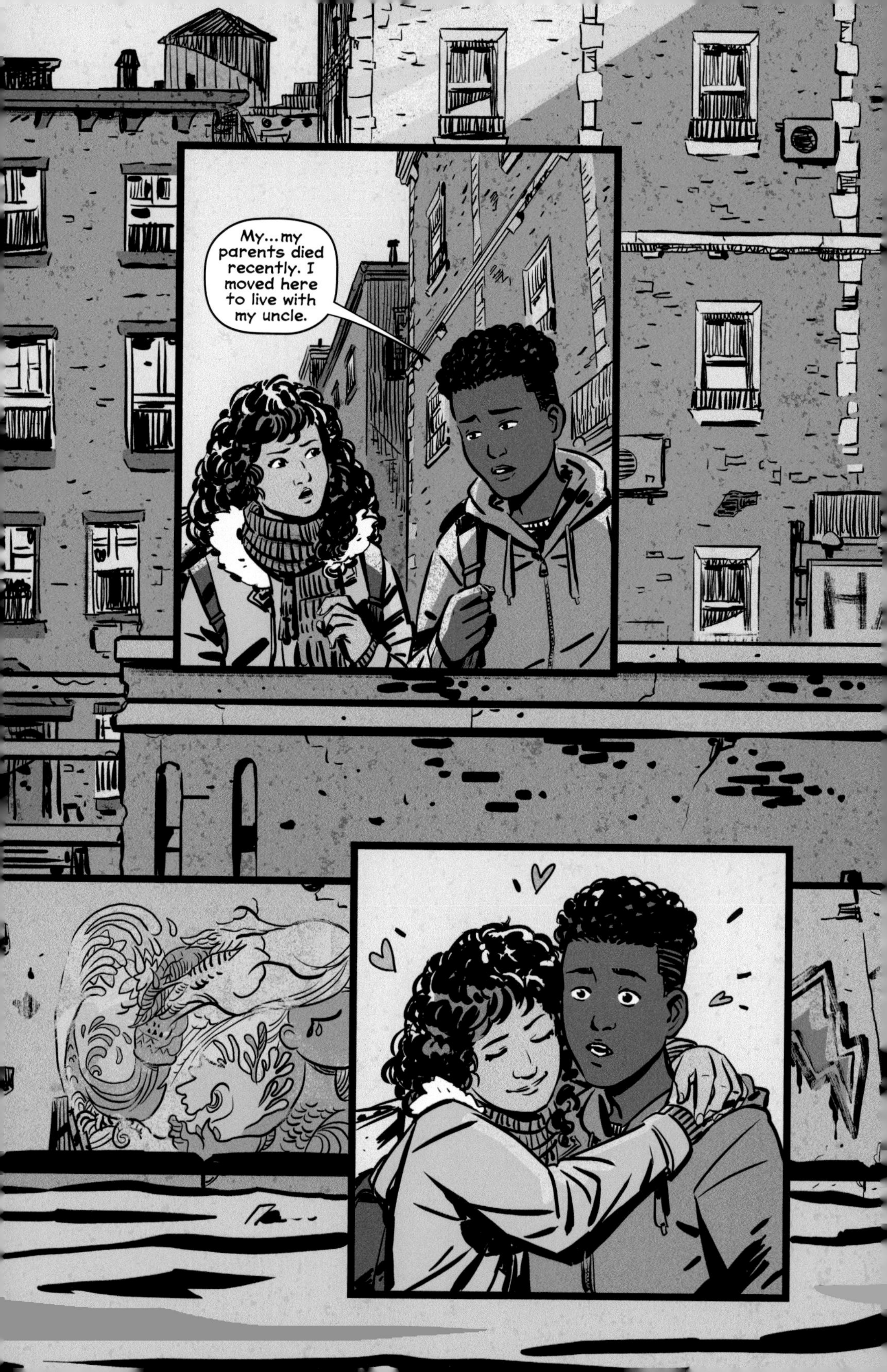
My...my parents died recently. I moved here to live with my uncle.

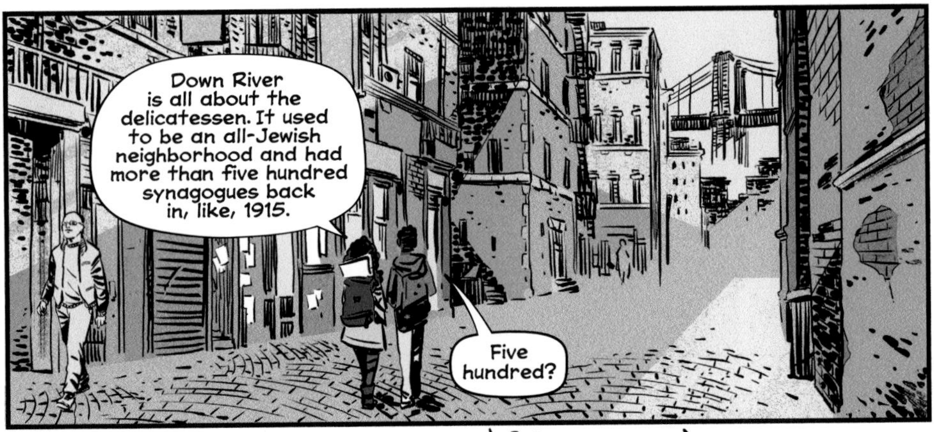
Down River is all about the delicatessen. It used to be an all-Jewish neighborhood and had more than five hundred synagogues back in, like, 1915.
Five hundred?

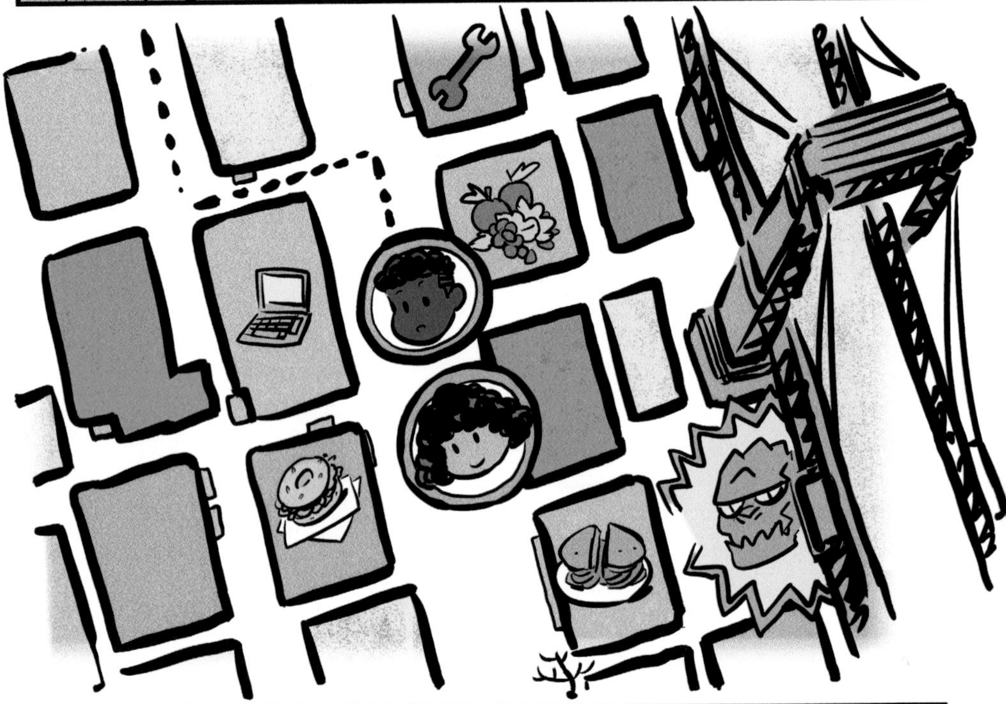

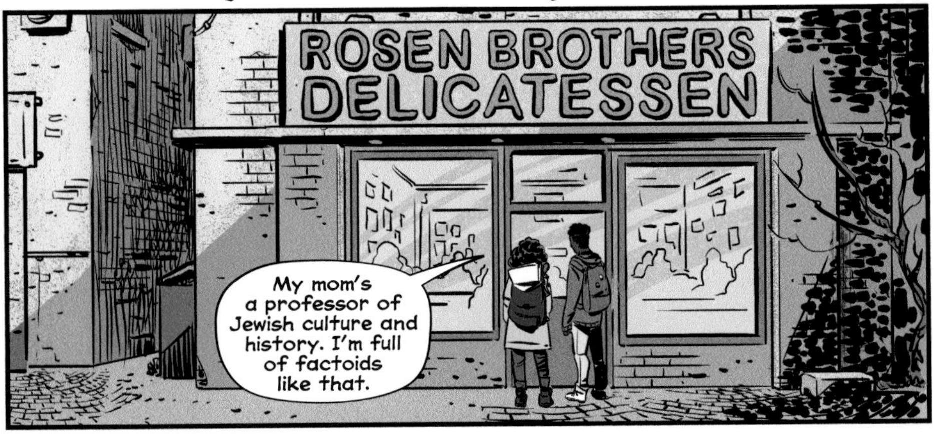
ROSEN BROTHERS DELICATESSEN
My mom's a professor of Jewish culture and history. I'm full of factoids like that.

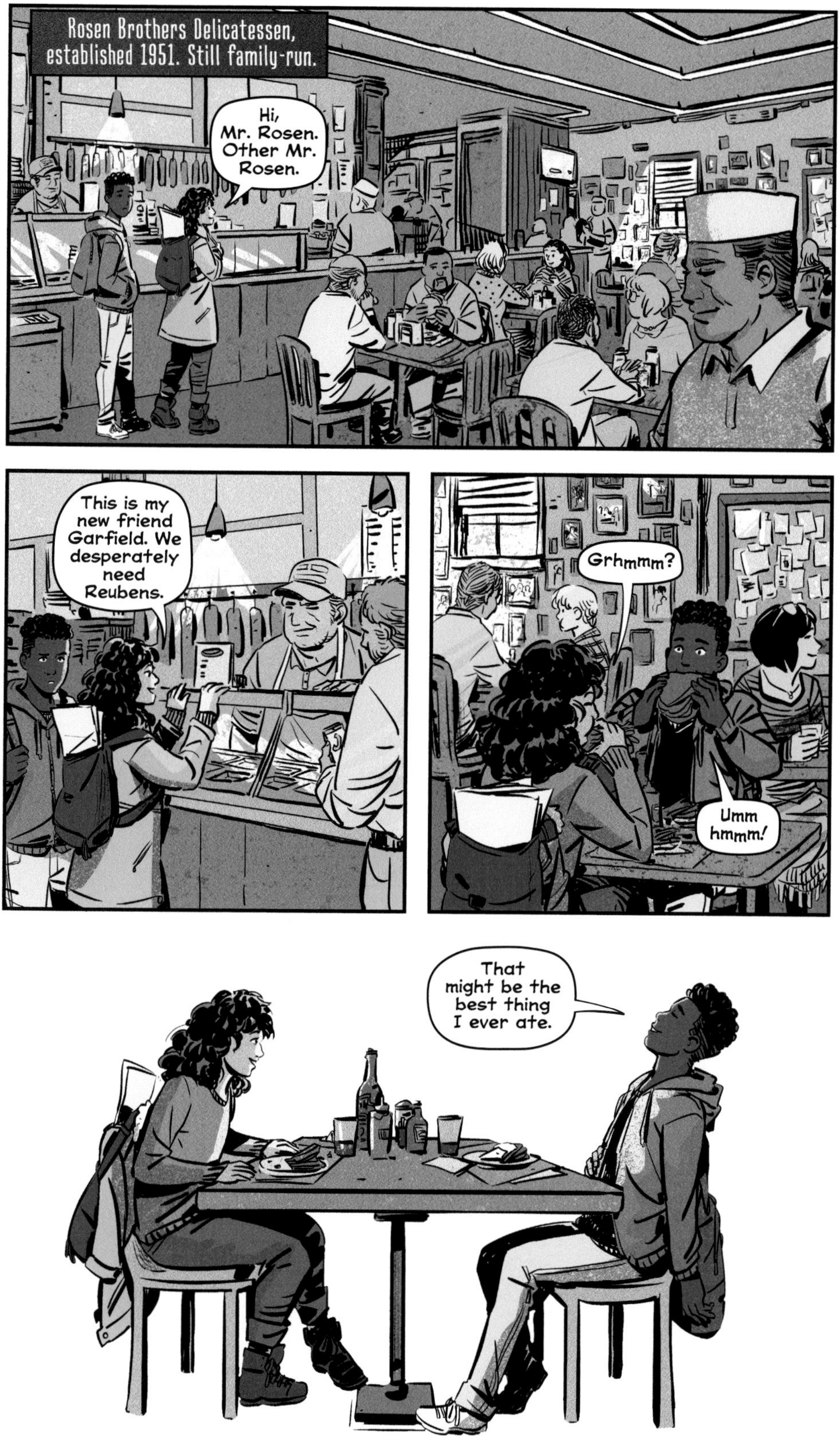
Rosen Brothers Delicatessen, established 1951. Still family-run.
Hi, Mr. Rosen. Other Mr. Rosen.
This is my new friend Garfield. We desperately need Reubens.
Grhmmm?
Umm hmmm!
That might be the best thing I ever ate.

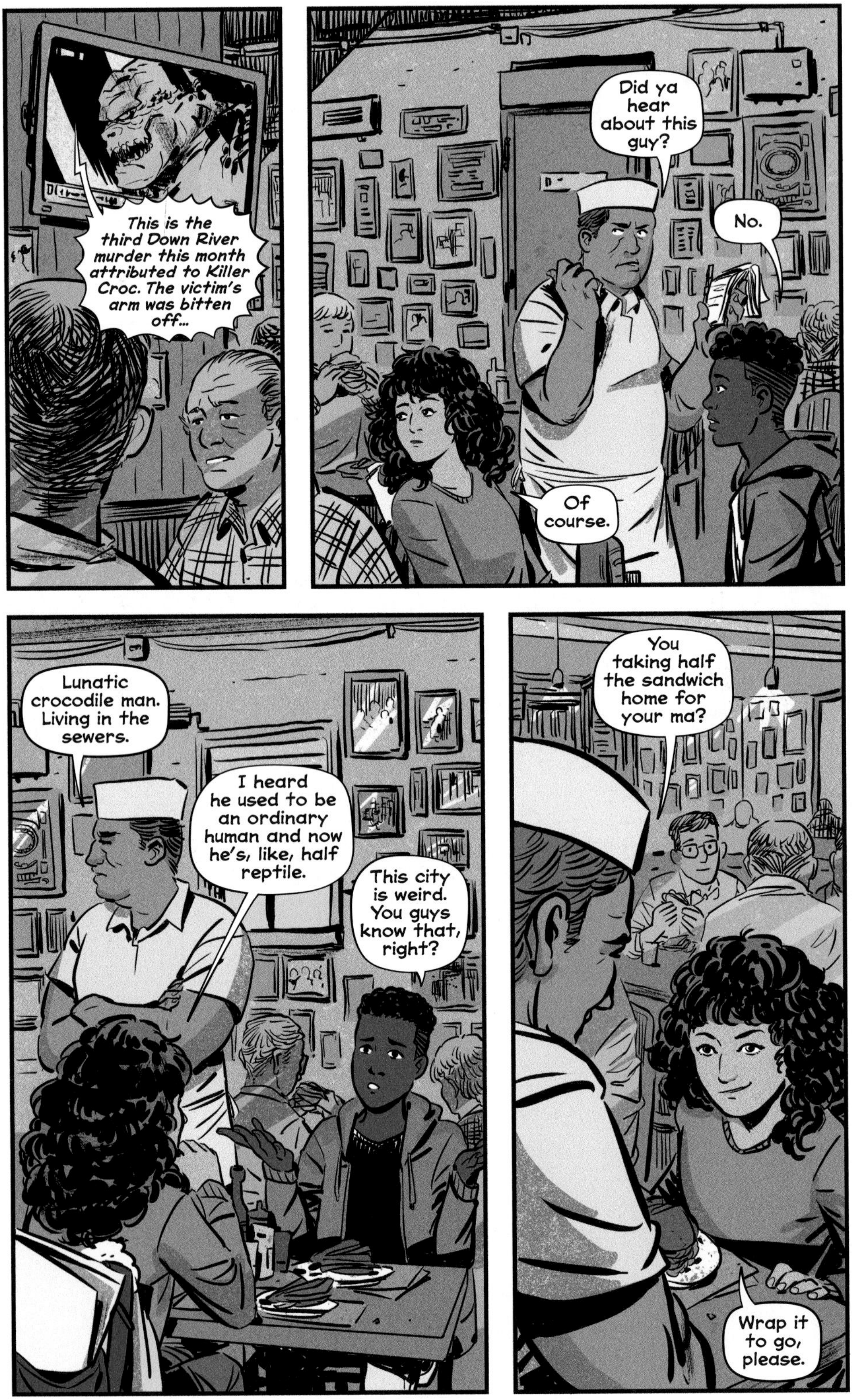

This is the third Down River murder this month attributed to Killer Croc. The victim's arm was bitten off...
Did ya hear about this guy?
No.
Of course.
Lunatic crocodile man. Living in the sewers.
I heard he used to be an ordinary human and now he's, like, half reptile.
This city is weird. You guys know that, right?
You taking half the sandwich home for your ma?
Wrap it to go, please.

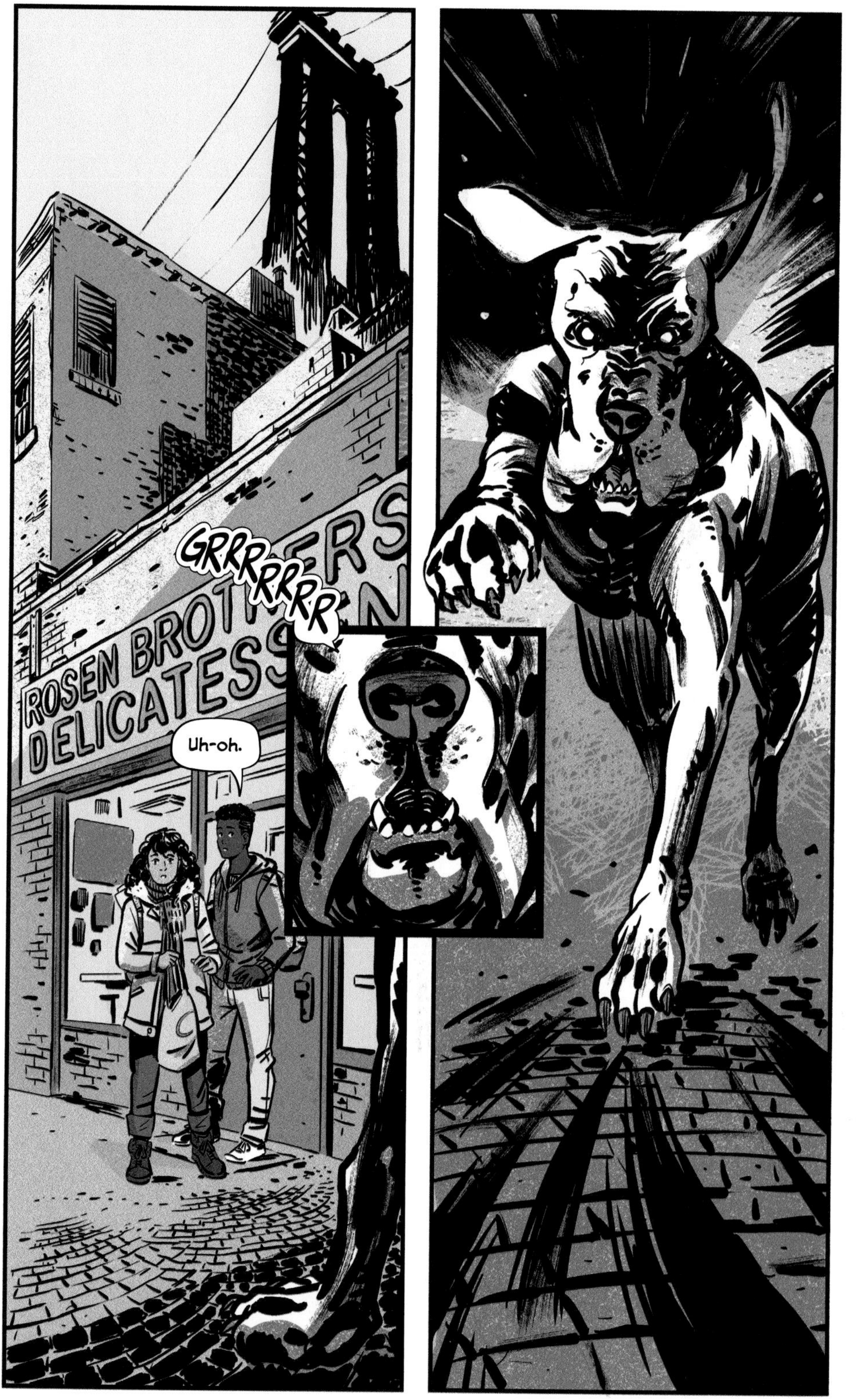
ROSEN BROTHERS
DELICATESSEN
GRRRRRRRR
Uh-oh.

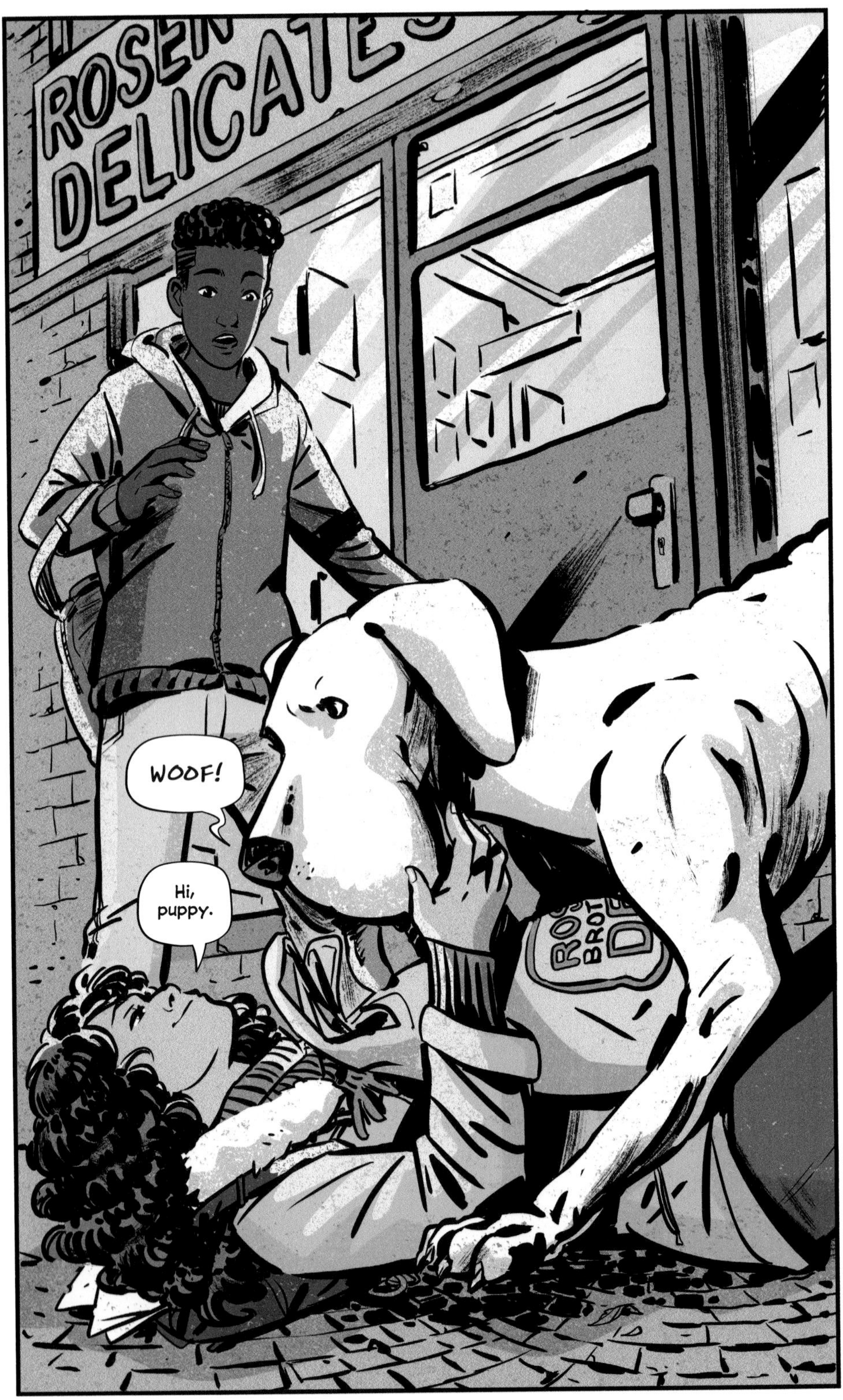
ROSEN
DELICATES
WOOF!
Hi, puppy.
ROS BROT DE

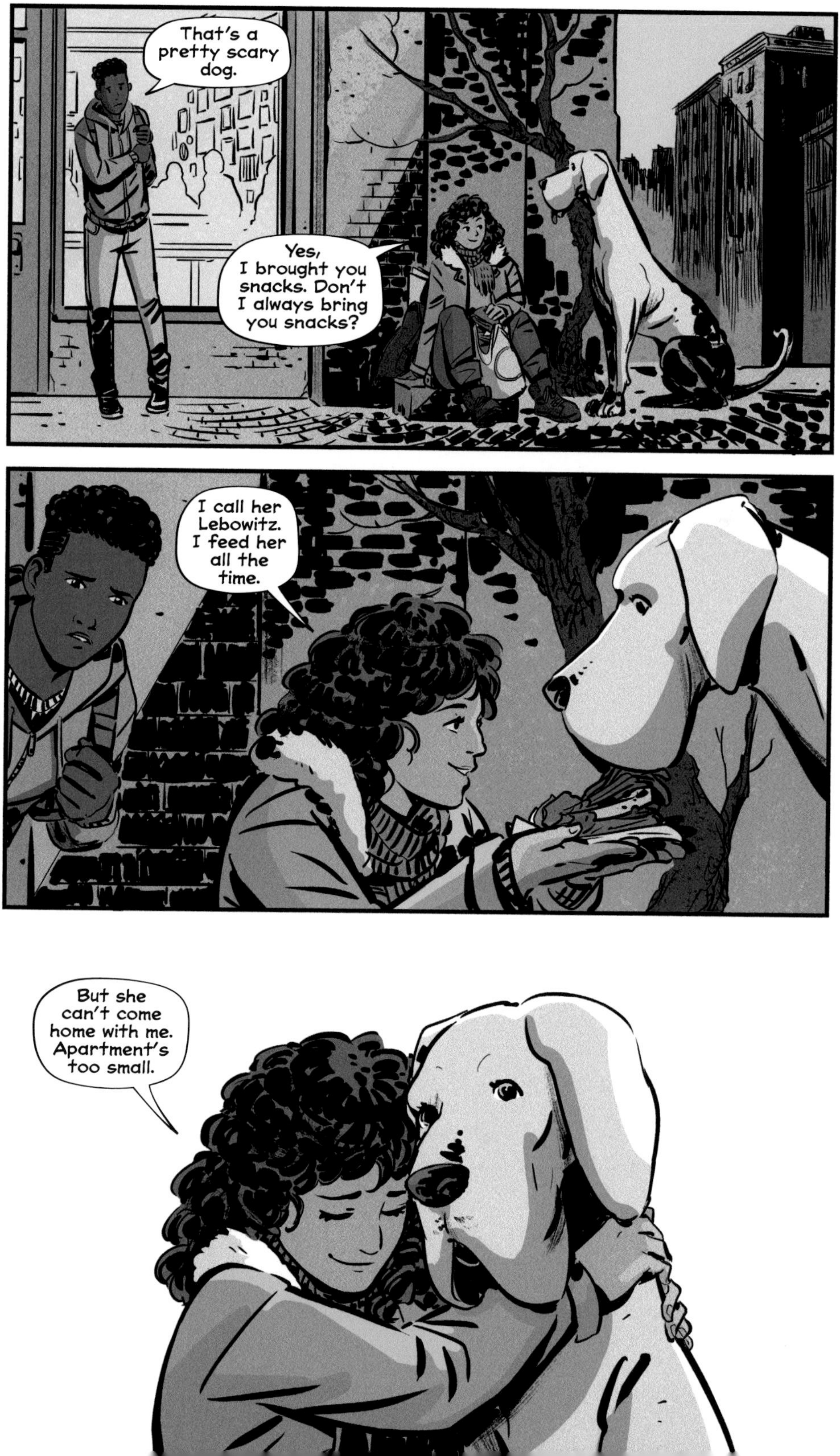
That's a pretty scary dog.
Yes, I brought you snacks. Don't I always bring you snacks?
I call her Lebowitz. I feed her all the time.
But she can't come home with me. Apartment's too small.

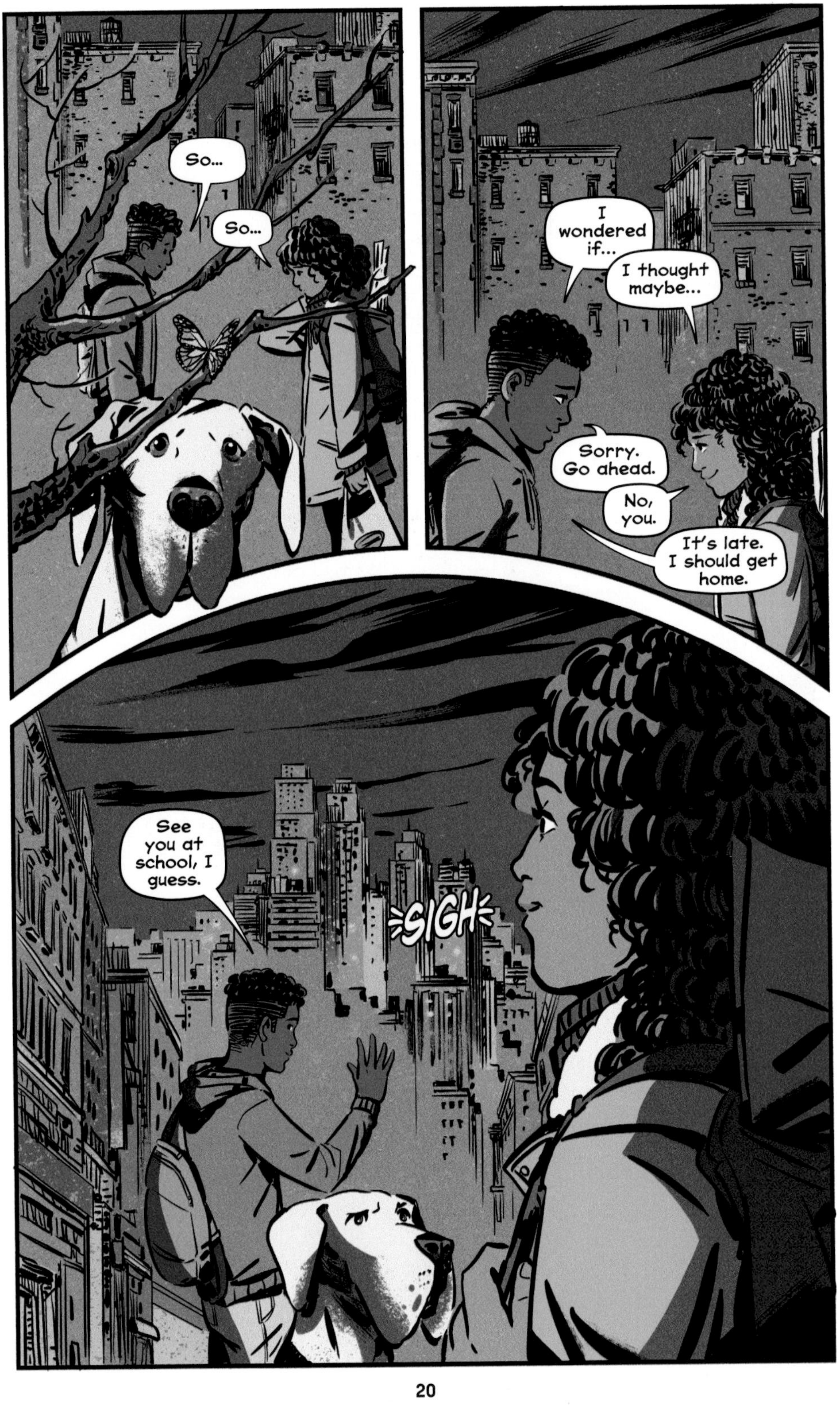
So...
So...
I wondered if...
I thought maybe...
Sorry. Go ahead.
No, you.
It's late. I should get home.
See you at school, I guess.
SIGH

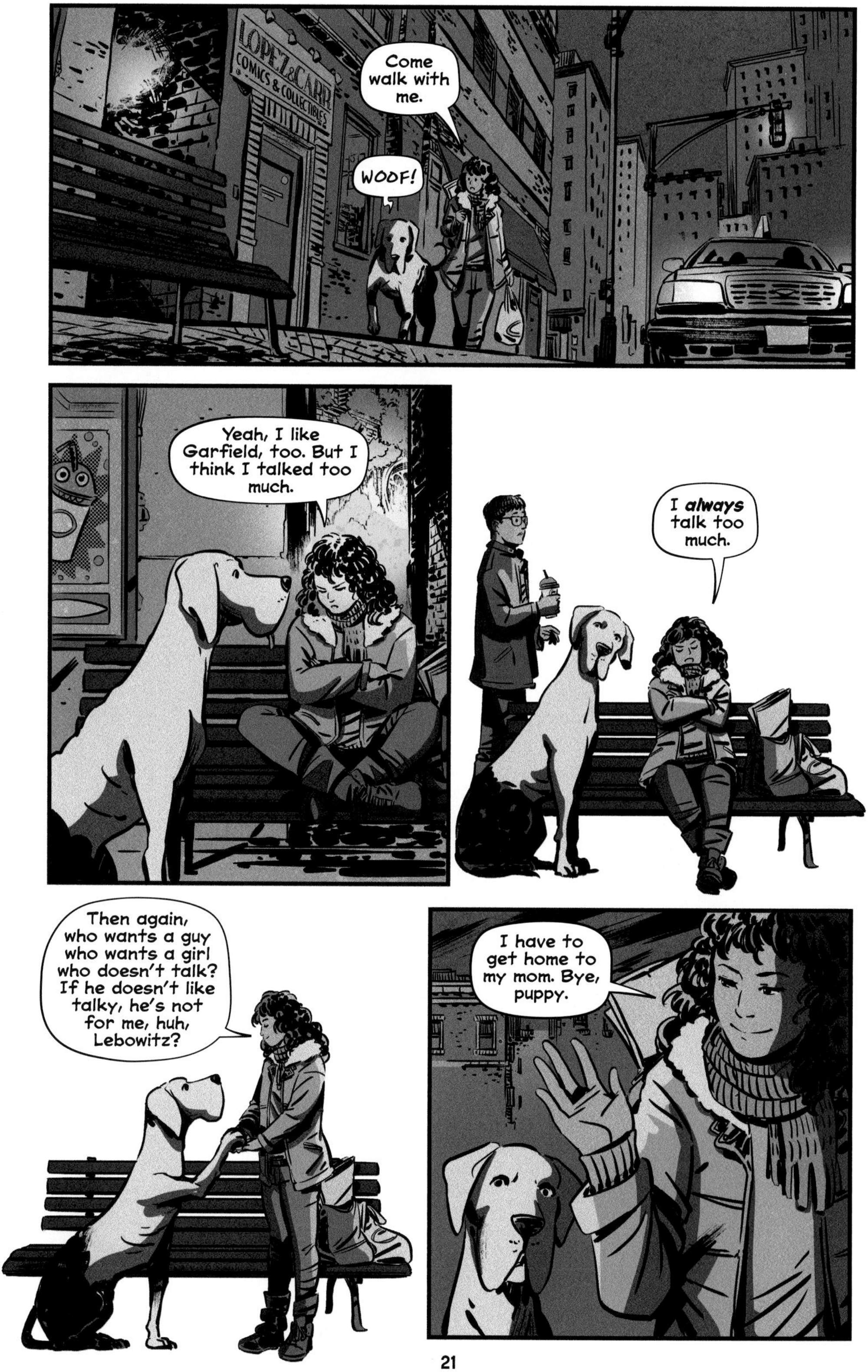
LOPEZ&CARR
COMICS & COLLECTIBLES
Come walk with me.
WOOF!
Yeah, I like Garfield, too. But I think I talked too much.
I *always* talk too much.
Then again, who wants a guy who wants a girl who doesn't talk? If he doesn't like talky, he's not for me, huh, Lebowitz?
I have to get home to my mom. Bye, puppy.

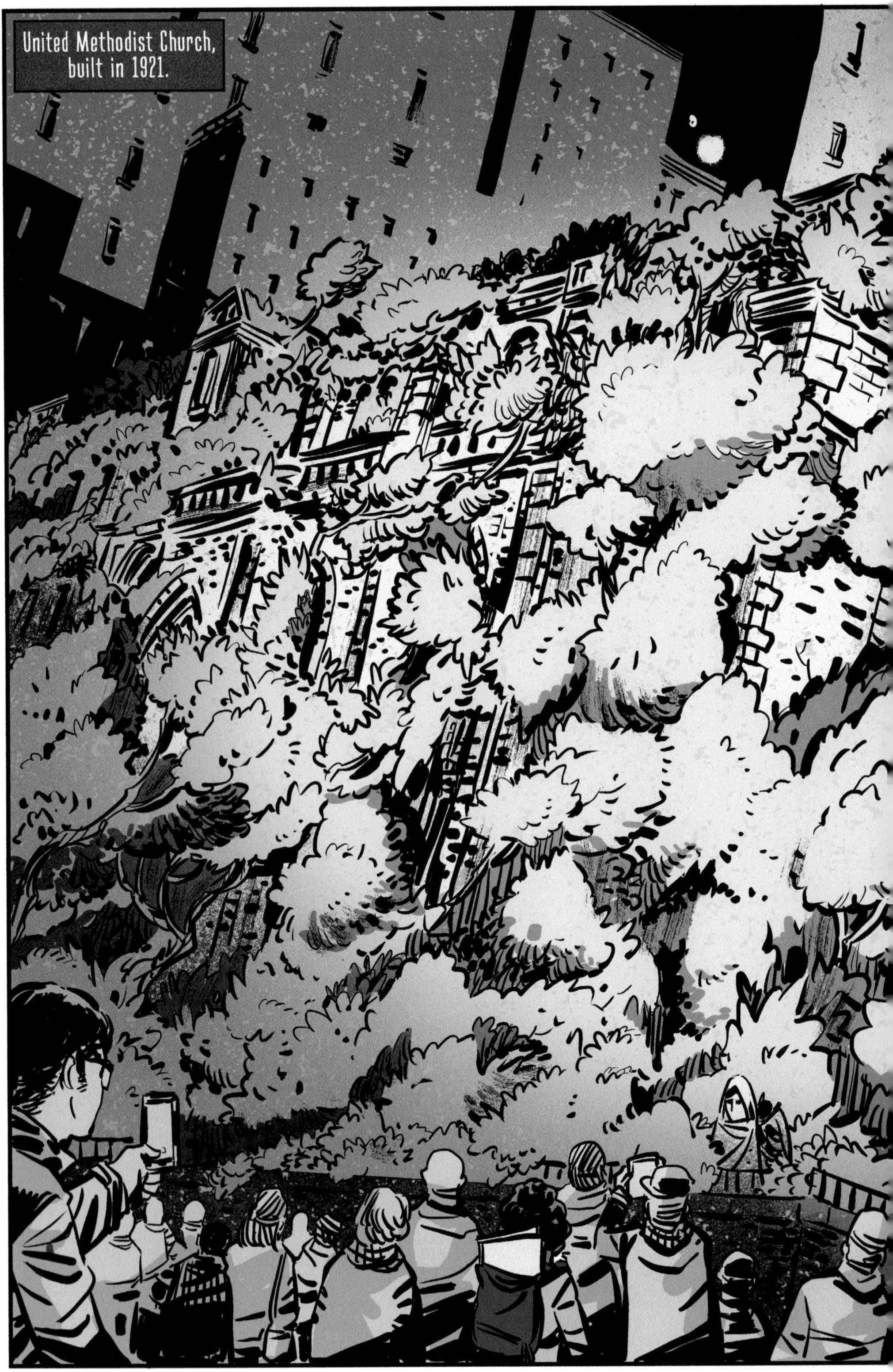
United Methodist Church, built in 1921.

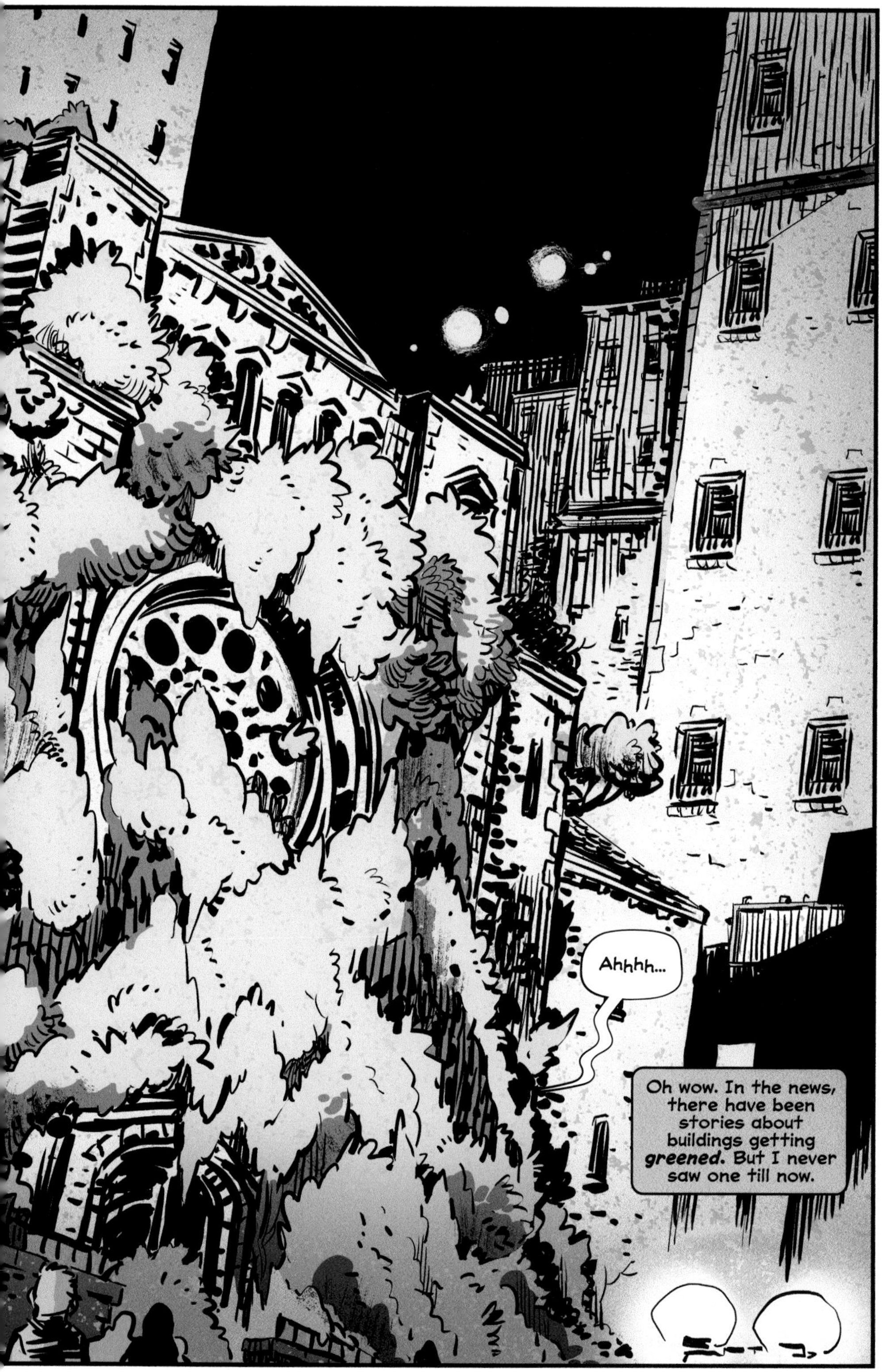
Ahhhh...
Oh wow. In the news, there have been stories about buildings getting *greened*. But I never saw one till now.

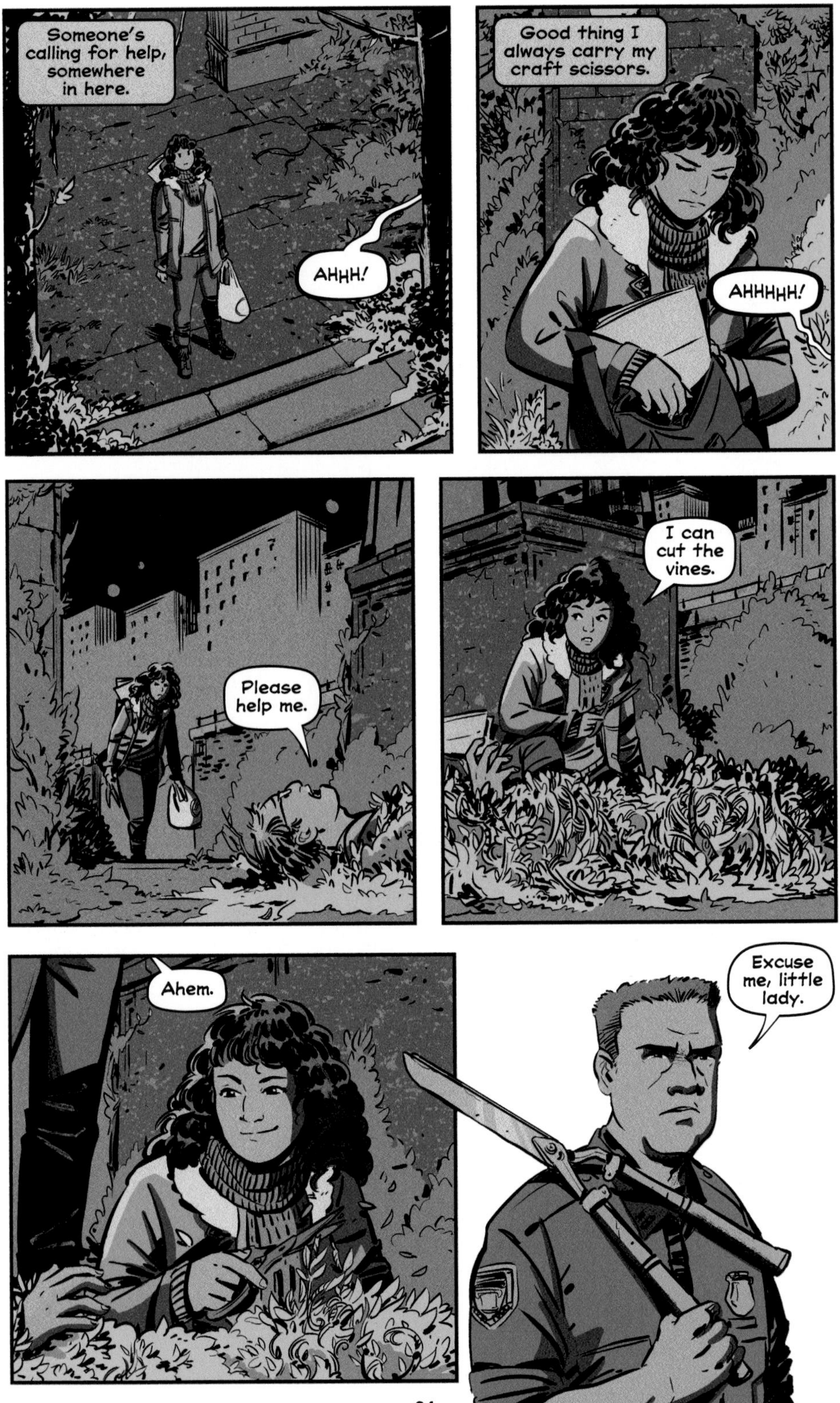
Someone's calling for help, somewhere in here.
AHHH!
Good thing I always carry my craft scissors.
AHHHHH!
Please help me.
I can cut the vines.
Ahem.
Excuse me, little lady.

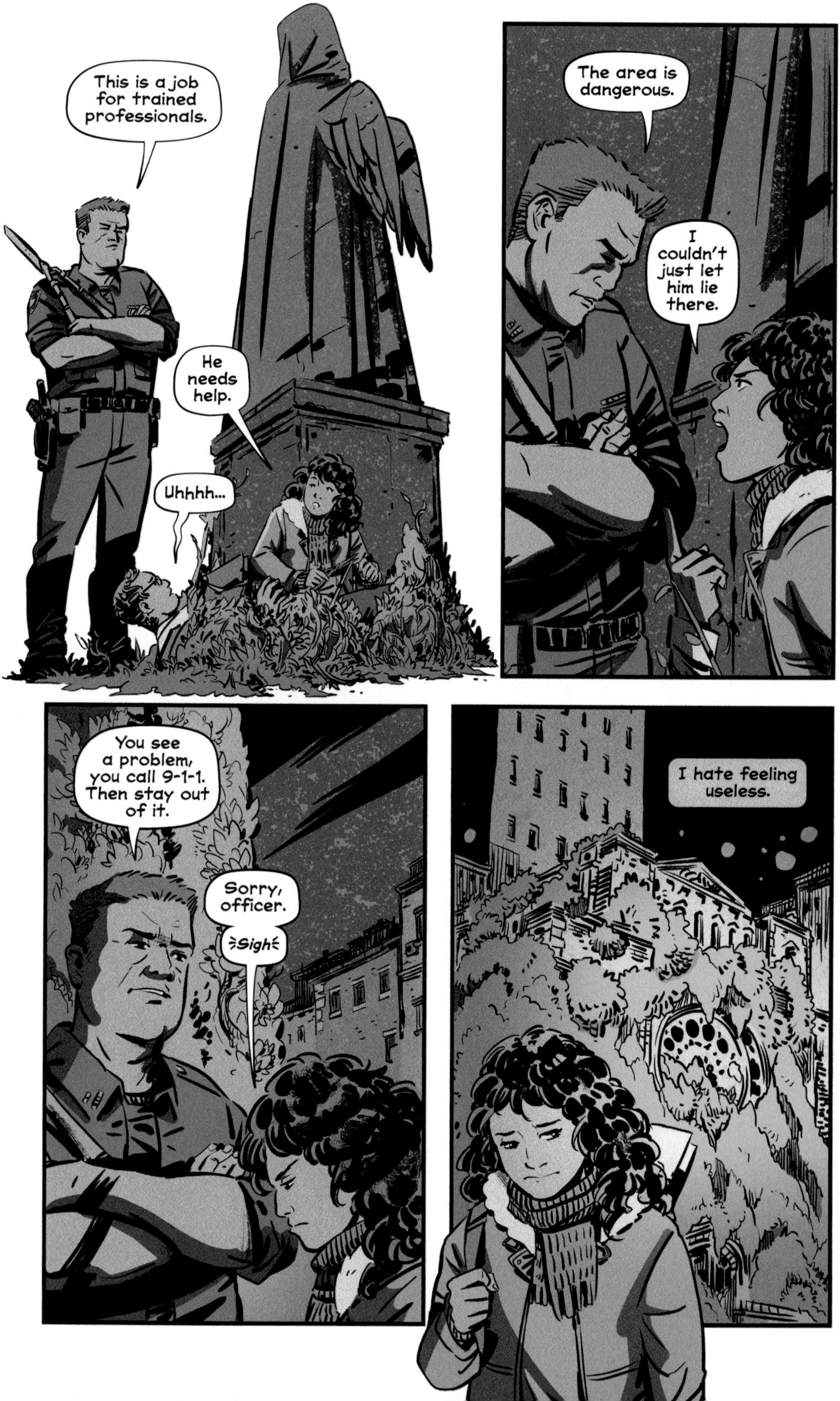
This is a job for trained professionals.
He needs help.
Uhhhh...
The area is dangerous.
I couldn't just let him lie there.
You see a problem, you call 9-1-1. Then stay out of it.
Sorry, officer.
Sigh
I hate feeling useless.

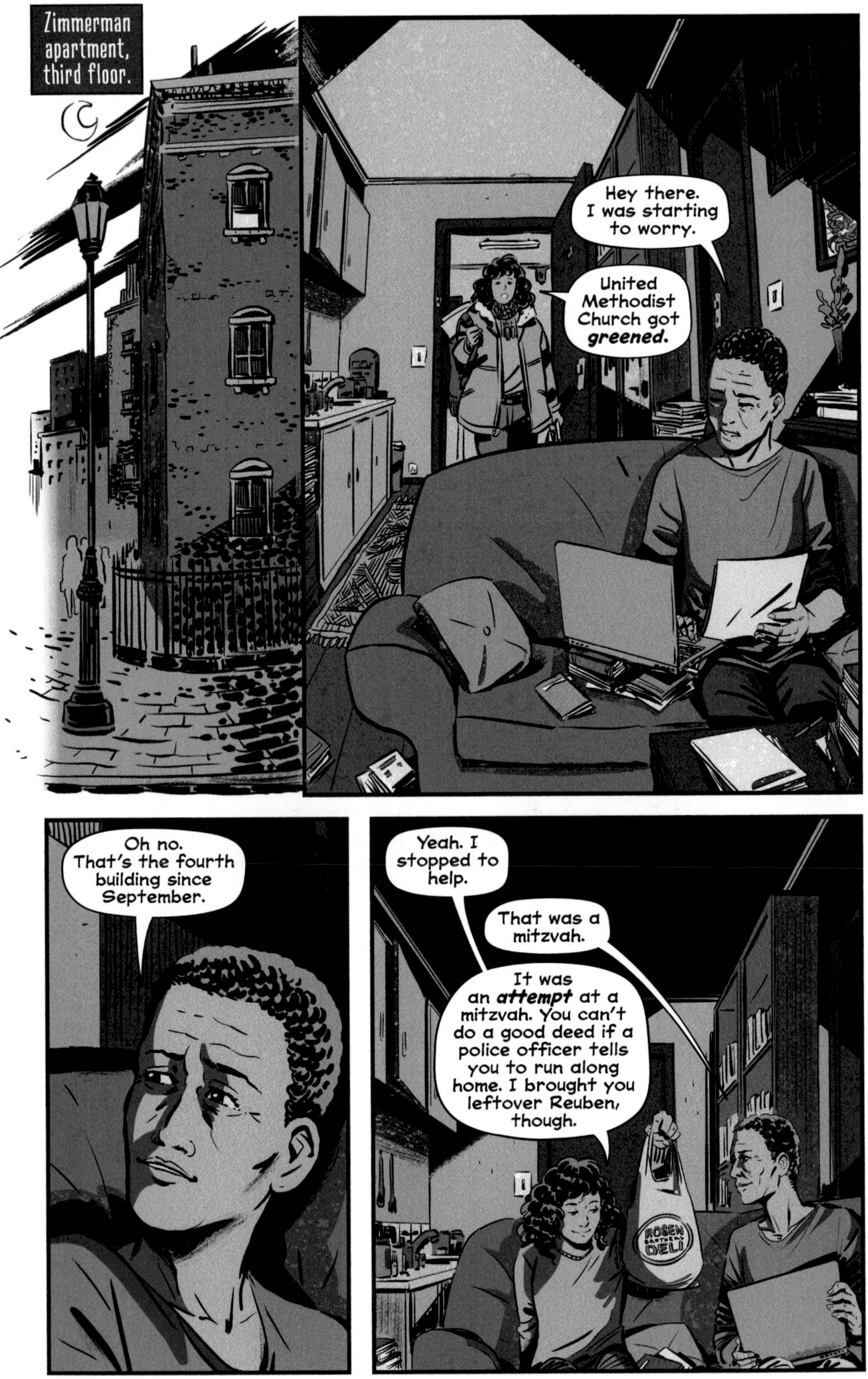
Zimmerman apartment, third floor.
Hey there. I was starting to worry.
United Methodist Church got *greened.*
Oh no. That's the fourth building since September.
Yeah. I stopped to help.
That was a mitzvah.
It was an *attempt* at a mitzvah. You can't do a good deed if a police officer tells you to run along home. I brought you leftover Reuben, though.
ROSEN DELI

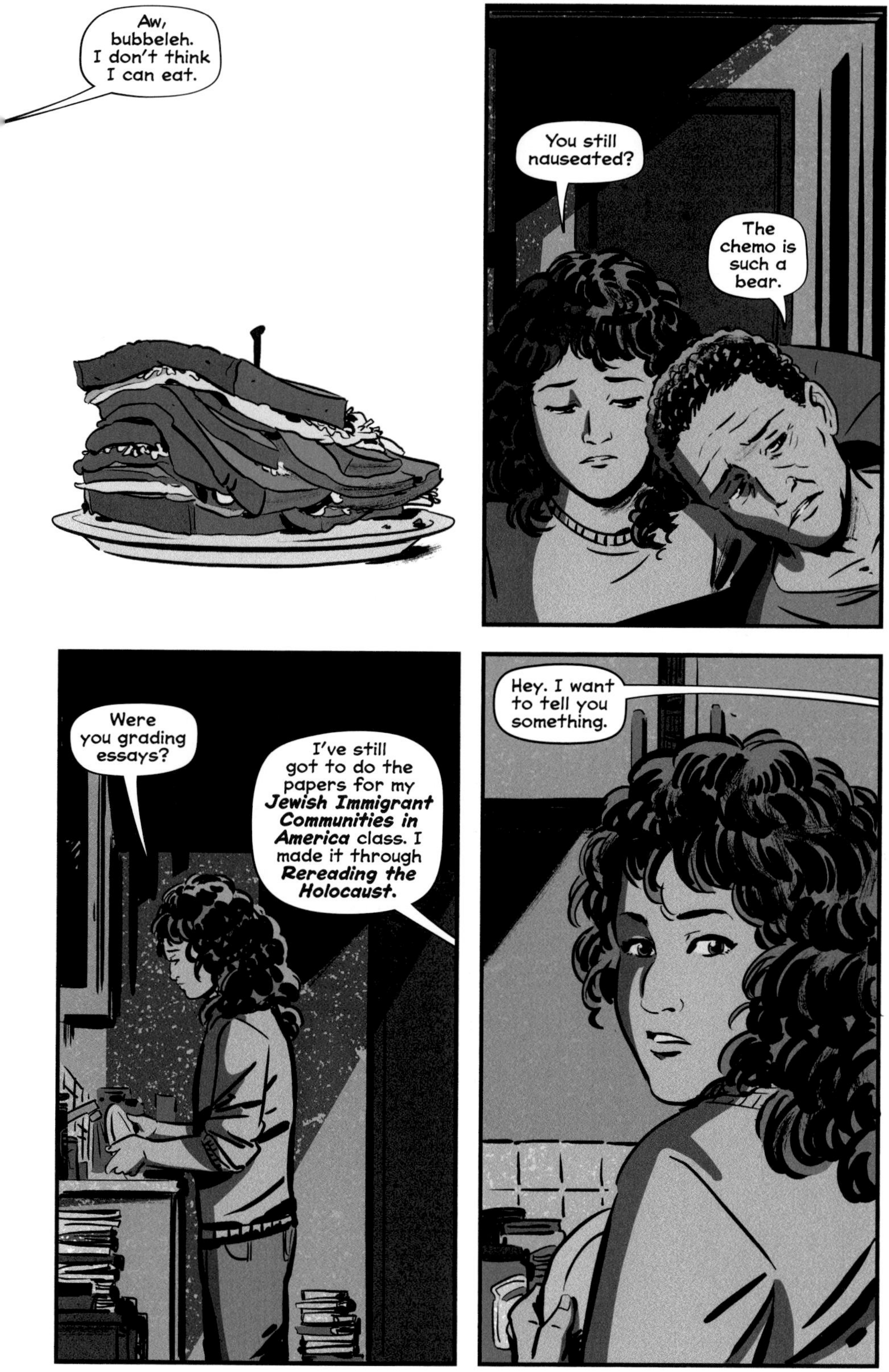

Aw, bubbeleh. I don't think I can eat.
You still nauseated?
The chemo is such a bear.
Were you grading essays?
I've still got to do the papers for my ***Jewish Immigrant Communities in America*** class. I made it through ***Rereading the Holocaust***.
Hey. I want to tell you something.

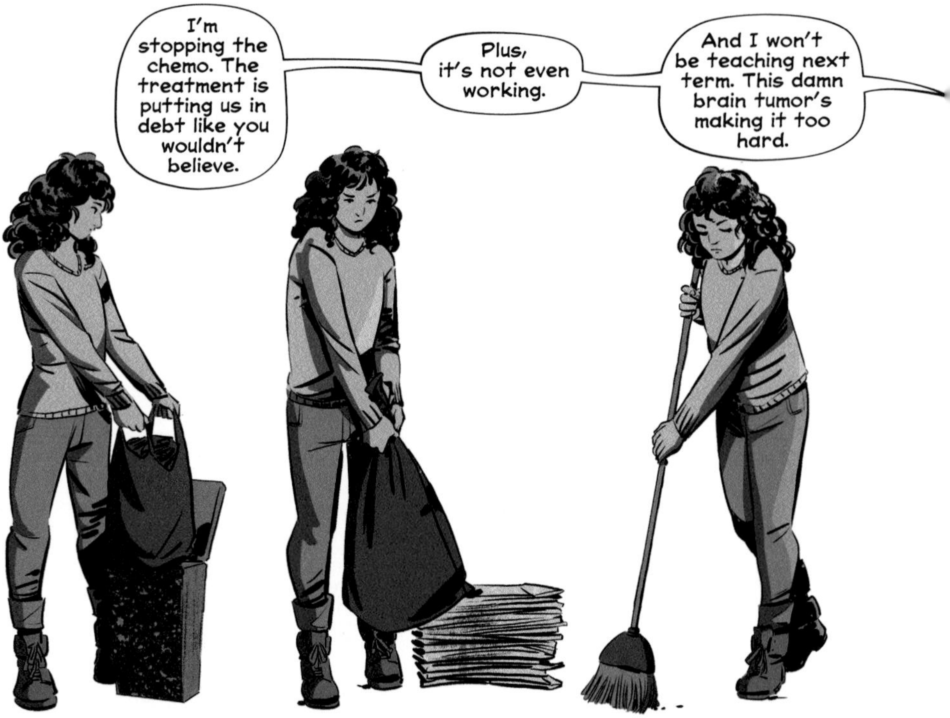
I'm stopping the chemo. The treatment is putting us in debt like you wouldn't believe.
Plus, it's not even working.
And I won't be teaching next term. This damn brain tumor's making it too hard.

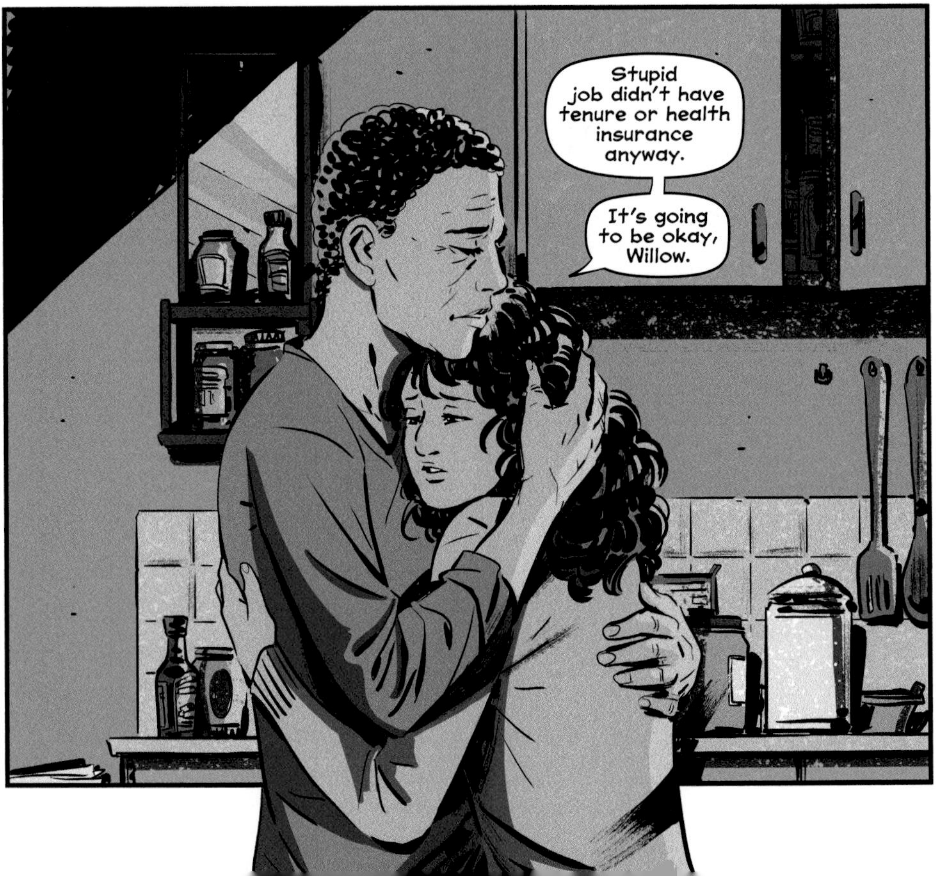
Stupid job didn't have tenure or health insurance anyway.
It's going to be okay, Willow.

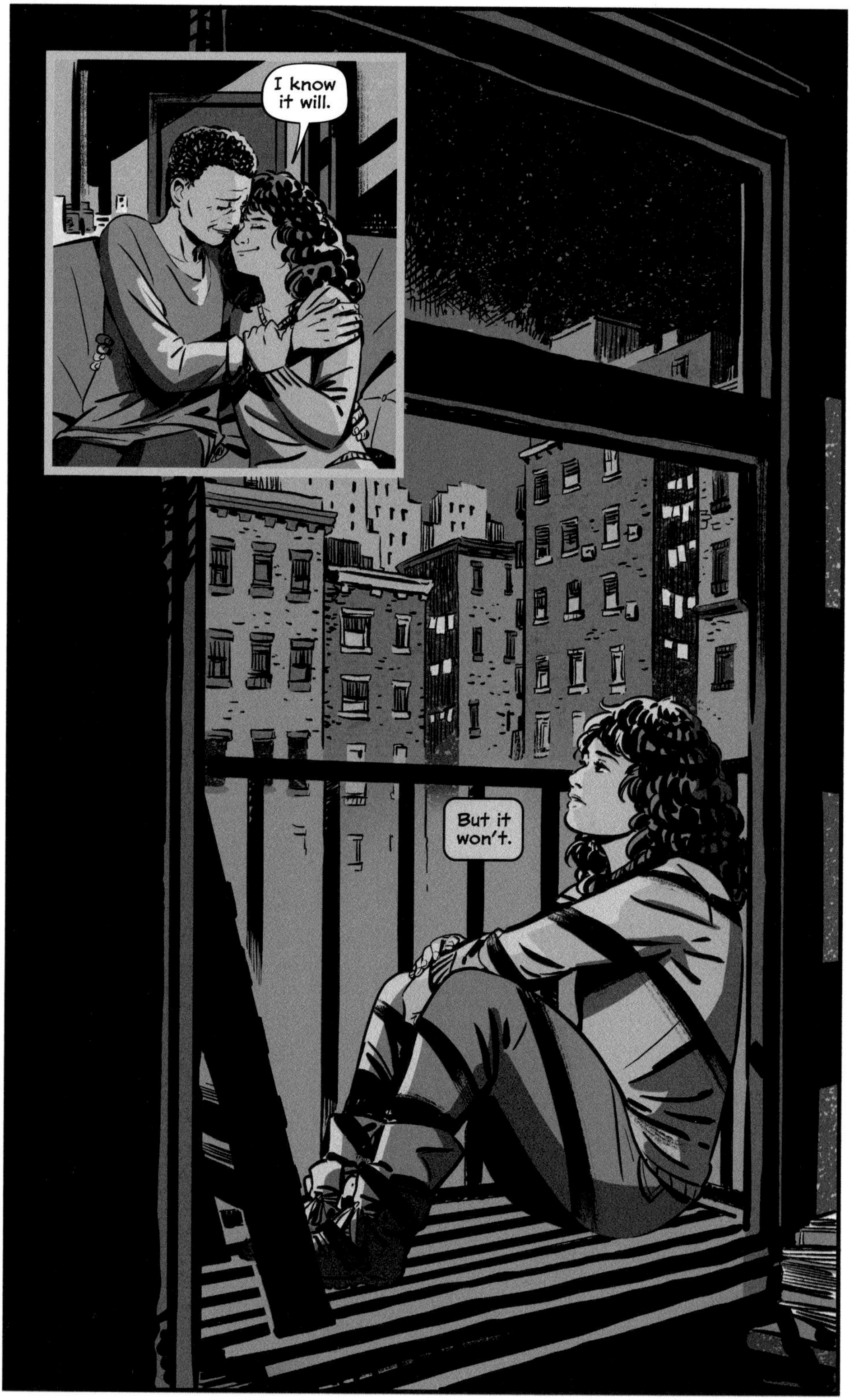
I know it will.
But it won't.

part two: **the puzzle box**

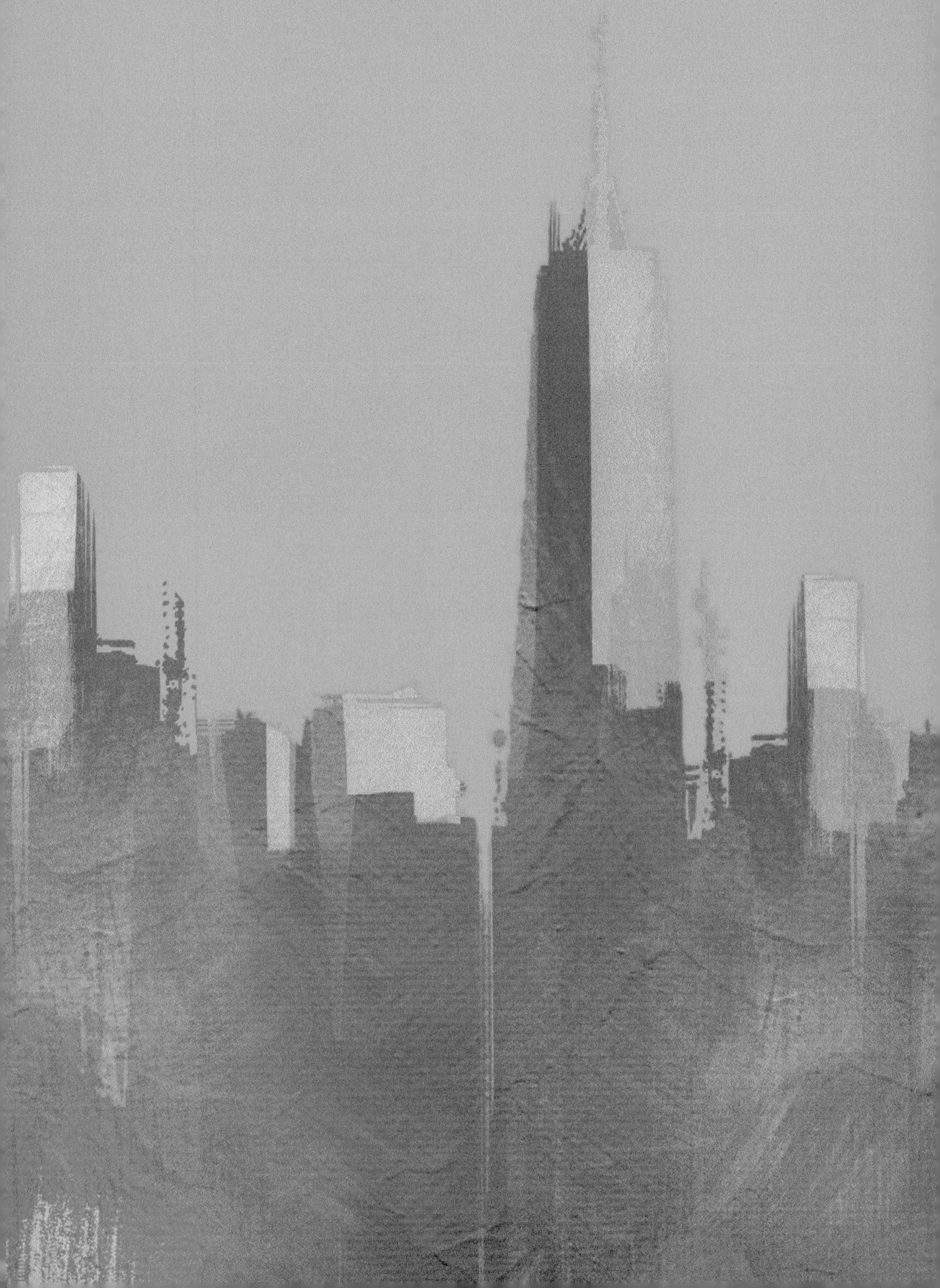

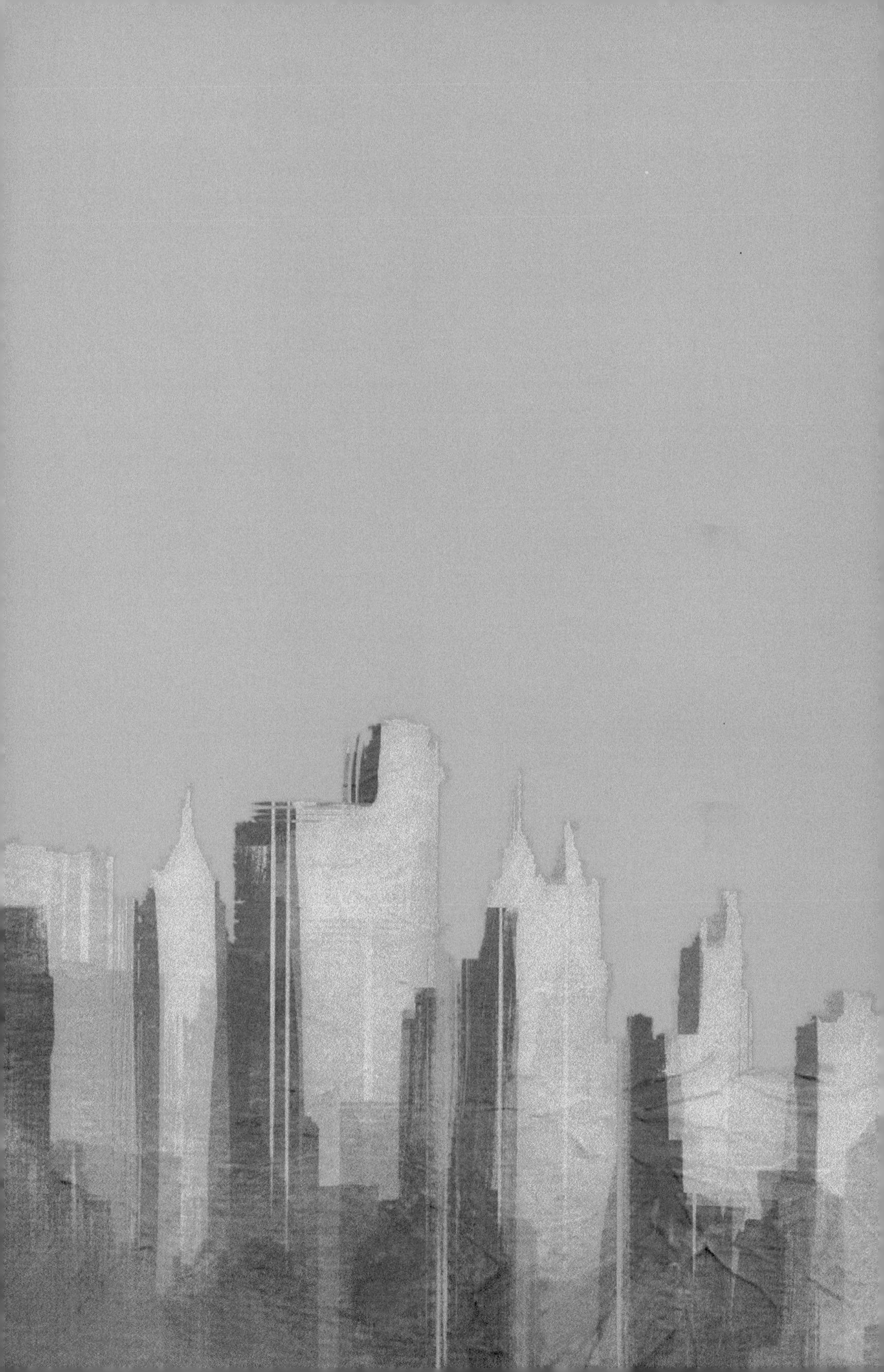

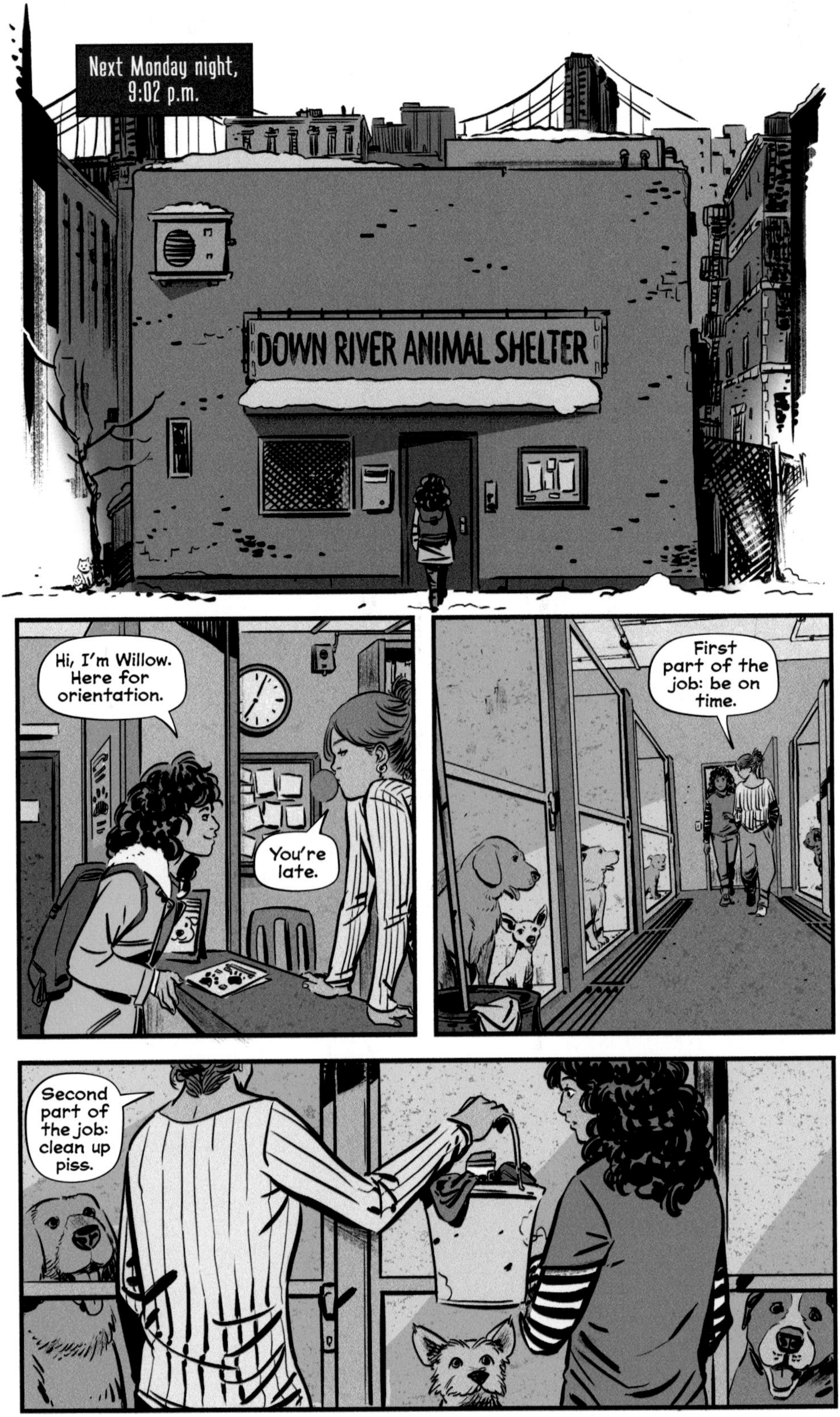
Next Monday night, 9:02 p.m.
DOWN RIVER ANIMAL SHELTER
Hi, I'm Willow. Here for orientation.
You're late.
First part of the job: be on time.
Second part of the job: clean up piss.

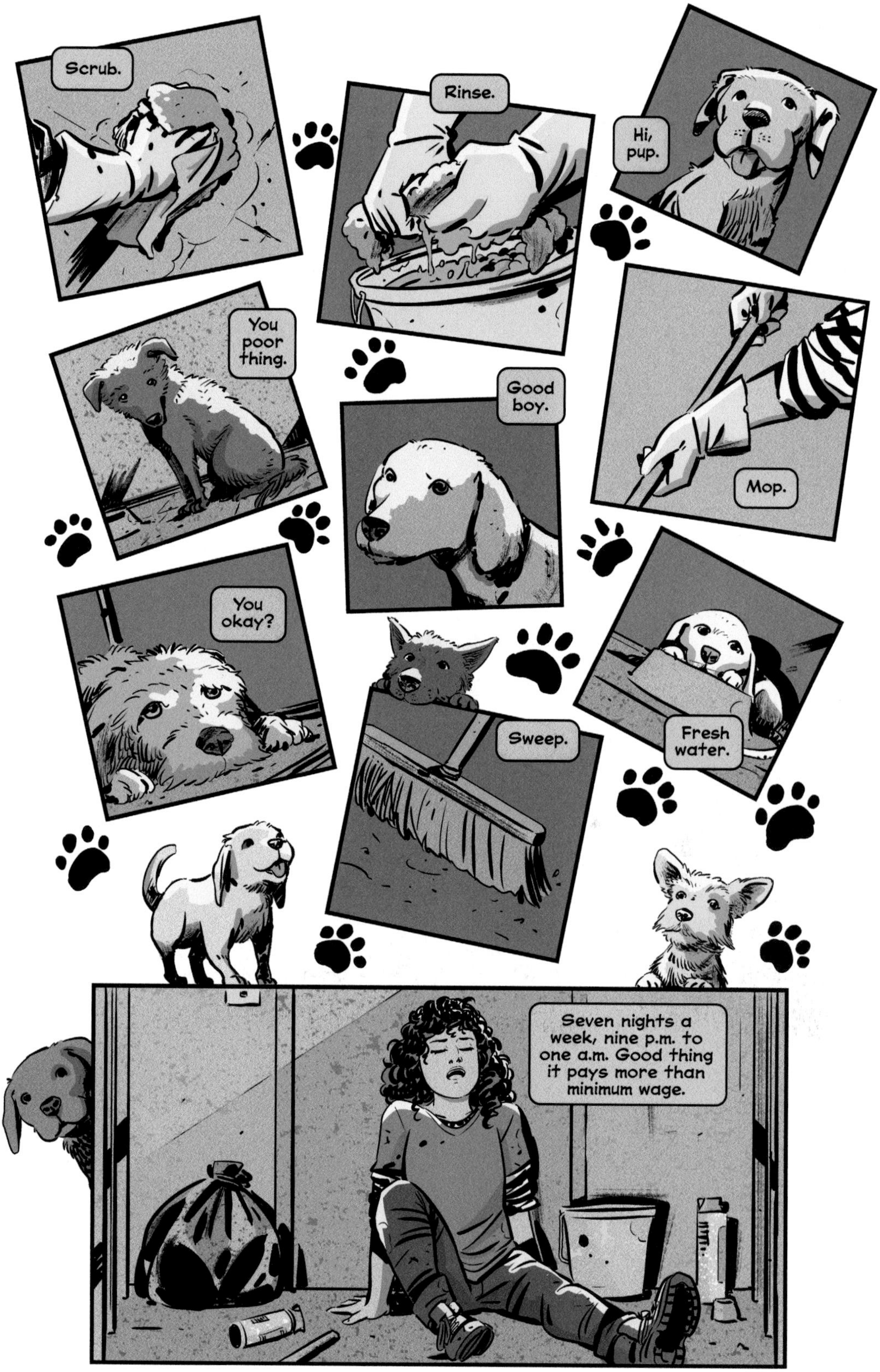
Scrub.
Rinse.
Hi, pup.
You poor thing.
Good boy.
Mop.
You okay?
Sweep.
Fresh water.
Seven nights a week, nine p.m. to one a.m. Good thing it pays more than minimum wage.

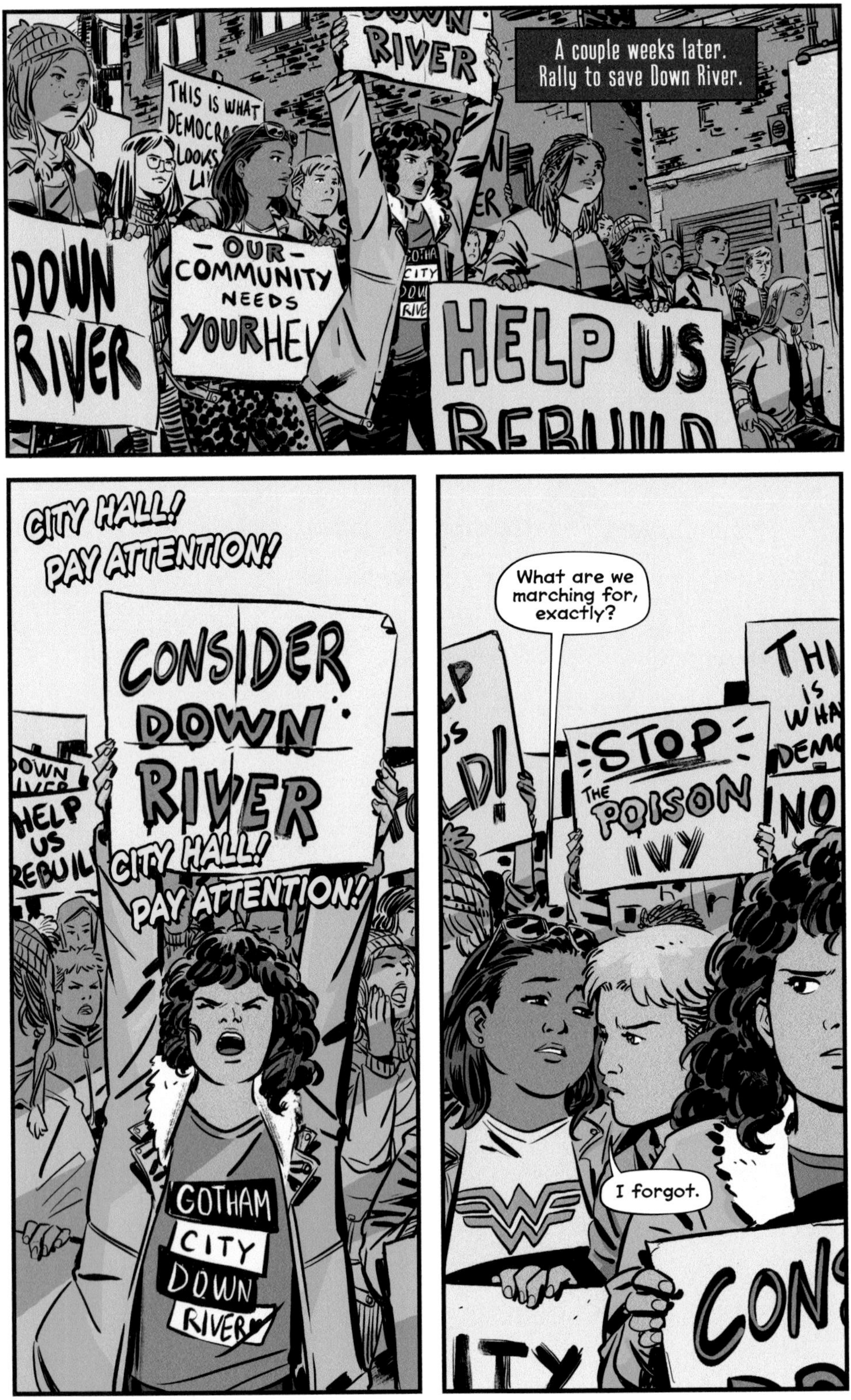
A couple weeks later.
Rally to save Down River.
RIVER
THIS IS WHAT
DOWN RIVER
OUR COMMUNITY NEEDS YOUR
HELP US
CITY HALL!
PAY ATTENTION!
CONSIDER DOWN RIVER
HELP US
CITY HALL!
PAY ATTENTION!
GOTHAM CITY DOWN RIVER
What are we marching for, exactly?
STOP THE POISON IVY
I forgot.

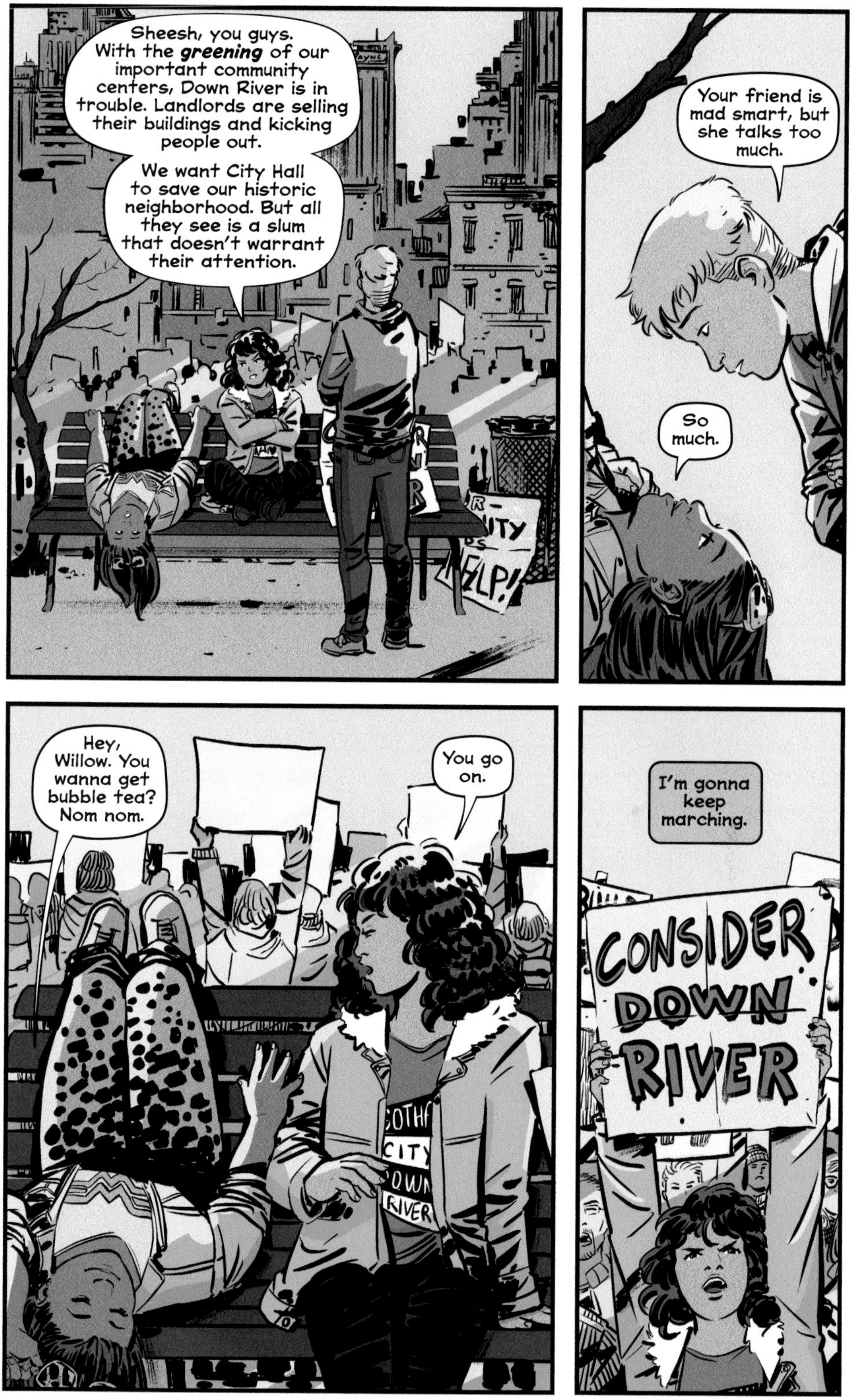

Sheesh, you guys. With the *greening* of our important community centers, Down River is in trouble. Landlords are selling their buildings and kicking people out.
We want City Hall to save our historic neighborhood. But all they see is a slum that doesn't warrant their attention.
Your friend is mad smart, but she talks too much.
So much.
Hey, Willow. You wanna get bubble tea? Nom nom.
You go on.
GOTHAM CITY DOWN RIVER
I'm gonna keep marching.
CONSIDER DOWN RIVER

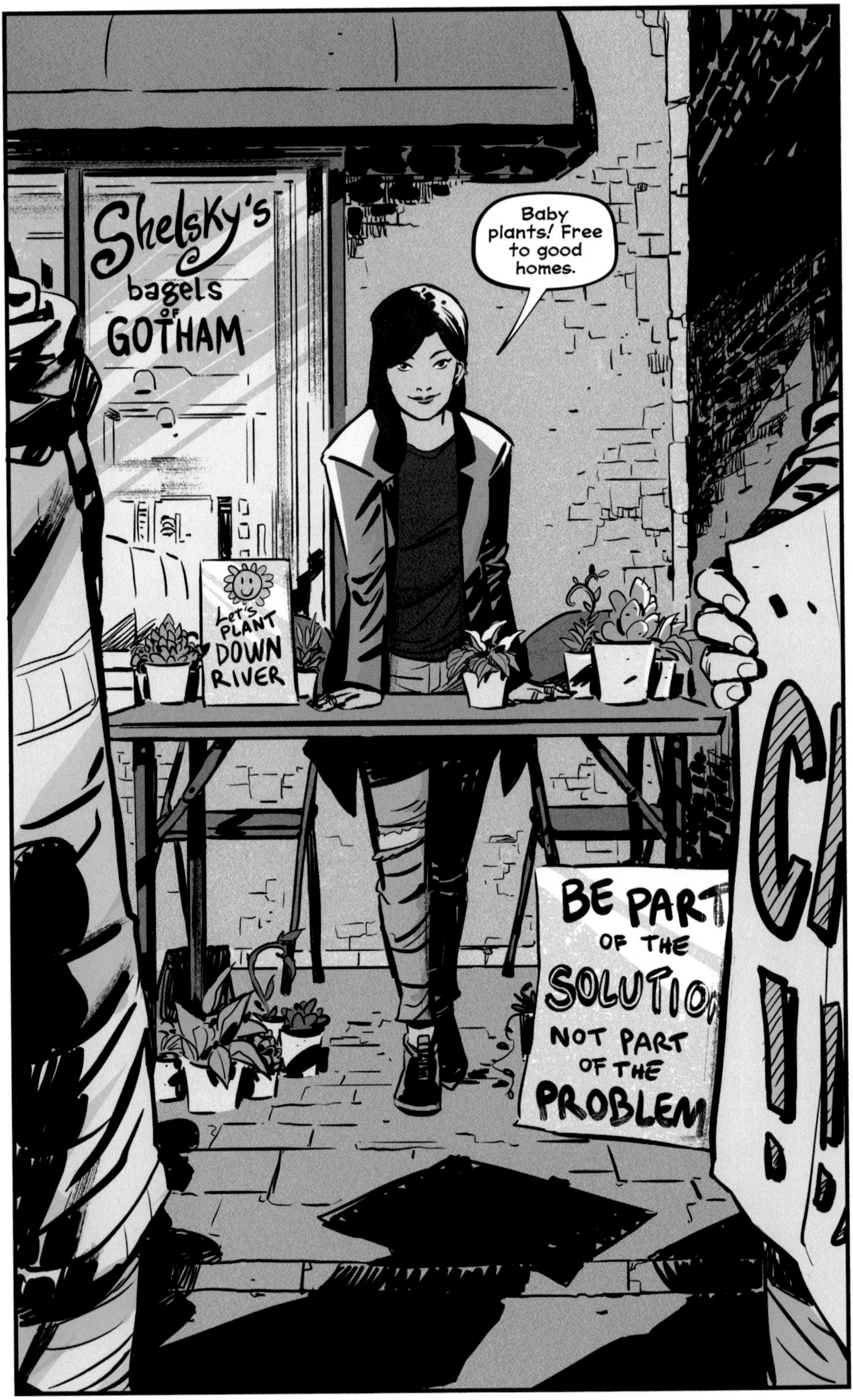
Shelsky's bagels of GOTHAM
Baby plants! Free to good homes.
Let's PLANT DOWN RIVER
BE PART OF THE SOLUTIO NOT PART OF THE PROBLEM

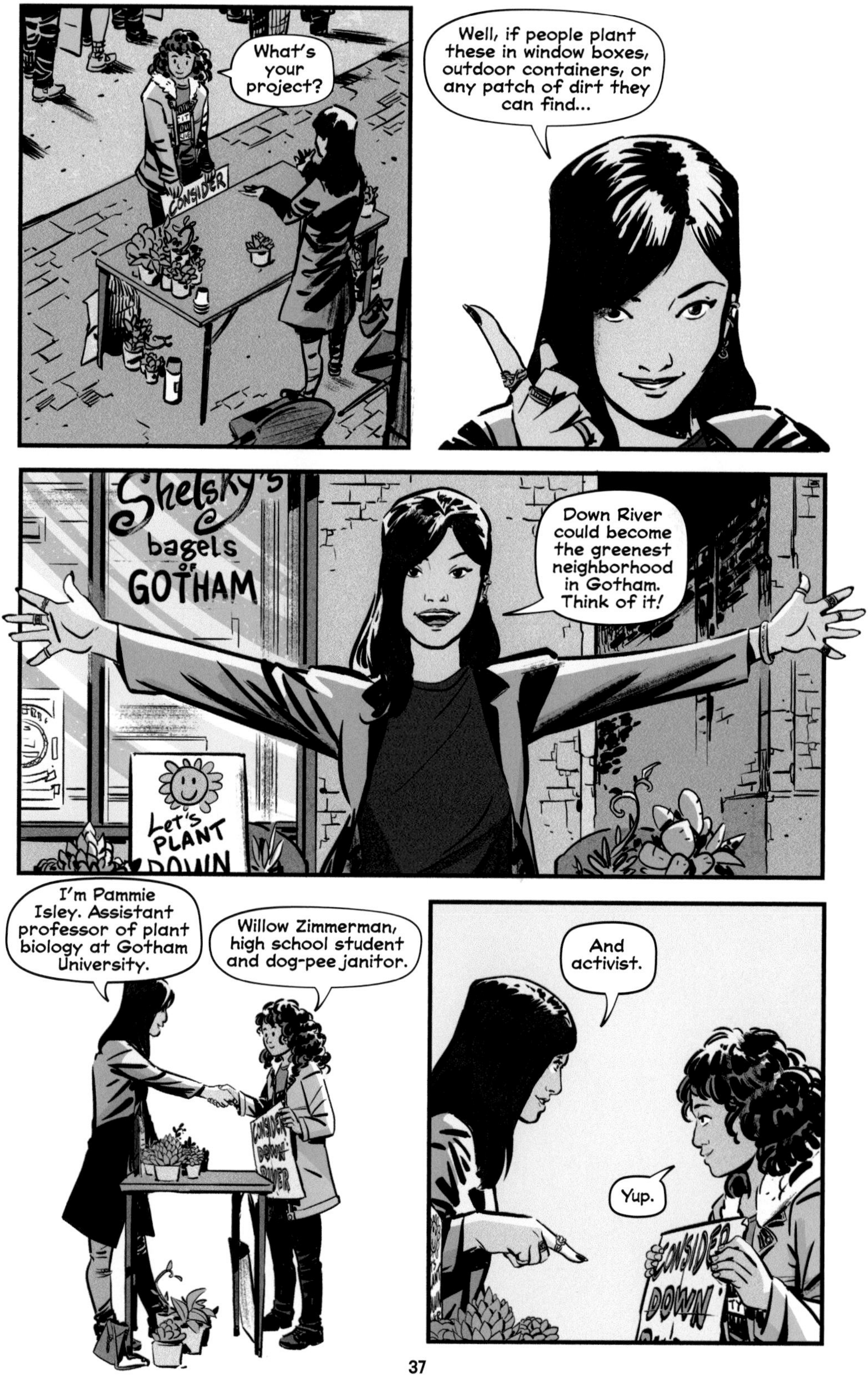
What's your project?
CONSIDER
Well, if people plant these in window boxes, outdoor containers, or any patch of dirt they can find...
Shelsky's
bagels of GOTHAM
Let's PLANT
Down River could become the greenest neighborhood in Gotham. Think of it!
I'm Pammie Isley. Assistant professor of plant biology at Gotham University.
Willow Zimmerman, high school student and dog-pee janitor.
CONSIDER DOWN RIVER
And activist.
Yup.

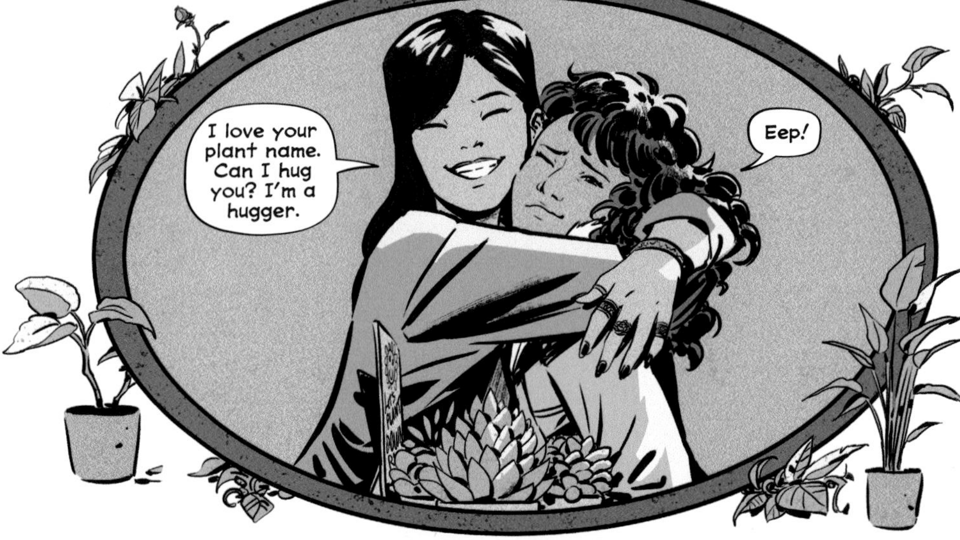
I love your plant name. Can I hug you? I'm a hugger.
Eep!

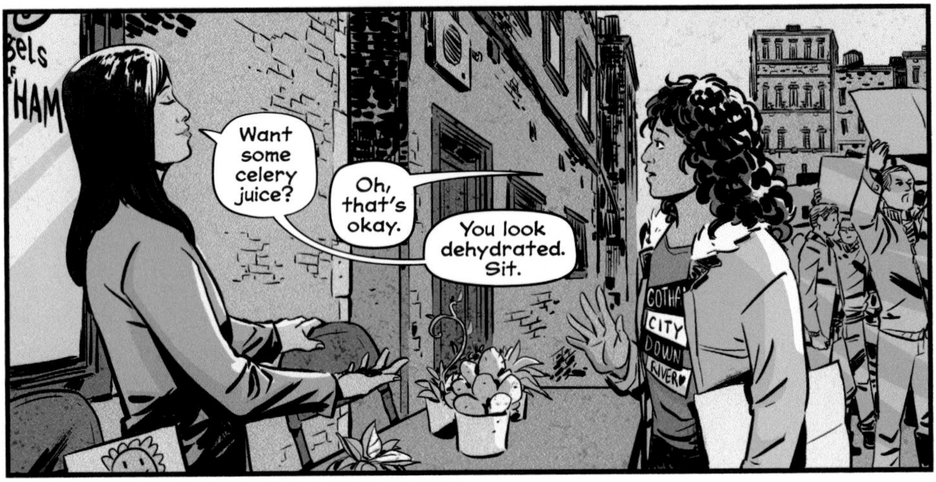
Bagels of Gotham
Want some celery juice?
Oh, that's okay.
You look dehydrated. Sit.
Gotham City Down River

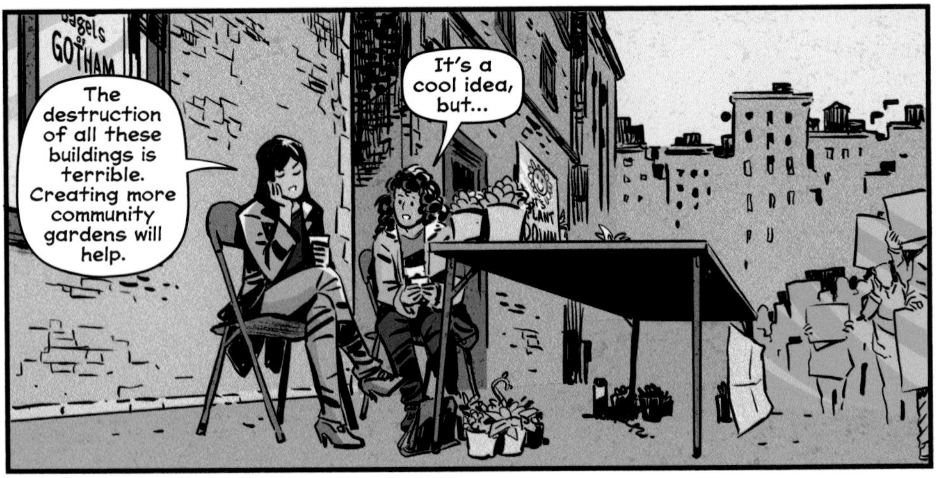
Bagels of Gotham
The destruction of all these buildings is terrible. Creating more community gardens will help.
It's a cool idea, but...

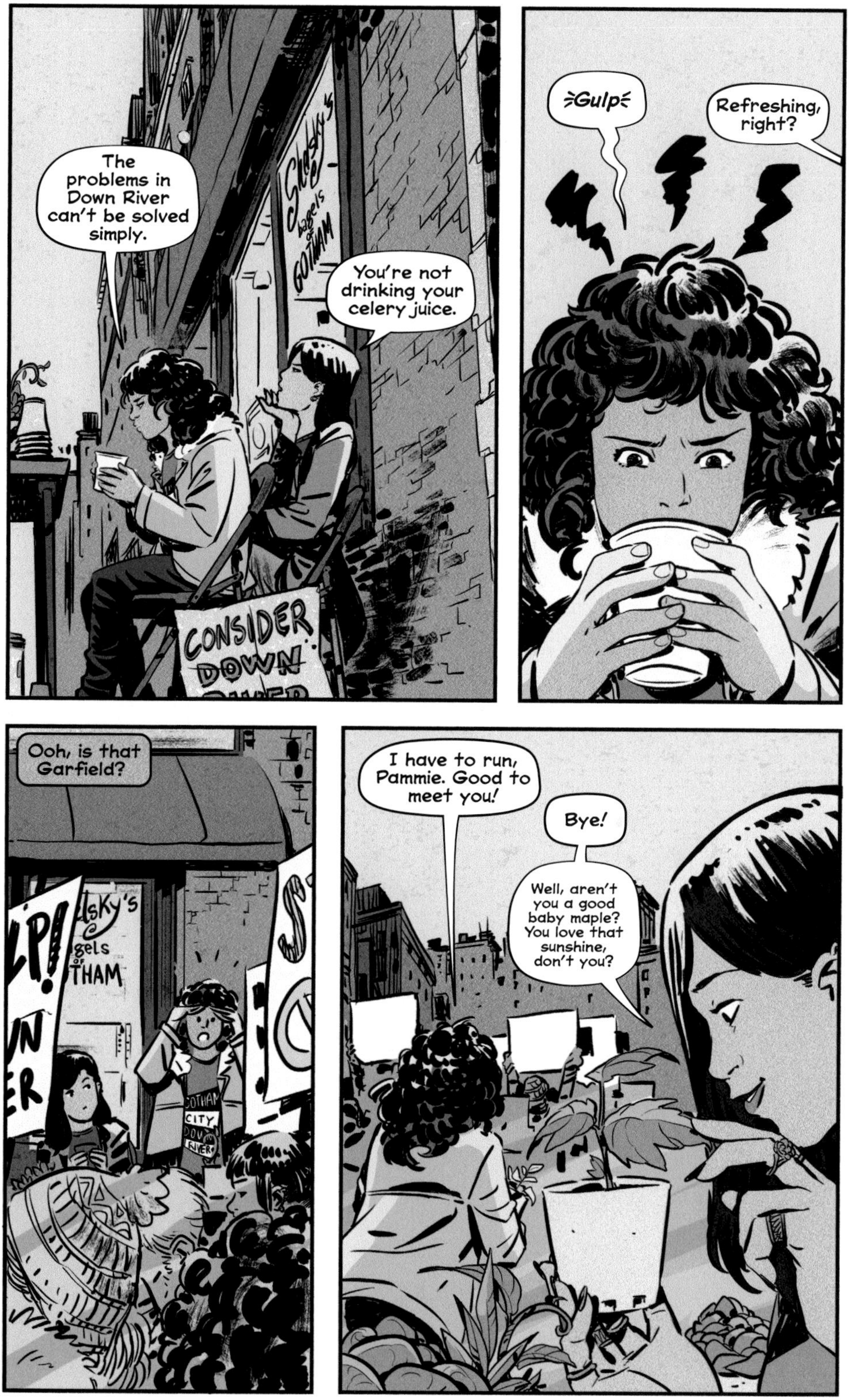
The problems in Down River can't be solved simply.
You're not drinking your celery juice.
Skolsky's bagels of Gotham
CONSIDER DOWN RIVER
Gulp
Refreshing, right?
Ooh, is that Garfield?
GOTHAM CITY DOWN RIVER
I have to run, Pammie. Good to meet you!
Bye!
Well, aren't you a good baby maple? You love that sunshine, don't you?

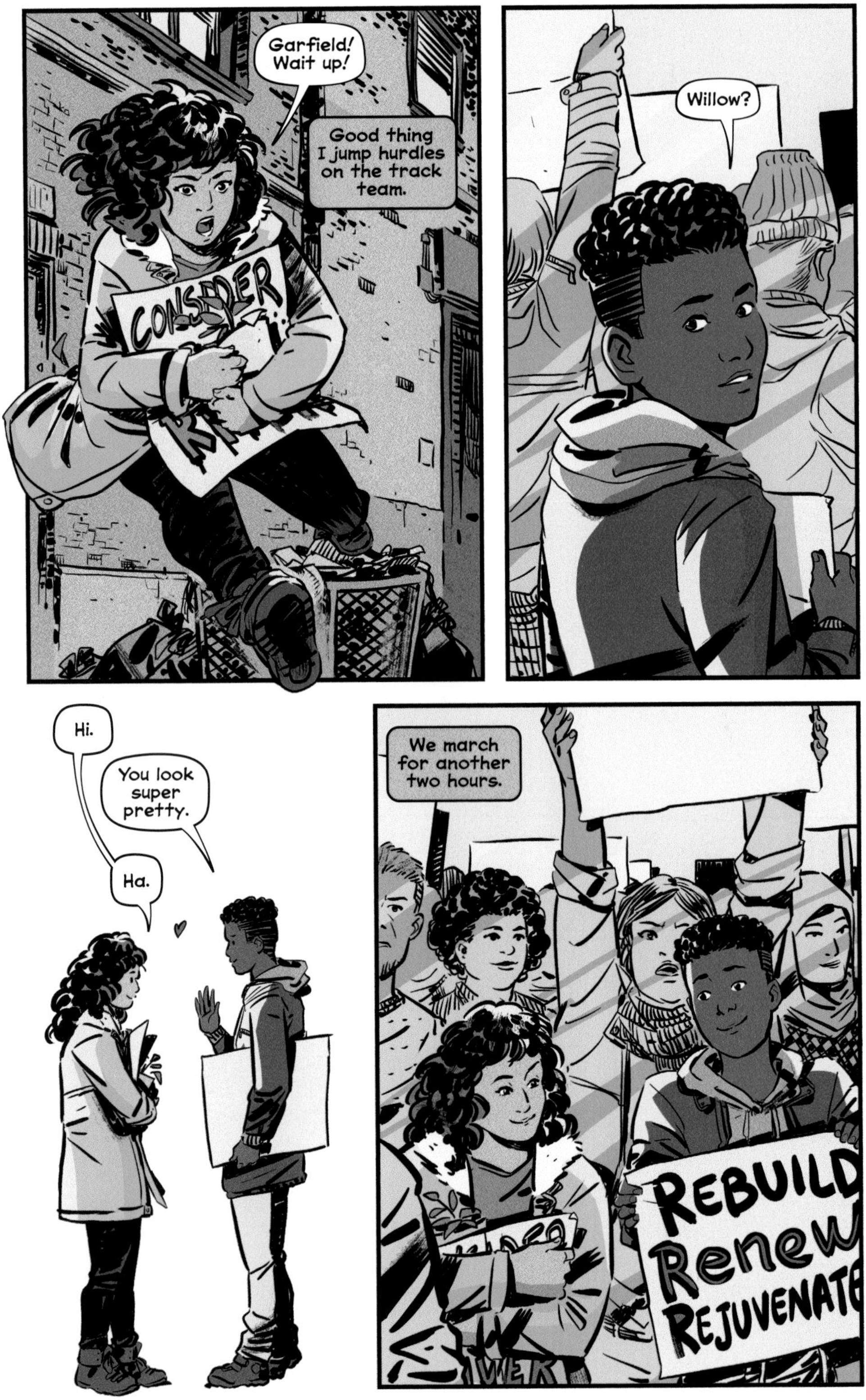
Garfield! Wait up!
Good thing I jump hurdles on the track team.
CONSIDER
Willow?
Hi.
You look super pretty.
Ha.
We march for another two hours.
REBUILD
Renew
REJUVENATE

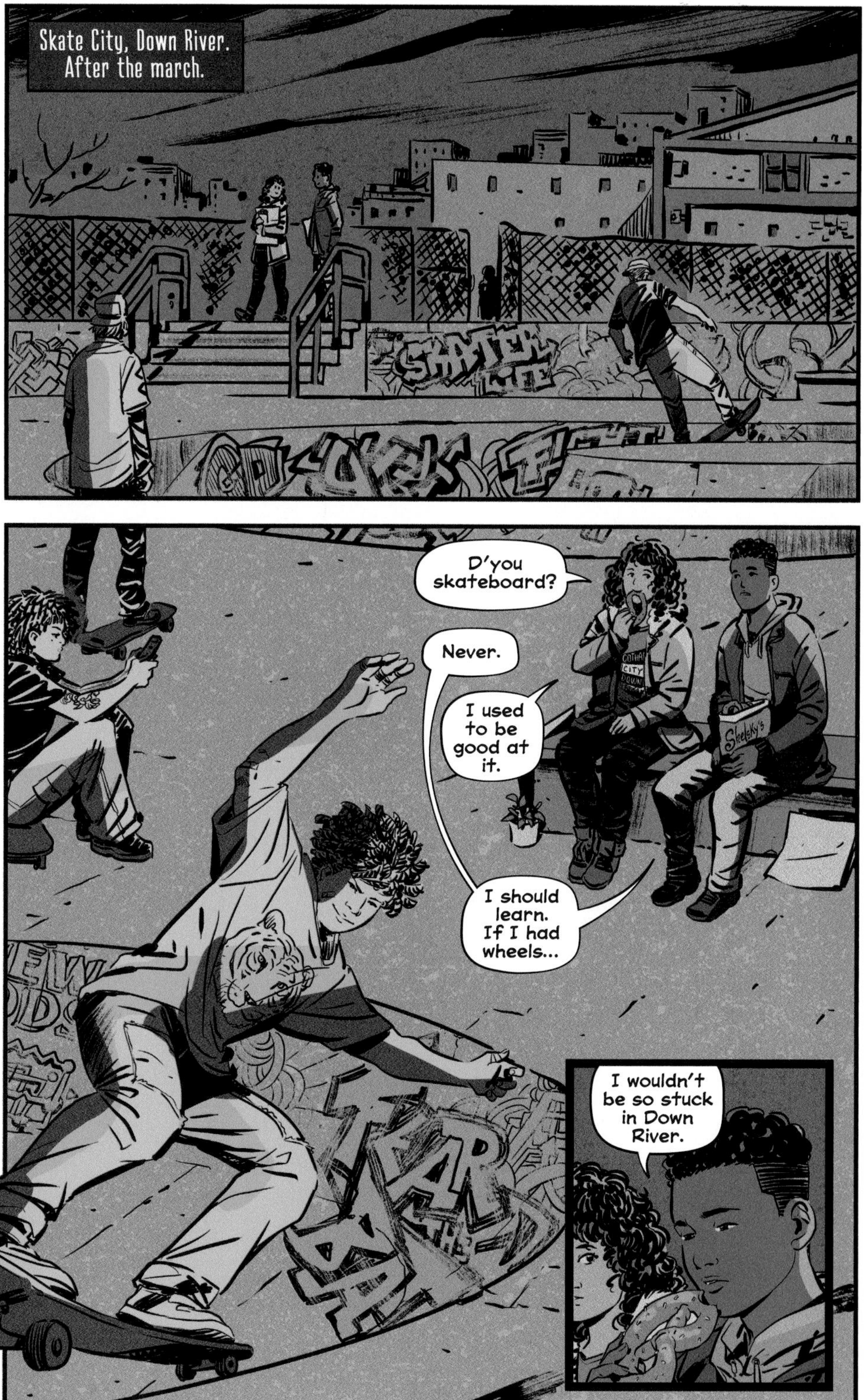
Skate City, Down River.
After the march.
SKATER LIFE
D'you skateboard?
Never.
I used to be good at it.
I should learn. If I had wheels...
I wouldn't be so stuck in Down River.

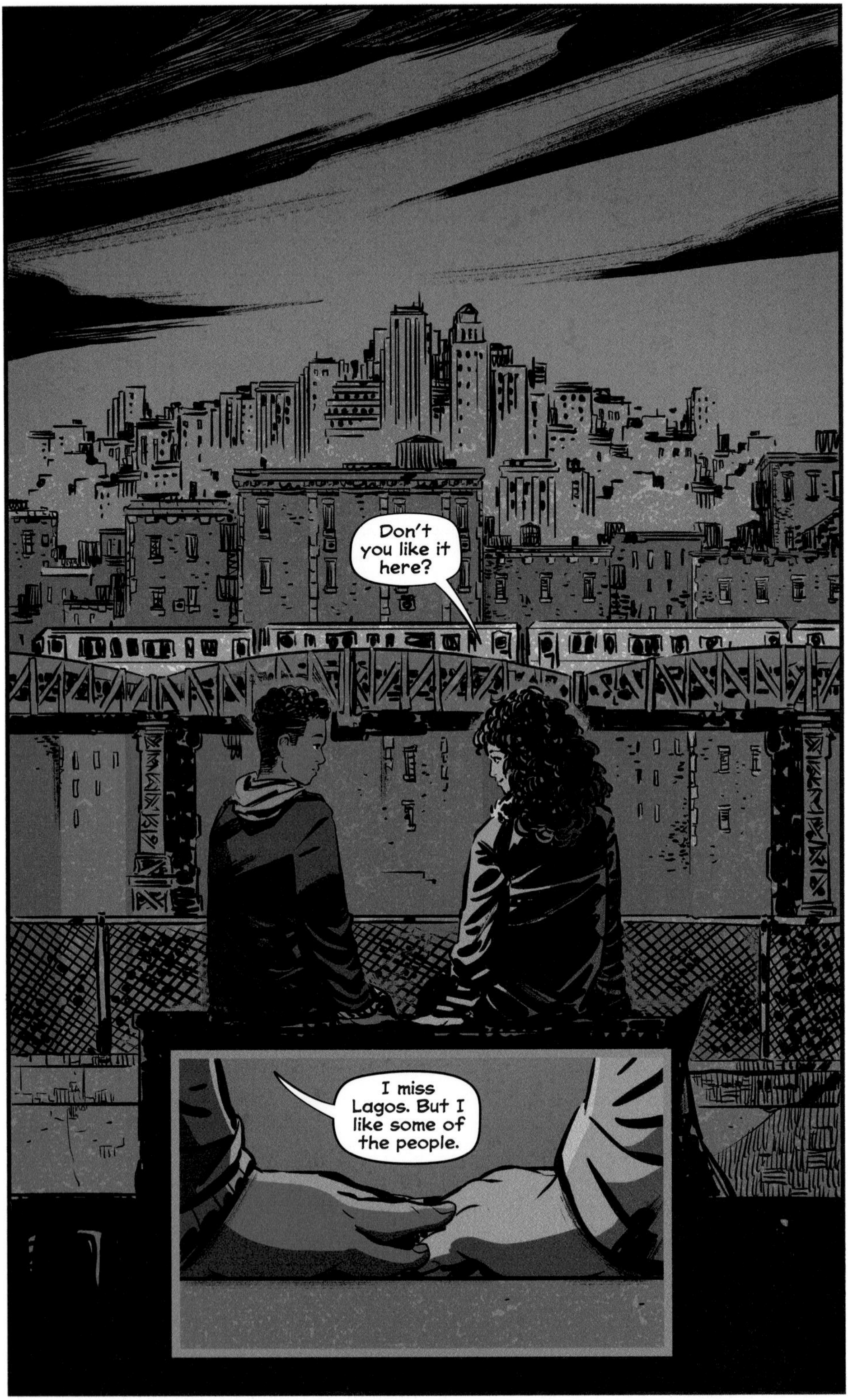
Don't you like it here?
I miss Lagos. But I like some of the people.

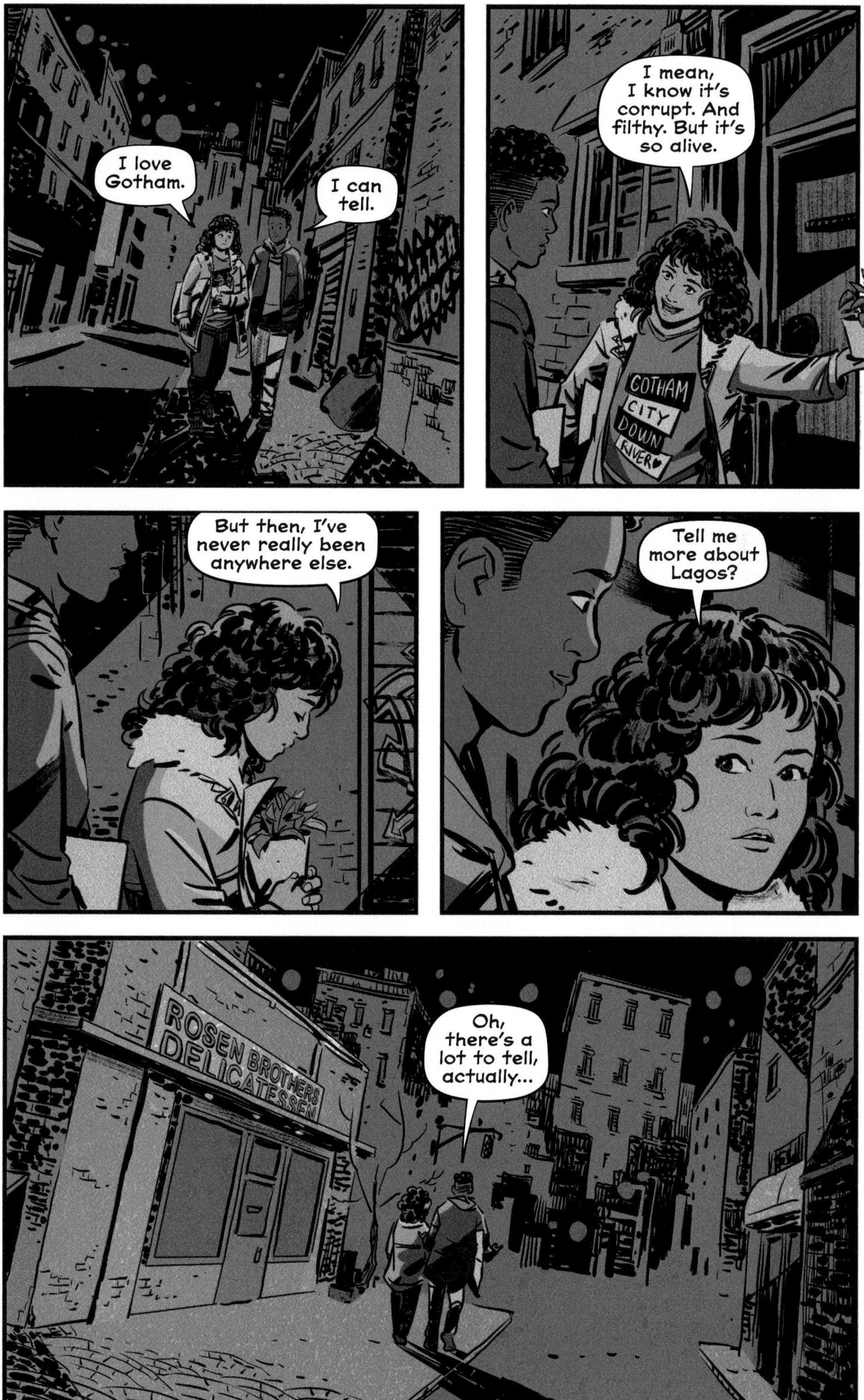
I love Gotham.
I can tell.
I mean, I know it's corrupt. And filthy. But it's so alive.
GOTHAM CITY DOWN RIVER
But then, I've never really been anywhere else.
Tell me more about Lagos?
ROSEN BROTHERS DELICATESSEN
Oh, there's a lot to tell, actually...

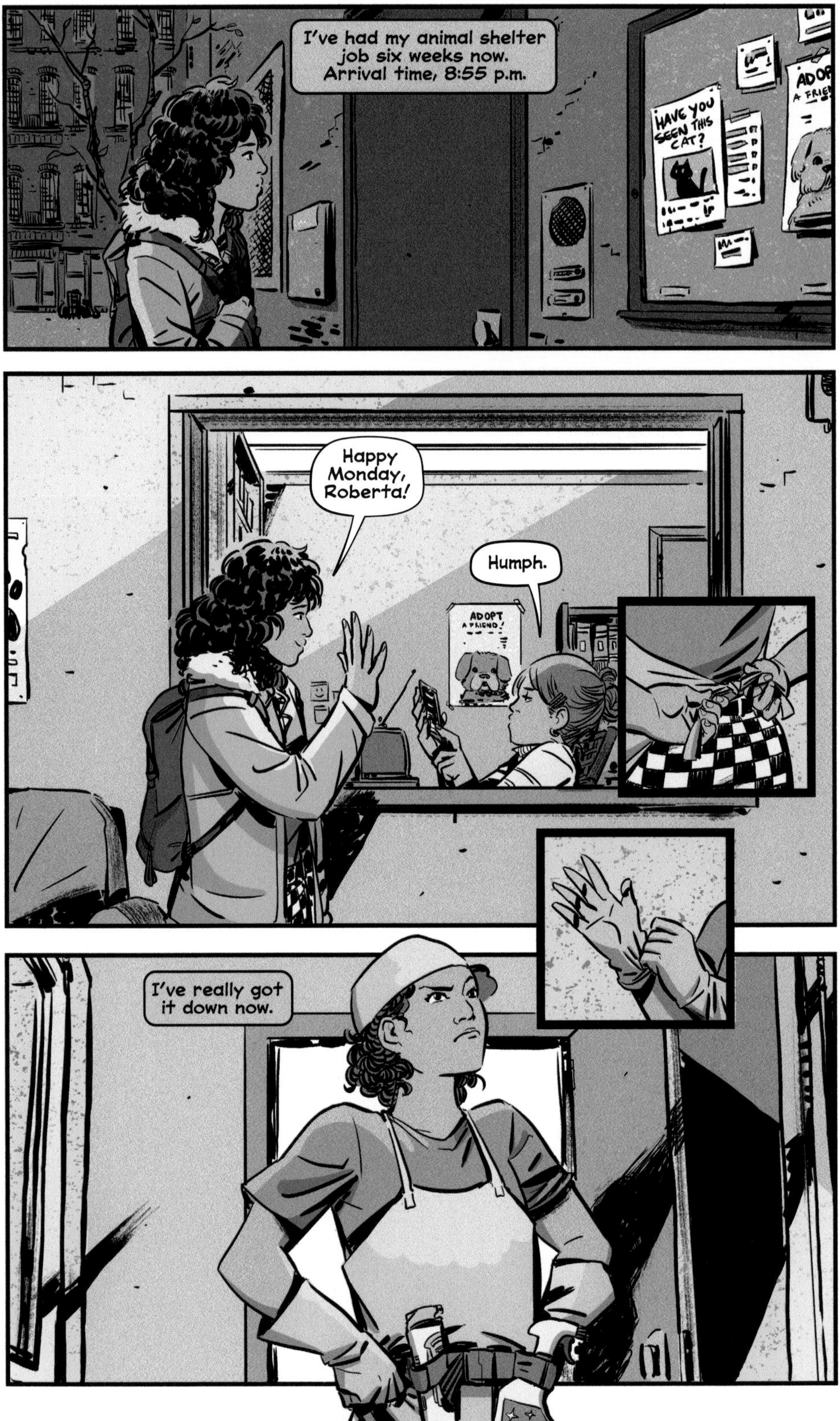
I've had my animal shelter job six weeks now. Arrival time, 8:55 p.m.
HAVE YOU SEEN THIS CAT?
ADOPT A FRIEND
Happy Monday, Roberta!
Humph.
ADOPT A FRIEND!
I've really got it down now.

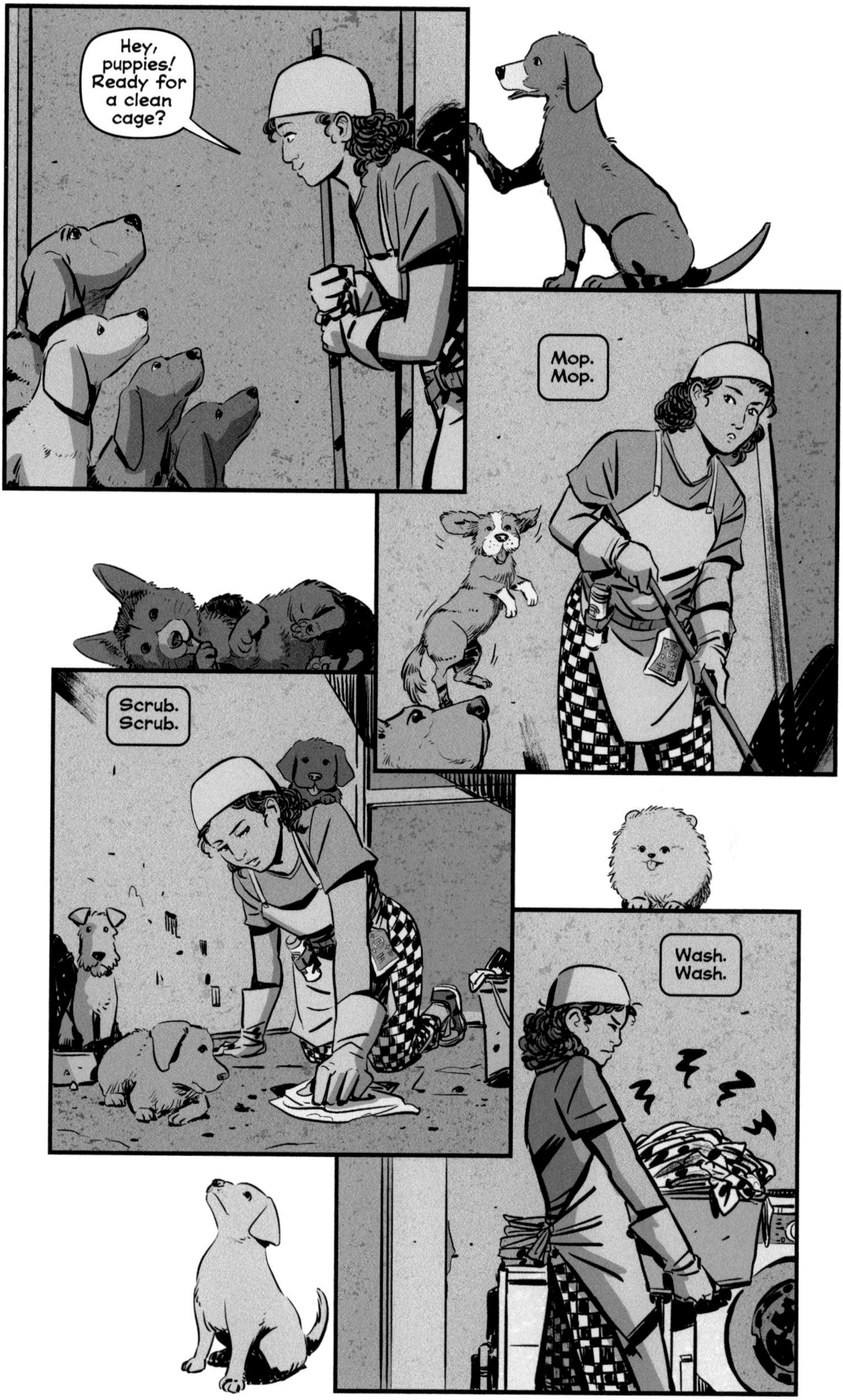
Hey, puppies! Ready for a clean cage?
Mop. Mop.
Scrub. Scrub.
Wash. Wash.

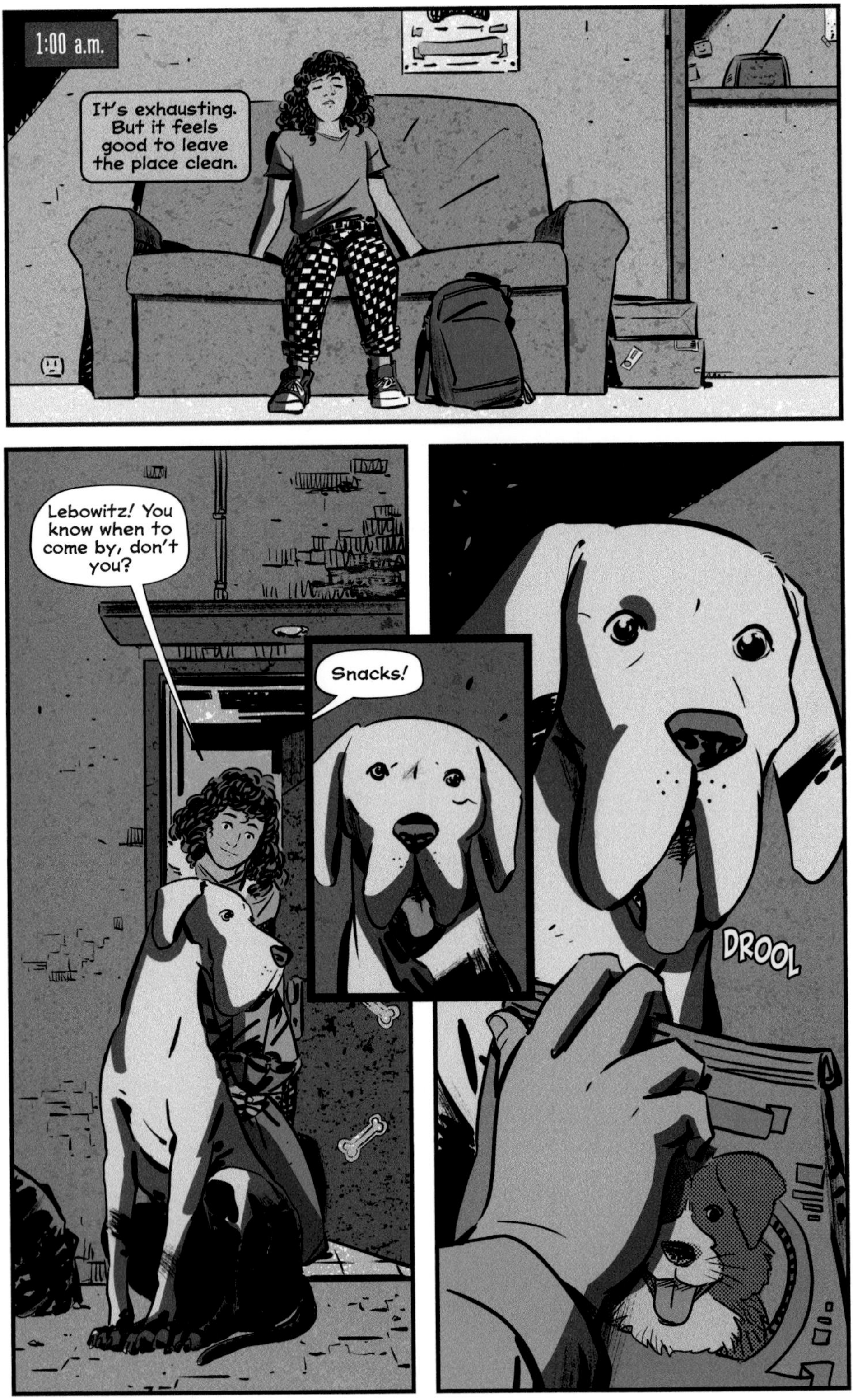
1:00 a.m.
It's exhausting. But it feels good to leave the place clean.
Lebowitz! You know when to come by, don't you?
Snacks!
DROOL

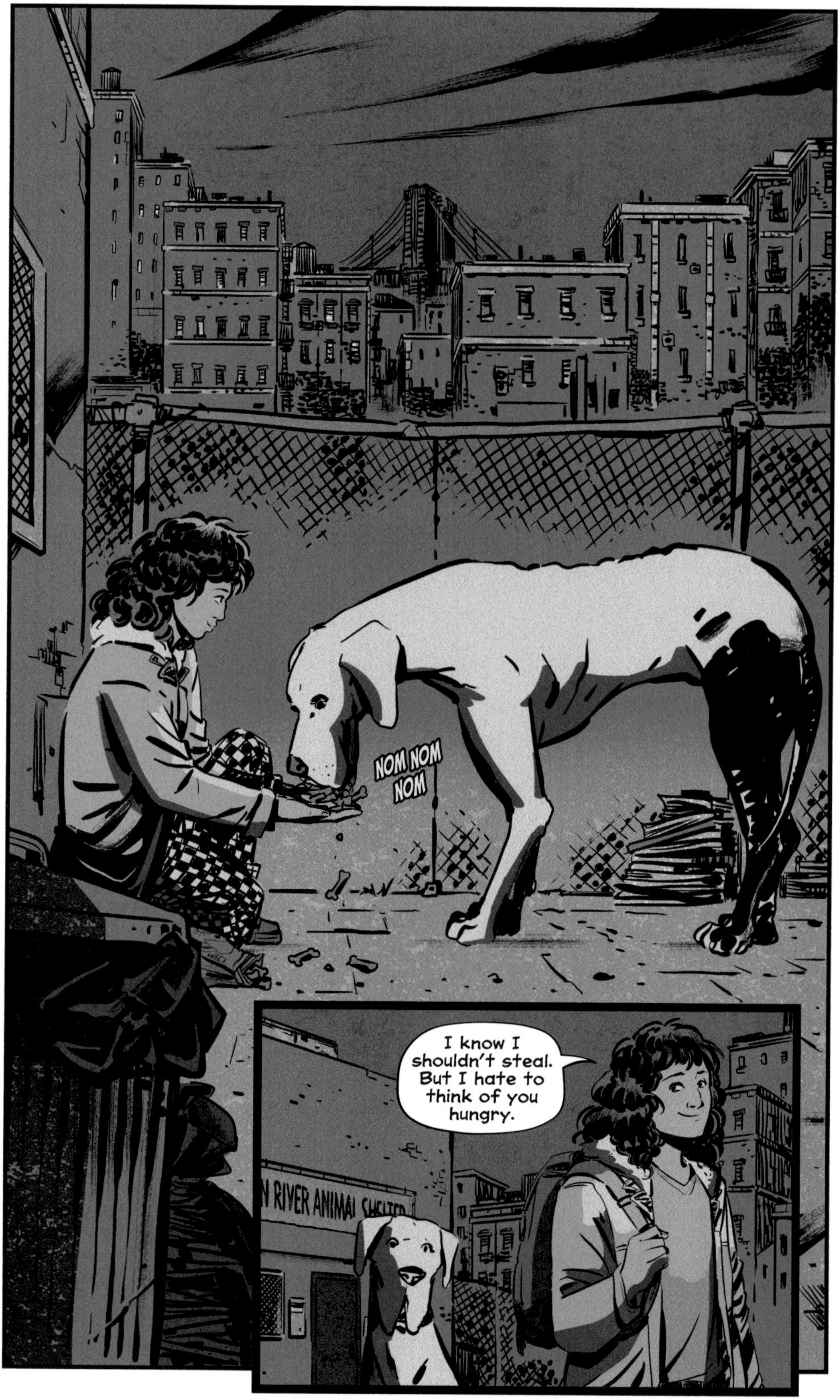
NOM NOM NOM
I know I shouldn't steal. But I hate to think of you hungry.
RIVER ANIMAL

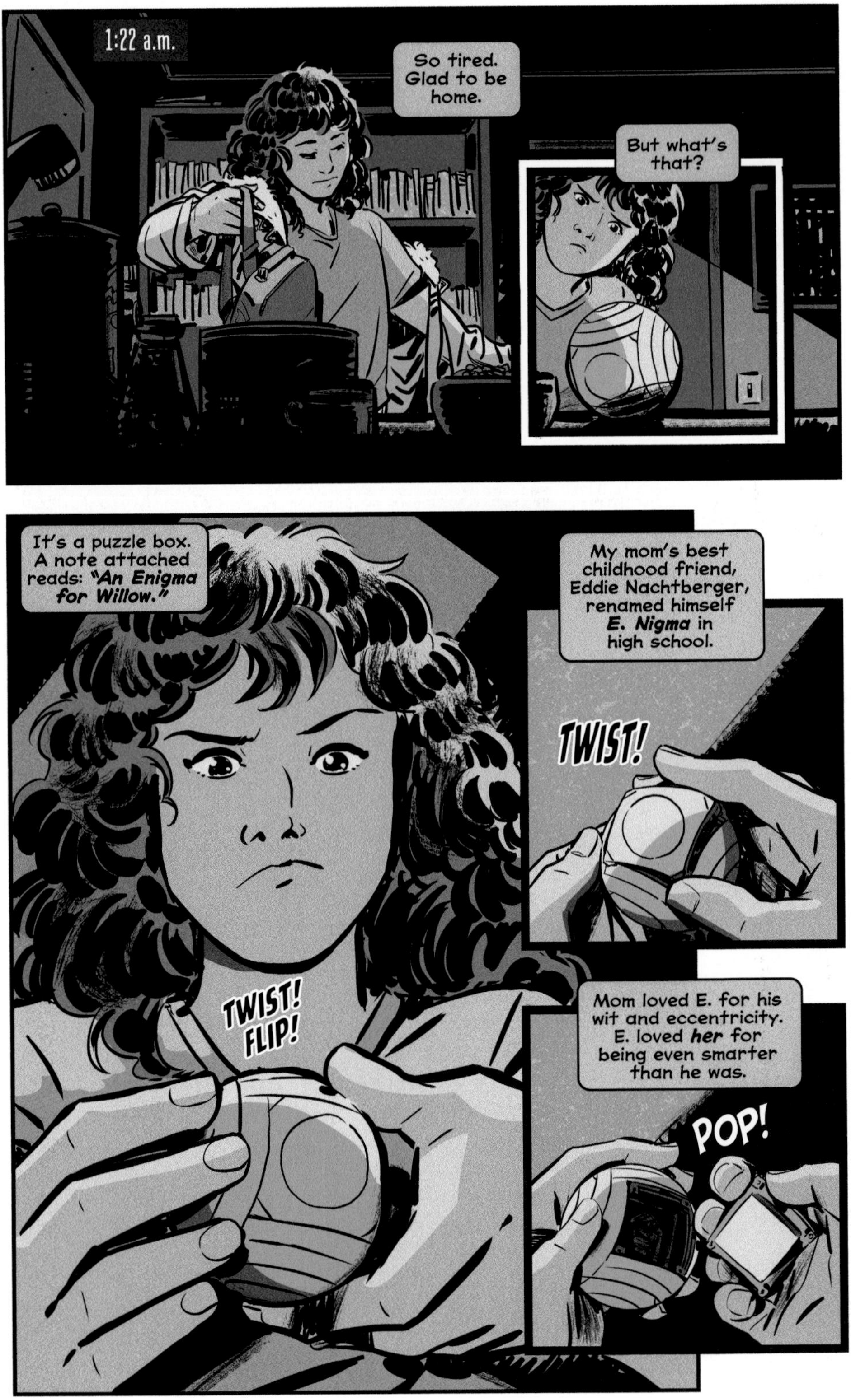
1:22 a.m.
So tired. Glad to be home.
But what's that?
It's a puzzle box. A note attached reads: "An Enigma for Willow."
TWIST! FLIP!
My mom's best childhood friend, Eddie Nachtberger, renamed himself E. Nigma in high school.
TWIST!
Mom loved E. for his wit and eccentricity. E. loved her for being even smarter than he was.
POP!

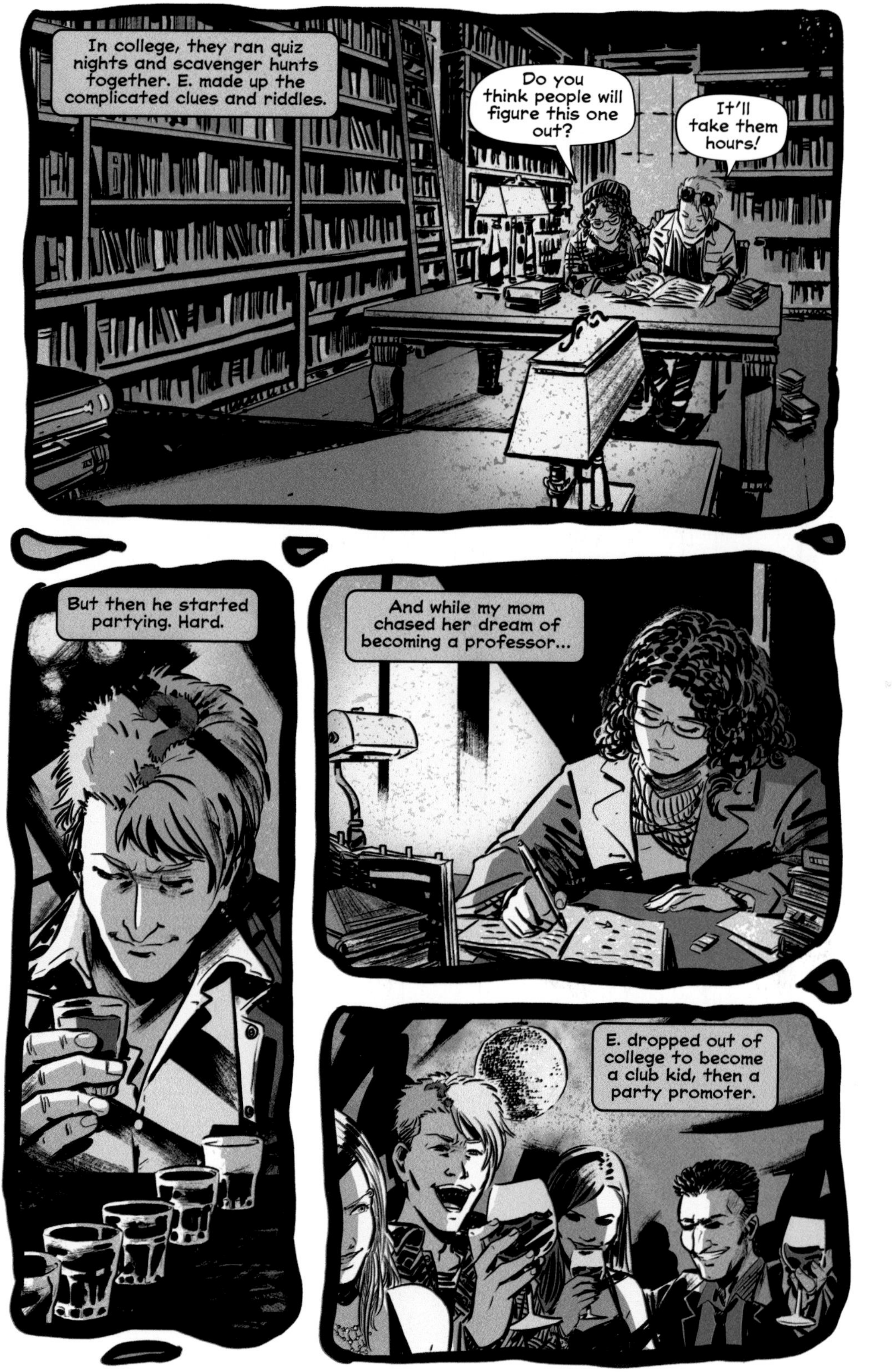

In college, they ran quiz nights and scavenger hunts together. E. made up the complicated clues and riddles.
Do you think people will figure this one out?
It'll take them hours!
But then he started partying. Hard.
And while my mom chased her dream of becoming a professor...
E. dropped out of college to become a club kid, then a party promoter.

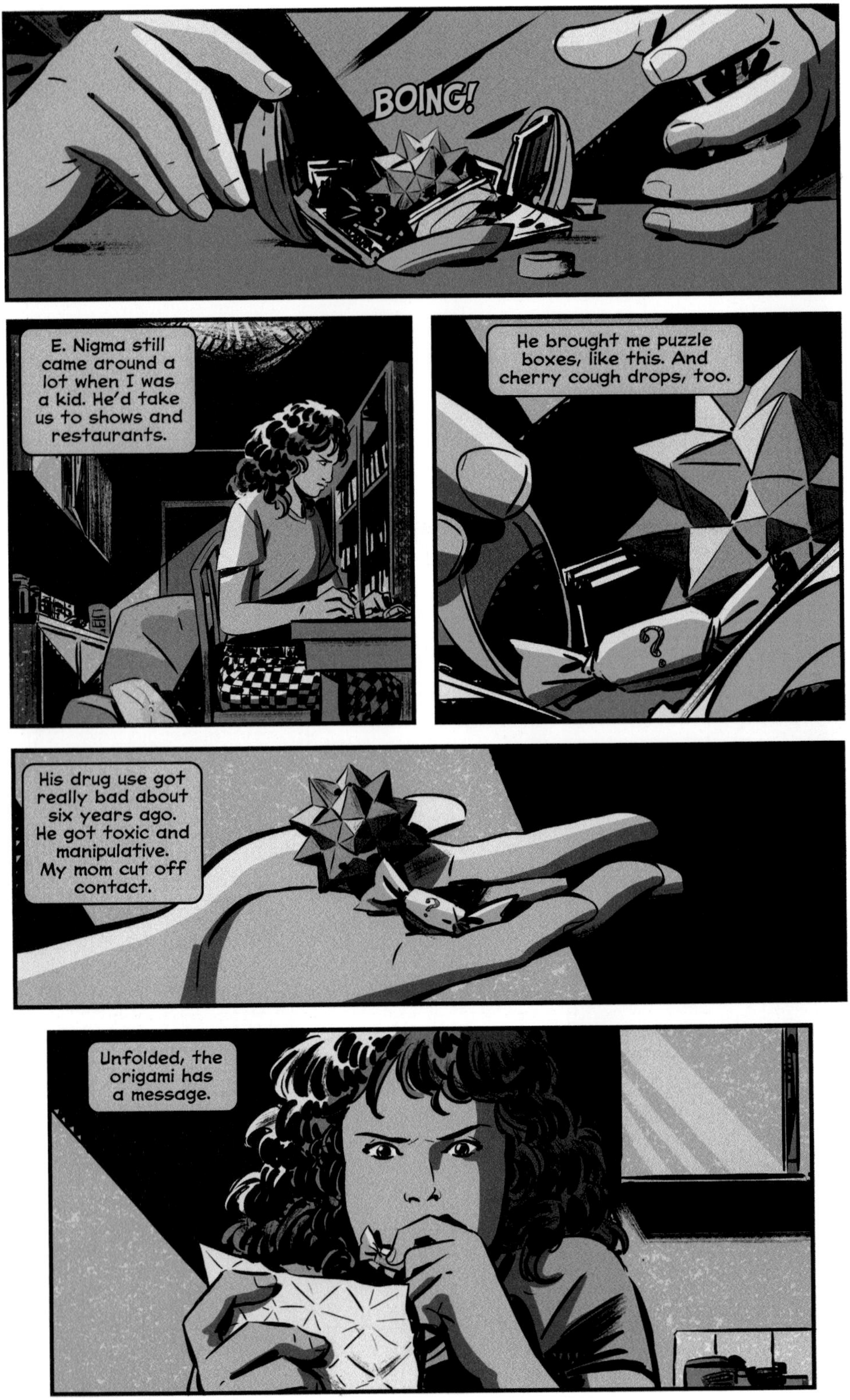
BOING!
E. Nigma still came around a lot when I was a kid. He'd take us to shows and restaurants.
He brought me puzzle boxes, like this. And cherry cough drops, too.
His drug use got really bad about six years ago. He got toxic and manipulative. My mom cut off contact.
Unfolded, the origami has a message.

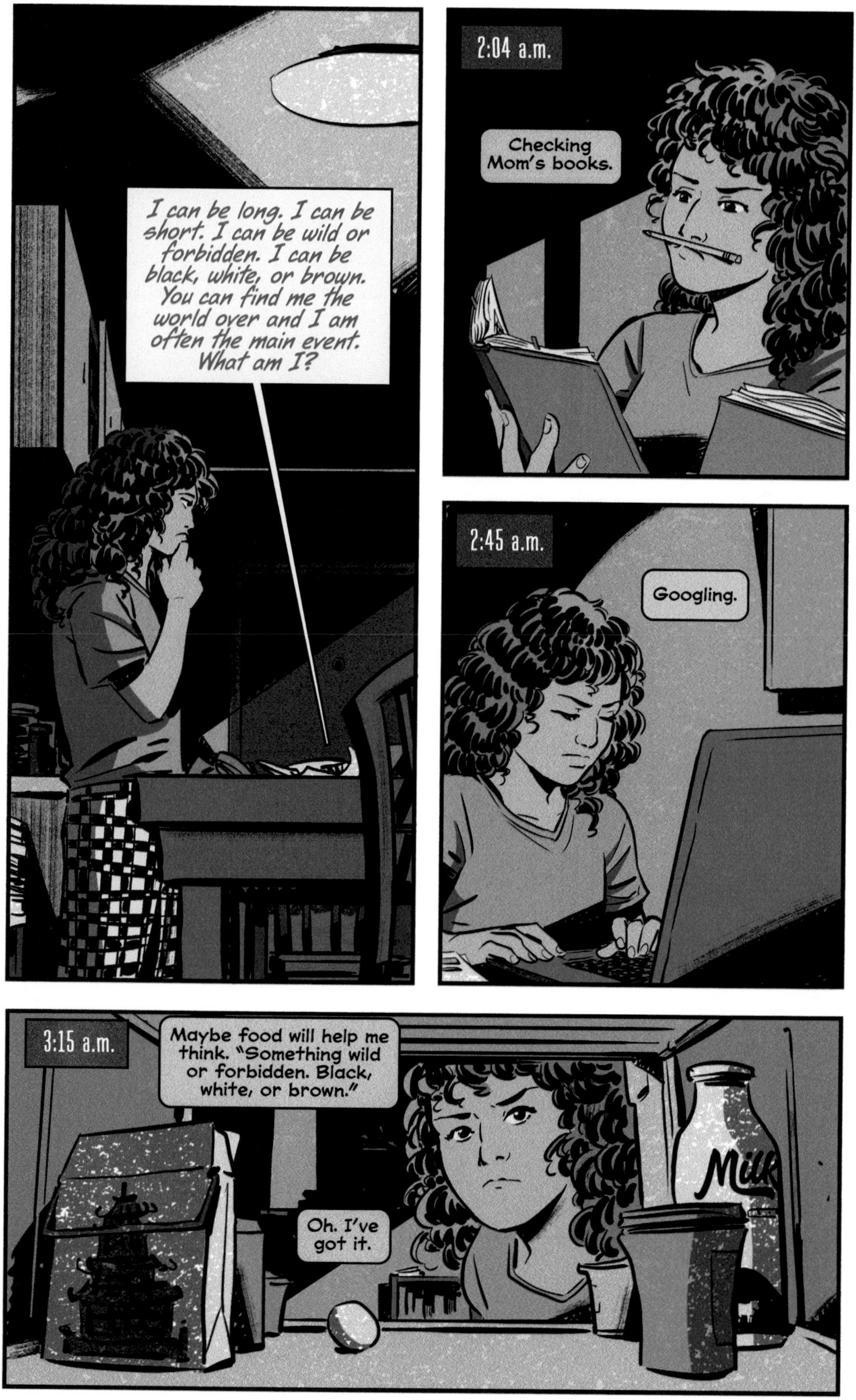
I can be long. I can be short. I can be wild or forbidden. I can be black, white, or brown. You can find me the world over and I am often the main event. What am I?
2:04 a.m.
Checking Mom's books.
2:45 a.m.
Googling.
3:15 a.m.
Maybe food will help me think. "Something wild or forbidden. Black, white, or brown."
Oh. I've got it.
Milk

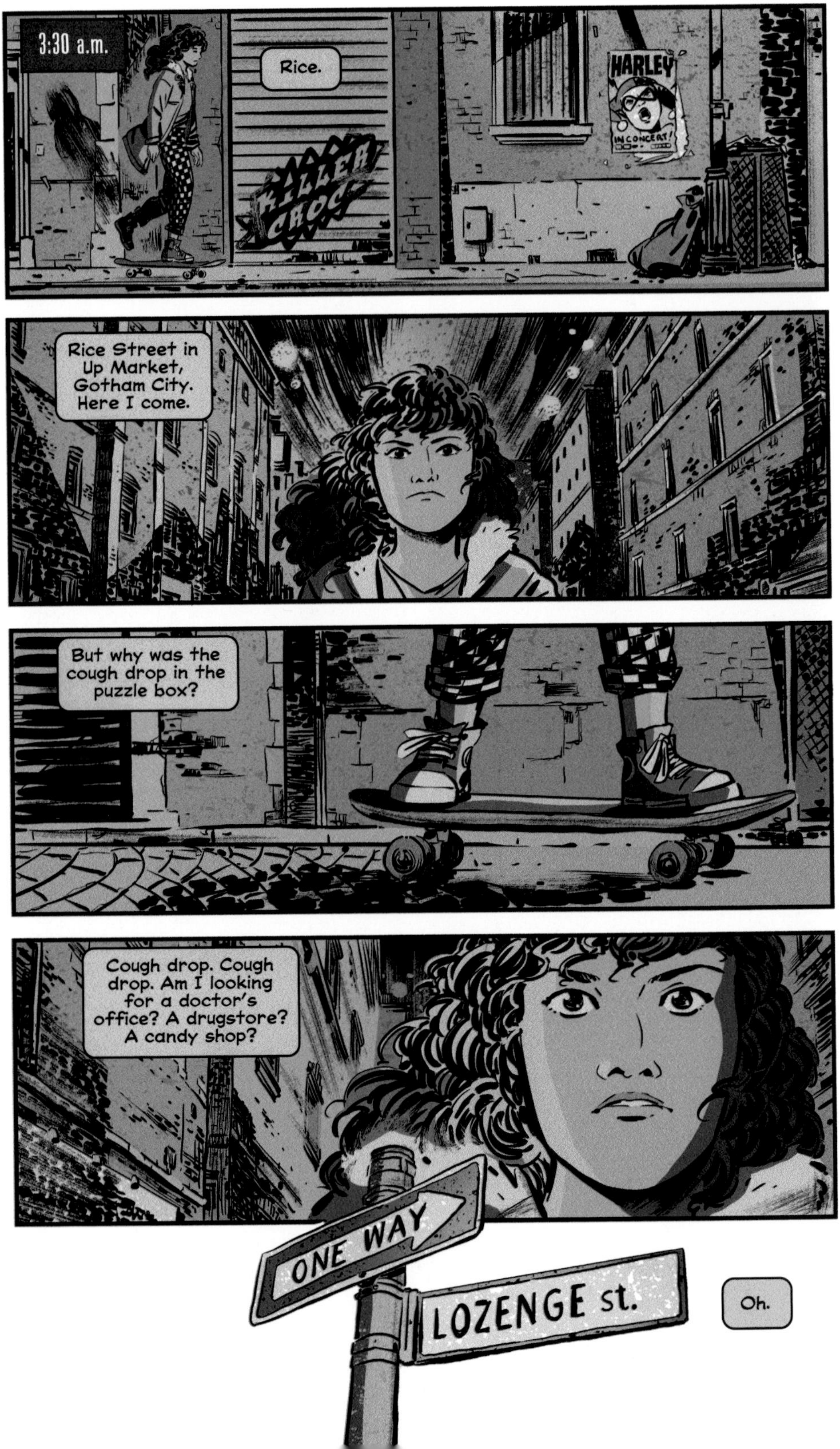
3:30 a.m.
Rice.
KILLER CROC
HARLEY
IN CONCERT!
Rice Street in Up Market, Gotham City. Here I come.
But why was the cough drop in the puzzle box?
Cough drop. Cough drop. Am I looking for a doctor's office? A drugstore? A candy shop?
ONE WAY
LOZENGE St.
Oh.

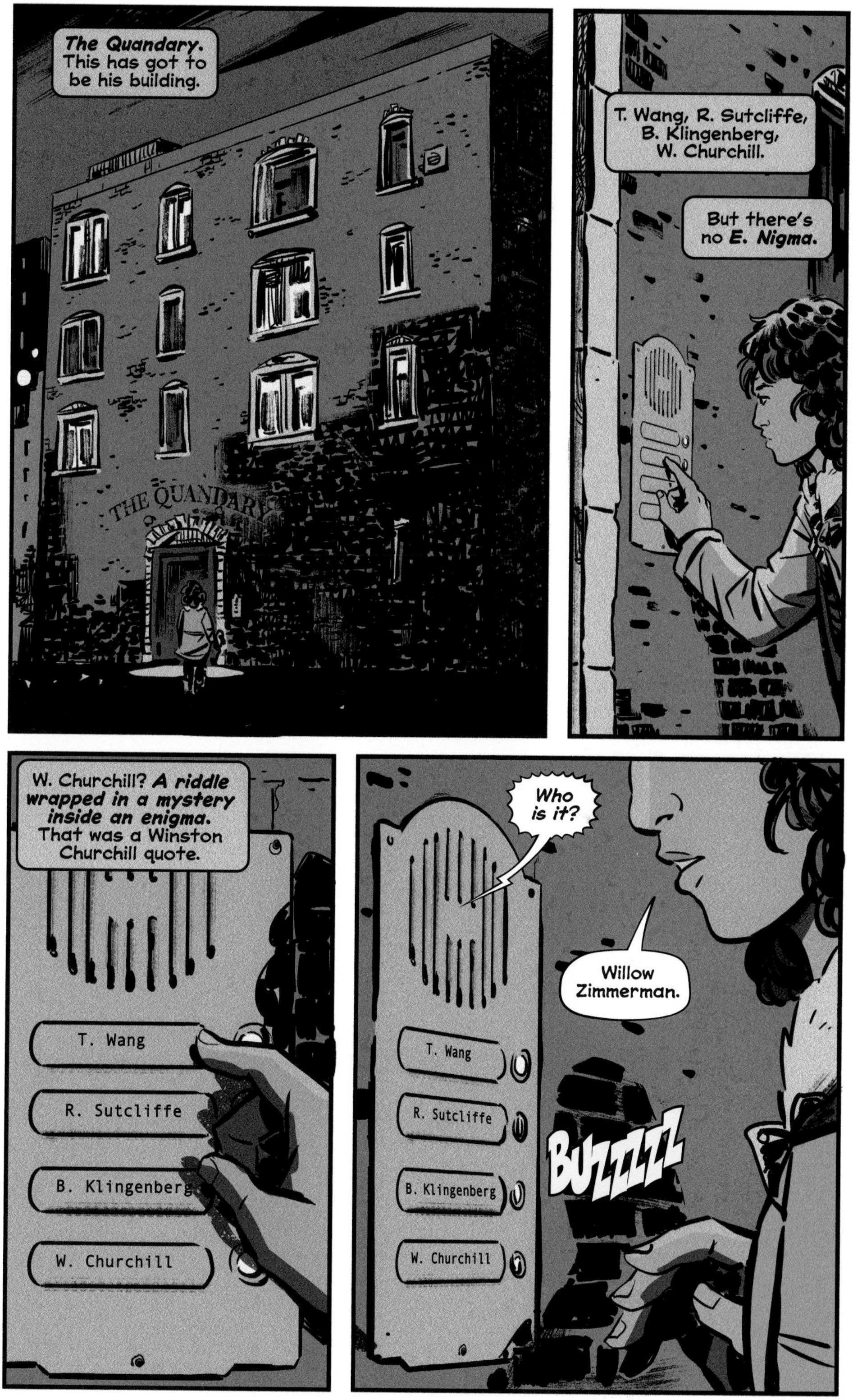
The Quandary. This has got to be his building.
THE QUANDARY
T. Wang, R. Sutcliffe, B. Klingenberg, W. Churchill.
But there's no E. Nigma.
W. Churchill? A riddle wrapped in a mystery inside an enigma. That was a Winston Churchill quote.
T. Wang
R. Sutcliffe
B. Klingenberg
W. Churchill
Who is it?
Willow Zimmerman.
T. Wang
R. Sutcliffe
B. Klingenberg
W. Churchill
BUZZZZZ

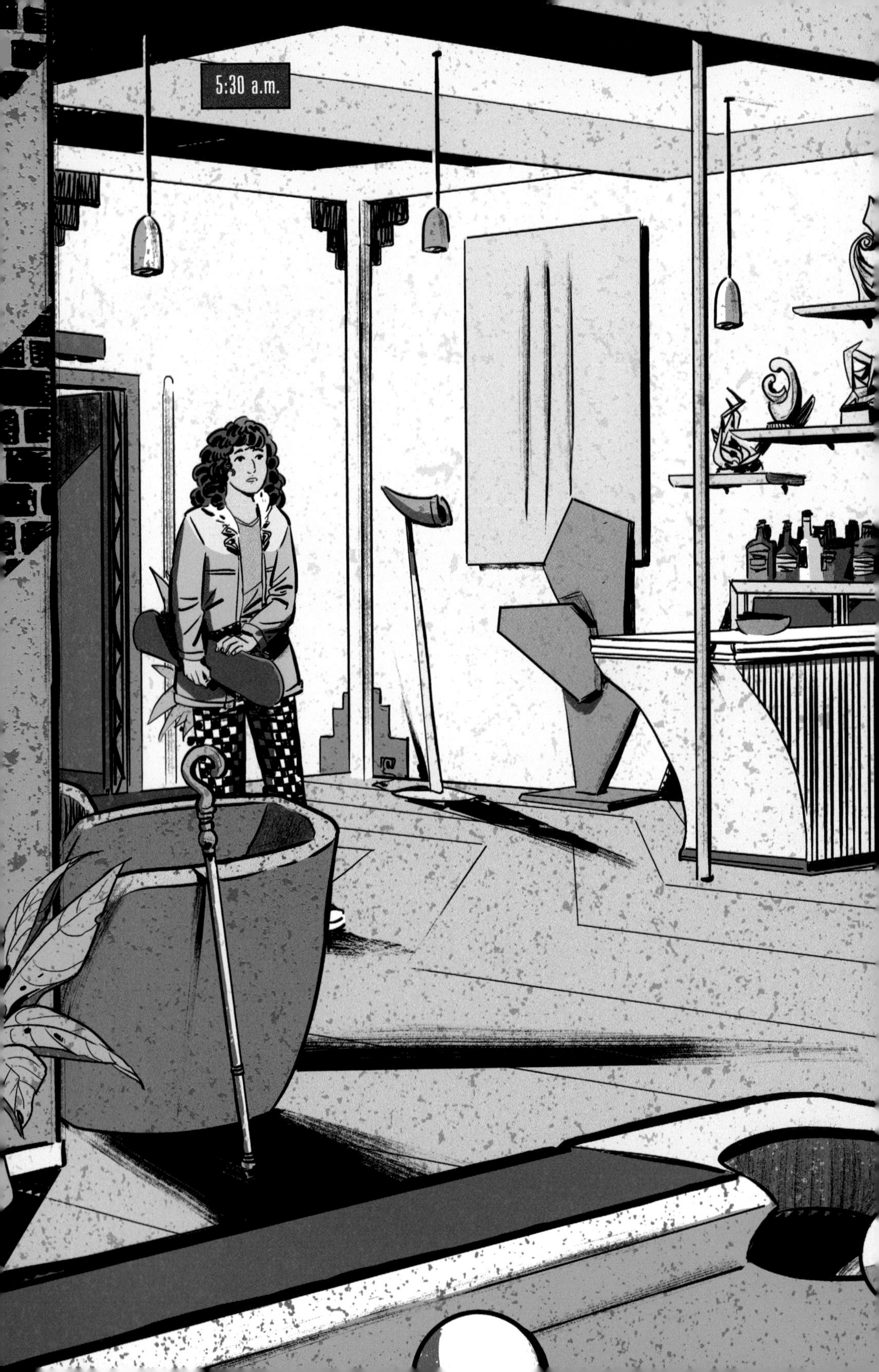
5:30 a.m.

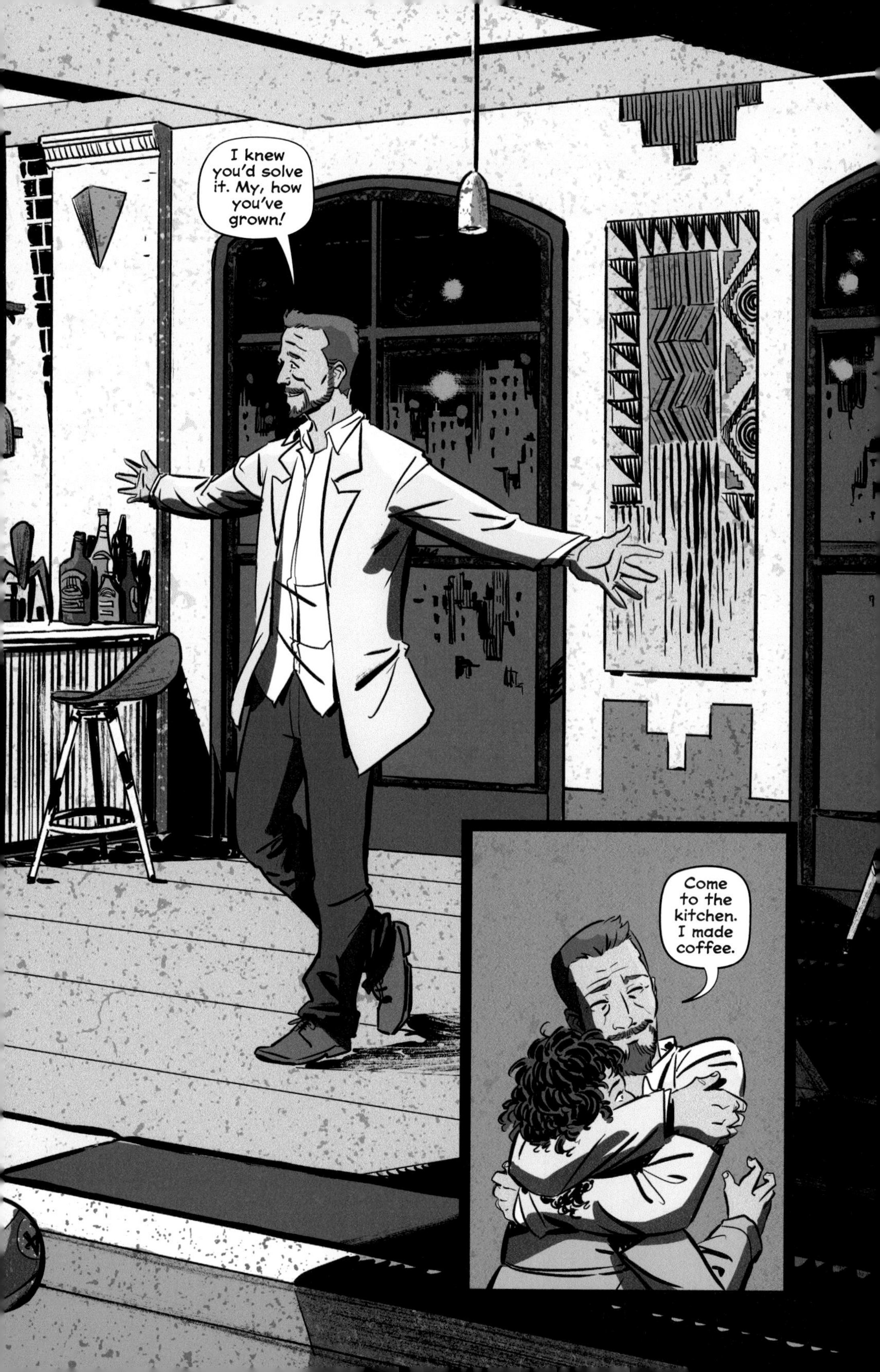
I knew you'd solve it. My, how you've grown!
Come to the kitchen. I made coffee.

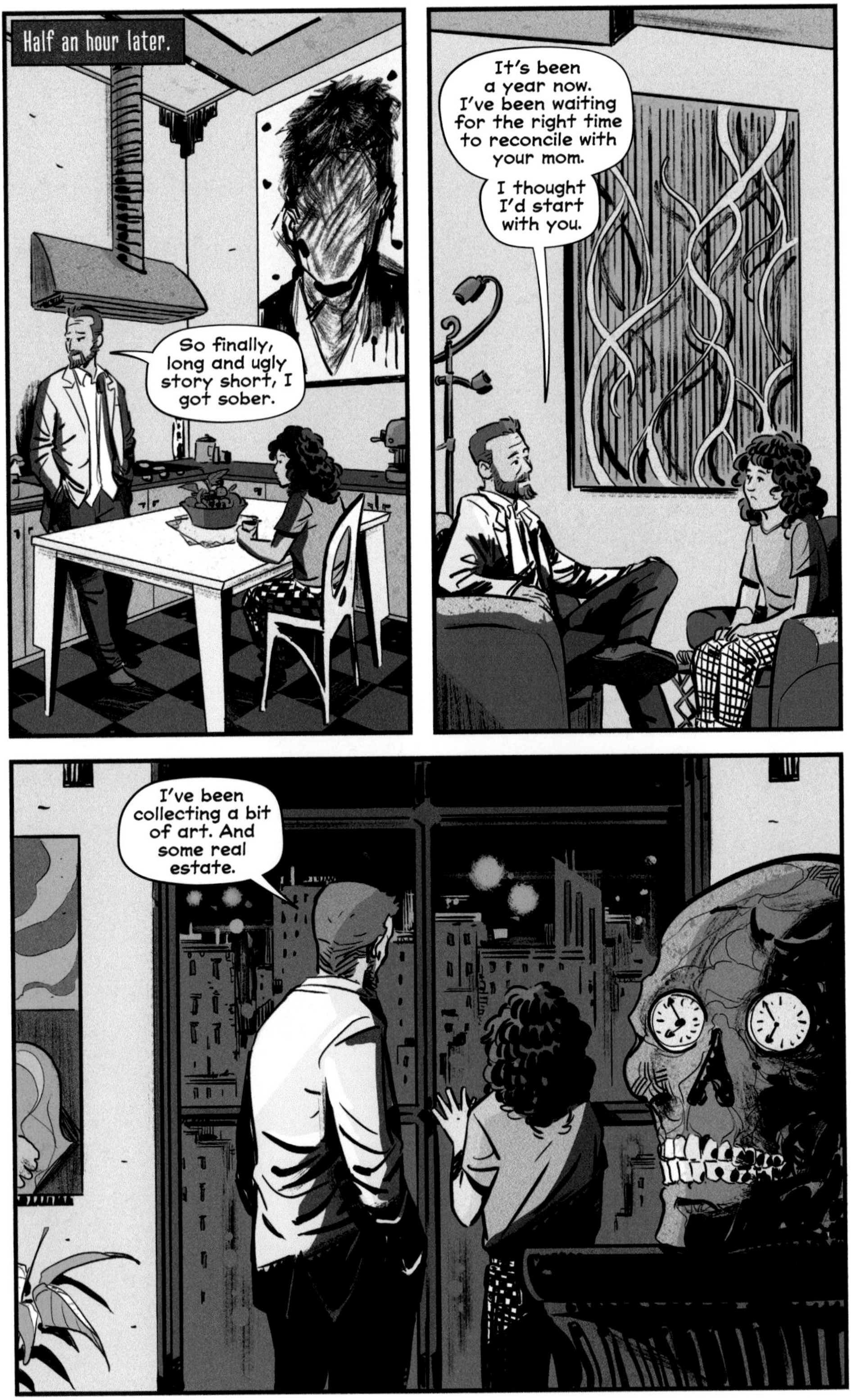
Half an hour later.
So finally, long and ugly story short, I got sober.
It's been a year now. I've been waiting for the right time to reconcile with your mom.
I thought I'd start with you.
I've been collecting a bit of art. And some real estate.

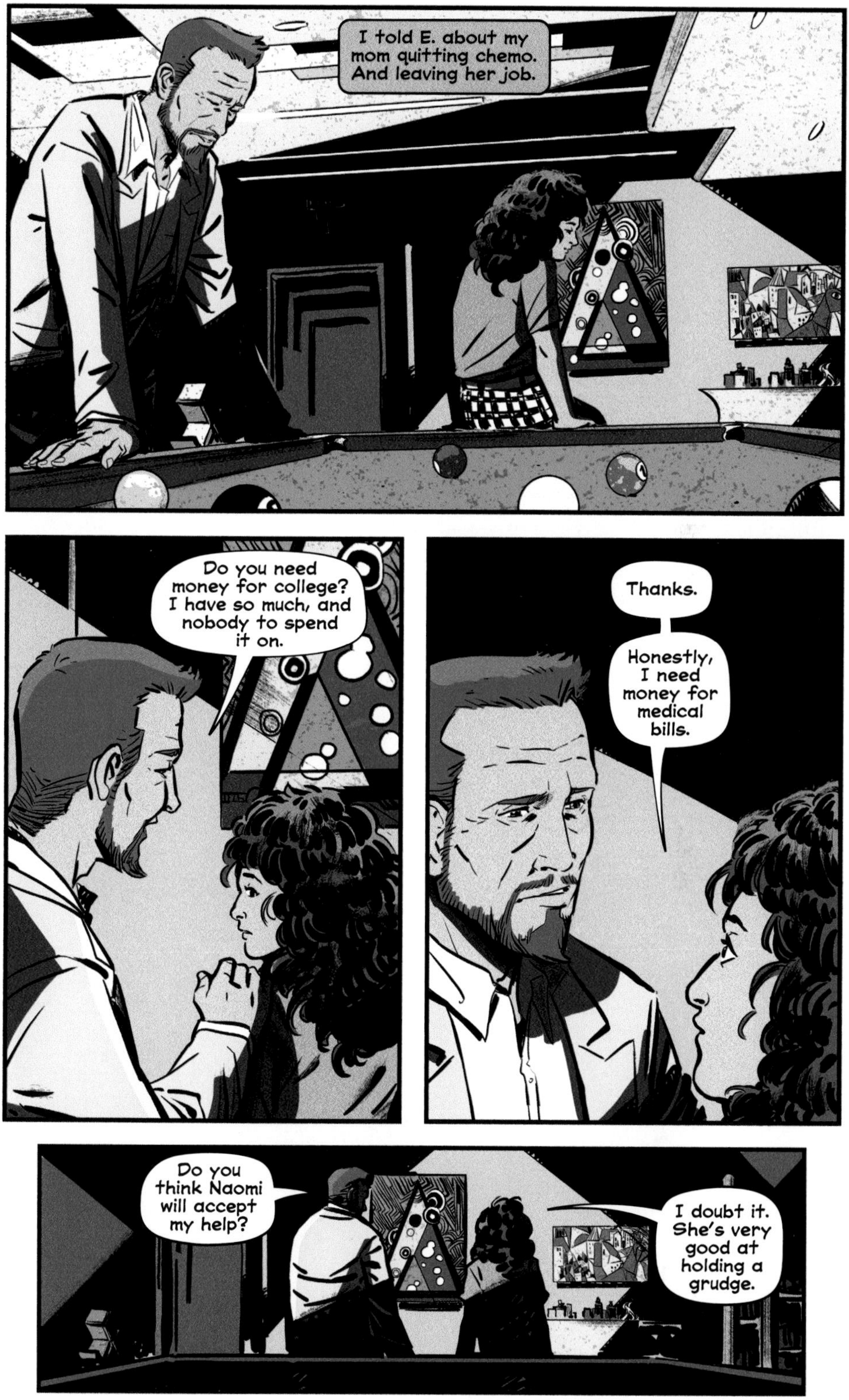
I told E. about my mom quitting chemo. And leaving her job.
Do you need money for college? I have so much, and nobody to spend it on.
Thanks.
Honestly, I need money for medical bills.
Do you think Naomi will accept my help?
I doubt it. She's very good at holding a grudge.

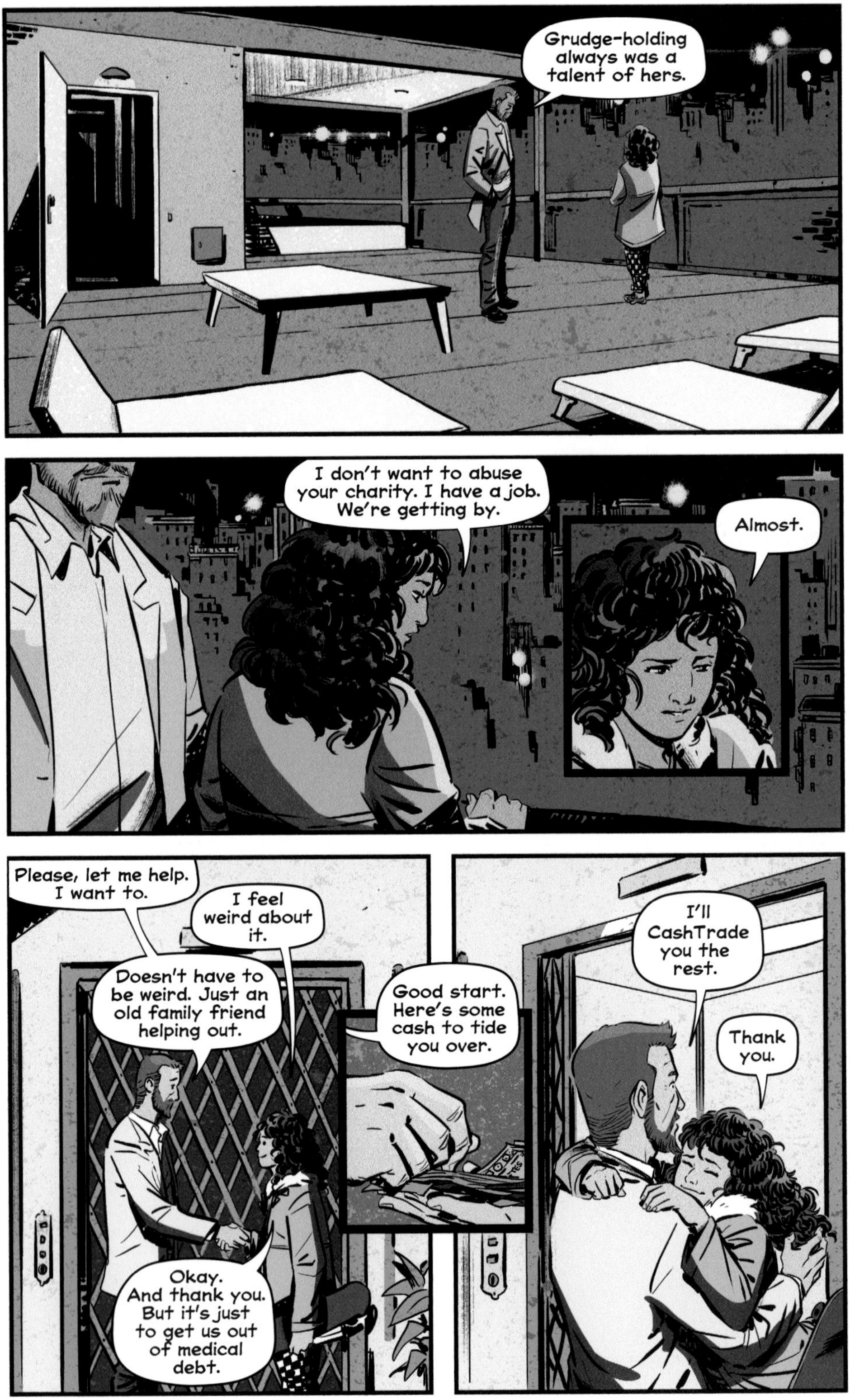
Grudge-holding always was a talent of hers.
I don't want to abuse your charity. I have a job. We're getting by.
Almost.
Please, let me help. I want to.
I feel weird about it.
Doesn't have to be weird. Just an old family friend helping out.
Okay. And thank you. But it's just to get us out of medical debt.
Good start. Here's some cash to tide you over.
I'll CashTrade you the rest.
Thank you.

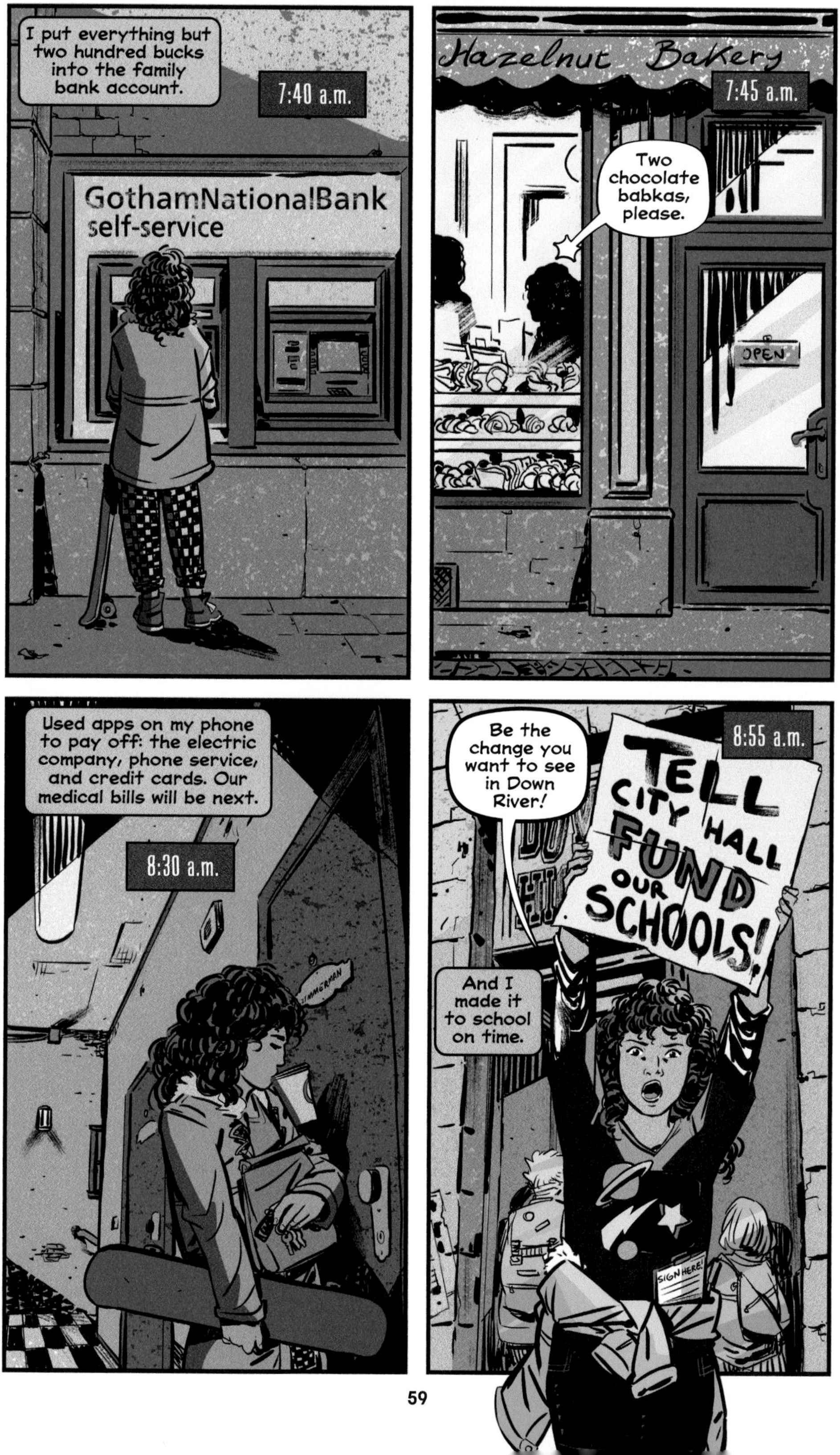
I put everything but two hundred bucks into the family bank account.
7:40 a.m.
GothamNationalBank self-service
Hazelnut Bakery
7:45 a.m.
Two chocolate babkas, please.
OPEN
Used apps on my phone to pay off: the electric company, phone service, and credit cards. Our medical bills will be next.
8:30 a.m.
ZIMMERMAN
Be the change you want to see in Down River!
8:55 a.m.
TELL CITY HALL FUND OUR SCHOOLS!
And I made it to school on time.
SIGN HERE!

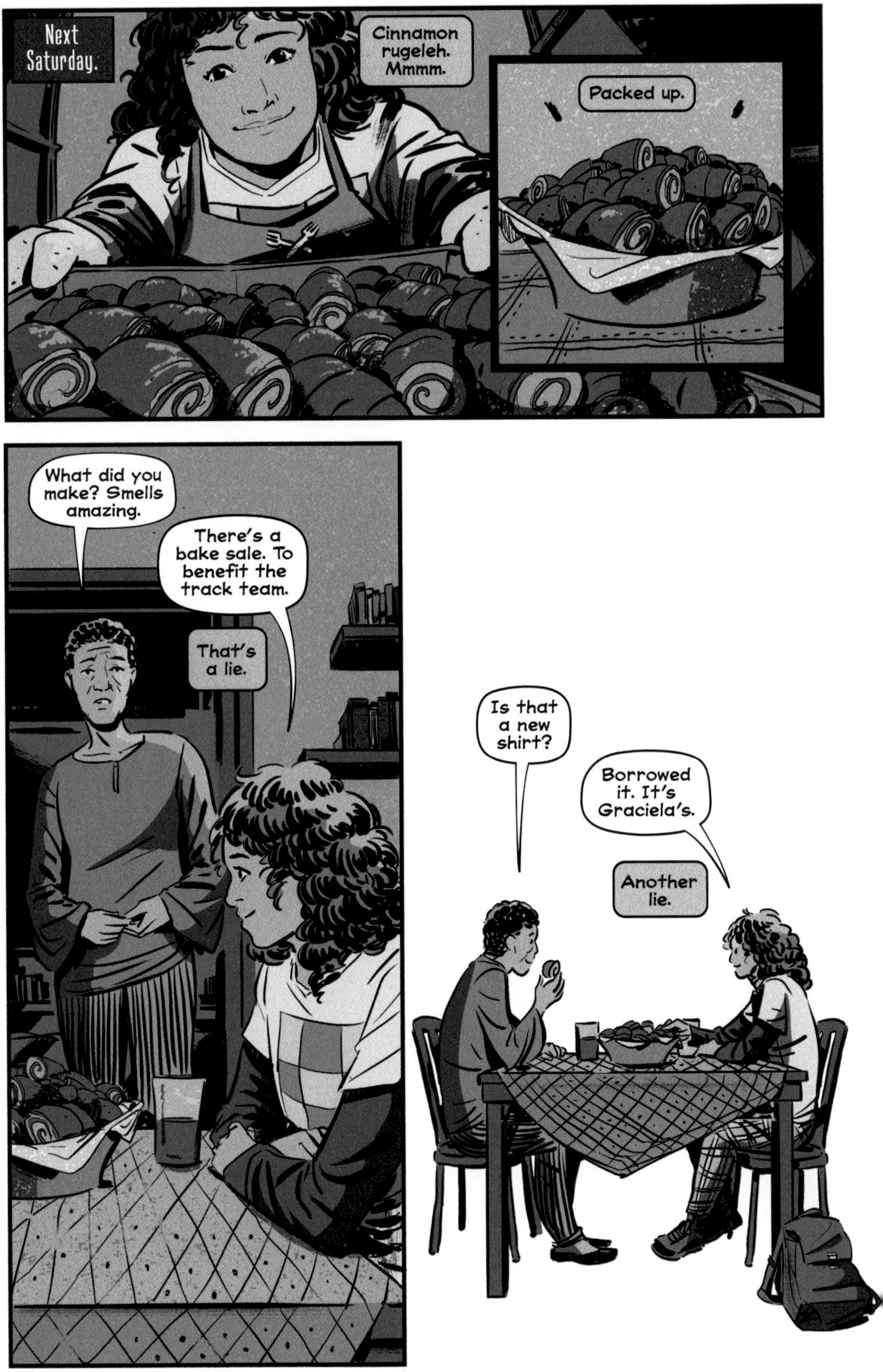
Next Saturday.
Cinnamon rugeleh. Mmmm.
Packed up.
What did you make? Smells amazing.
There's a bake sale. To benefit the track team.
That's a lie.
Is that a new shirt?
Borrowed it. It's Graciela's.
Another lie.

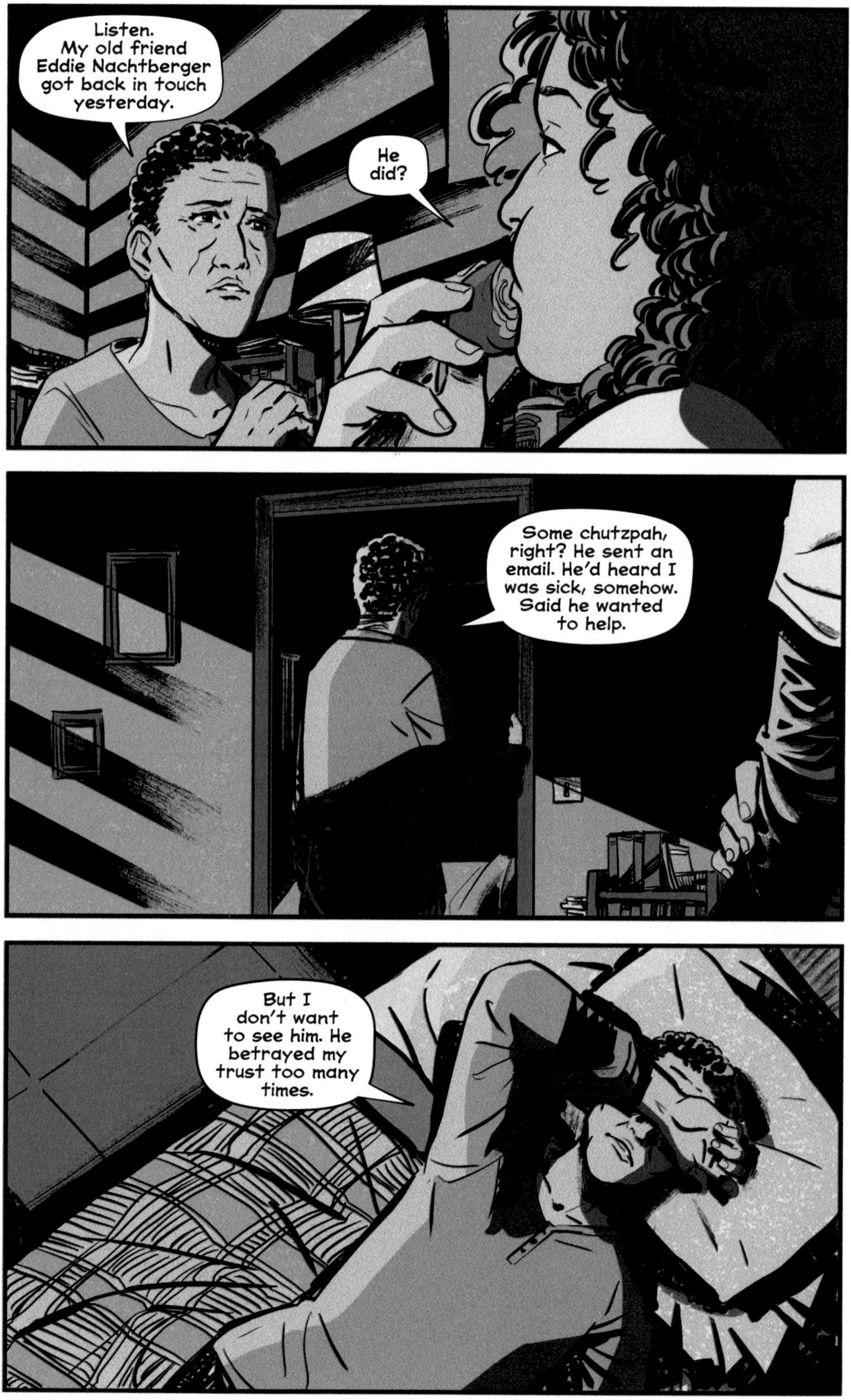
Listen. My old friend Eddie Nachtberger got back in touch yesterday.
He did?
Some chutzpah, right? He sent an email. He'd heard I was sick, somehow. Said he wanted to help.
But I don't want to see him. He betrayed my trust too many times.

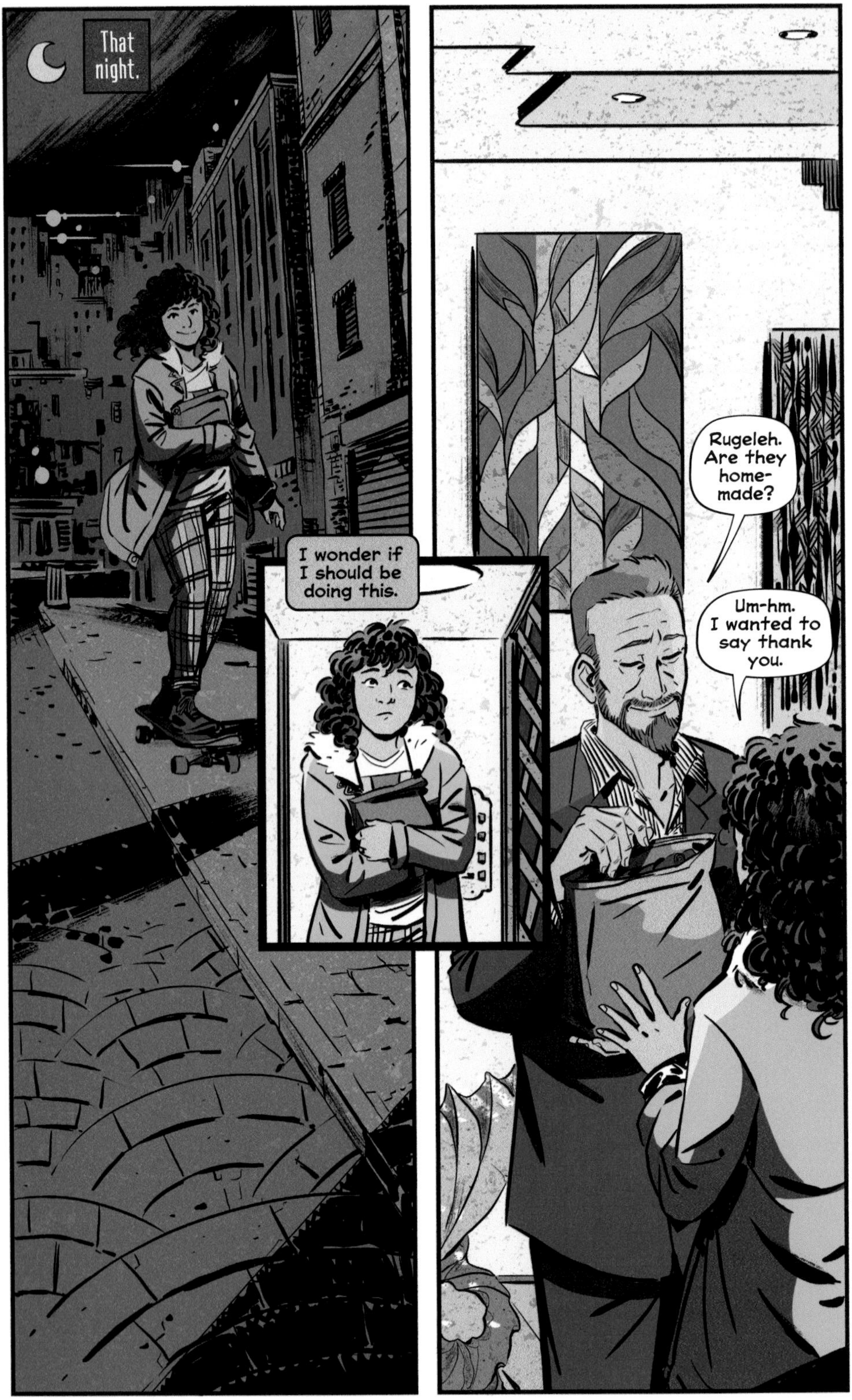
That night.
I wonder if I should be doing this.
Rugeleh. Are they home-made?
Um-hm. I wanted to say thank you.

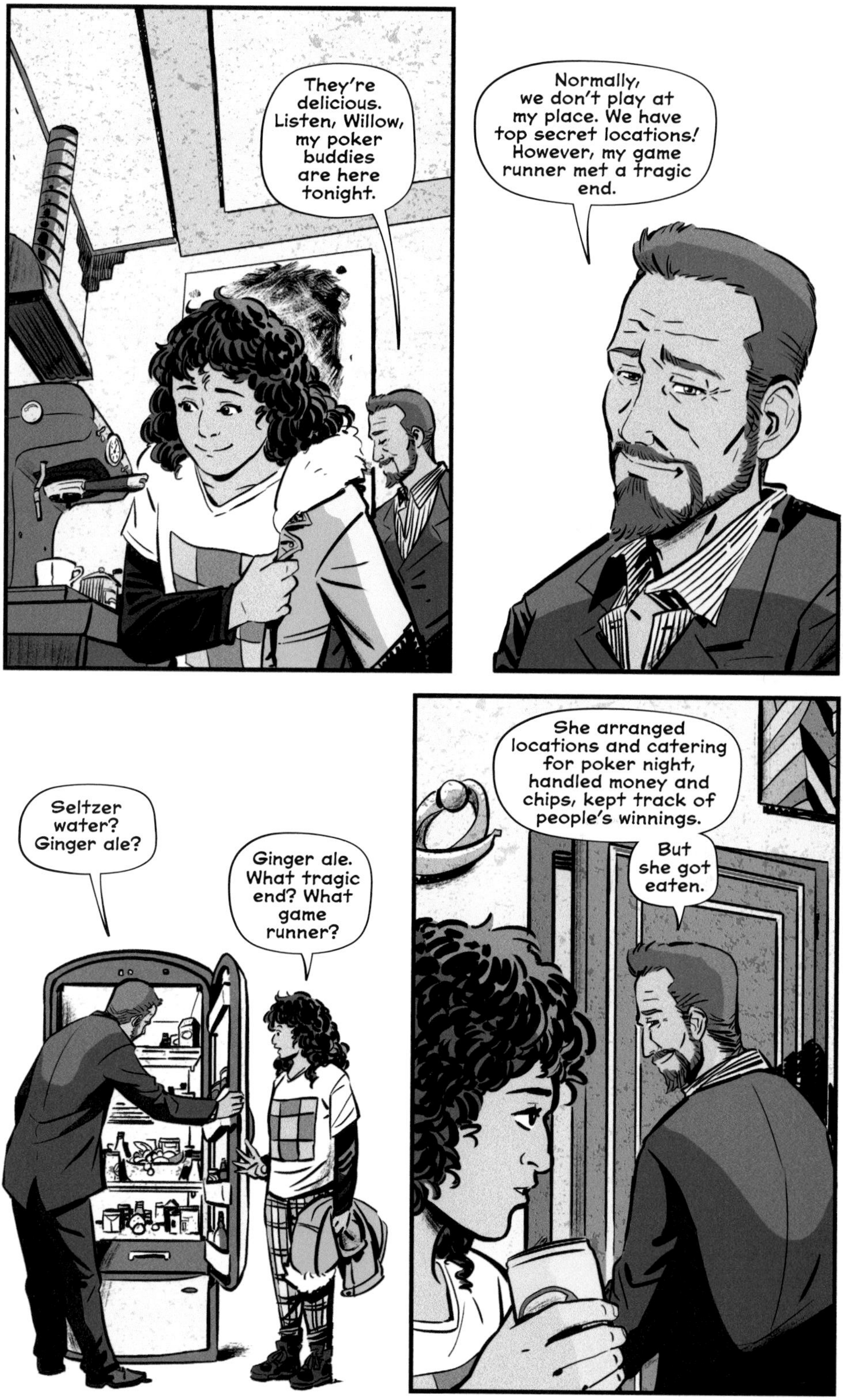
They're delicious. Listen, Willow, my poker buddies are here tonight.
Normally, we don't play at my place. We have top secret locations! However, my game runner met a tragic end.
Seltzer water? Ginger ale?
Ginger ale. What tragic end? What game runner?
She arranged locations and catering for poker night, handled money and chips, kept track of people's winnings.
But she got eaten.

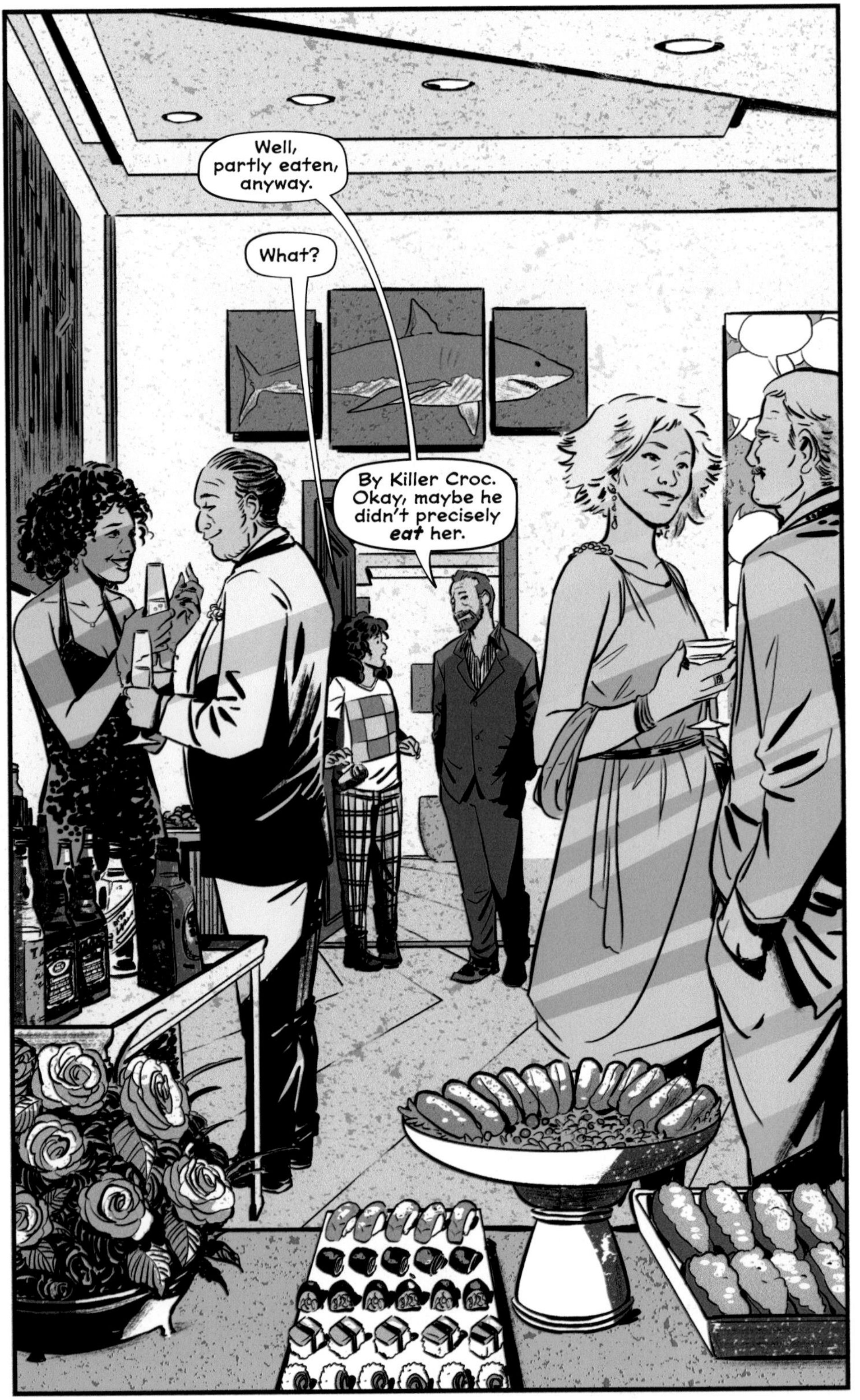
Well, partly eaten, anyway.
What?
By Killer Croc. Okay, maybe he didn't precisely *eat* her.

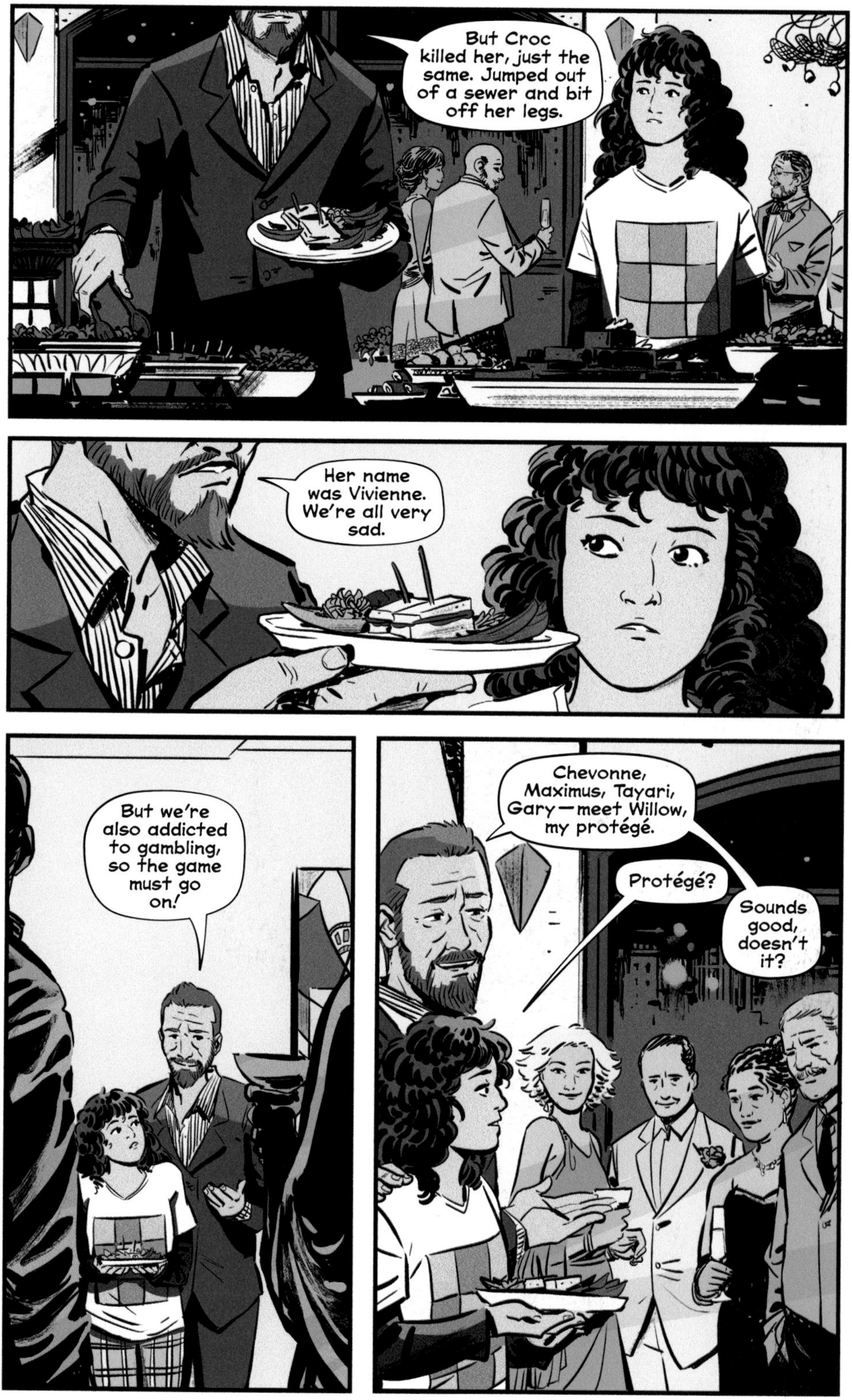
But Croc killed her, just the same. Jumped out of a sewer and bit off her legs.
Her name was Vivienne. We're all very sad.
But we're also addicted to gambling, so the game must go on!
Chevonne, Maximus, Tayari, Gary—meet Willow, my protégé.
Protégé?
Sounds good, doesn't it?

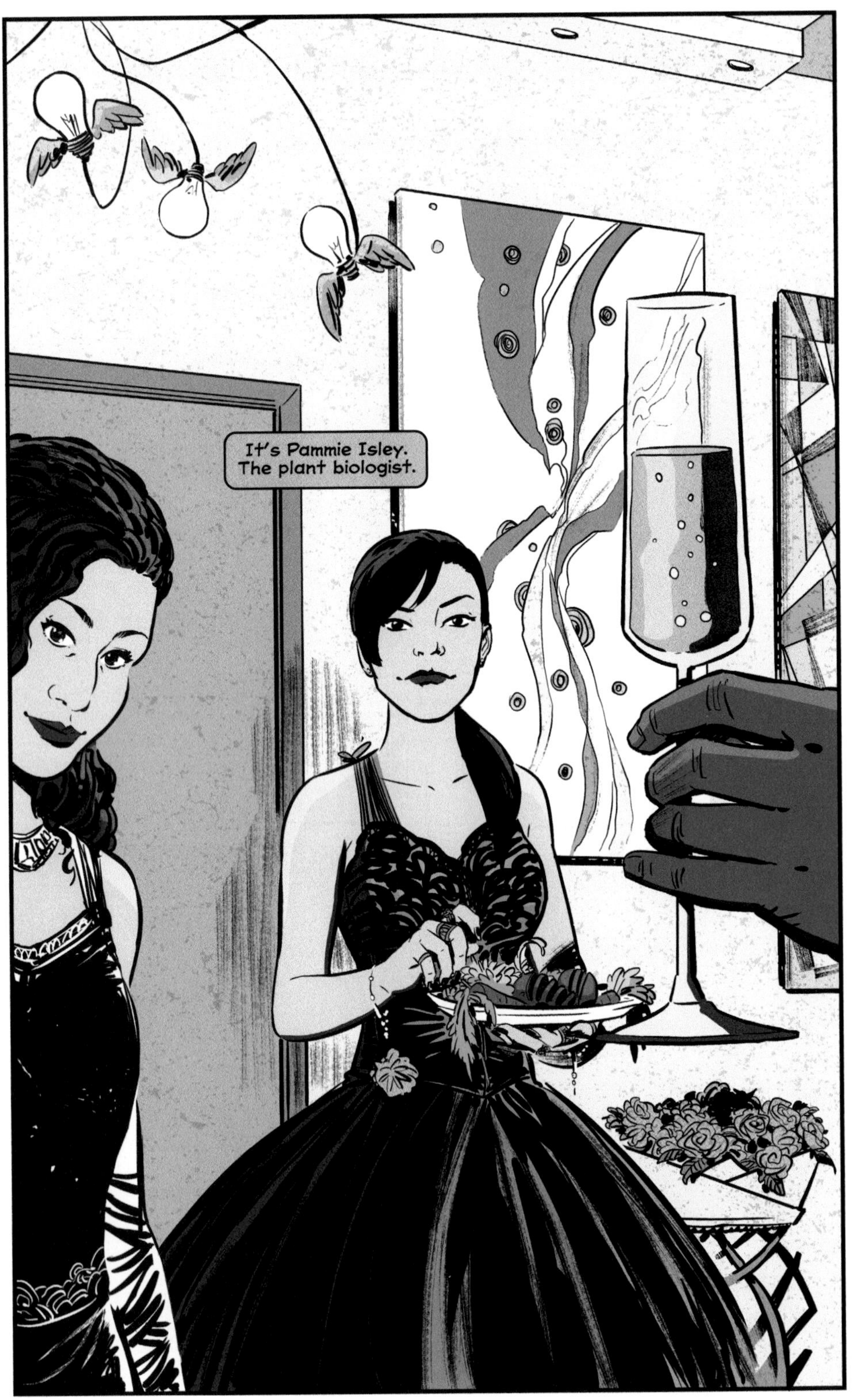
It's Pammie Isley.
The plant biologist.

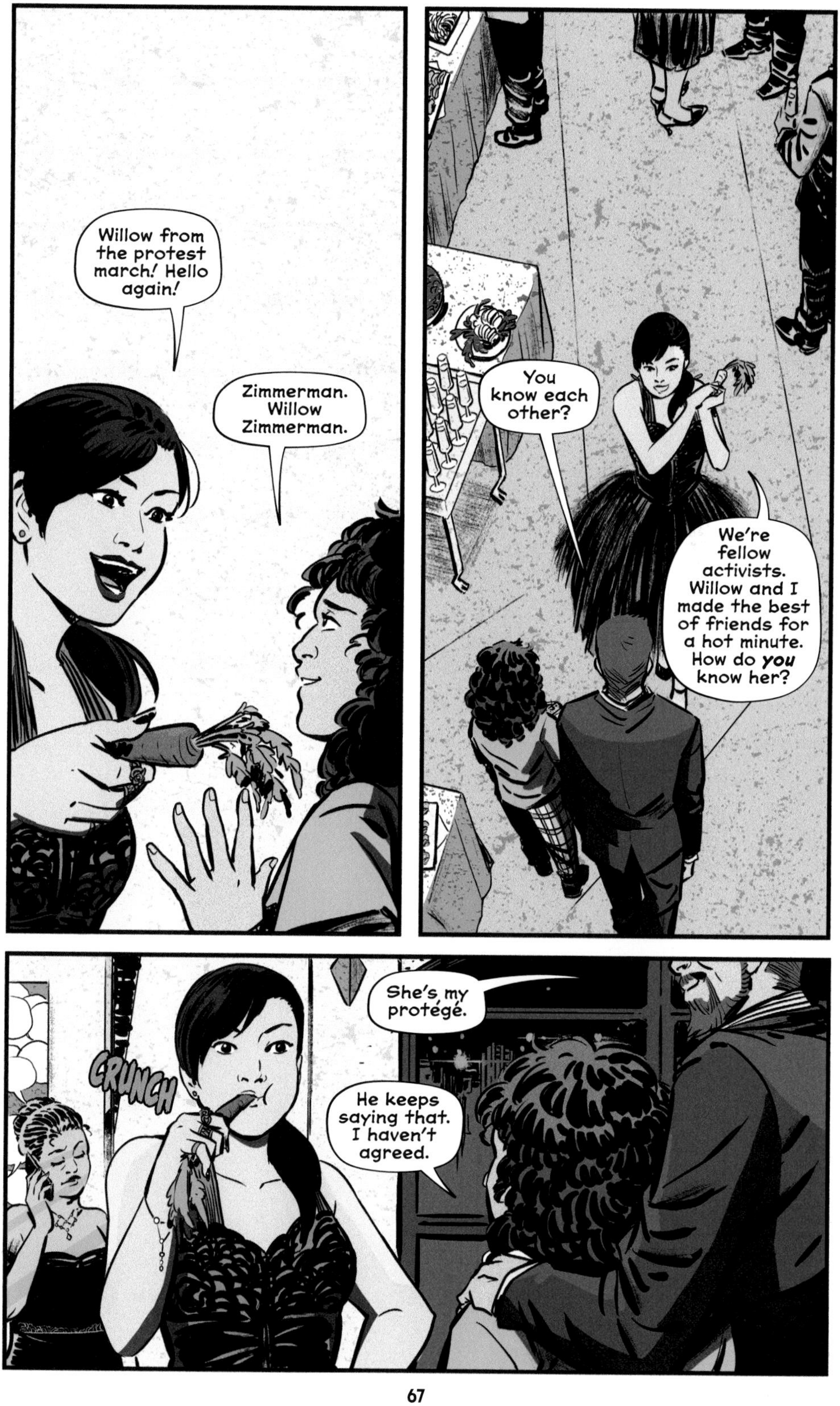

Willow from the protest march! Hello again!
Zimmerman. Willow Zimmerman.
You know each other?
We're fellow activists. Willow and I made the best of friends for a hot minute. How do *you* know her?
She's my protégé.
CRUNCH
He keeps saying that. I haven't agreed.

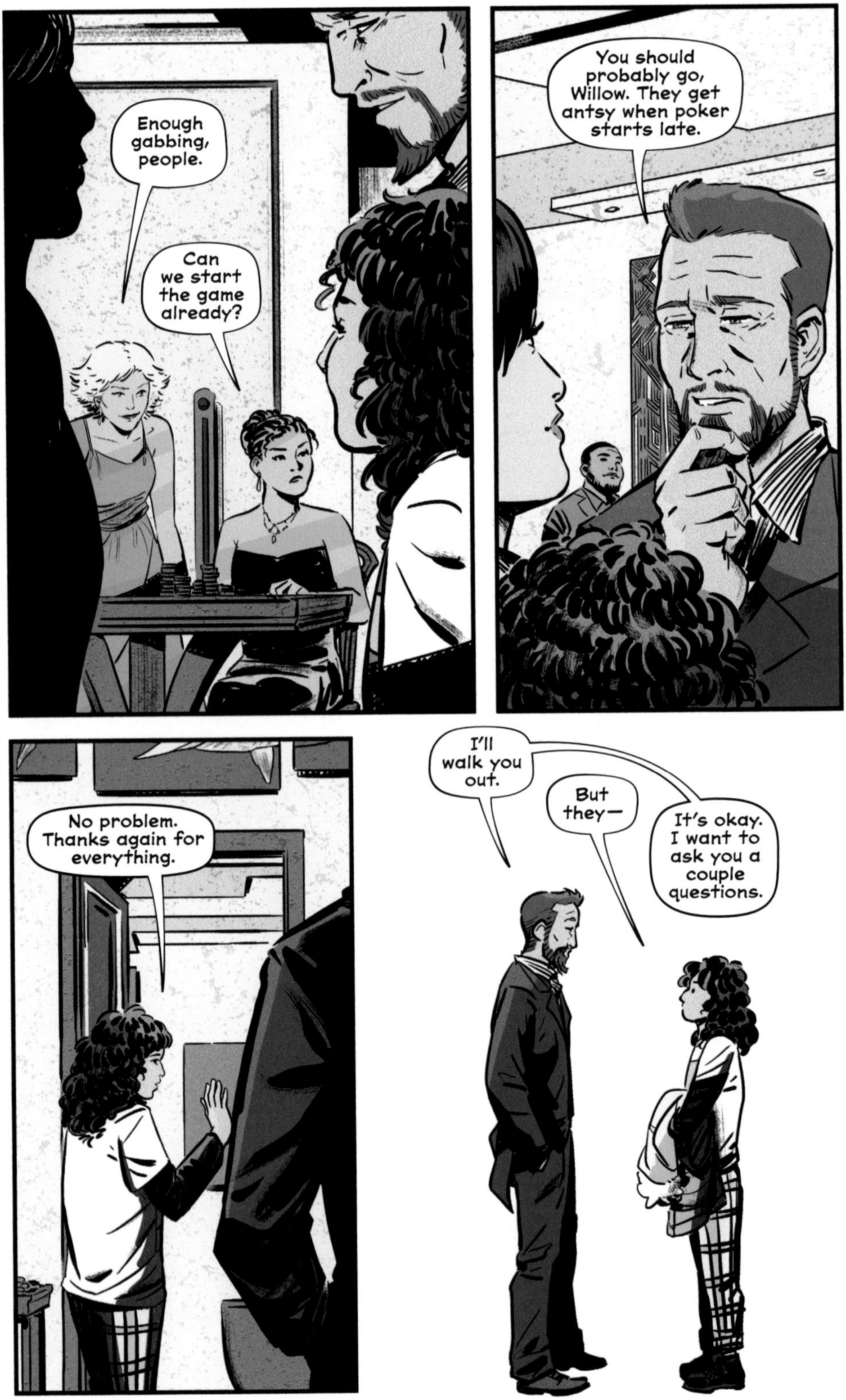
Enough gabbing, people.
Can we start the game already?
You should probably go, Willow. They get antsy when poker starts late.
No problem. Thanks again for everything.
I'll walk you out.
But they—
It's okay. I want to ask you a couple questions.

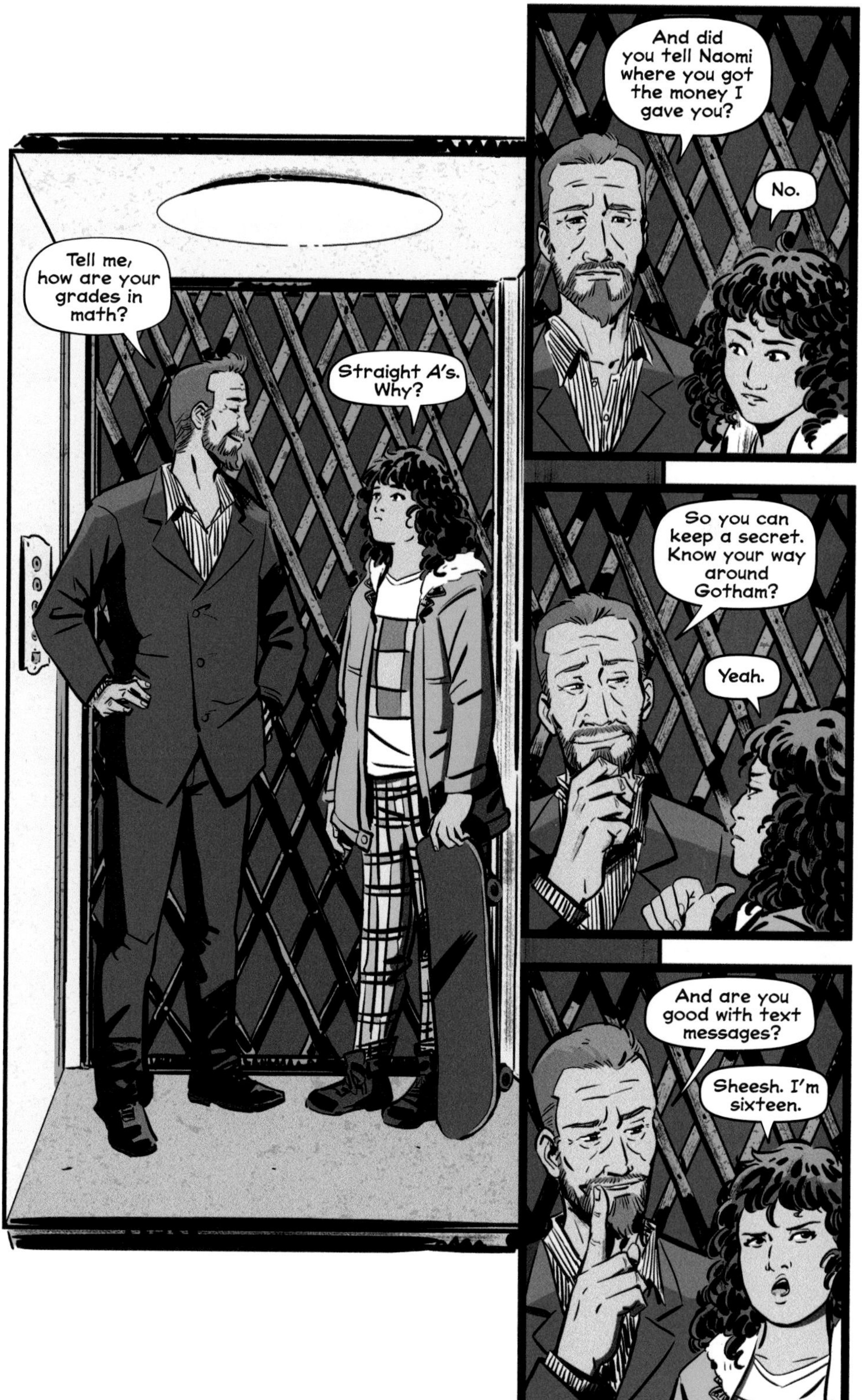
Tell me, how are your grades in math?
Straight A's. Why?
And did you tell Naomi where you got the money I gave you?
No.
So you can keep a secret. Know your way around Gotham?
Yeah.
And are you good with text messages?
Sheesh. I'm sixteen.

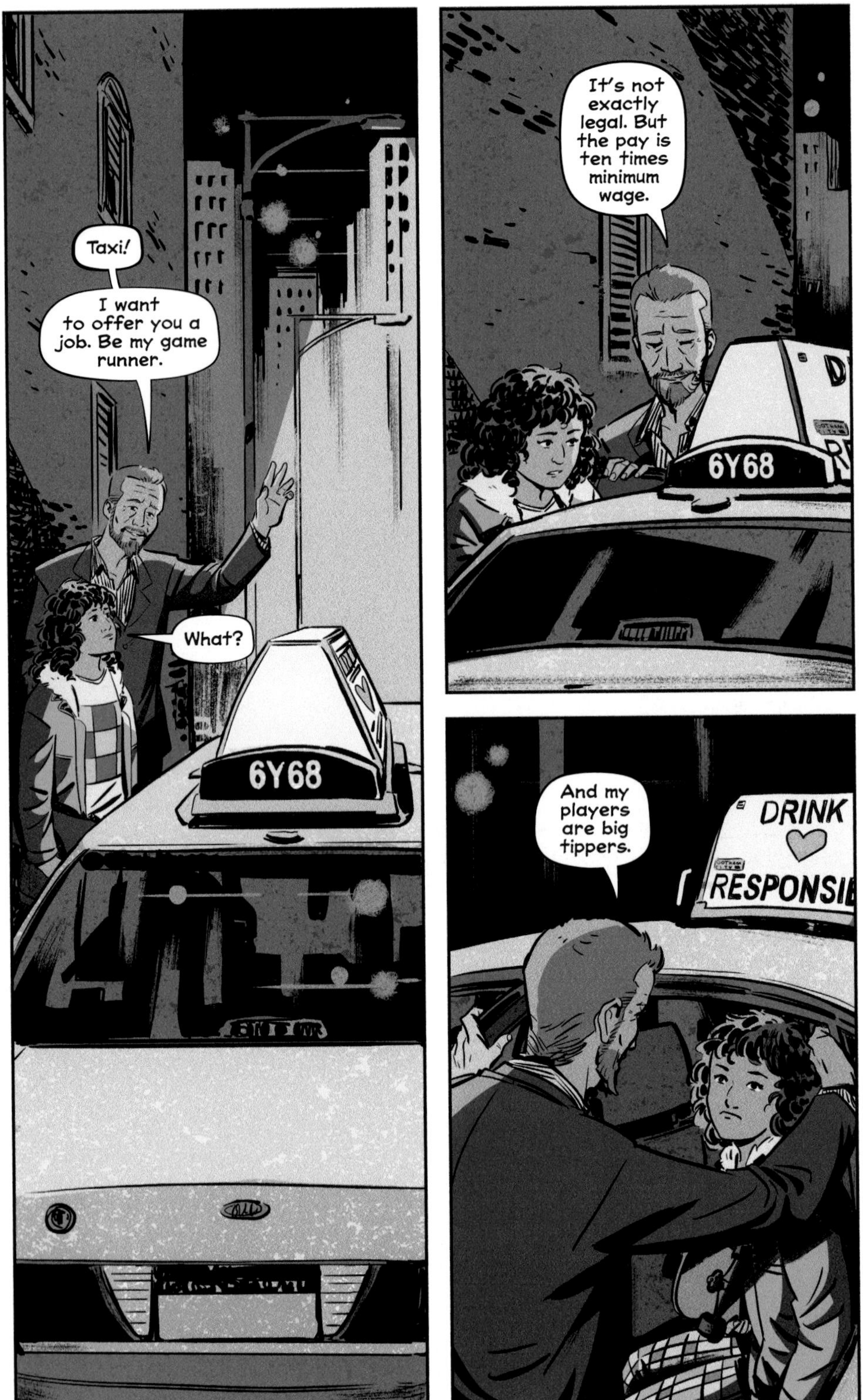
Taxi!
I want to offer you a job. Be my game runner.
What?
6Y68
It's not exactly legal. But the pay is ten times minimum wage.
6Y68
And my players are big tippers.
DRINK

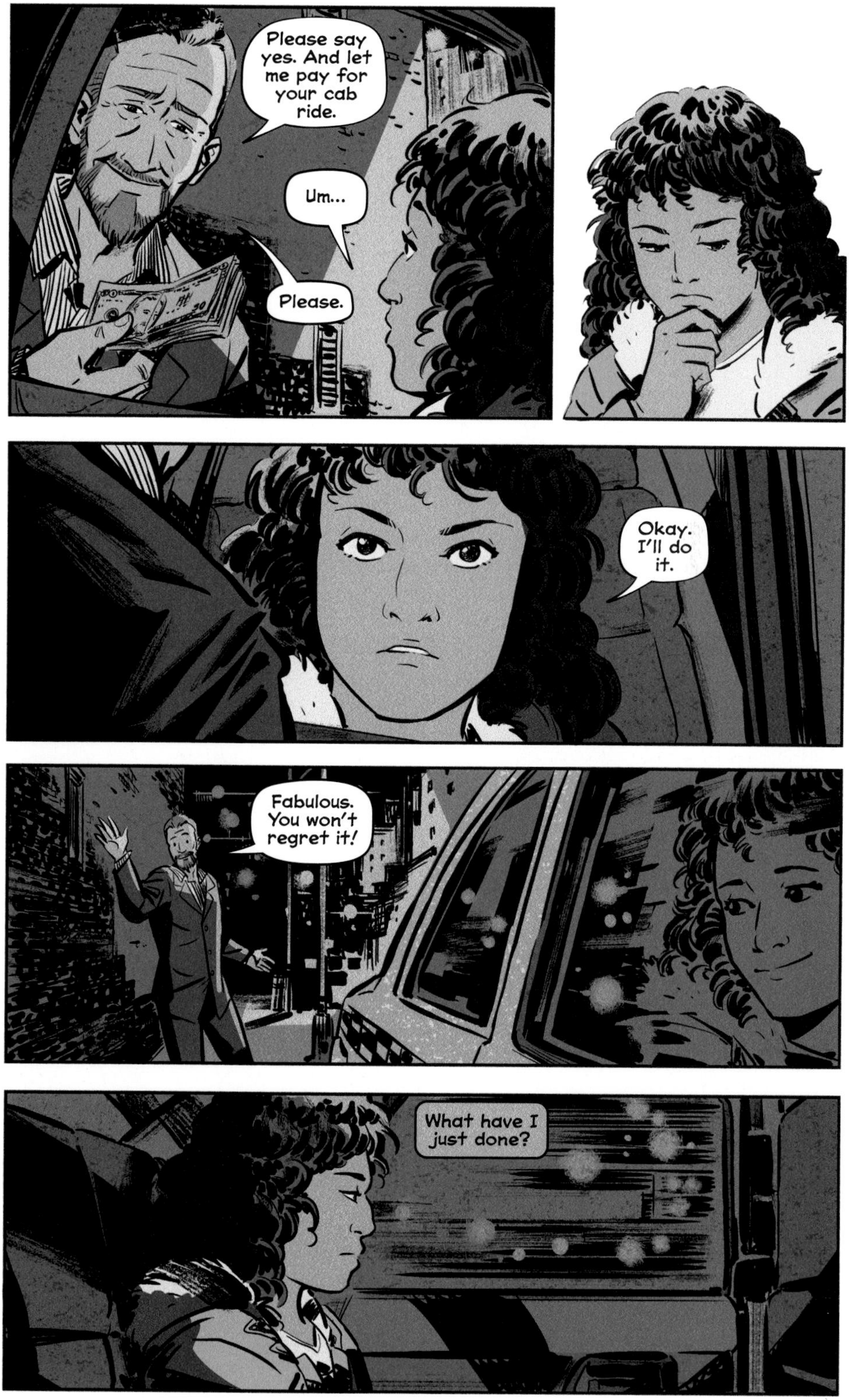
Please say yes. And let me pay for your cab ride.
Um...
Please.
Okay. I'll do it.
Fabulous. You won't regret it!
What have I just done?

part three: **a dirty job**

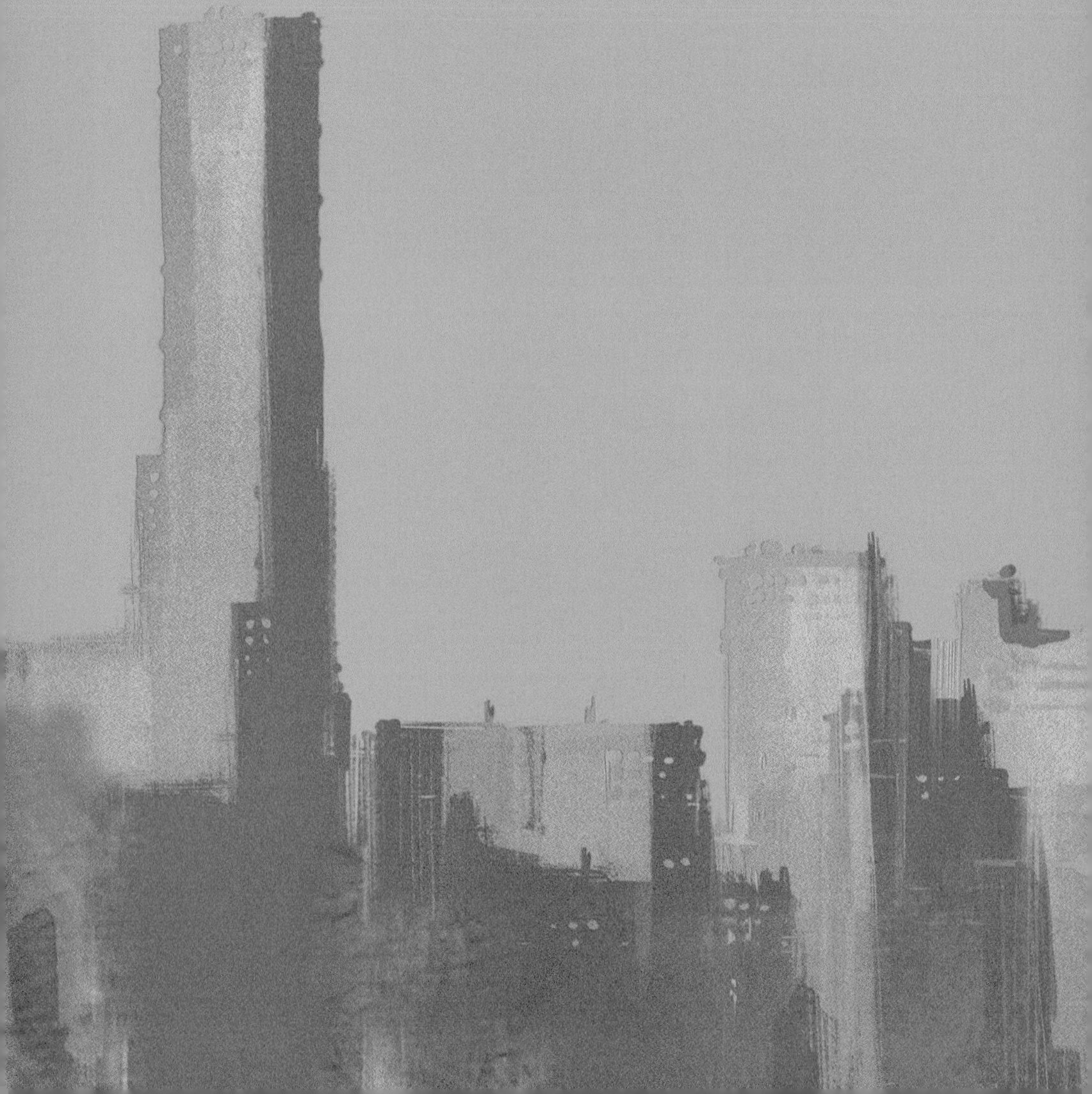

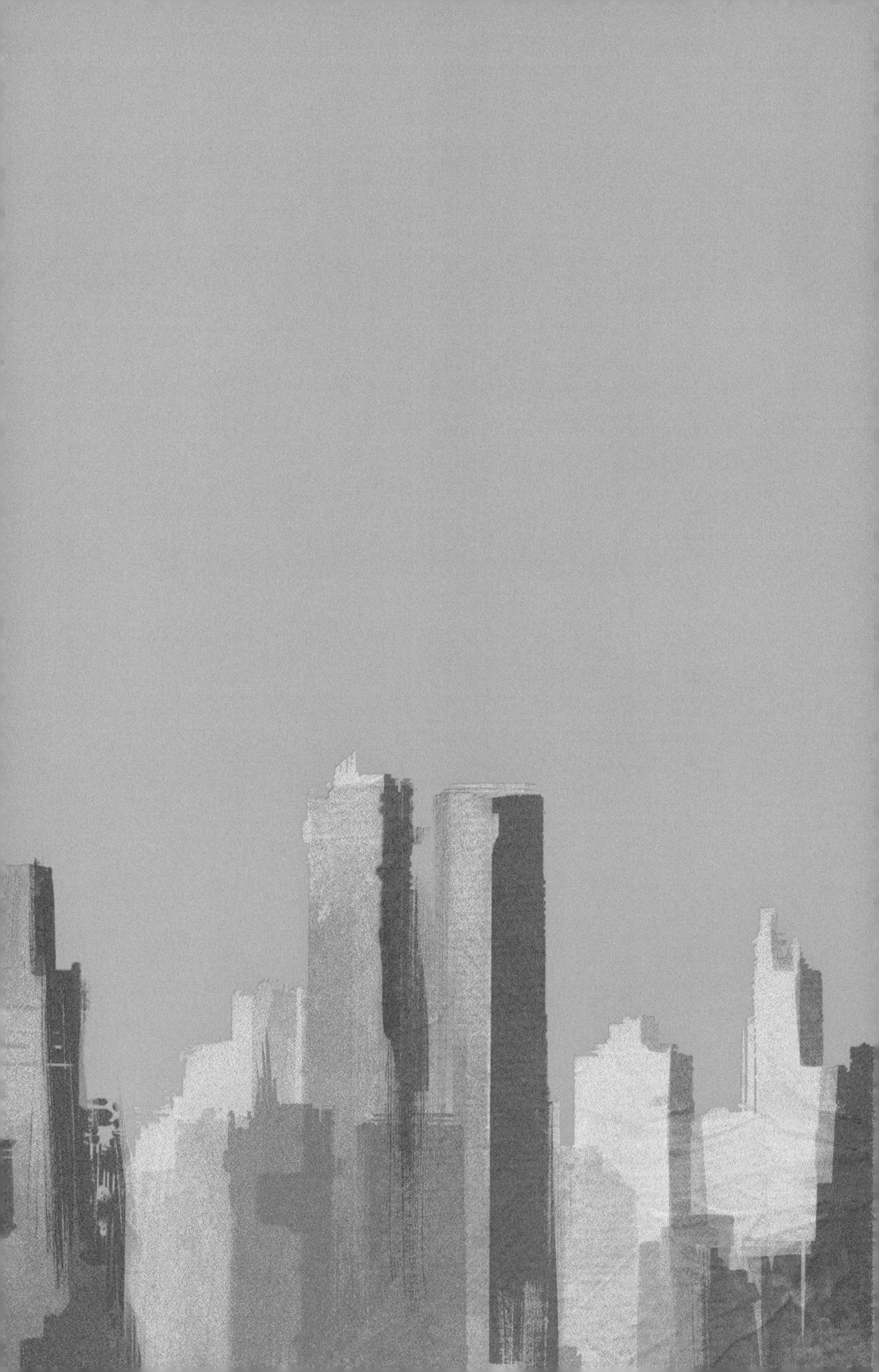

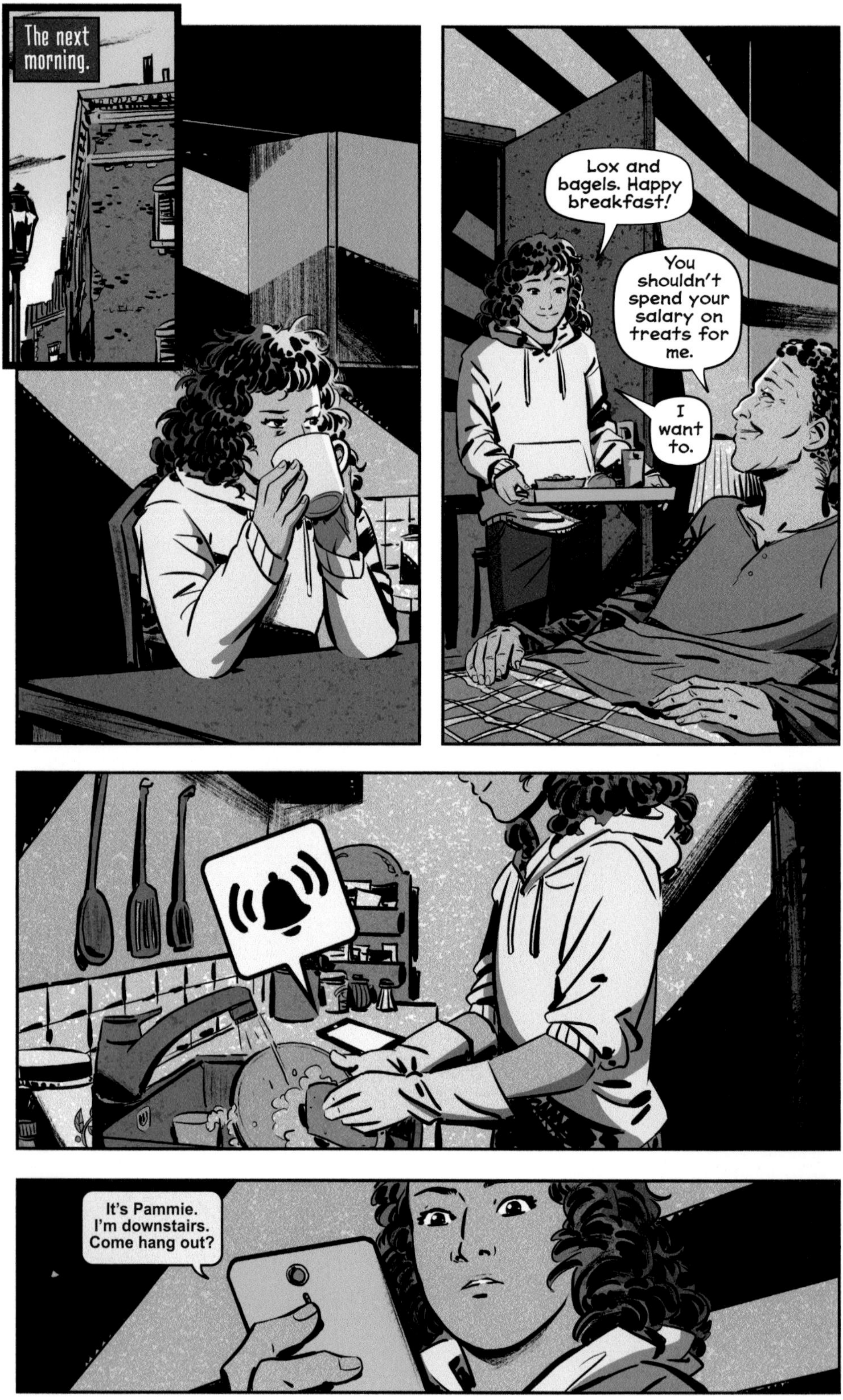

The next morning.
Lox and bagels. Happy breakfast!
You shouldn't spend your salary on treats for me.
I want to.
It's Pammie. I'm downstairs. Come hang out?

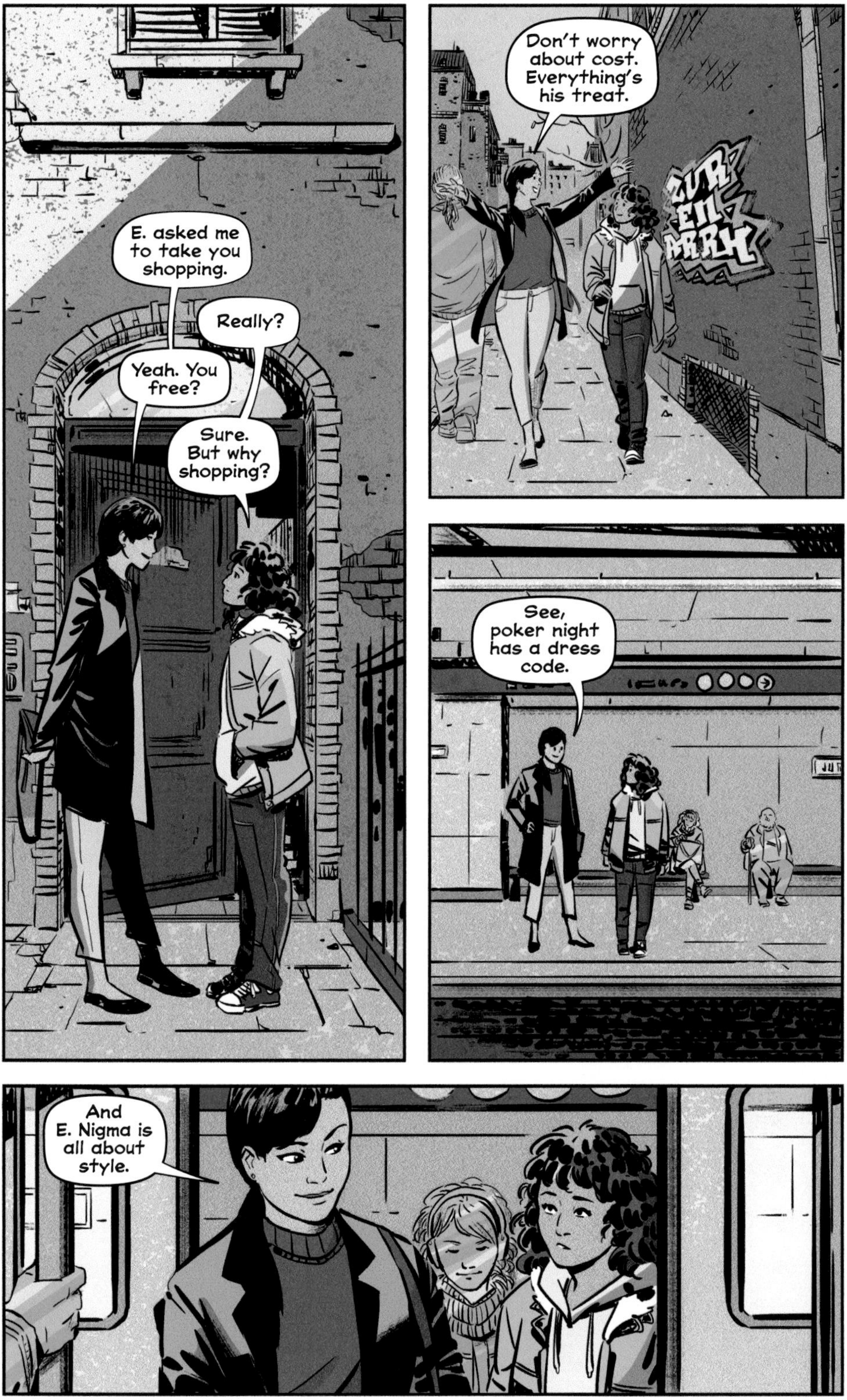
E. asked me to take you shopping.
Really?
Yeah. You free?
Sure. But why shopping?
Don't worry about cost. Everything's his treat.
See, poker night has a dress code.
And E. Nigma is all about style.

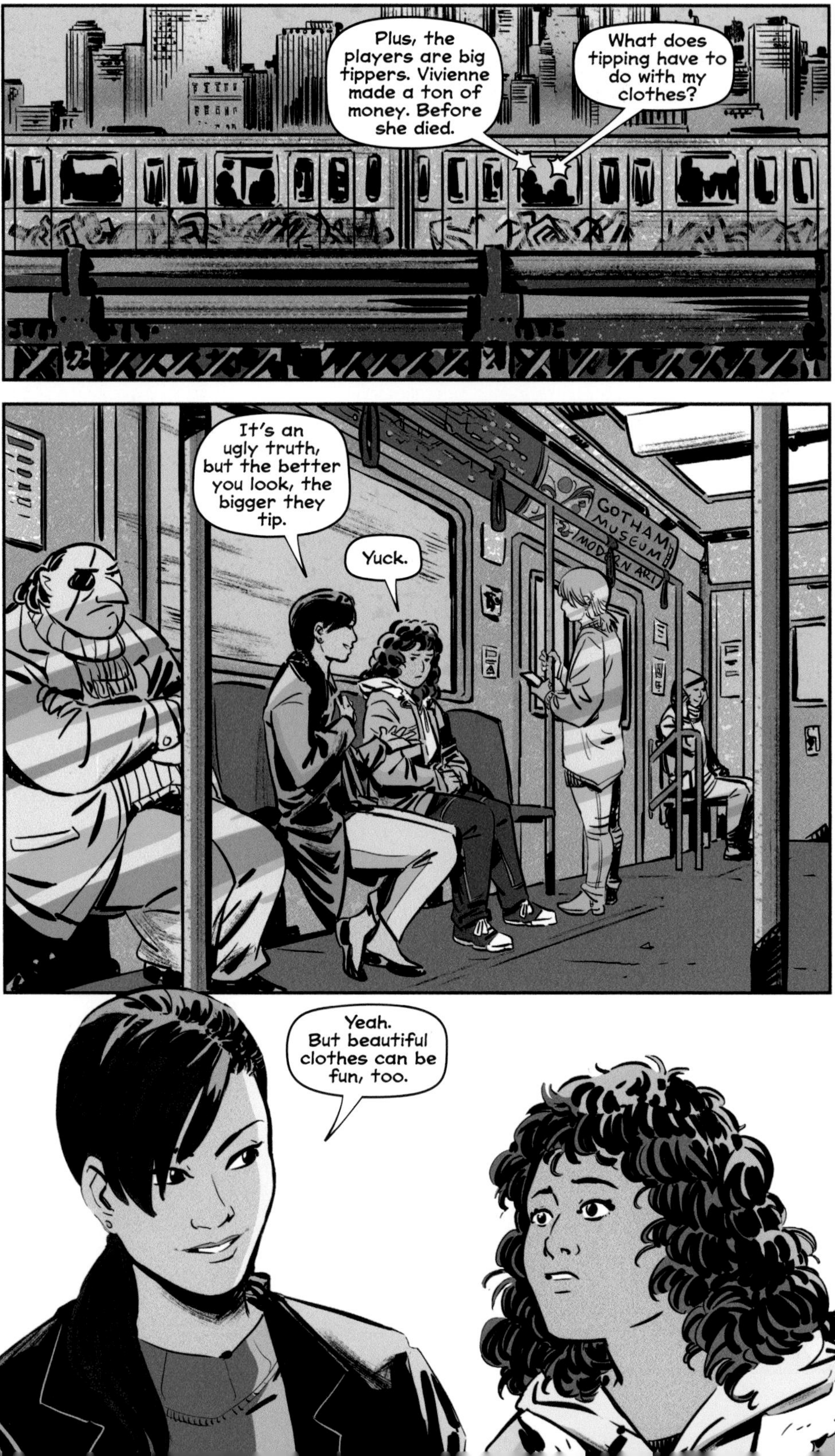

Plus, the players are big tippers. Vivienne made a ton of money. Before she died.
What does tipping have to do with my clothes?
It's an ugly truth, but the better you look, the bigger they tip.
Yuck.
GOTHAM MUSEUM MODERN ART
Yeah. But beautiful clothes can be fun, too.

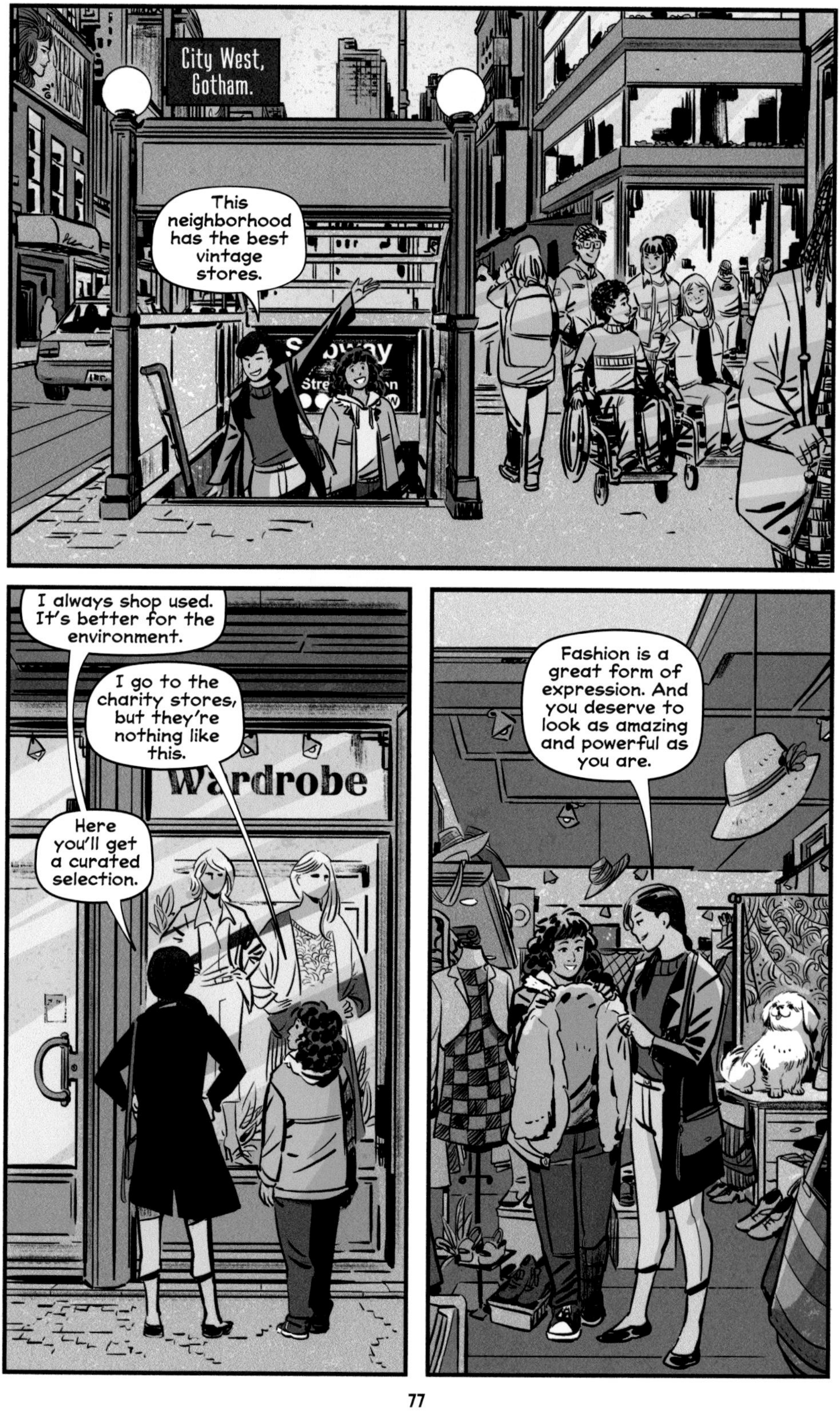
City West, Gotham.
This neighborhood has the best vintage stores.
I always shop used. It's better for the environment.
I go to the charity stores, but they're nothing like this.
Wardrobe
Here you'll get a curated selection.
Fashion is a great form of expression. And you deserve to look as amazing and powerful as you are.

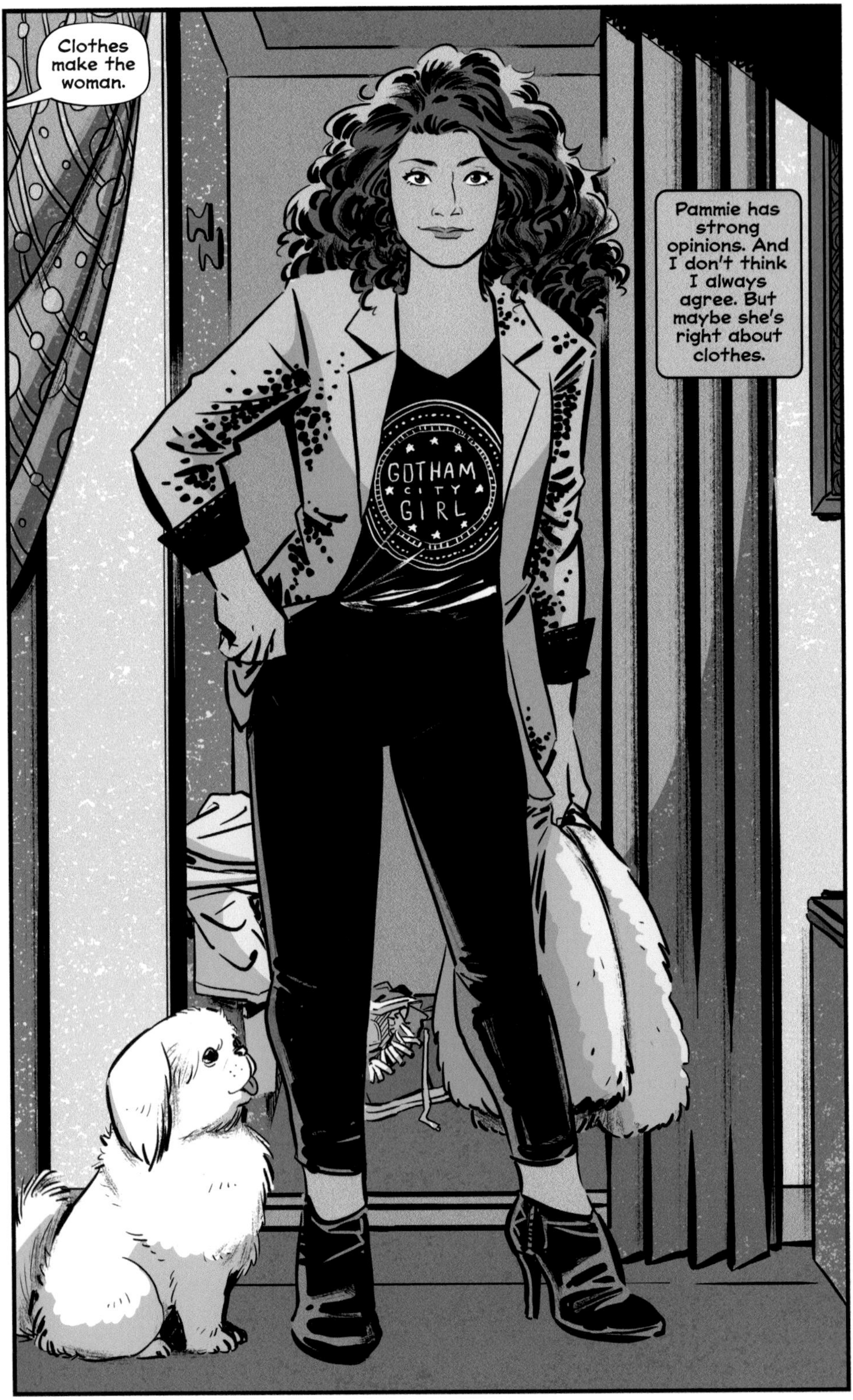
Clothes make the woman.
Pammie has strong opinions. And I don't think I always agree. But maybe she's right about clothes.
GOTHAM CITY GIRL

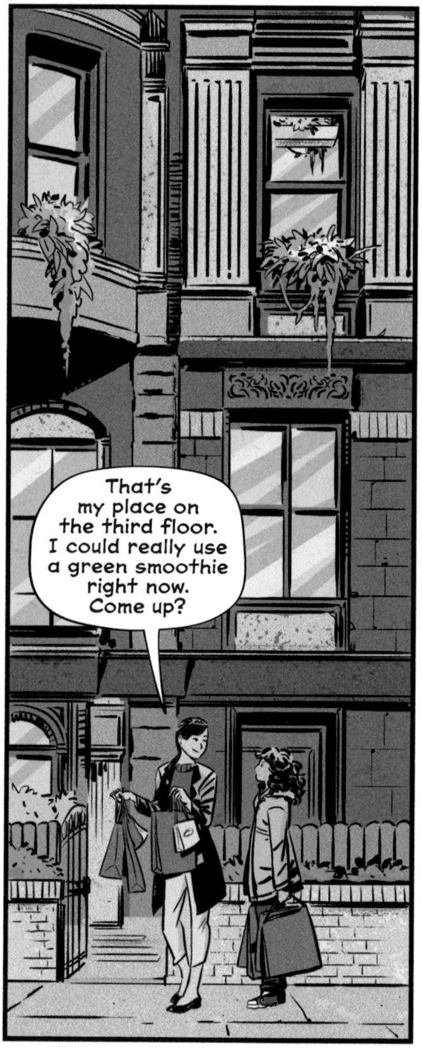
That's my place on the third floor. I could really use a green smoothie right now. Come up?

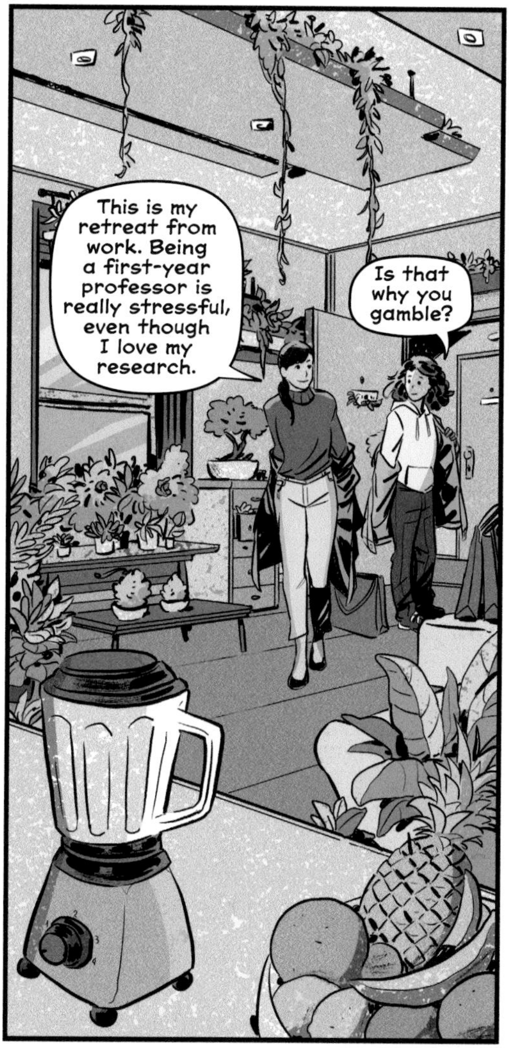
This is my retreat from work. Being a first-year professor is really stressful, even though I love my research.
Is that why you gamble?

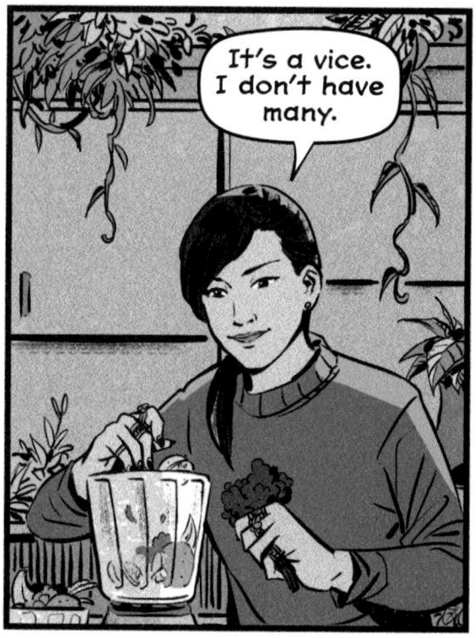
It's a vice. I don't have many.

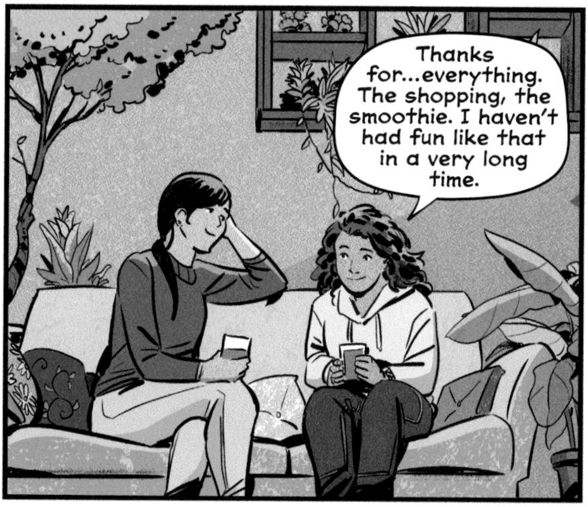
Thanks for...everything. The shopping, the smoothie. I haven't had fun like that in a very long time.

Next week. After school.

That's right, poker night in a ballet studio.

E., you asked for a new secret location every time and this is a good one.

Yes... Yes...No. I arranged for the most amazing dim sum.

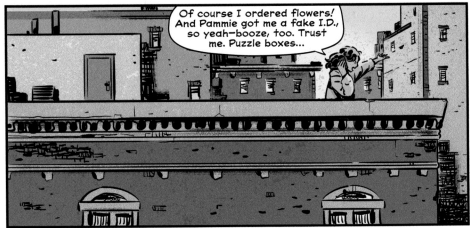

Of course I ordered flowers! And Pammie got me a fake I.D., so yeah—booze, too. Trust me. Puzzle boxes...

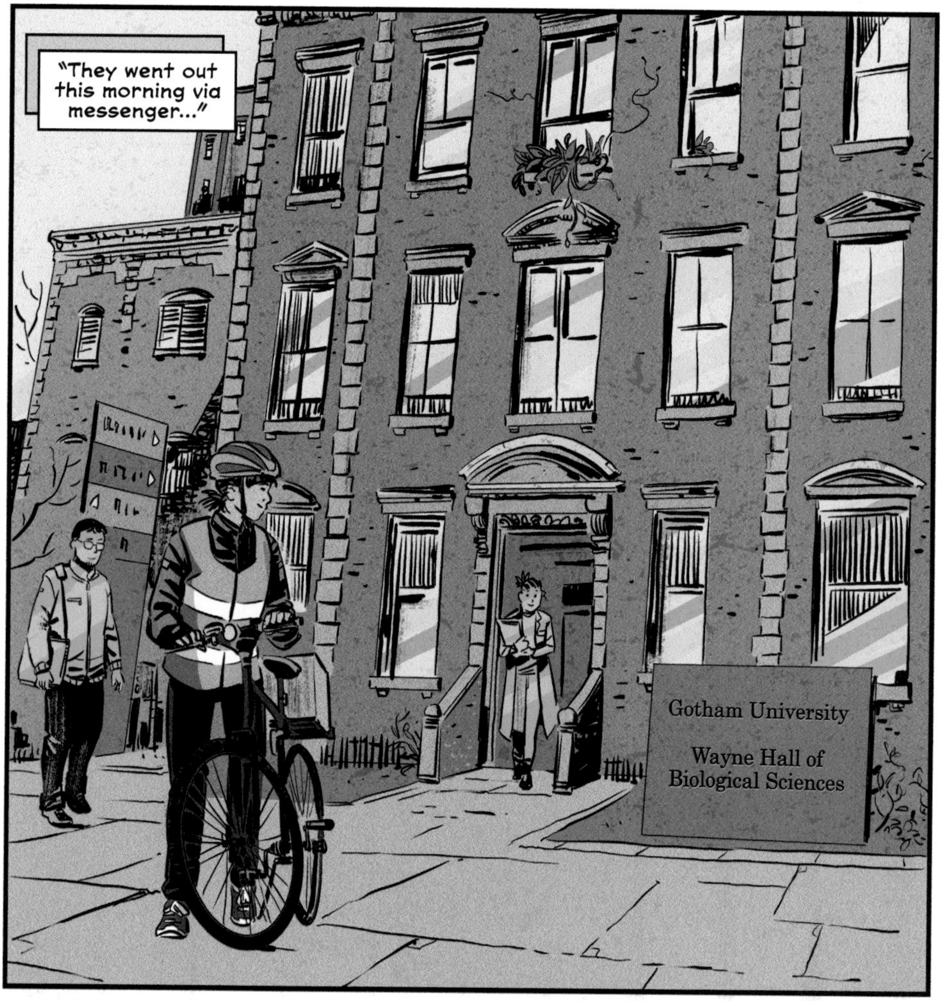
"They went out this morning via messenger..."
Gotham University
Wayne Hall of Biological Sciences

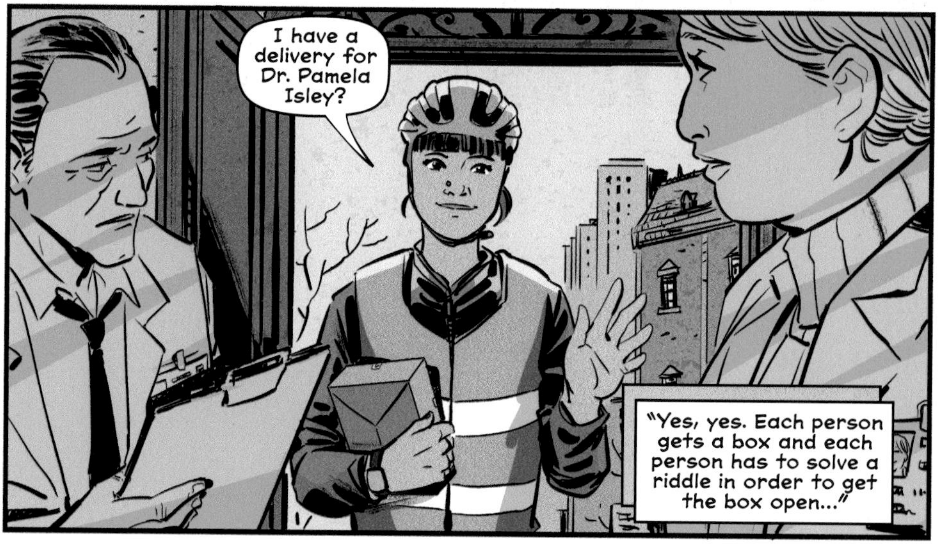
I have a delivery for Dr. Pamela Isley?
"Yes, yes. Each person gets a box and each person has to solve a riddle in order to get the box open..."

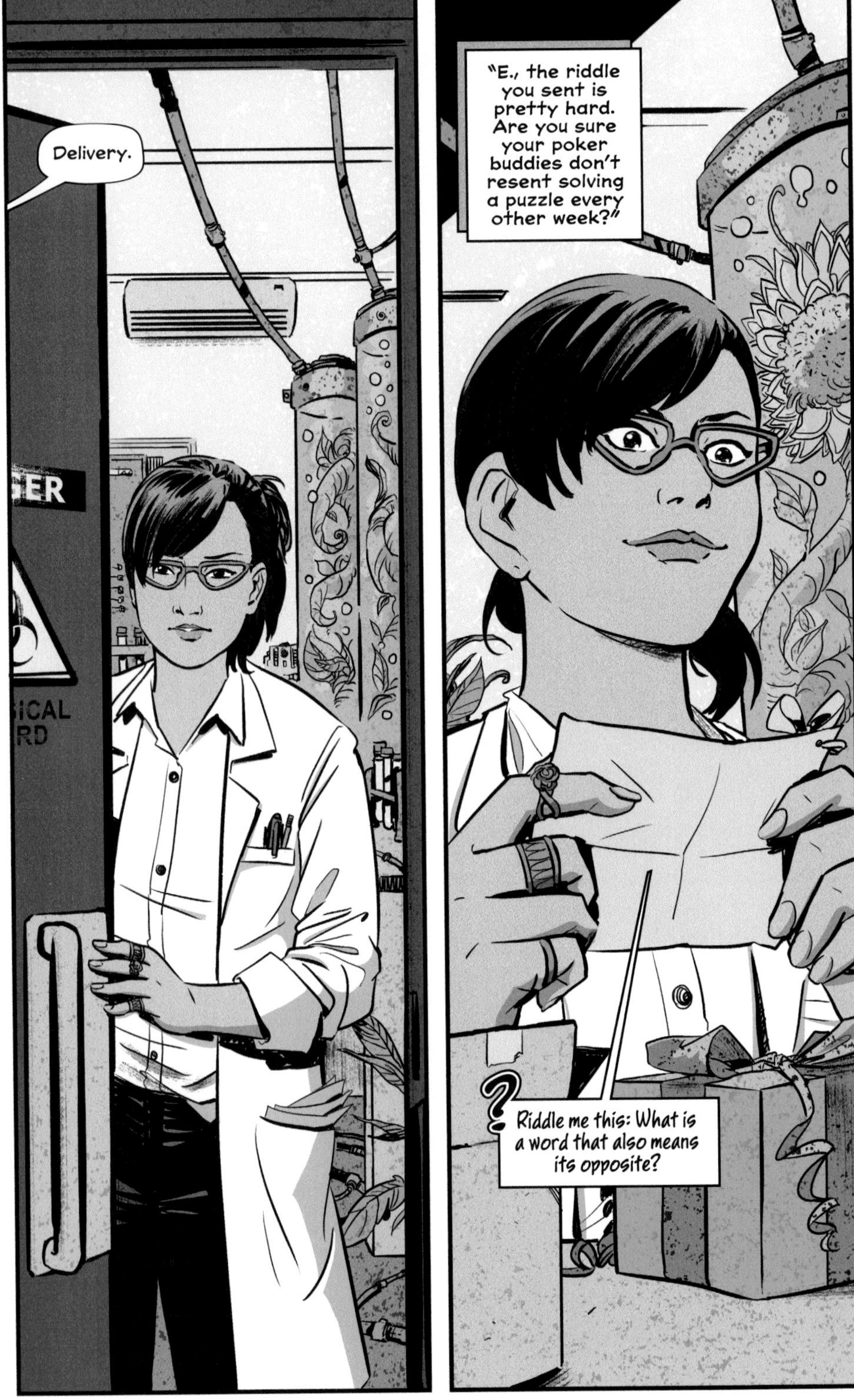
Delivery.
"E., the riddle you sent is pretty hard. Are you sure your poker buddies don't resent solving a puzzle every other week?"
Riddle me this: What is a word that also means its opposite?

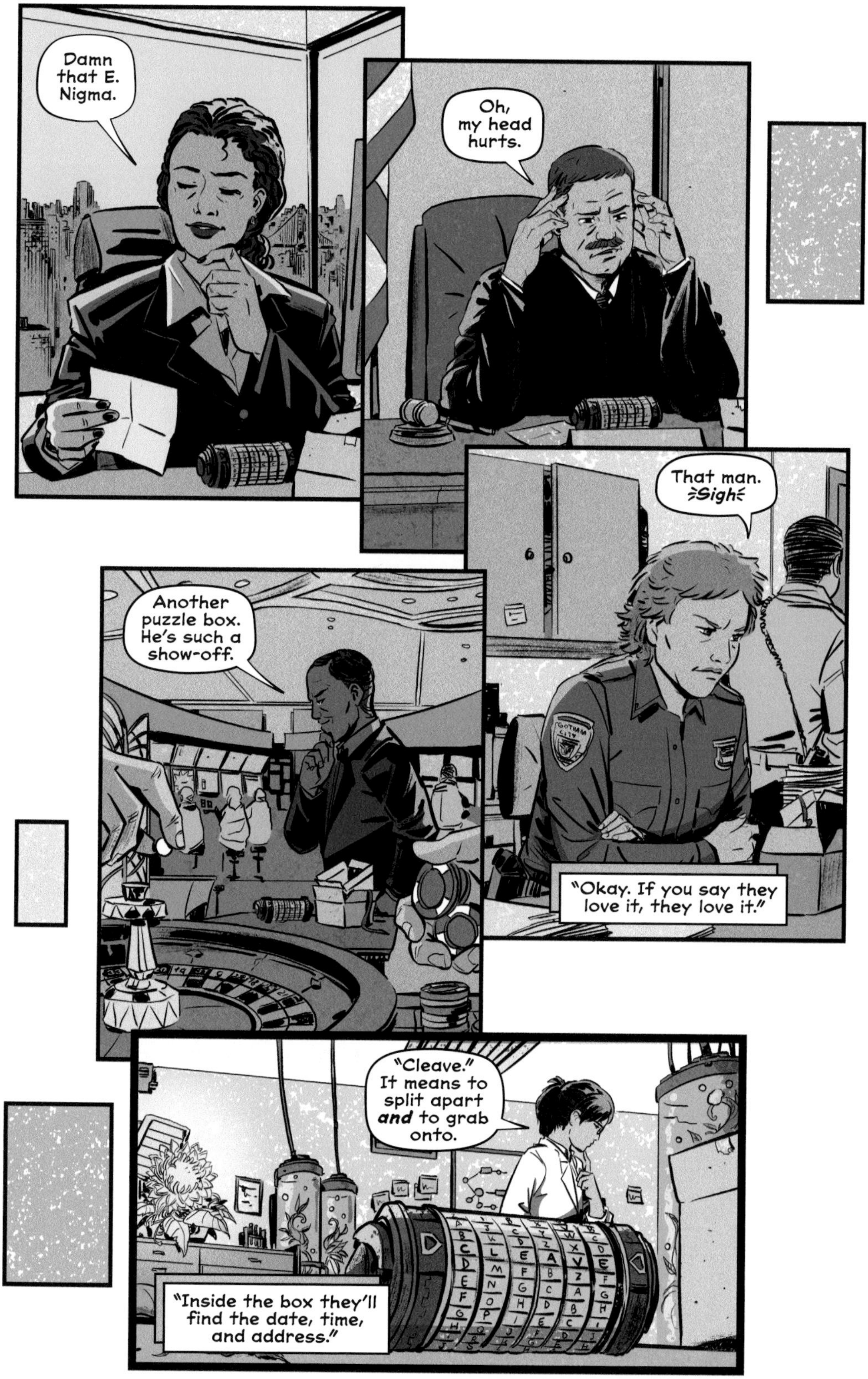
Damn that E. Nigma.
Oh, my head hurts.
That man. *Sigh*
"Okay. If you say they love it, they love it."
Another puzzle box. He's such a show-off.
"Cleave." It means to split apart **and** to grab onto.
"Inside the box they'll find the date, time, and address."
CLEAVE

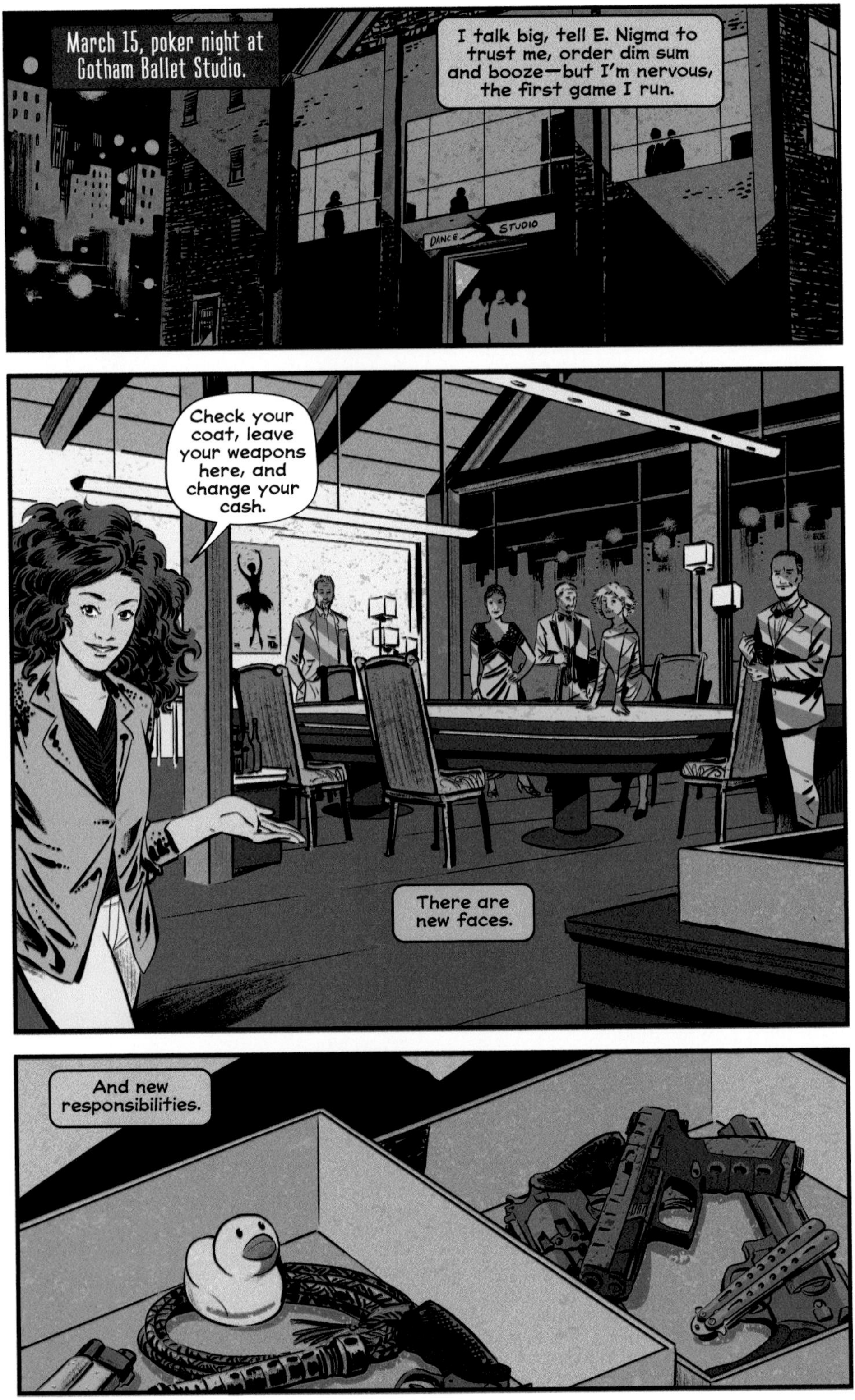
March 15, poker night at Gotham Ballet Studio.
I talk big, tell E. Nigma to trust me, order dim sum and booze—but I'm nervous, the first game I run.
DANCE STUDIO
Check your coat, leave your weapons here, and change your cash.
There are new faces.
And new responsibilities.

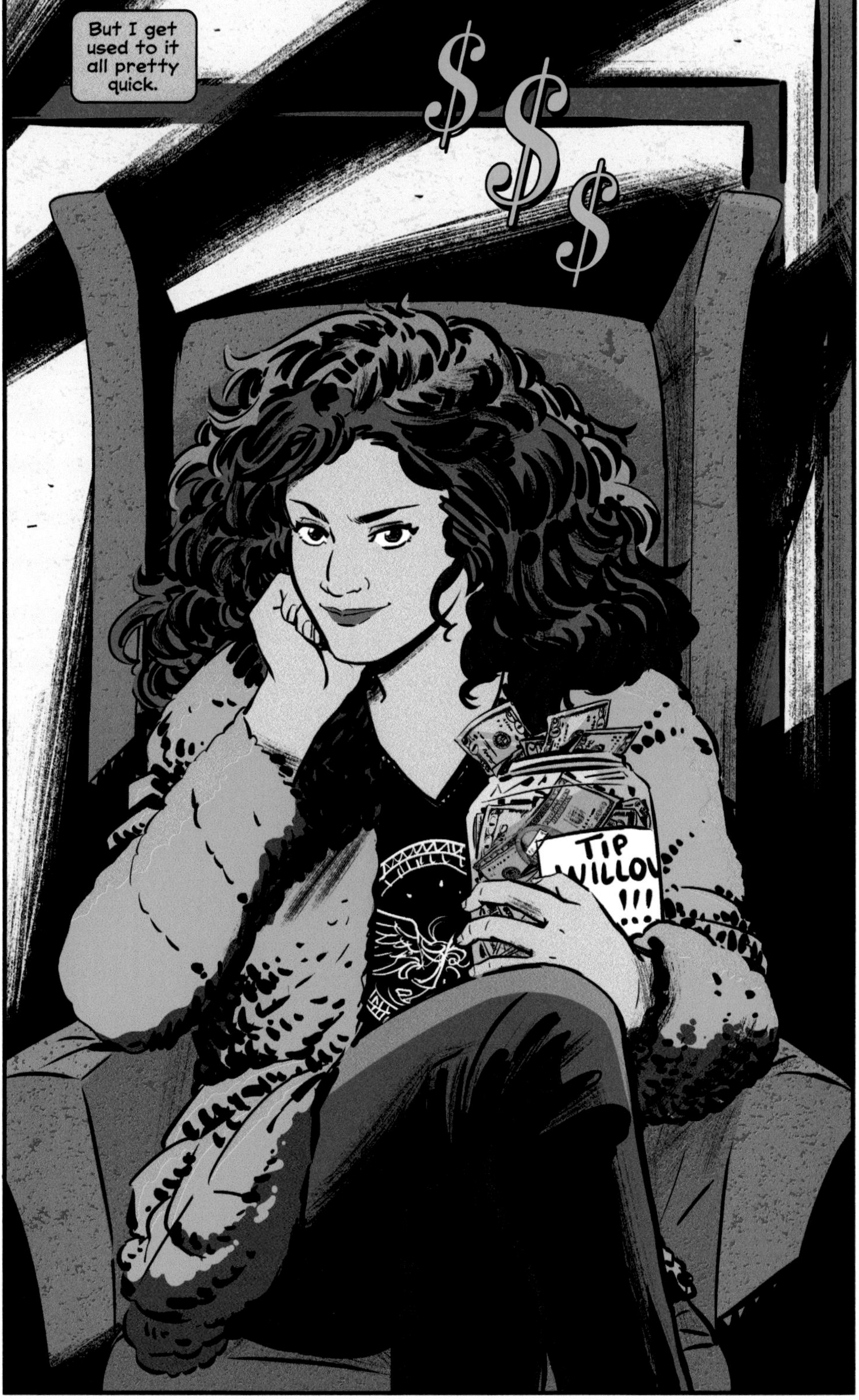
But I get used to it all pretty quick.
$$$
TIP WILLOW !!!

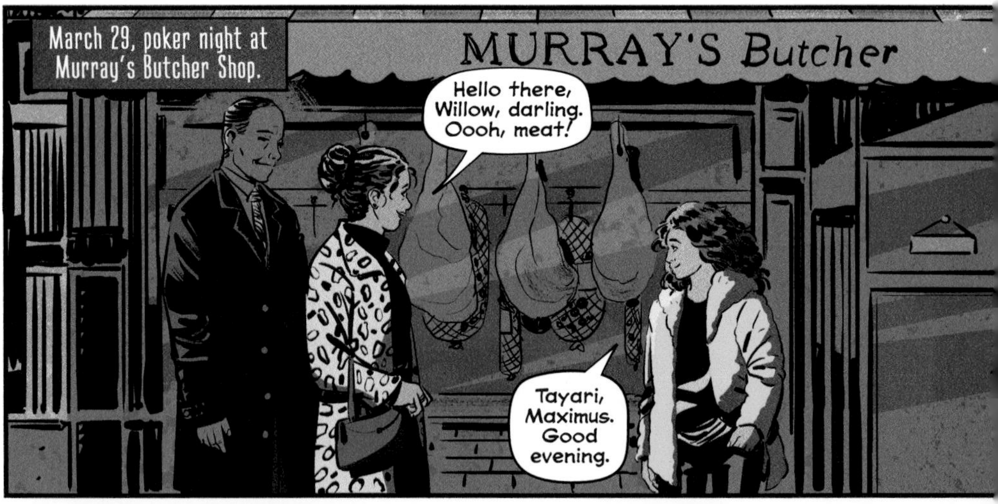
March 29, poker night at Murray's Butcher Shop.
MURRAY'S Butcher
Hello there, Willow, darling. Oooh, meat!
Tayari, Maximus. Good evening.

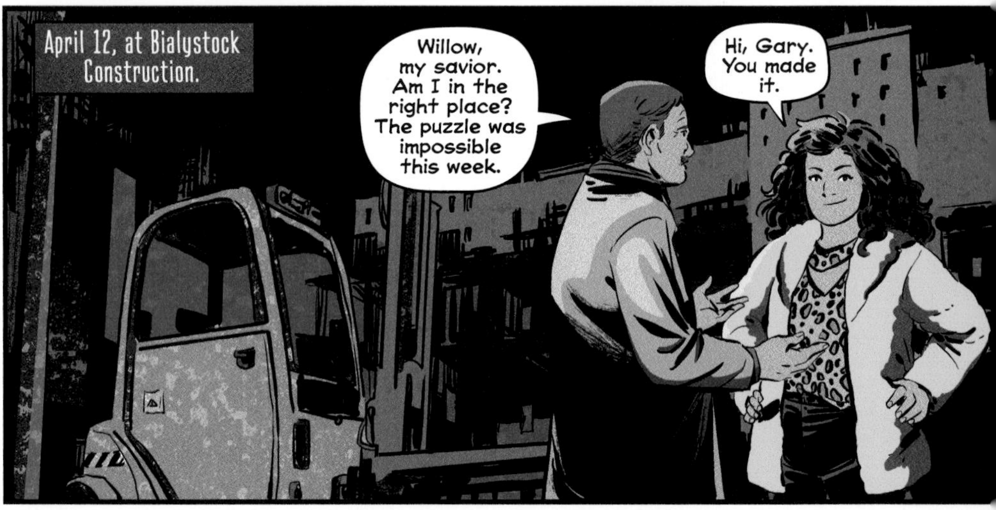
April 12, at Bialystock Construction.
Willow, my savior. Am I in the right place? The puzzle was impossible this week.
Hi, Gary. You made it.

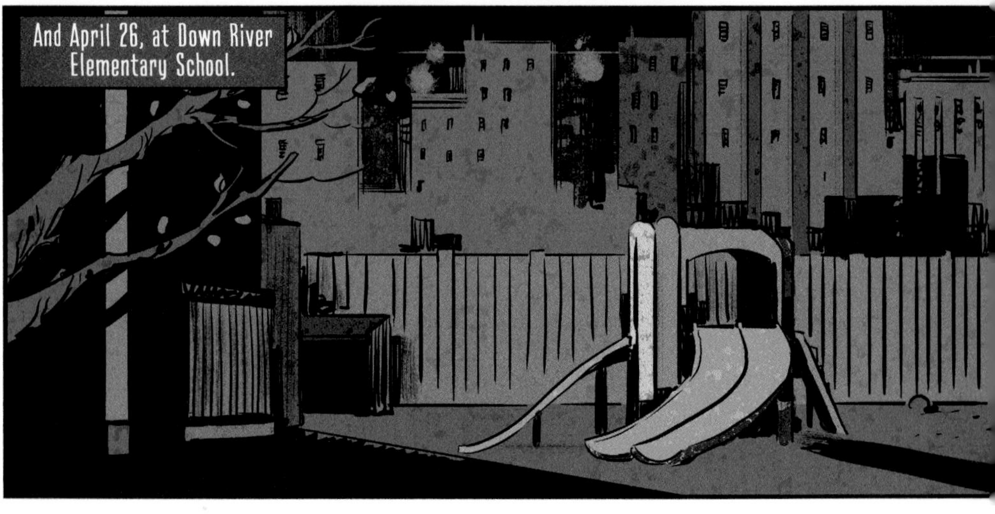
And April 26, at Down River Elementary School.

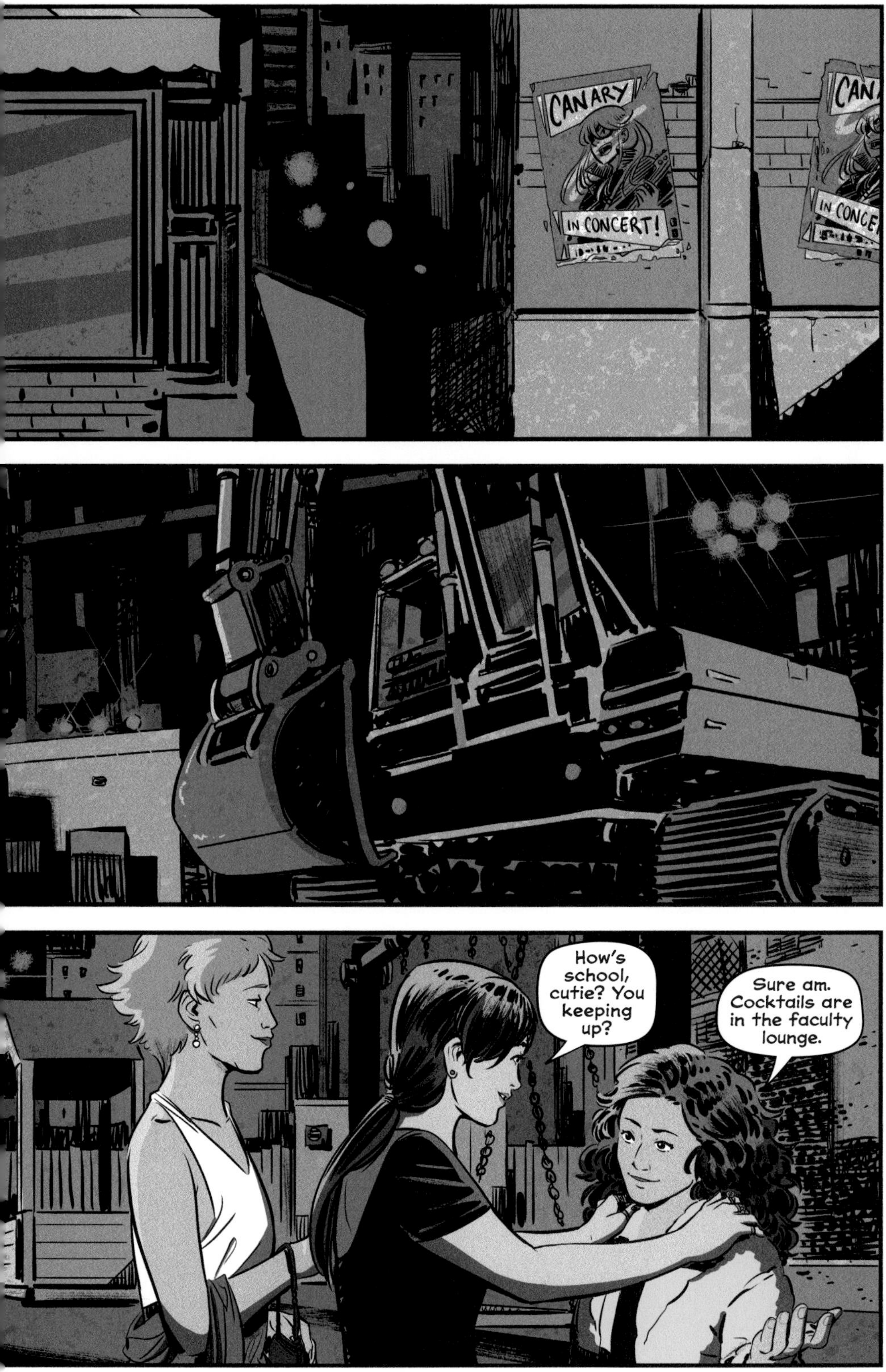
CANARY
IN CONCERT!
How's school, cutie? You keeping up?
Sure am. Cocktails are in the faculty lounge.

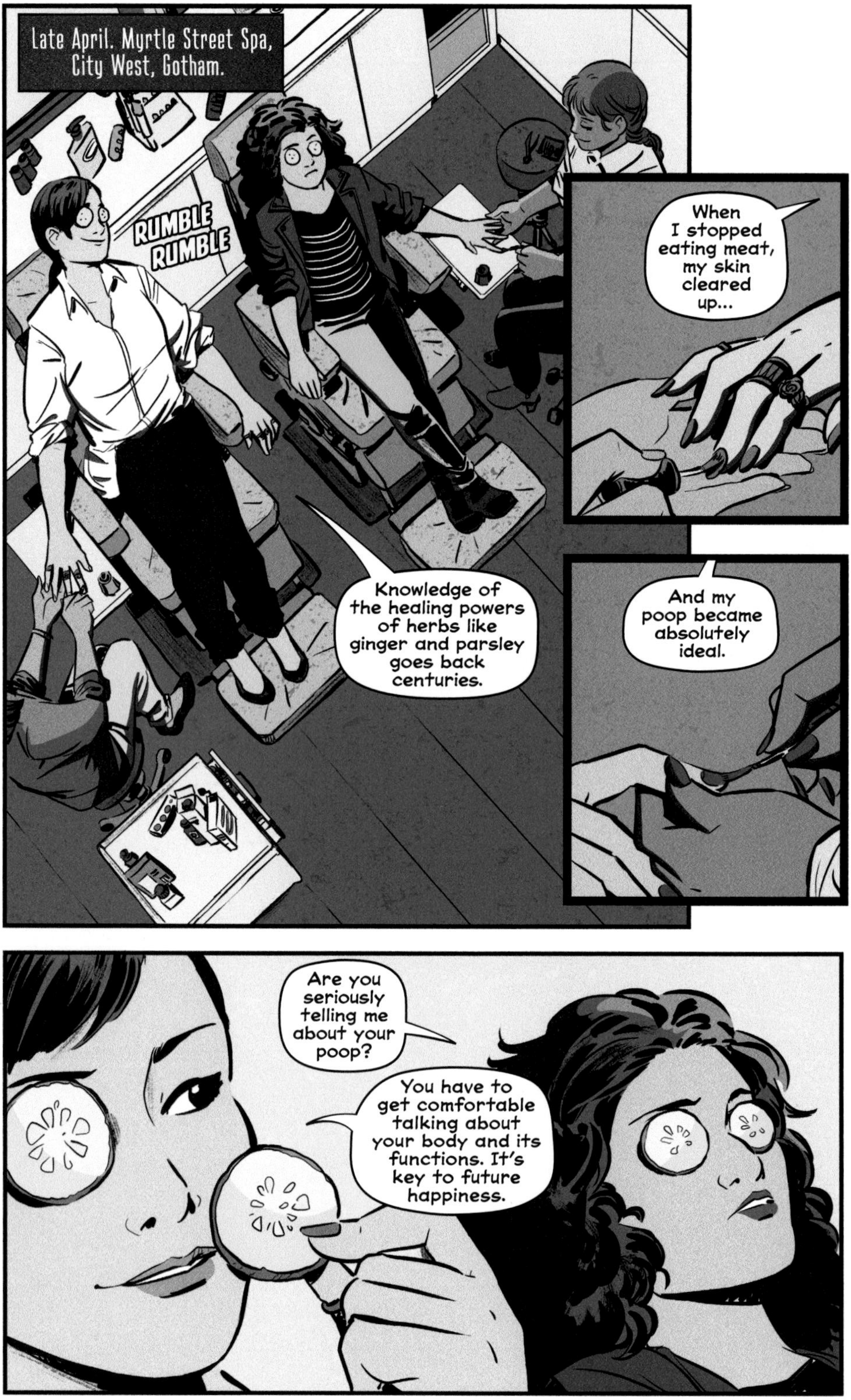
Late April. Myrtle Street Spa, City West, Gotham.
RUMBLE RUMBLE
Knowledge of the healing powers of herbs like ginger and parsley goes back centuries.
When I stopped eating meat, my skin cleared up...
And my poop became absolutely ideal.
Are you seriously telling me about your poop?
You have to get comfortable talking about your body and its functions. It's key to future happiness.

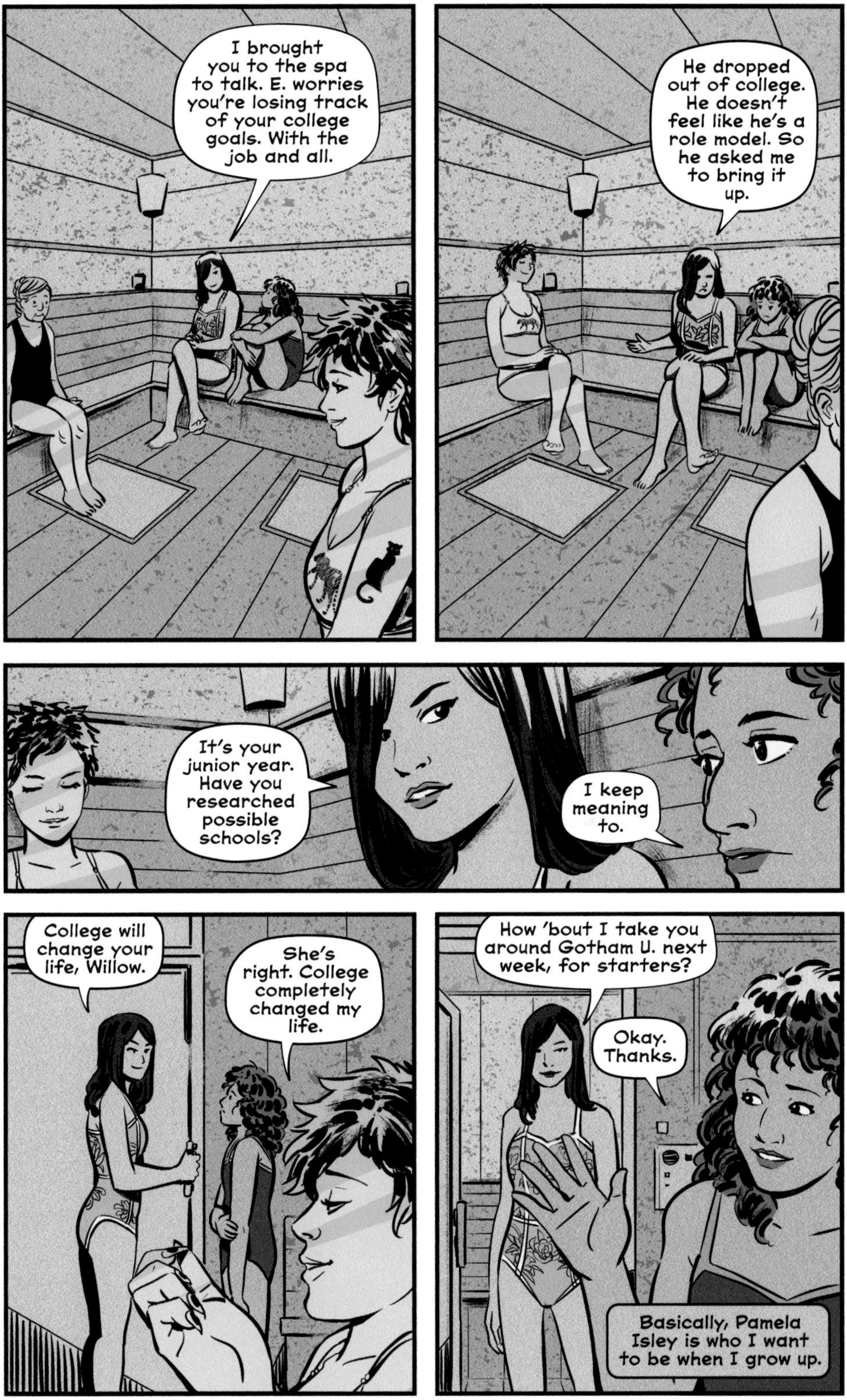
I brought you to the spa to talk. E. worries you're losing track of your college goals. With the job and all.
He dropped out of college. He doesn't feel like he's a role model. So he asked me to bring it up.
It's your junior year. Have you researched possible schools?
I keep meaning to.
College will change your life, Willow.
She's right. College completely changed my life.
How 'bout I take you around Gotham U. next week, for starters?
Okay. Thanks.
Basically, Pamela Isley is who I want to be when I grow up.

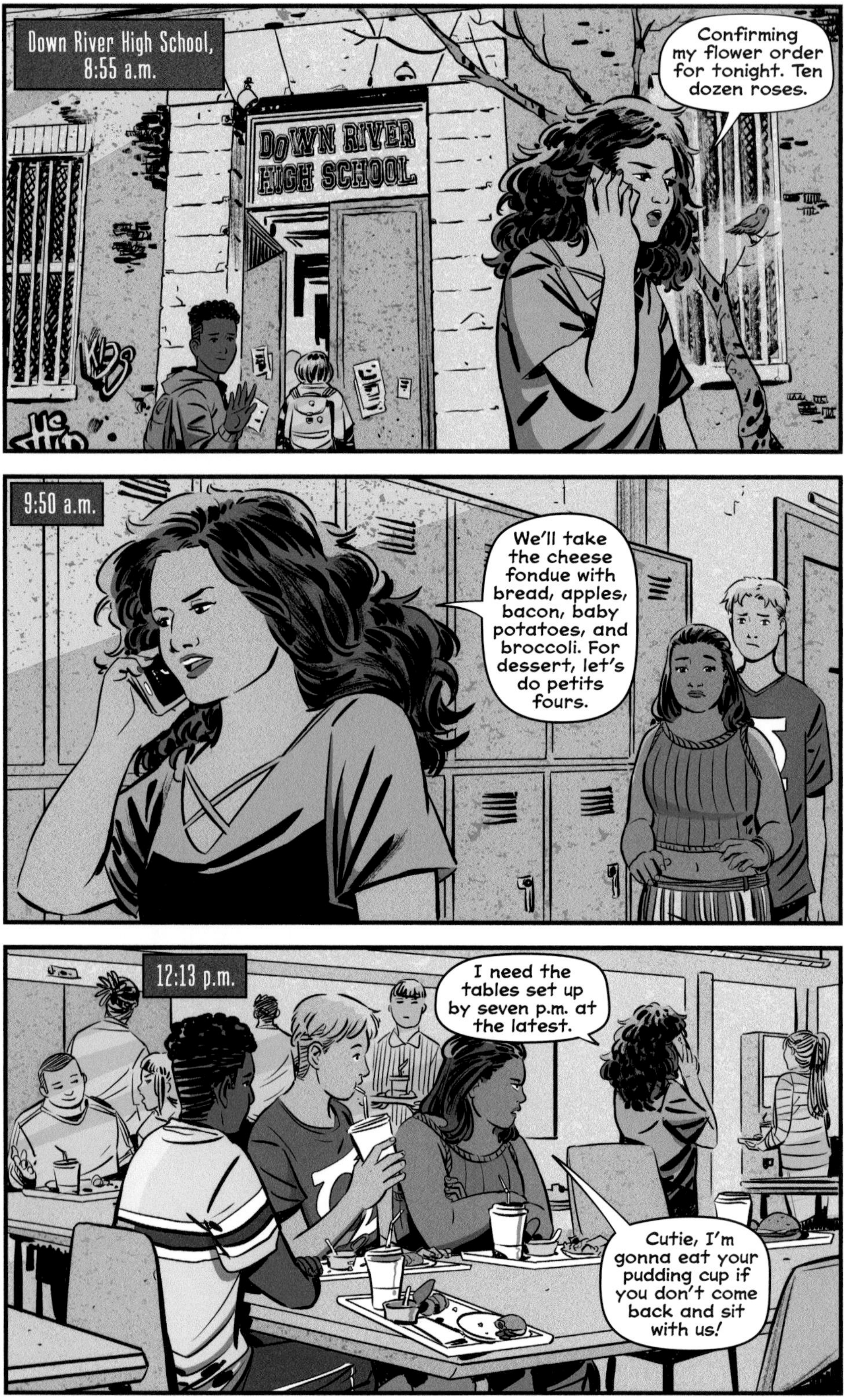
Down River High School, 8:55 a.m.
DOWN RIVER HIGH SCHOOL
Confirming my flower order for tonight. Ten dozen roses.
9:50 a.m.
We'll take the cheese fondue with bread, apples, bacon, baby potatoes, and broccoli. For dessert, let's do petits fours.
12:13 p.m.
I need the tables set up by seven p.m. at the latest.
Cutie, I'm gonna eat your pudding cup if you don't come back and sit with us!

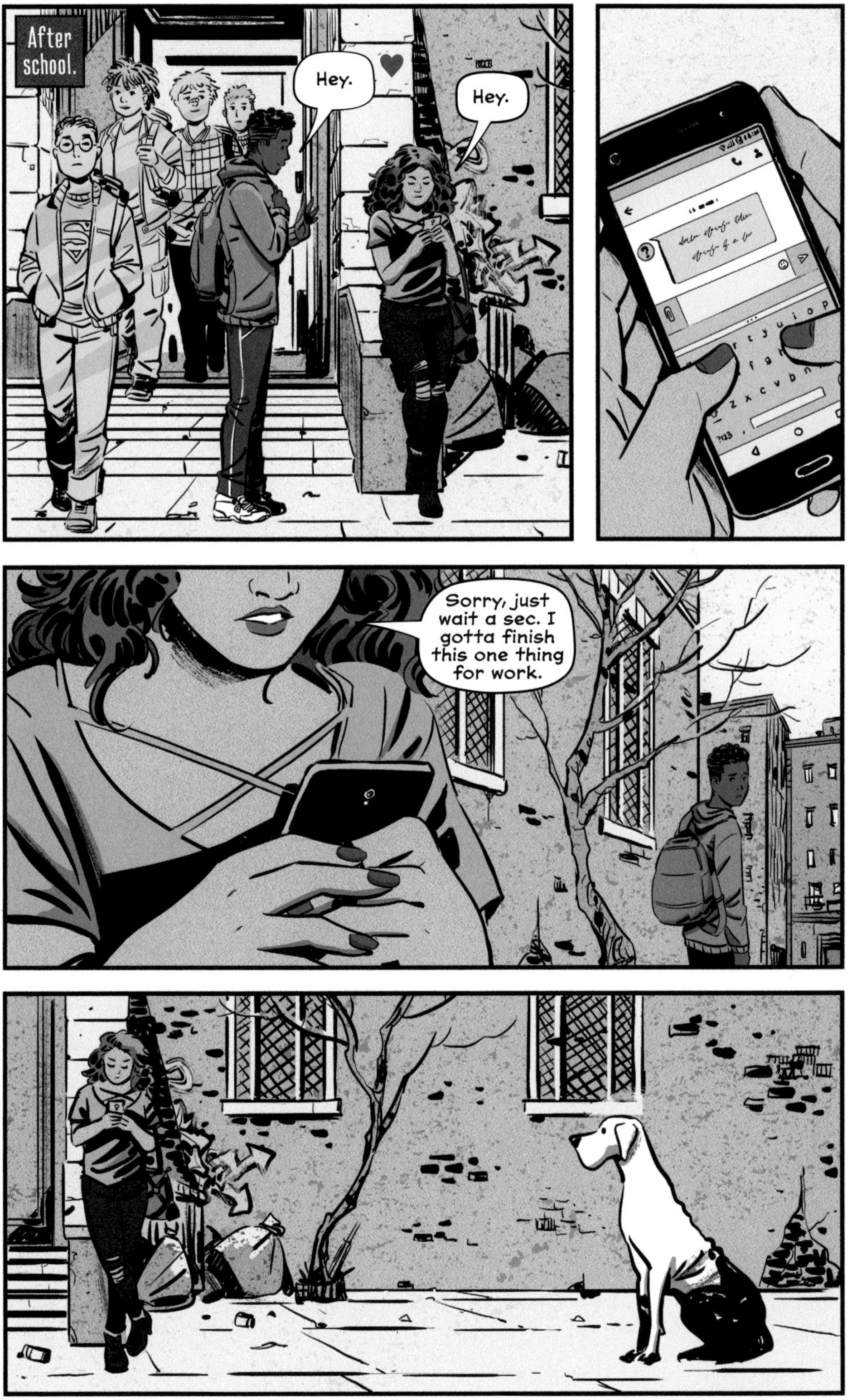
After school.
Hey.
Hey.
Sorry, just wait a sec. I gotta finish this one thing for work.

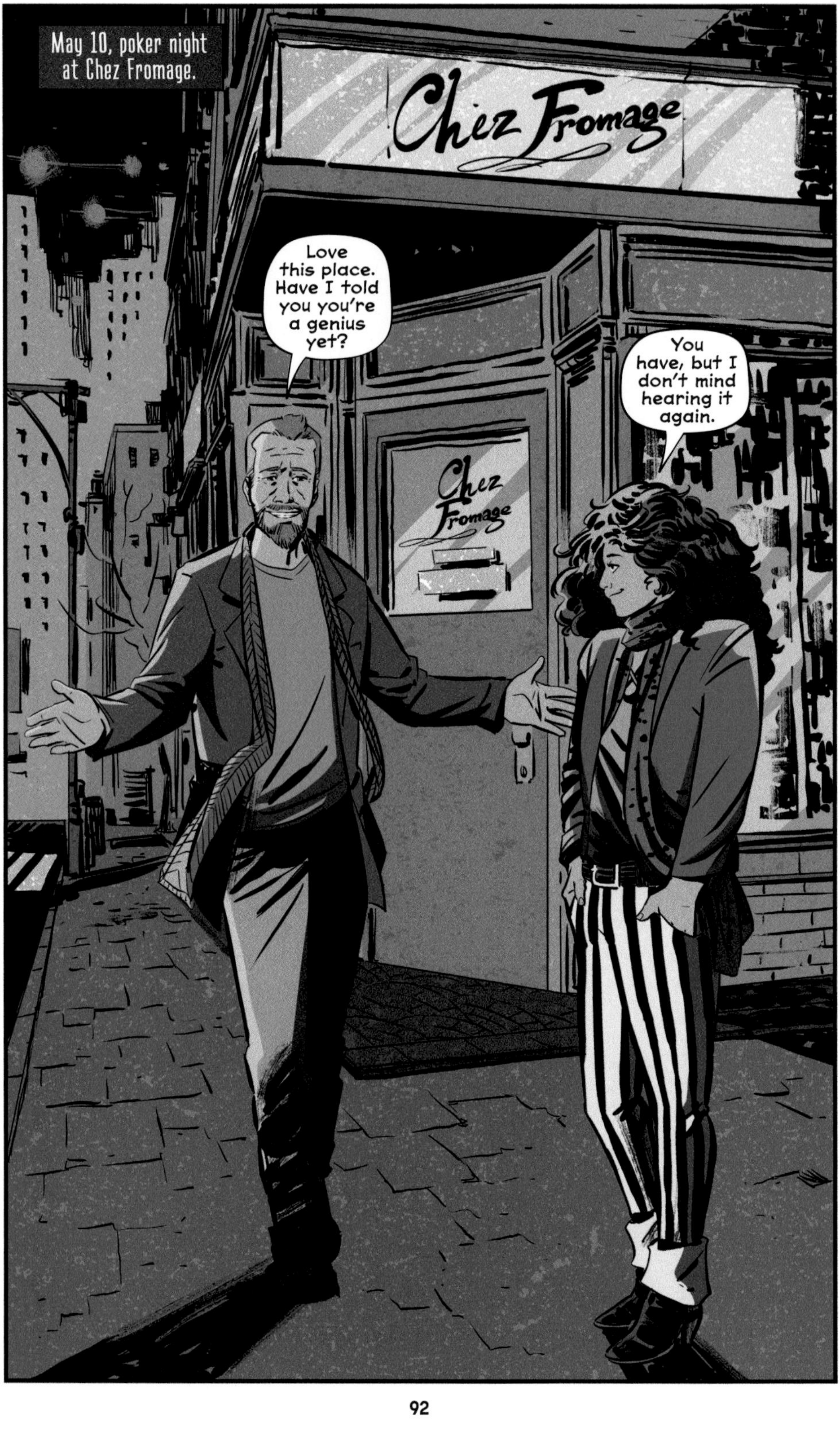
May 10, poker night at Chez Fromage.
Chez Fromage
Love this place. Have I told you you're a genius yet?
Chez Fromage
You have, but I don't mind hearing it again.

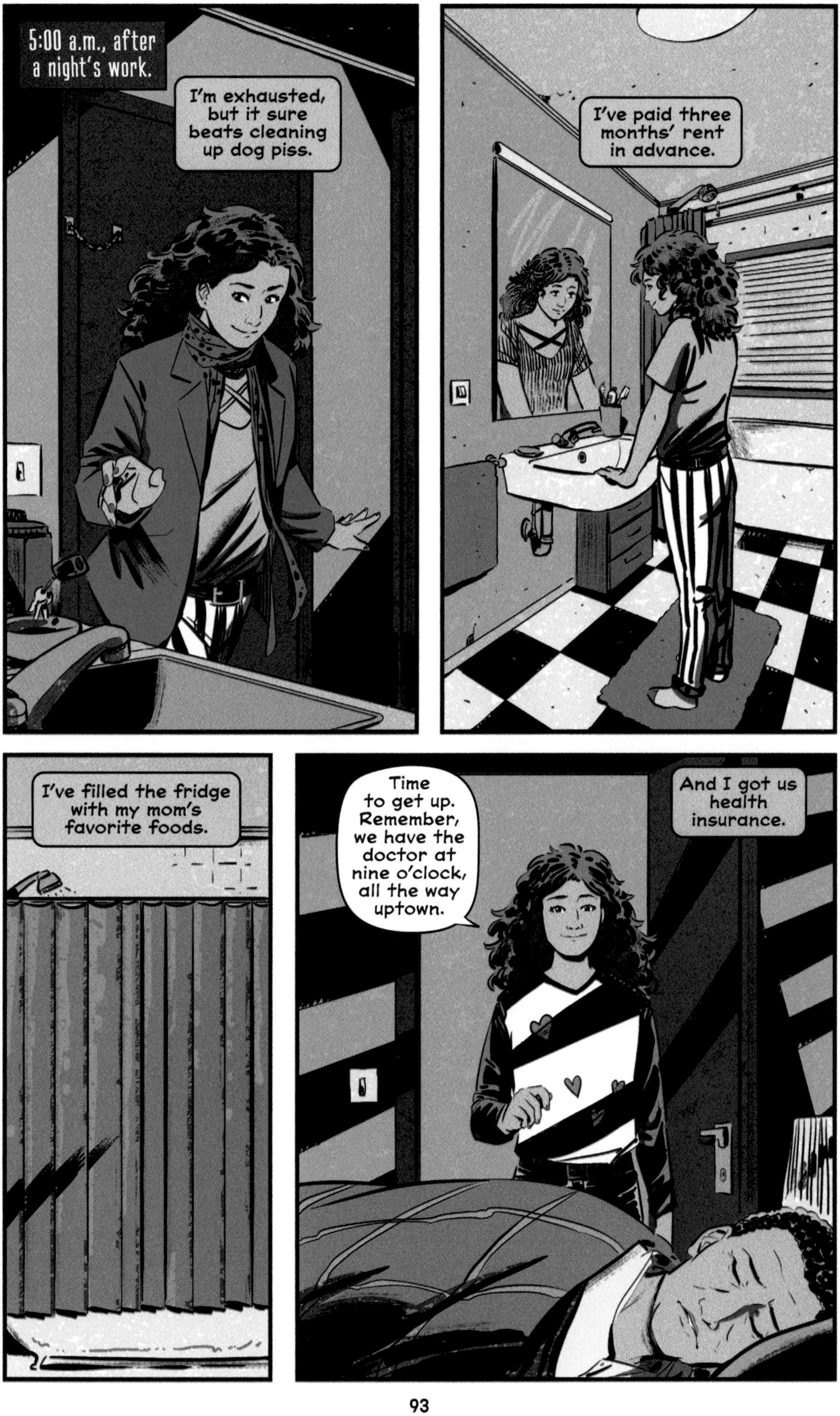
5:00 a.m., after a night's work.
I'm exhausted, but it sure beats cleaning up dog piss.
I've paid three months' rent in advance.
I've filled the fridge with my mom's favorite foods.
Time to get up. Remember, we have the doctor at nine o'clock, all the way uptown.
And I got us health insurance.

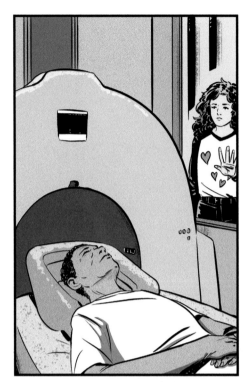

We can begin radiation immediately.

And the scans we took today will let us know what other courses of action are open to us.

It's good you came back in, Naomi.

94

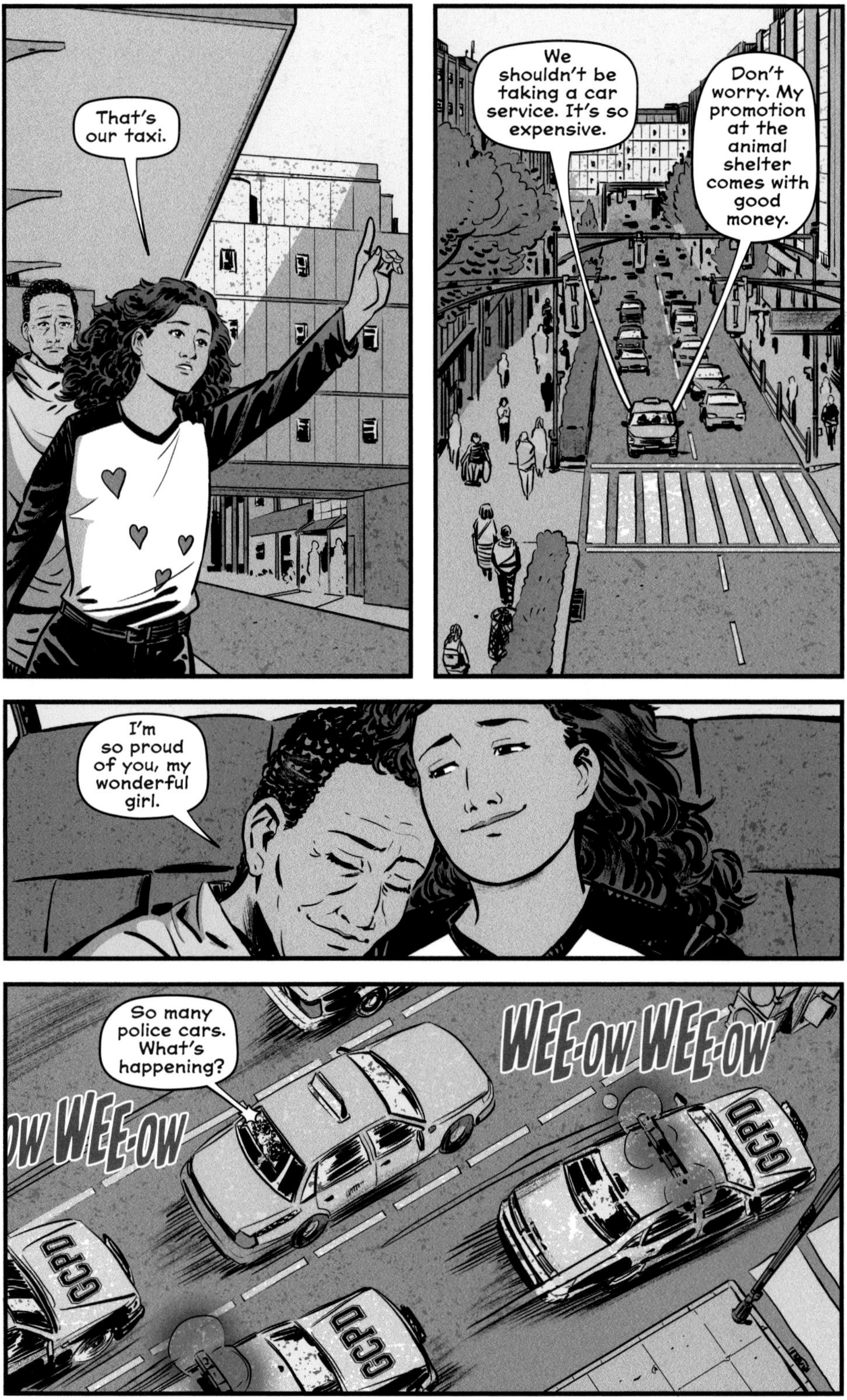
That's our taxi.
We shouldn't be taking a car service. It's so expensive.
Don't worry. My promotion at the animal shelter comes with good money.
I'm so proud of you, my wonderful girl.
So many police cars. What's happening?
WEE-OW WEE-OW
OW WEE-OW
GCPD
GCPD
GCPD
GCPD

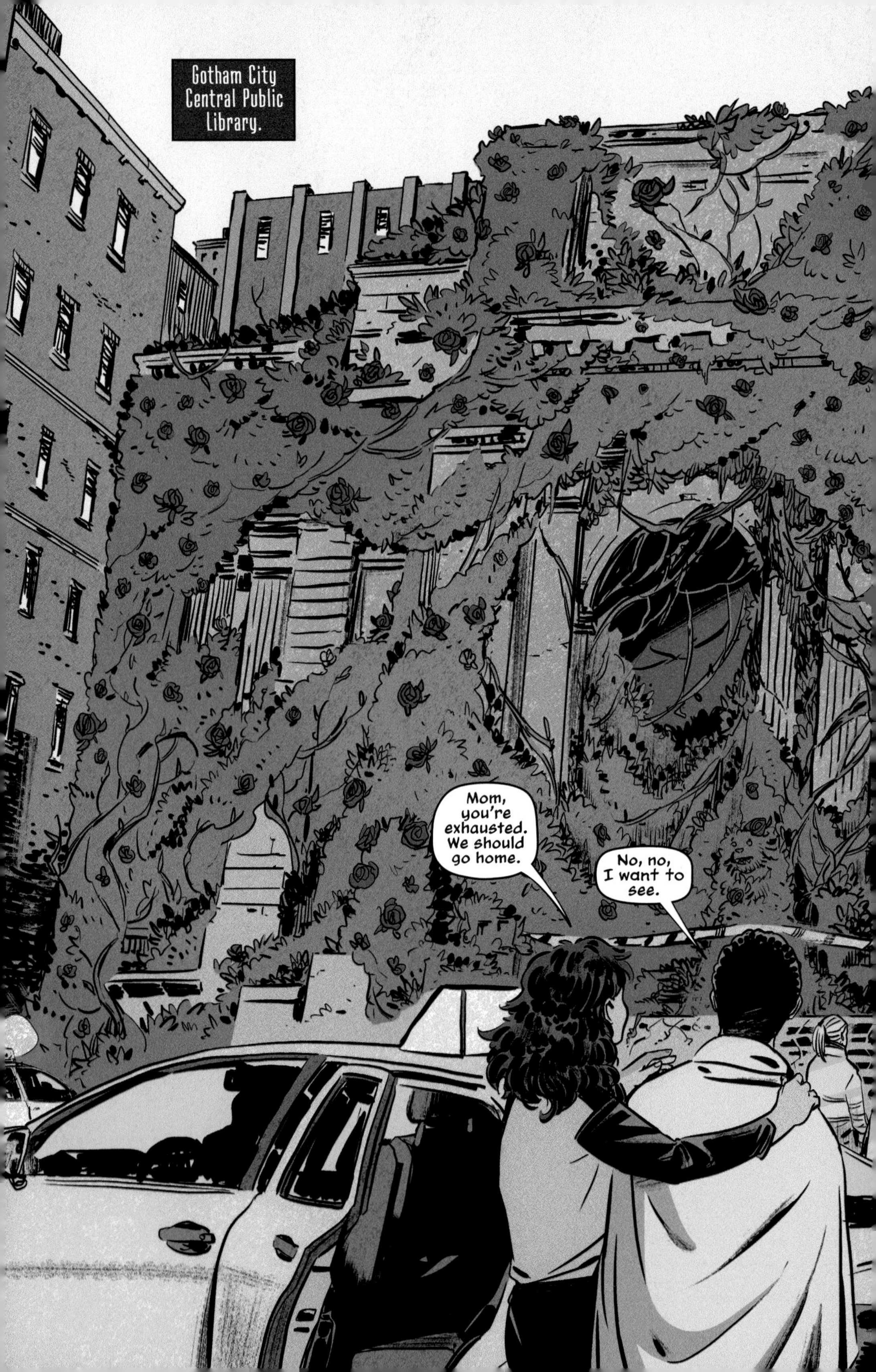
Gotham City Central Public Library.
Mom, you're exhausted. We should go home.
No, no, I want to see.

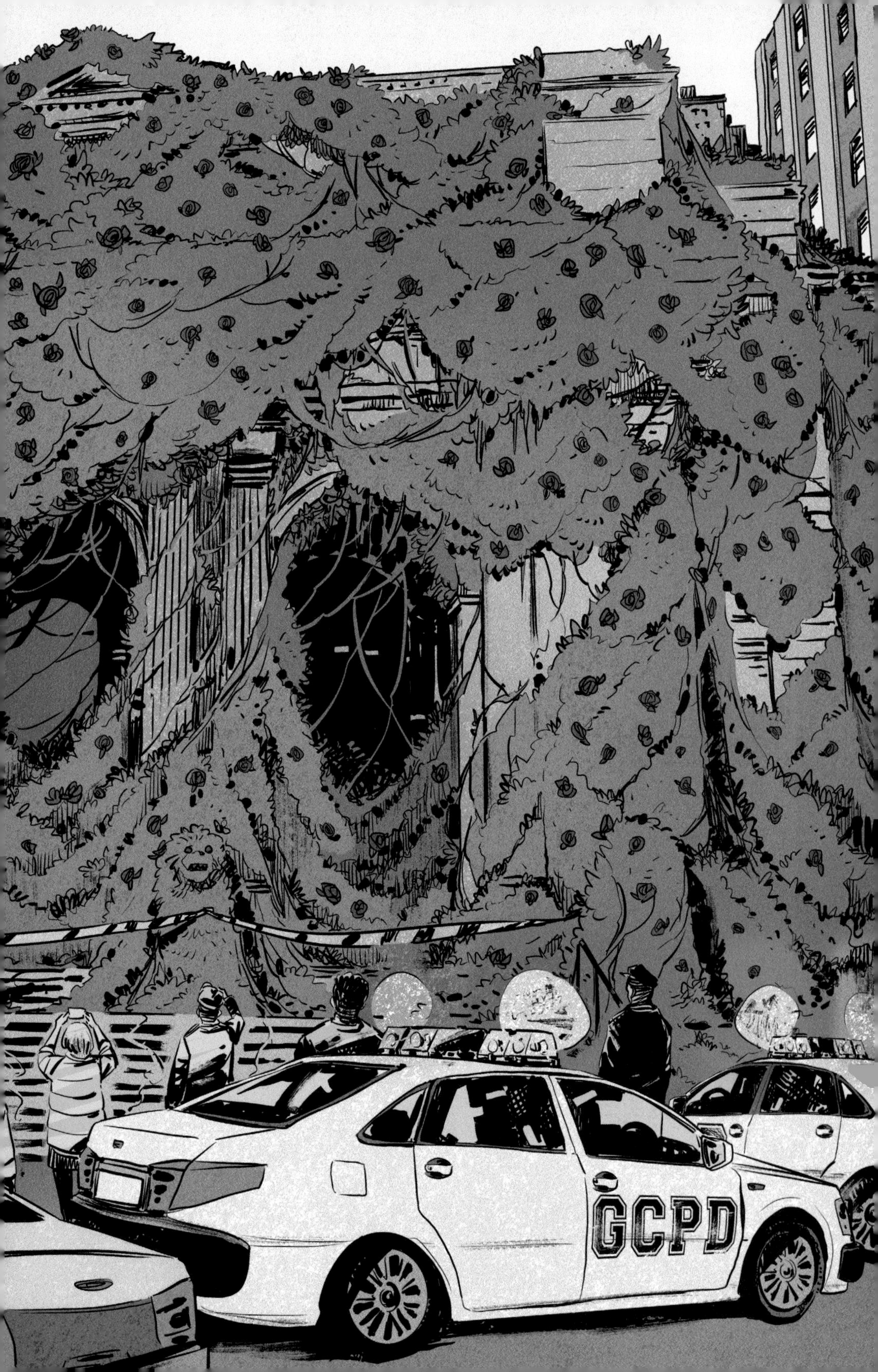
GCPD

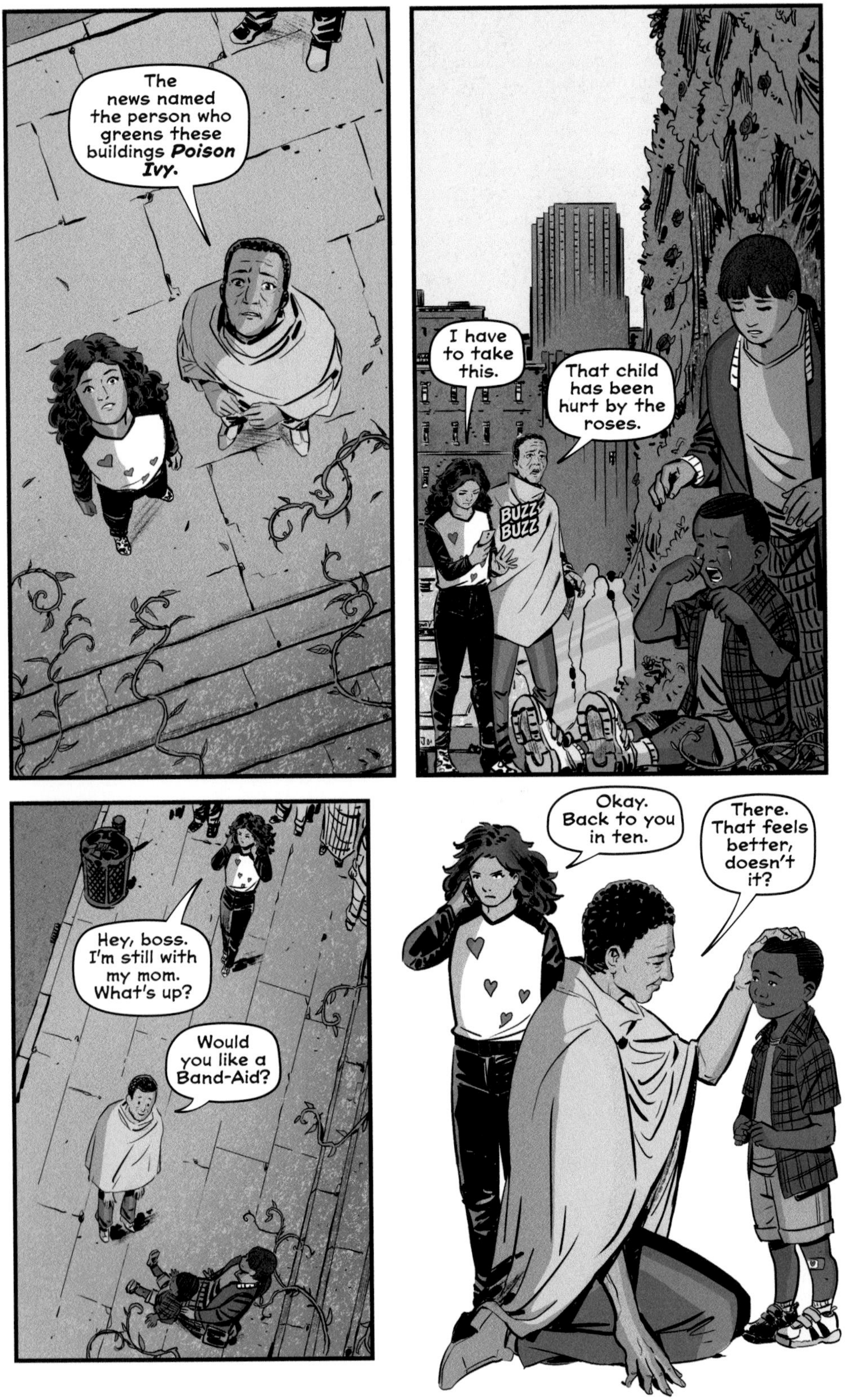
The news named the person who greens these buildings *Poison Ivy*.
I have to take this.
That child has been hurt by the roses.
BUZZ BUZZ
Hey, boss. I'm still with my mom. What's up?
Would you like a Band-Aid?
Okay. Back to you in ten.
There. That feels better, doesn't it?

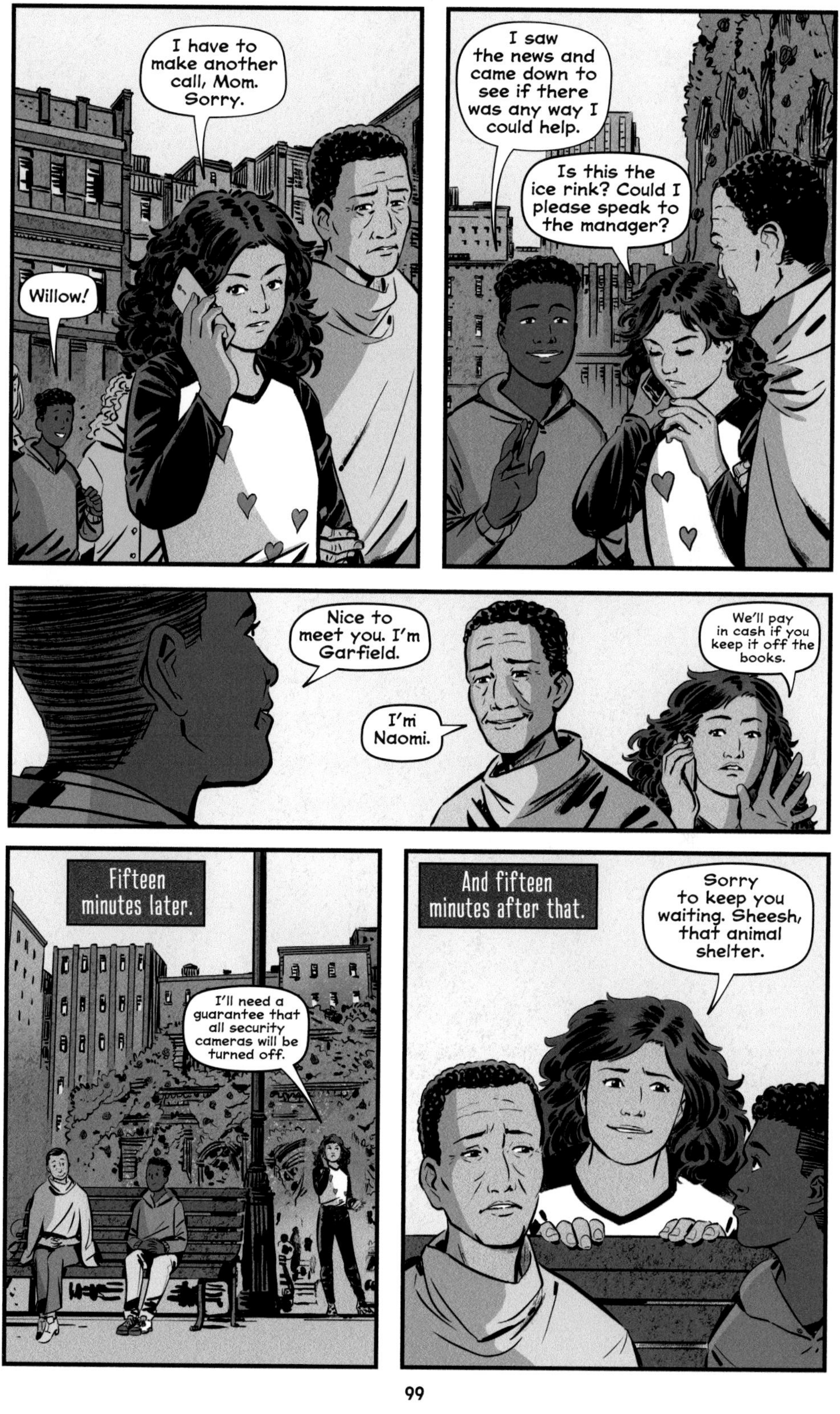
I have to make another call, Mom. Sorry.
Willow!
I saw the news and came down to see if there was any way I could help.
Is this the ice rink? Could I please speak to the manager?
Nice to meet you. I'm Garfield.
I'm Naomi.
We'll pay in cash if you keep it off the books.
Fifteen minutes later.
I'll need a guarantee that all security cameras will be turned off.
And fifteen minutes after that.
Sorry to keep you waiting. Sheesh, that animal shelter.

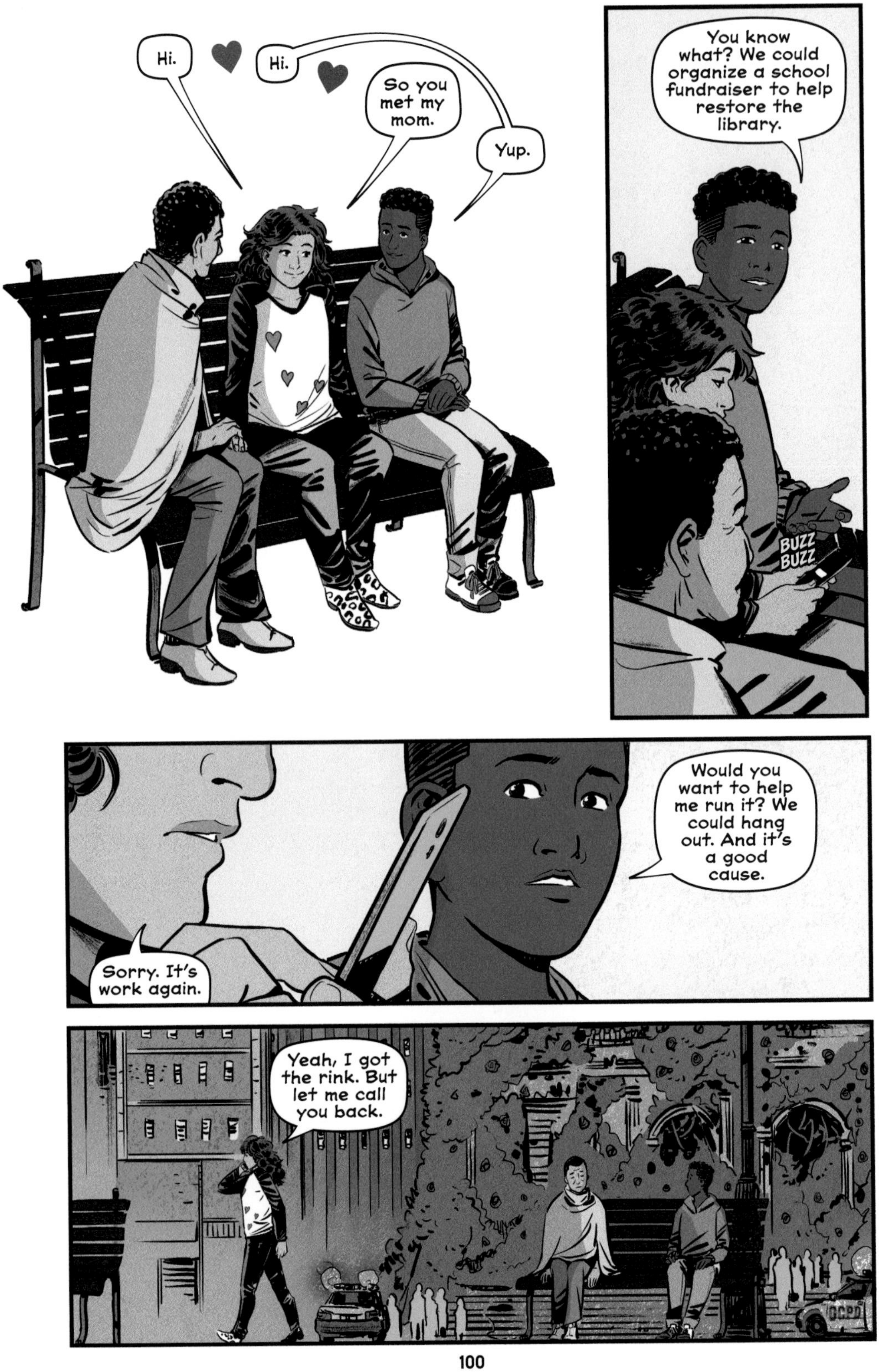
Hi.
Hi.
So you met my mom.
Yup.
You know what? We could organize a school fundraiser to help restore the library.
BUZZ BUZZ
Sorry. It's work again.
Would you want to help me run it? We could hang out. And it's a good cause.
Yeah, I got the rink. But let me call you back.
GCPD

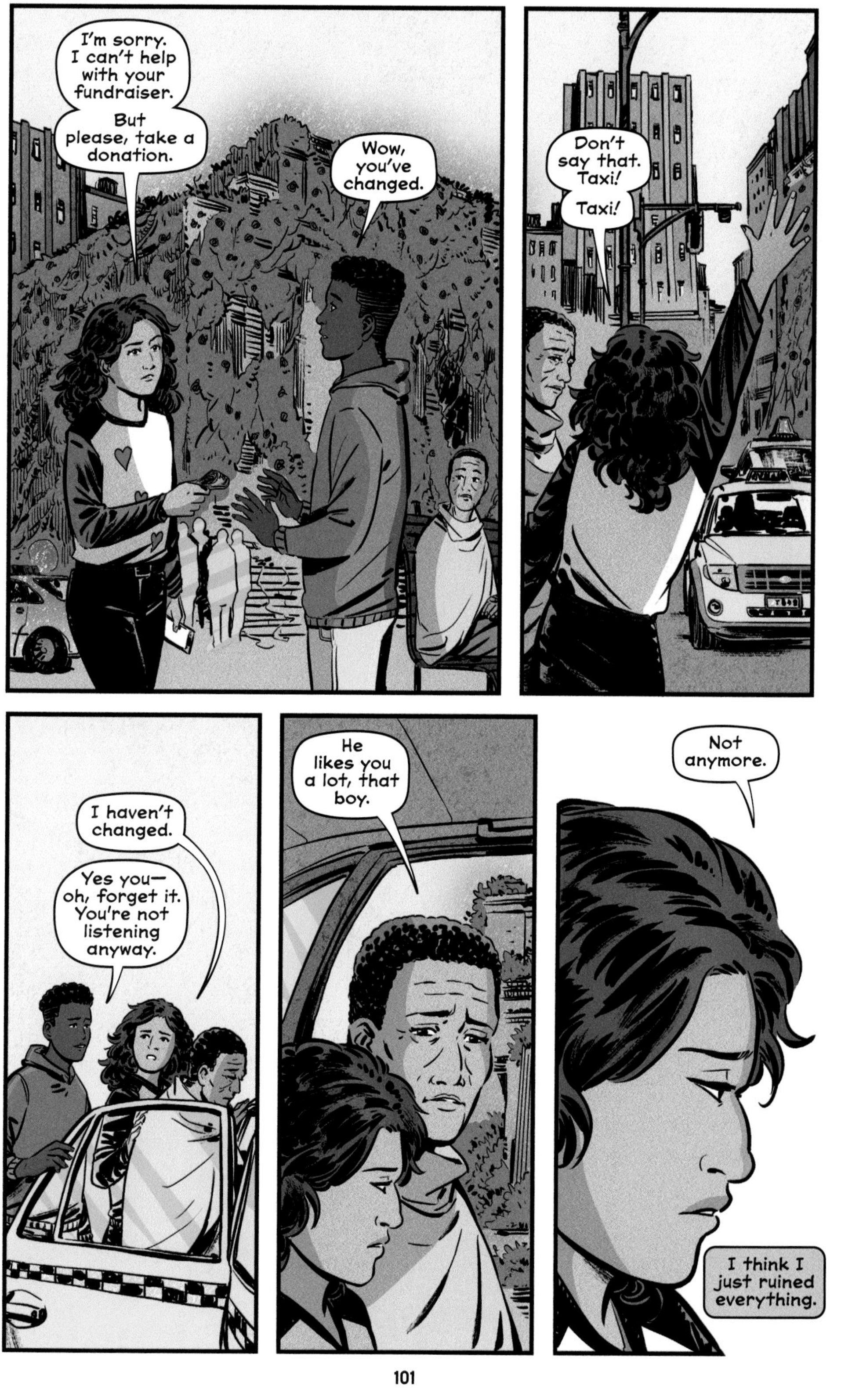
I'm sorry. I can't help with your fundraiser.
But please, take a donation.
Wow, you've changed.
Don't say that. Taxi!
Taxi!
I haven't changed.
Yes you— oh, forget it. You're not listening anyway.
He likes you a lot, that boy.
Not anymore.
I think I just ruined everything.

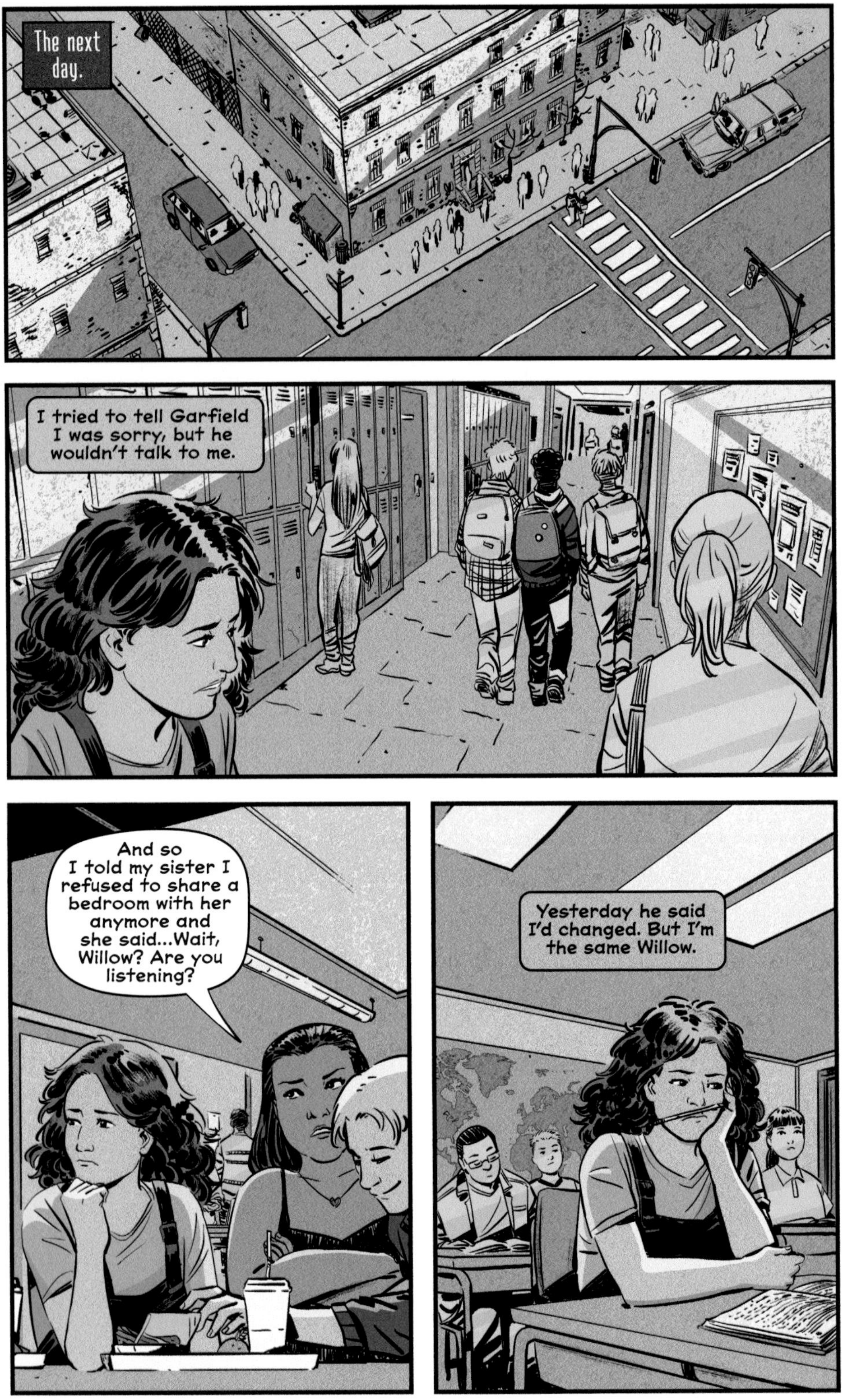
The next day.
I tried to tell Garfield I was sorry, but he wouldn't talk to me.
And so I told my sister I refused to share a bedroom with her anymore and she said...Wait, Willow? Are you listening?
Yesterday he said I'd changed. But I'm the same Willow.

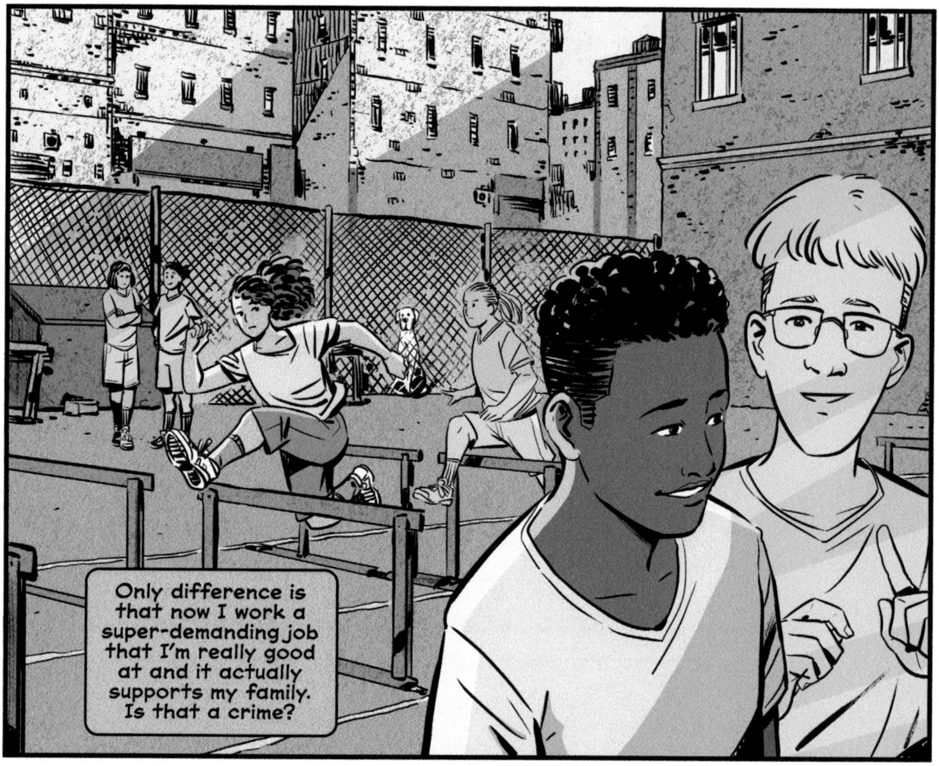
Only difference is that now I work a super-demanding job that I'm really good at and it actually supports my family. Is that a crime?

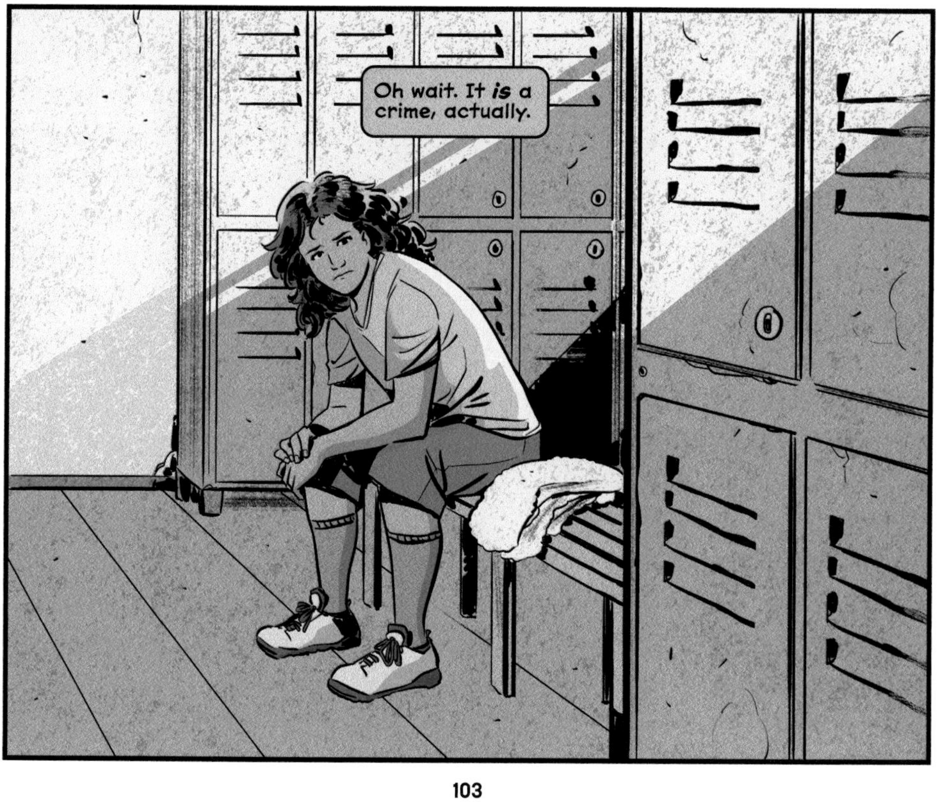
Oh wait. It *is* a crime, actually.

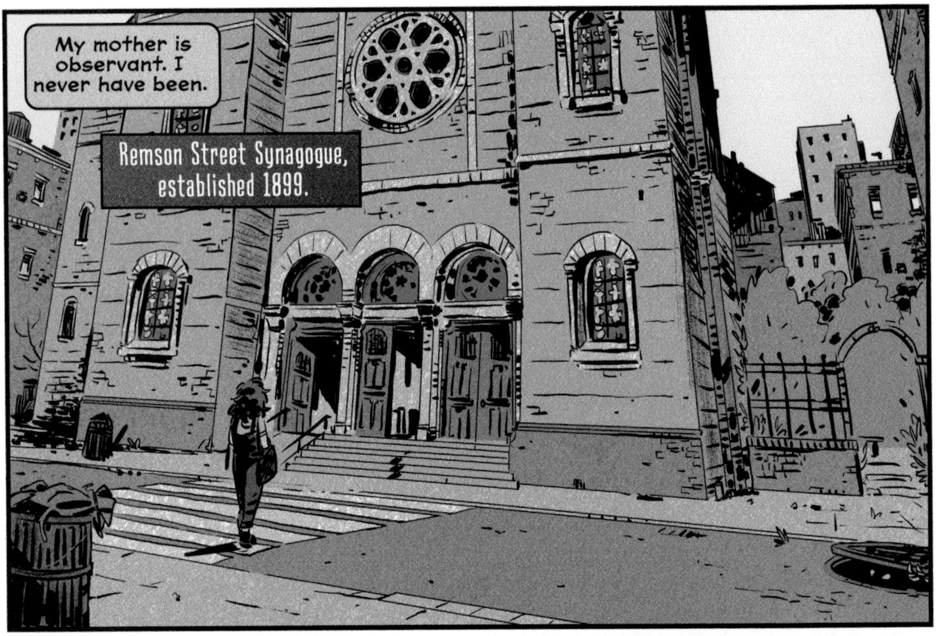
My mother is observant. I never have been.
Remson Street Synagogue, established 1899.

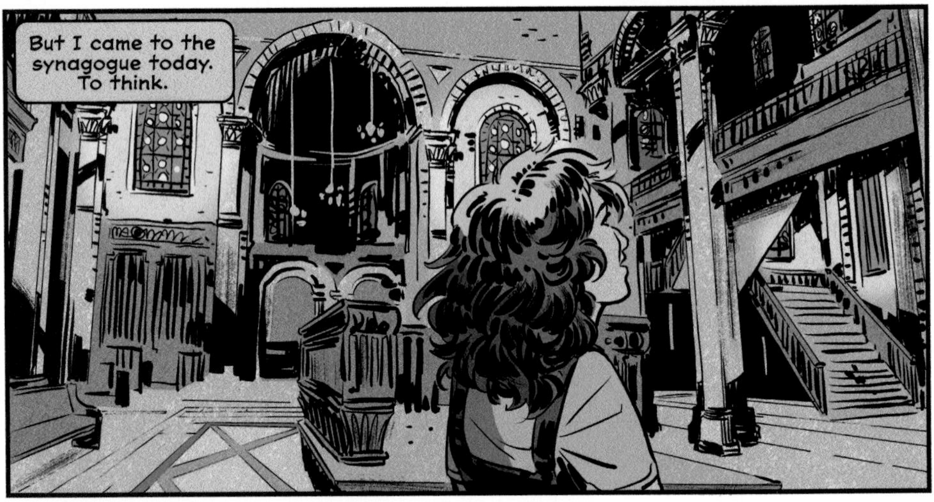
But I came to the synagogue today. To think.

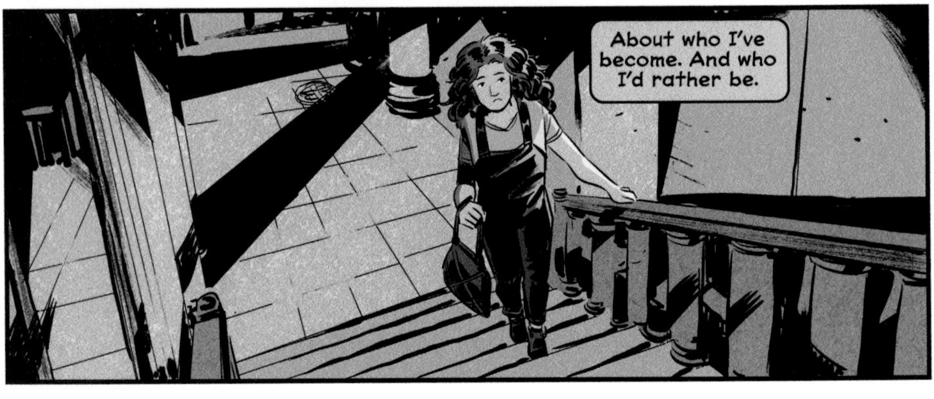
About who I've become. And who I'd rather be.

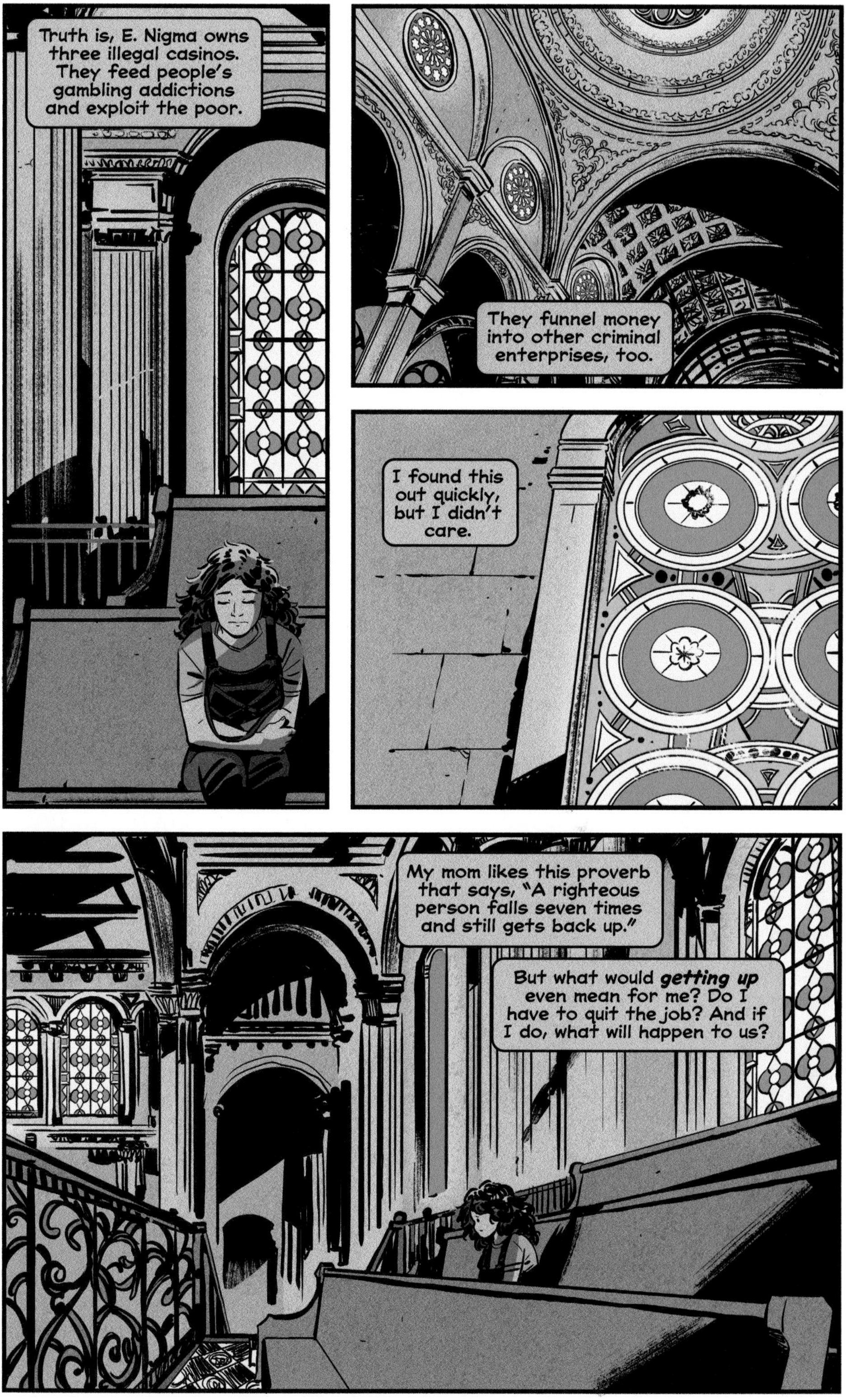
Truth is, E. Nigma owns three illegal casinos. They feed people's gambling addictions and exploit the poor.
They funnel money into other criminal enterprises, too.
I found this out quickly, but I didn't care.
My mom likes this proverb that says, "A righteous person falls seven times and still gets back up."
But what would ***getting up*** even mean for me? Do I have to quit the job? And if I do, what will happen to us?

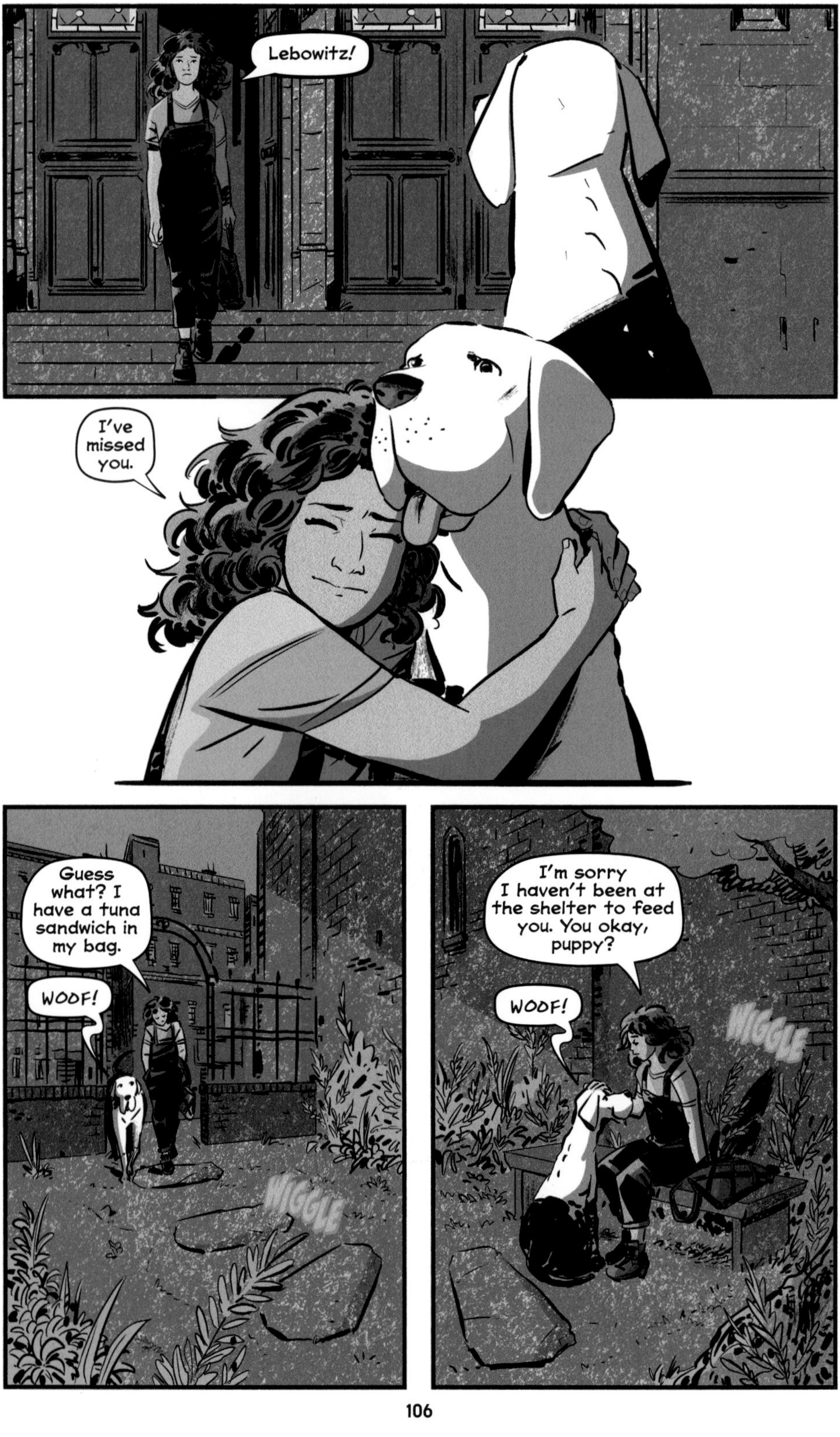
Lebowitz!
I've missed you.
Guess what? I have a tuna sandwich in my bag.
WOOF!
WIGGLE
I'm sorry I haven't been at the shelter to feed you. You okay, puppy?
WOOF!
WIGGLE

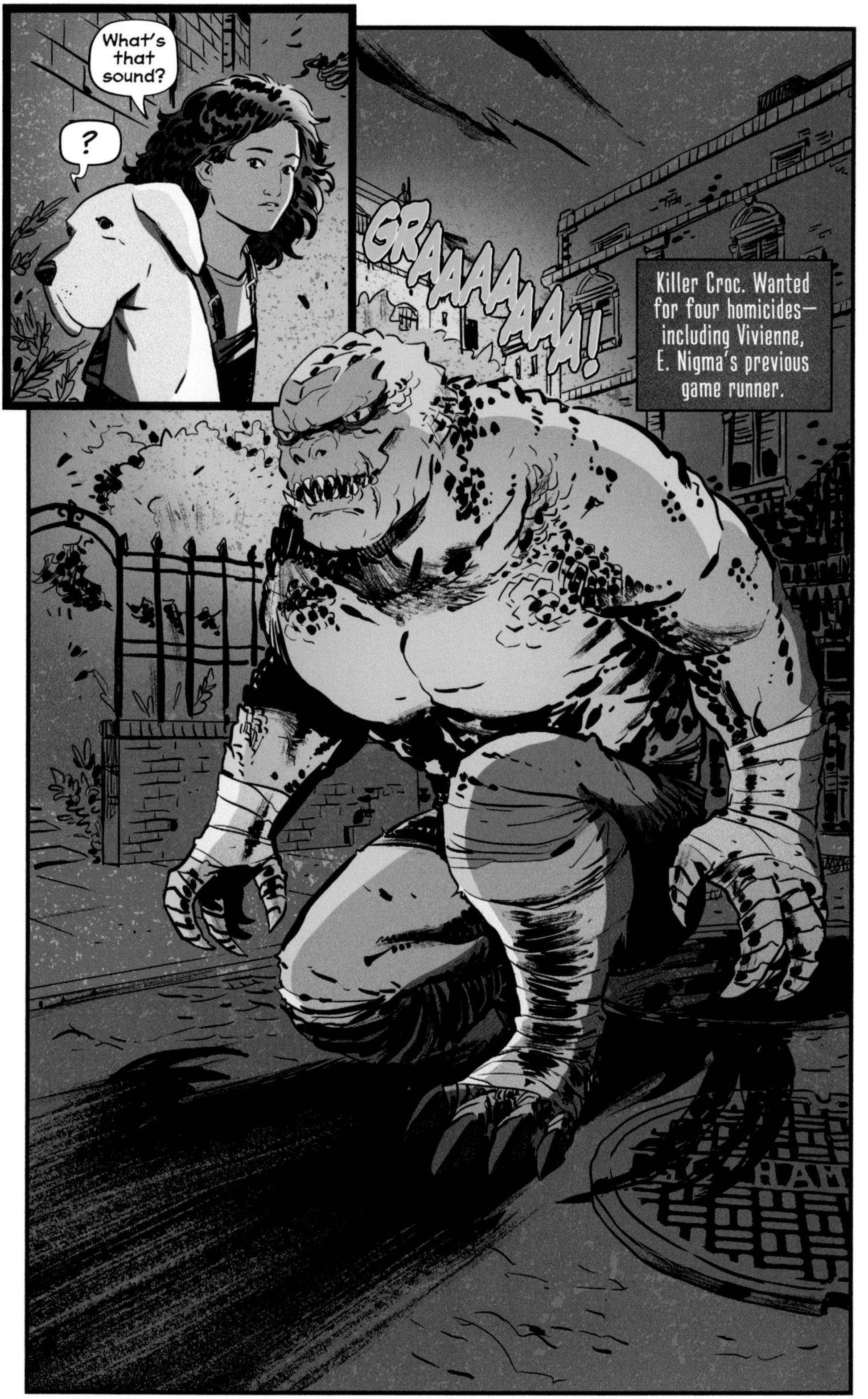
What's that sound?
?
GRAAAAAAAAA!
Killer Croc. Wanted for four homicides—including Vivienne, E. Nigma's previous game runner.

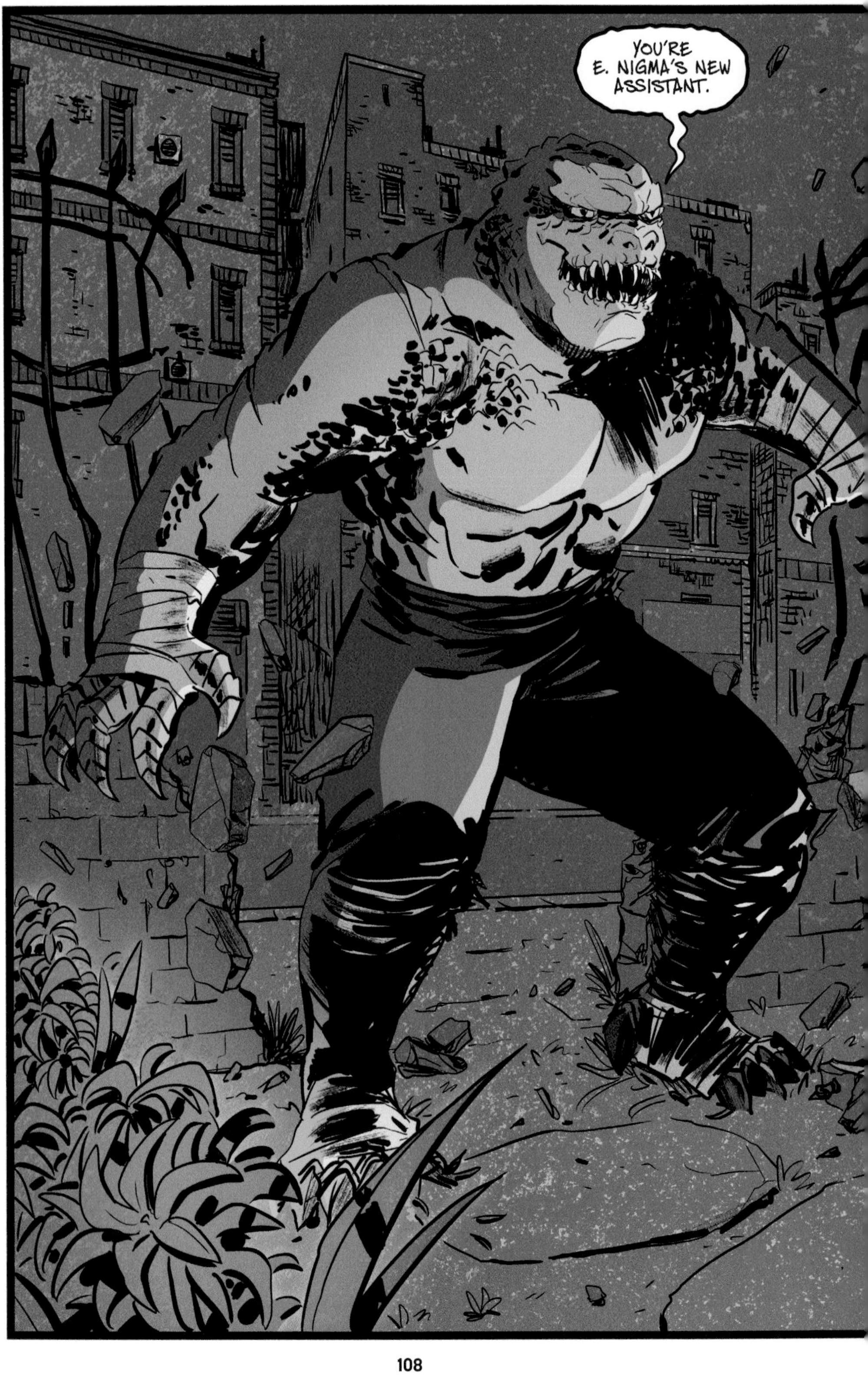
YOU'RE E. NIGMA'S NEW ASSISTANT.

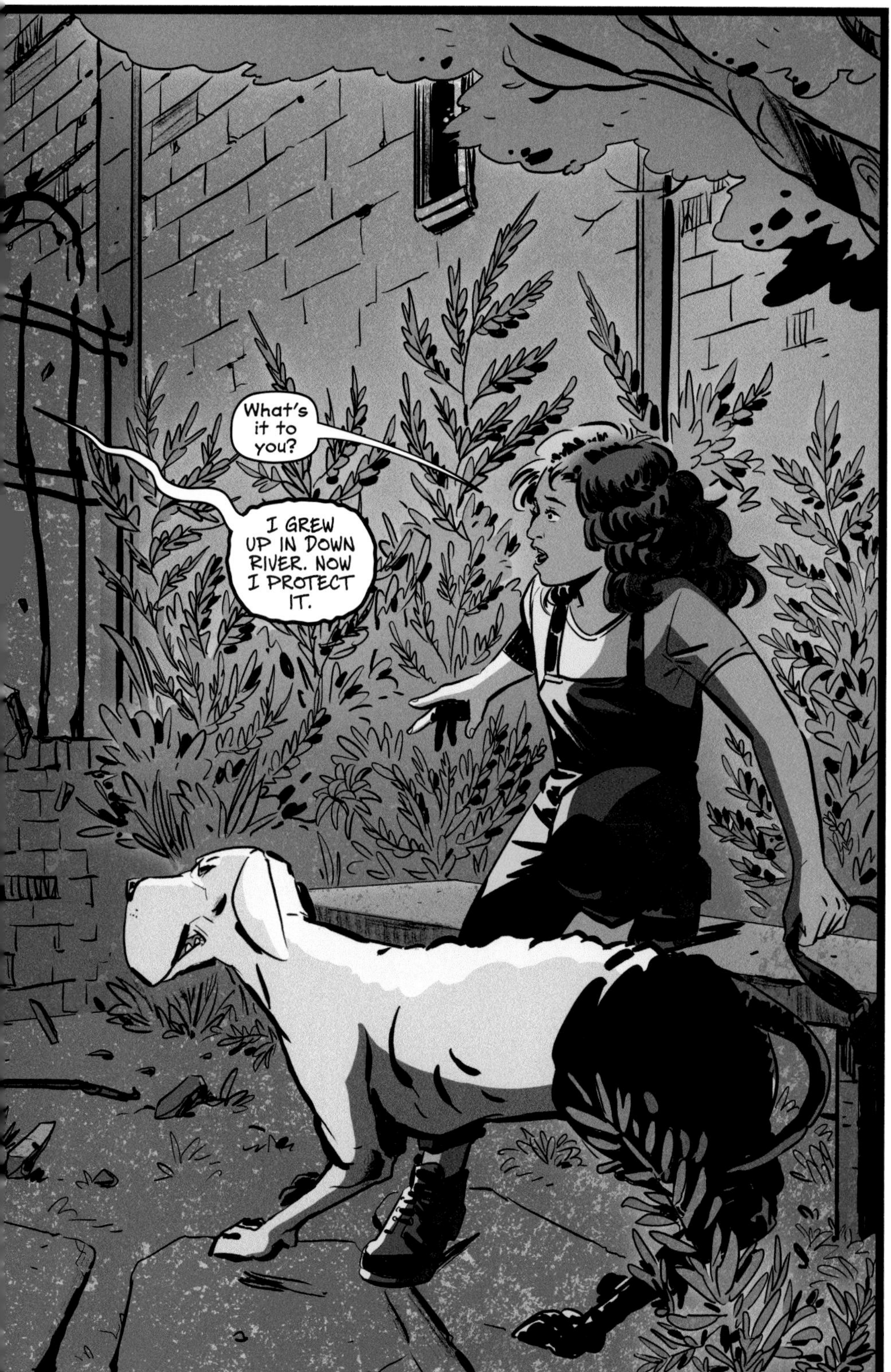
What's it to you?
I GREW UP IN DOWN RIVER. NOW I PROTECT IT.

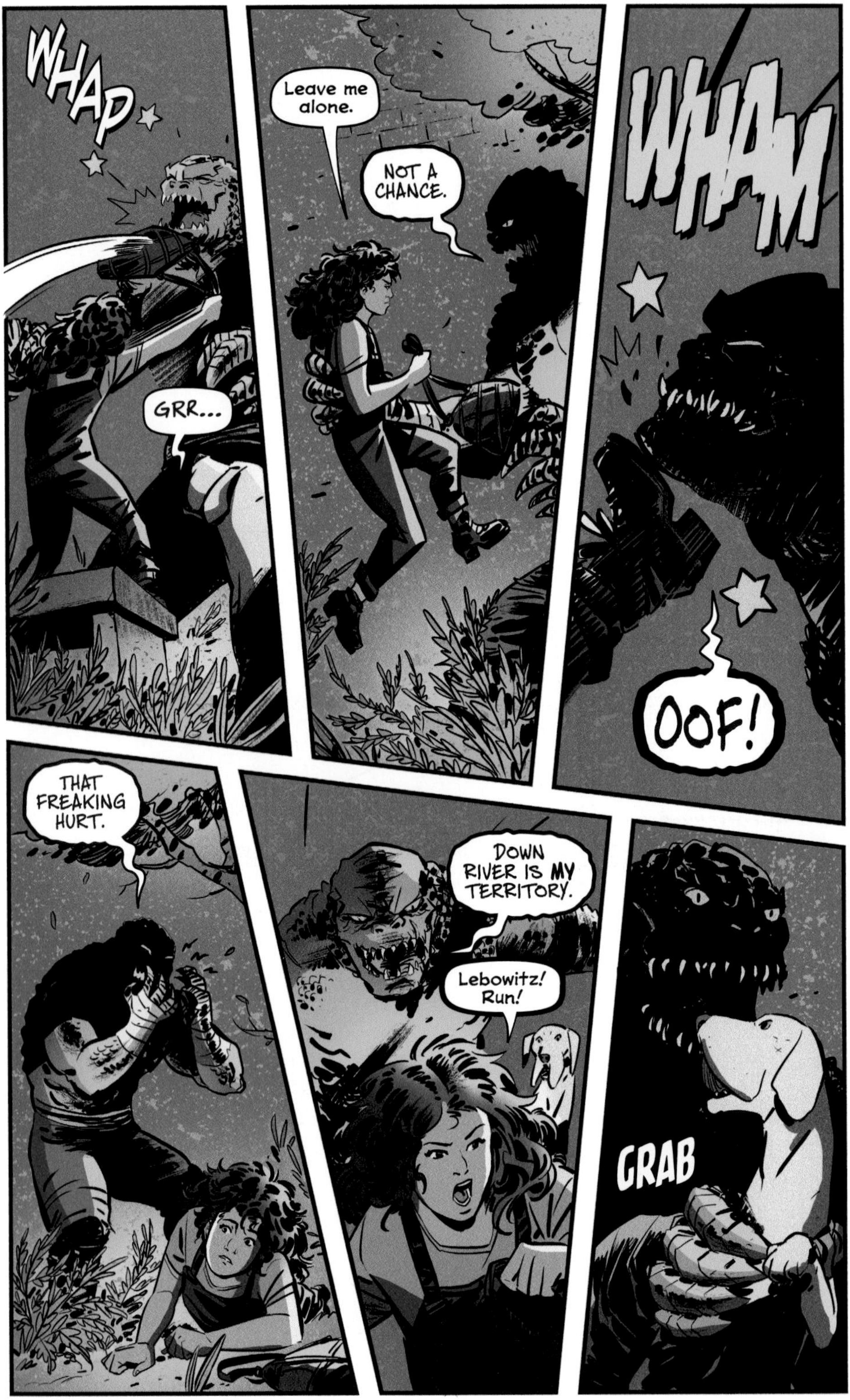
WHAP
GRR...
Leave me alone.
NOT A CHANCE.
WHAM
OOF!
THAT FREAKING HURT.
DOWN RIVER IS MY TERRITORY.
Lebowitz! Run!
GRAB

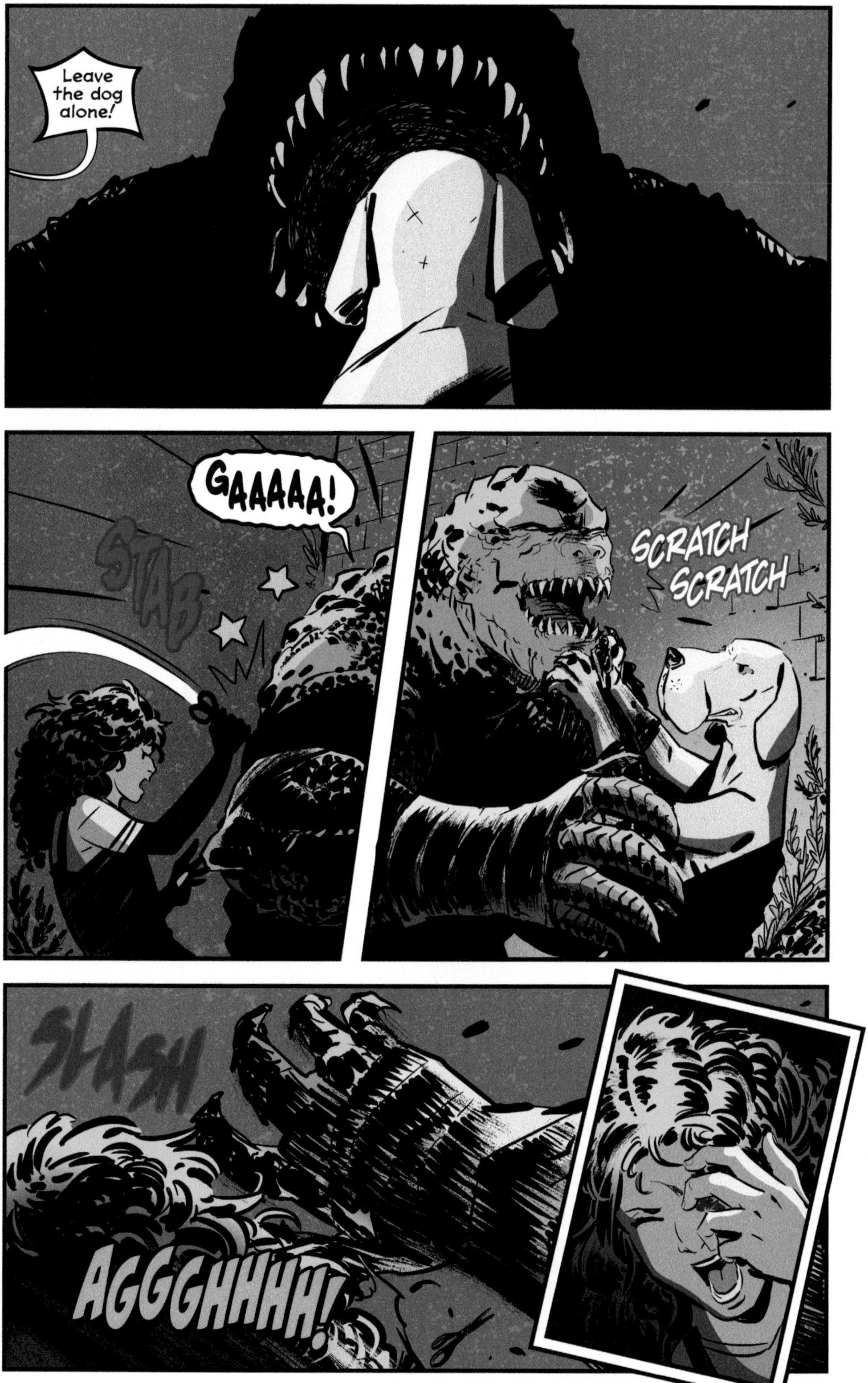
Leave the dog alone!
GAAAAA!
STAB
SCRATCH SCRATCH
SLASH
AGGGHHHH!

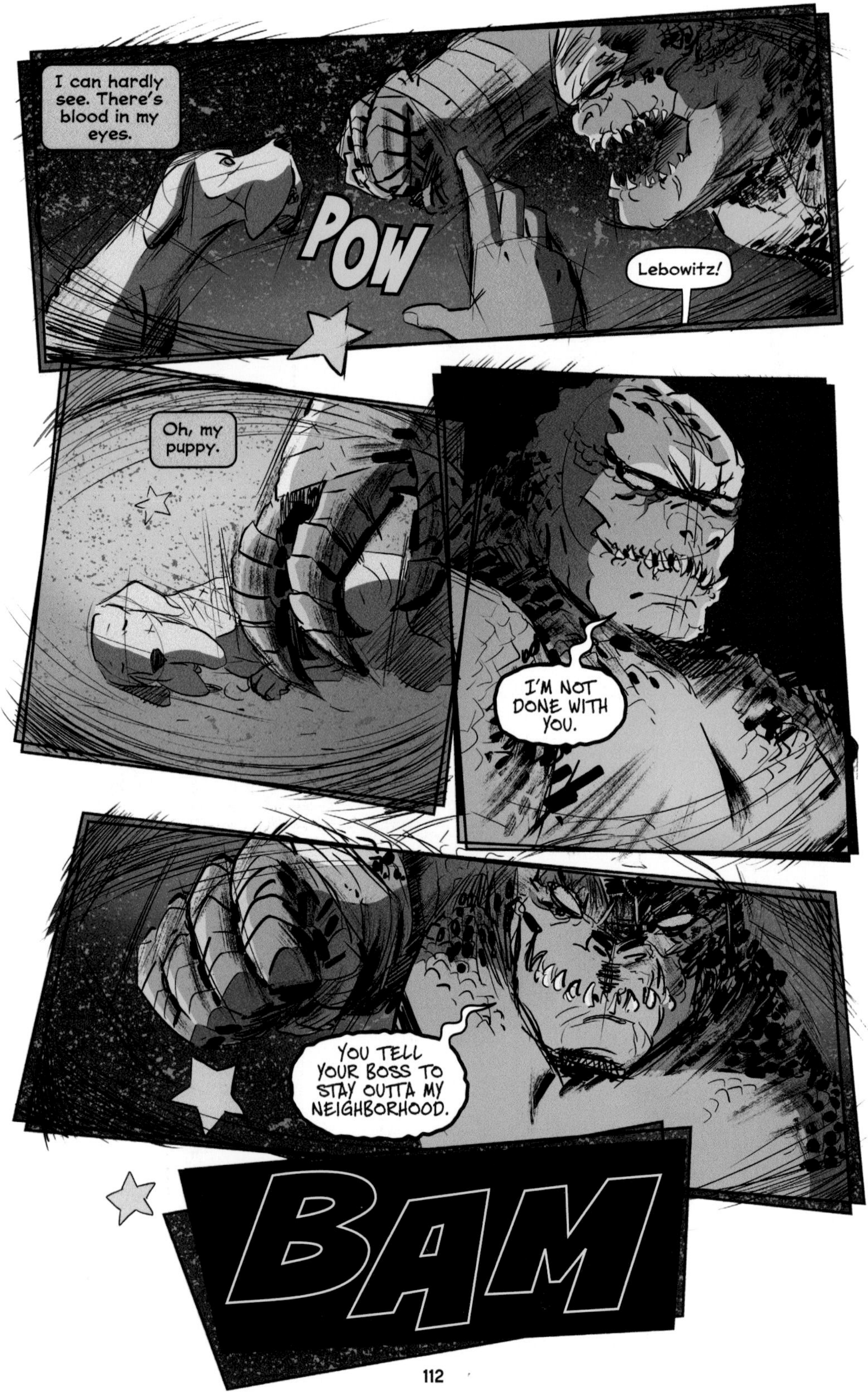
I can hardly see. There's blood in my eyes.
POW
Lebowitz!
Oh, my puppy.
I'M NOT DONE WITH YOU.
YOU TELL YOUR BOSS TO STAY OUTTA MY NEIGHBORHOOD.
BAM

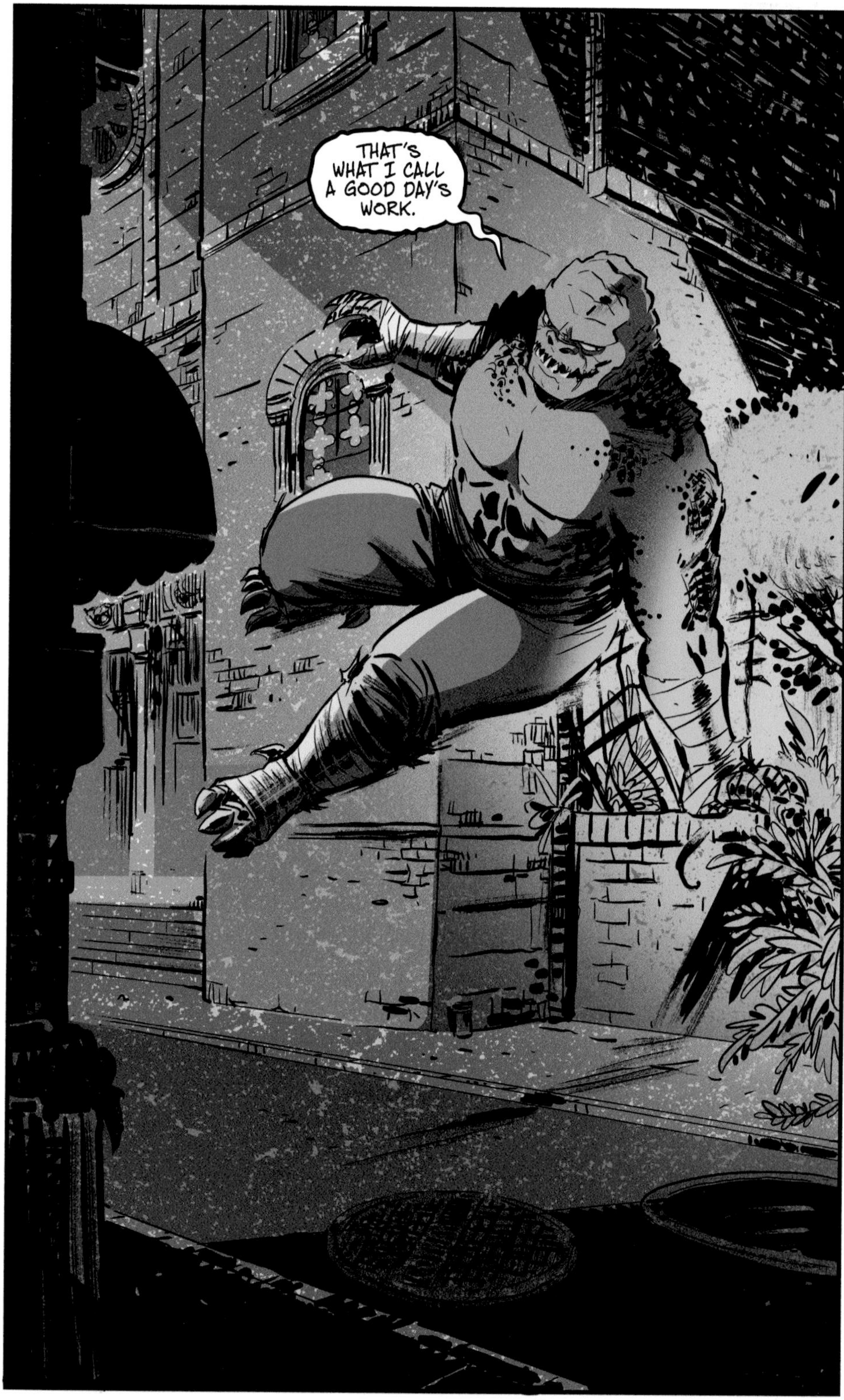
THAT'S WHAT I CALL A GOOD DAY'S WORK.

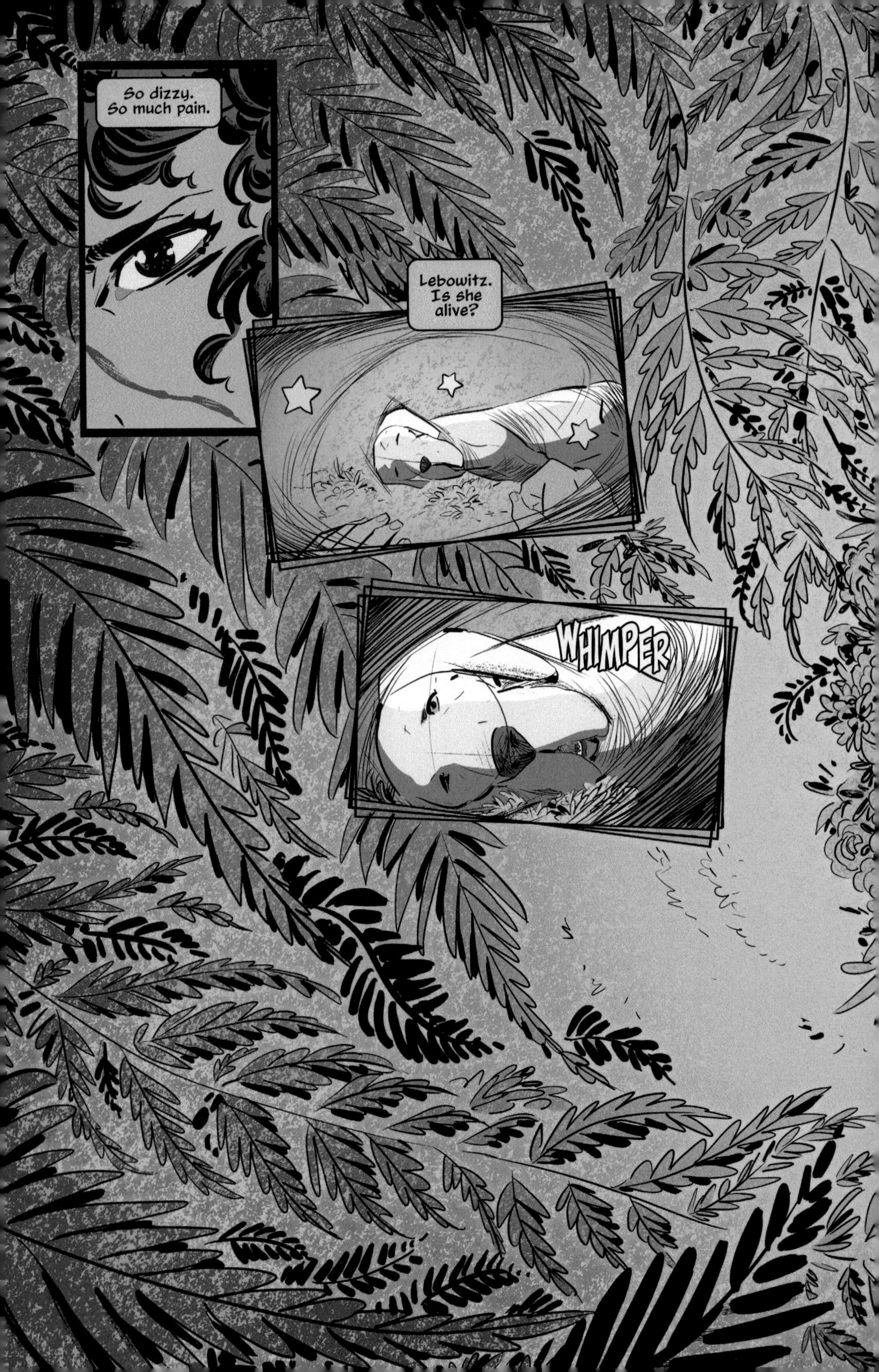
So dizzy. So much pain.
Lebowitz. Is she alive?
WHIMPER

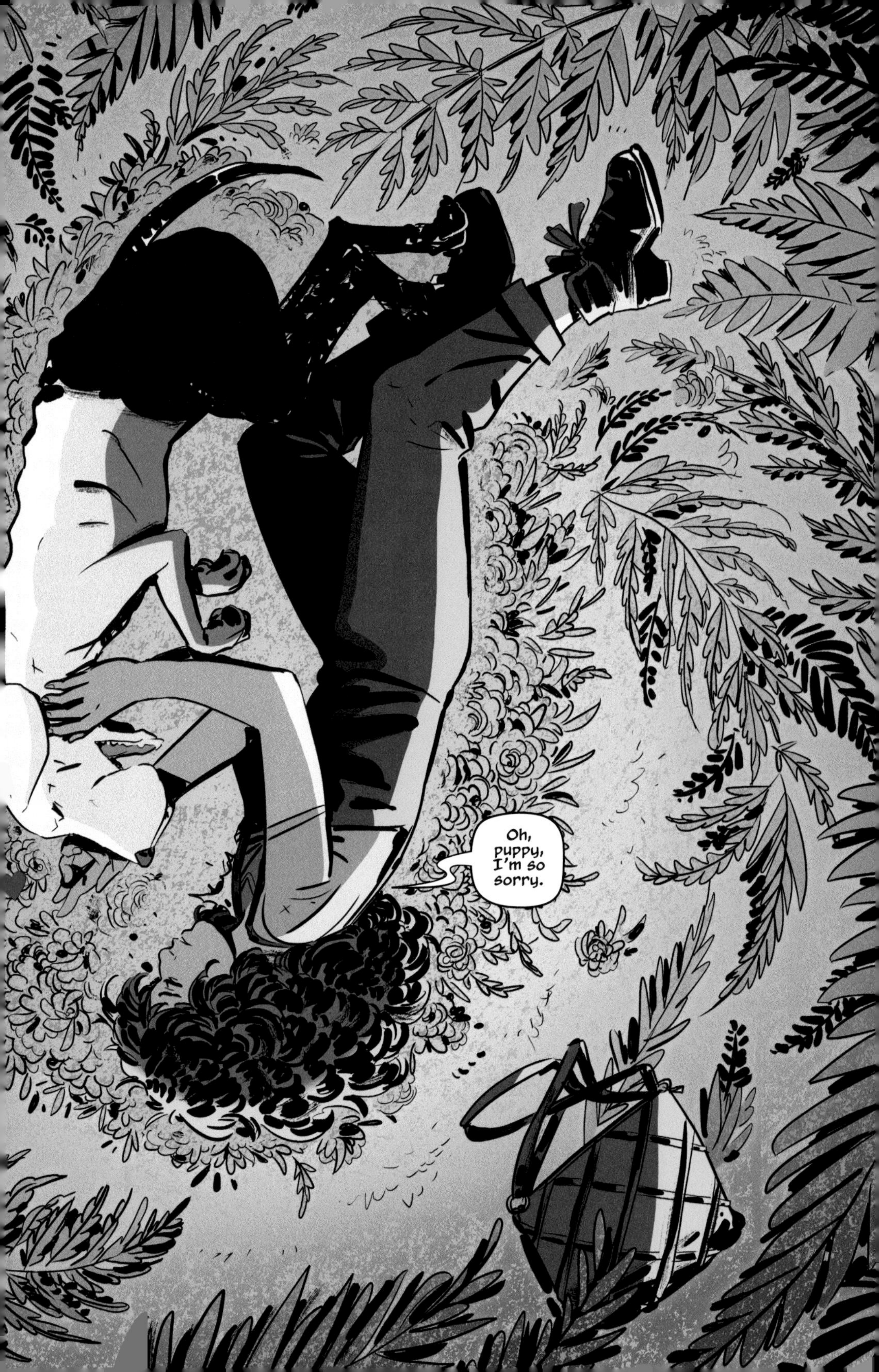
Oh, puppy, I'm so sorry.

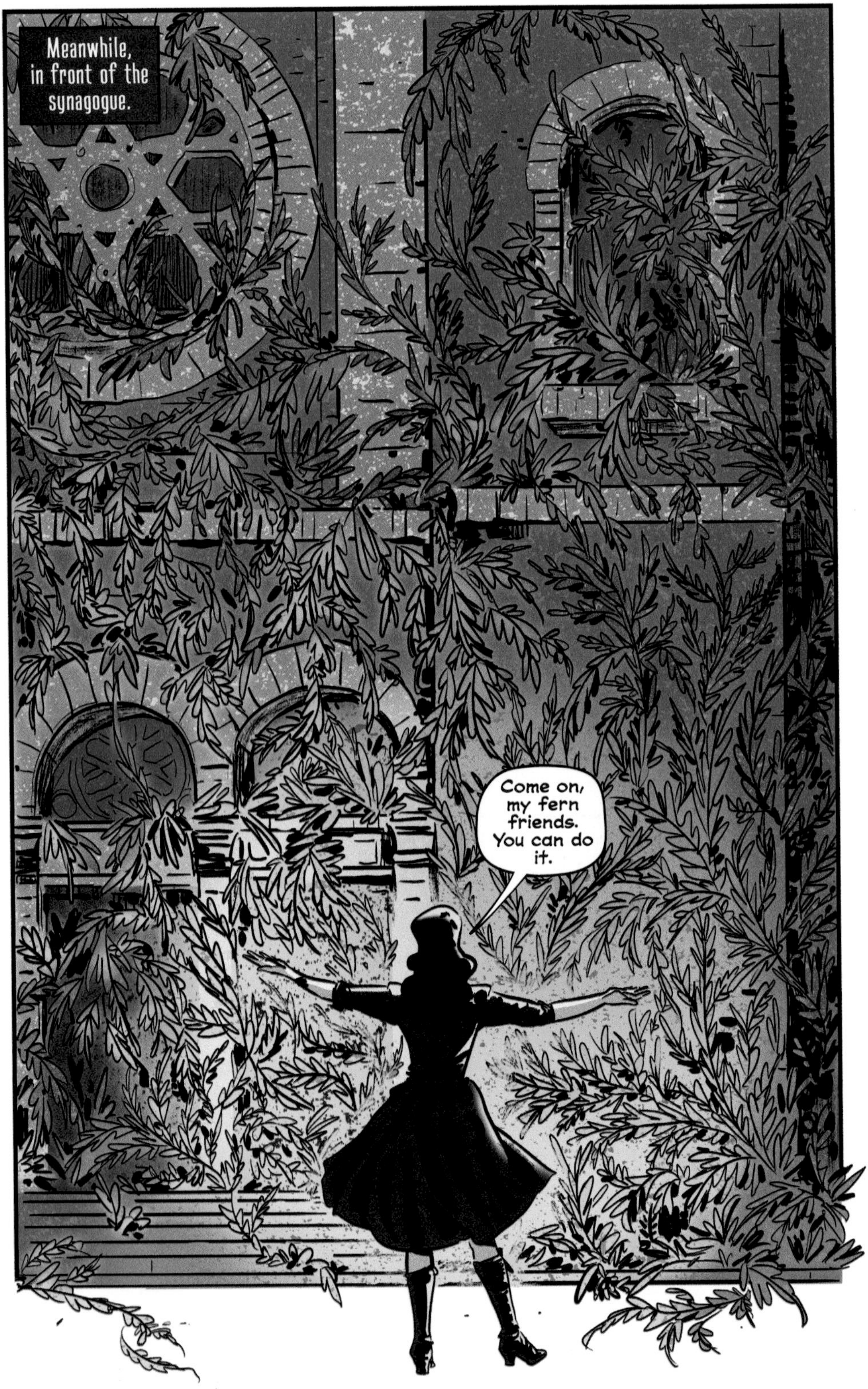
Meanwhile, in front of the synagogue.
Come on, my fern friends. You can do it.

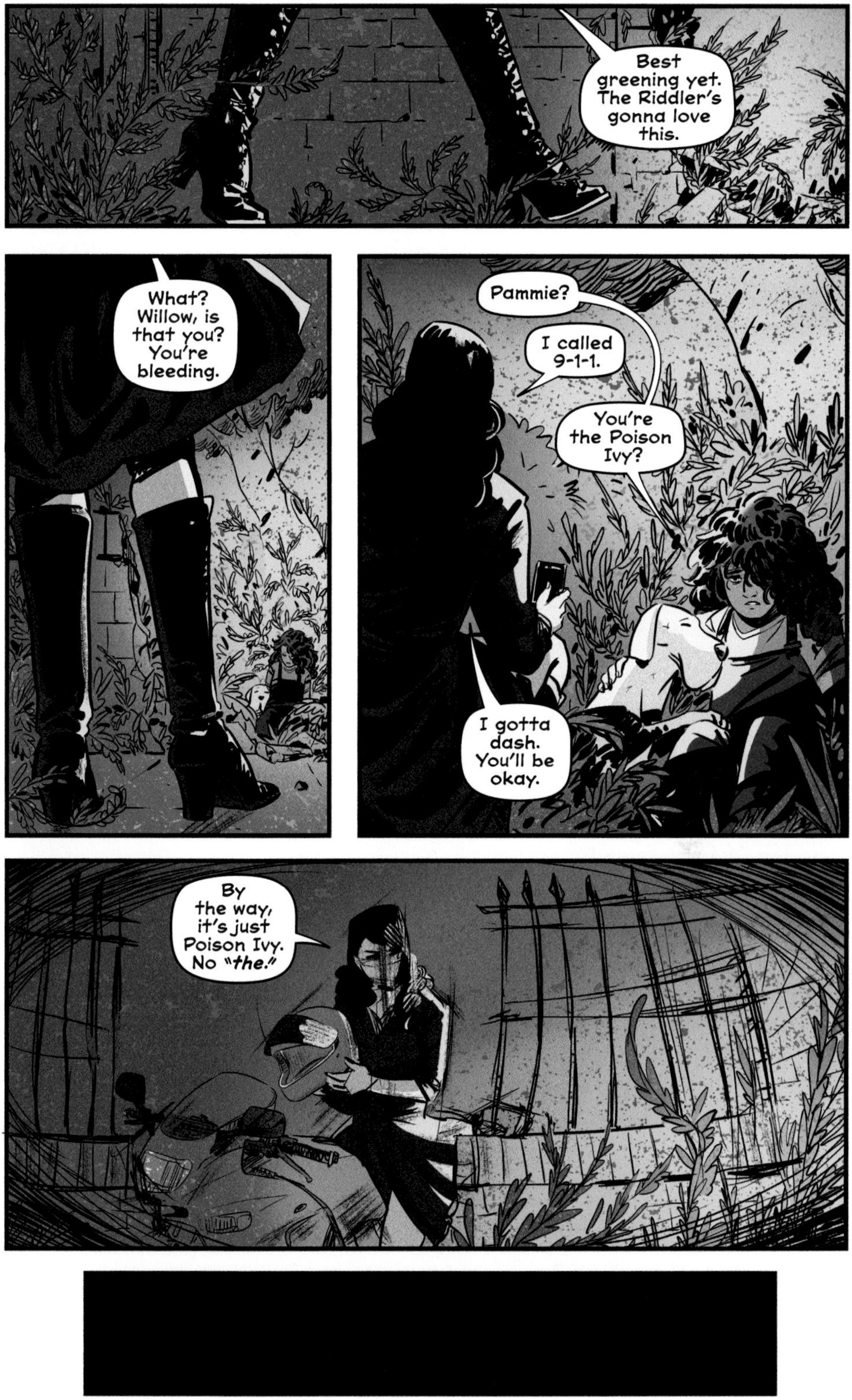
Best greening yet. The Riddler's gonna love this.
What? Willow, is that you? You're bleeding.
Pammie?
I called 9-1-1.
You're the Poison Ivy?
I gotta dash. You'll be okay.
By the way, it's just Poison Ivy. No "the."

part four: **what doesn't kill you makes you stronger**

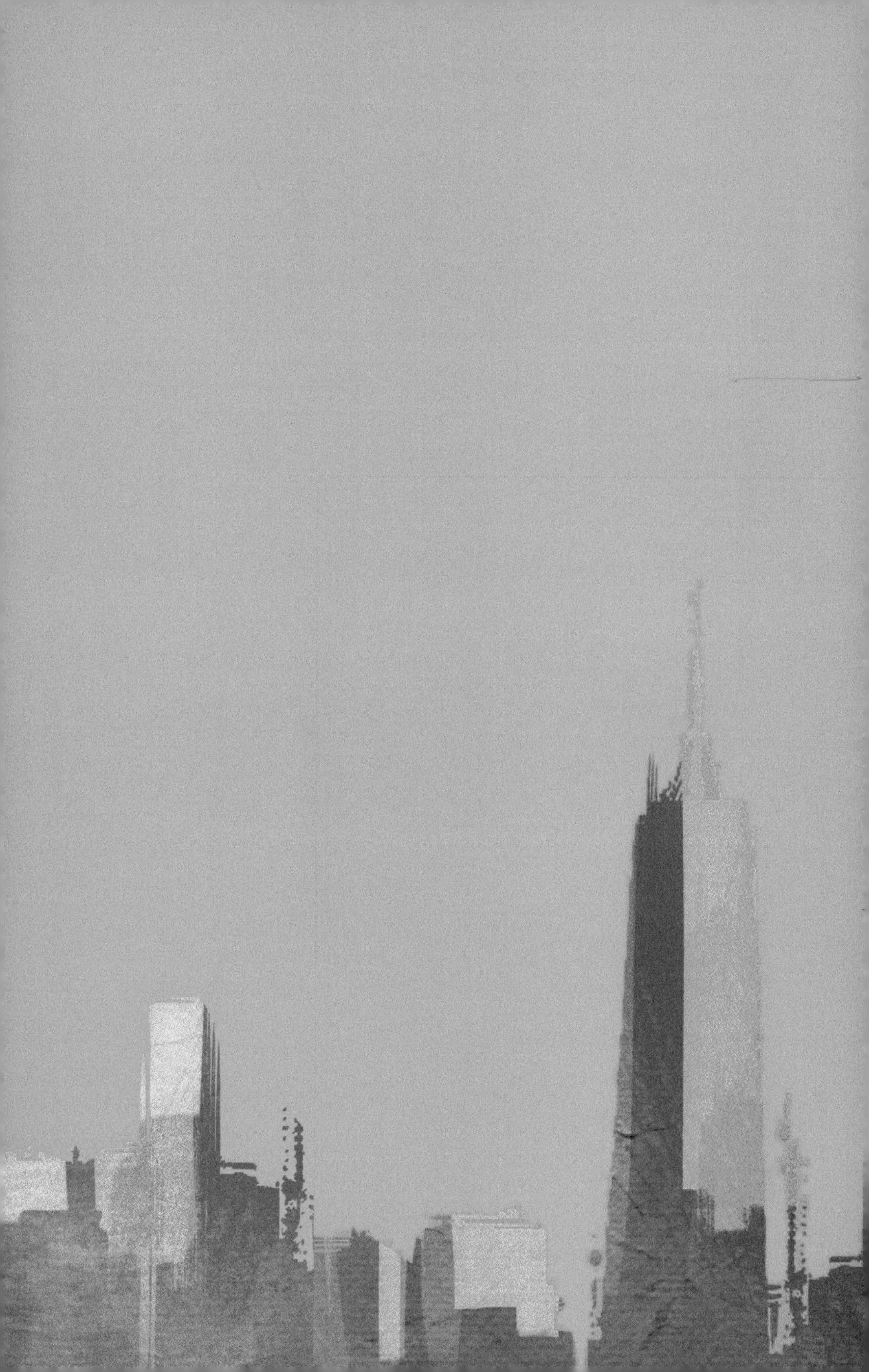

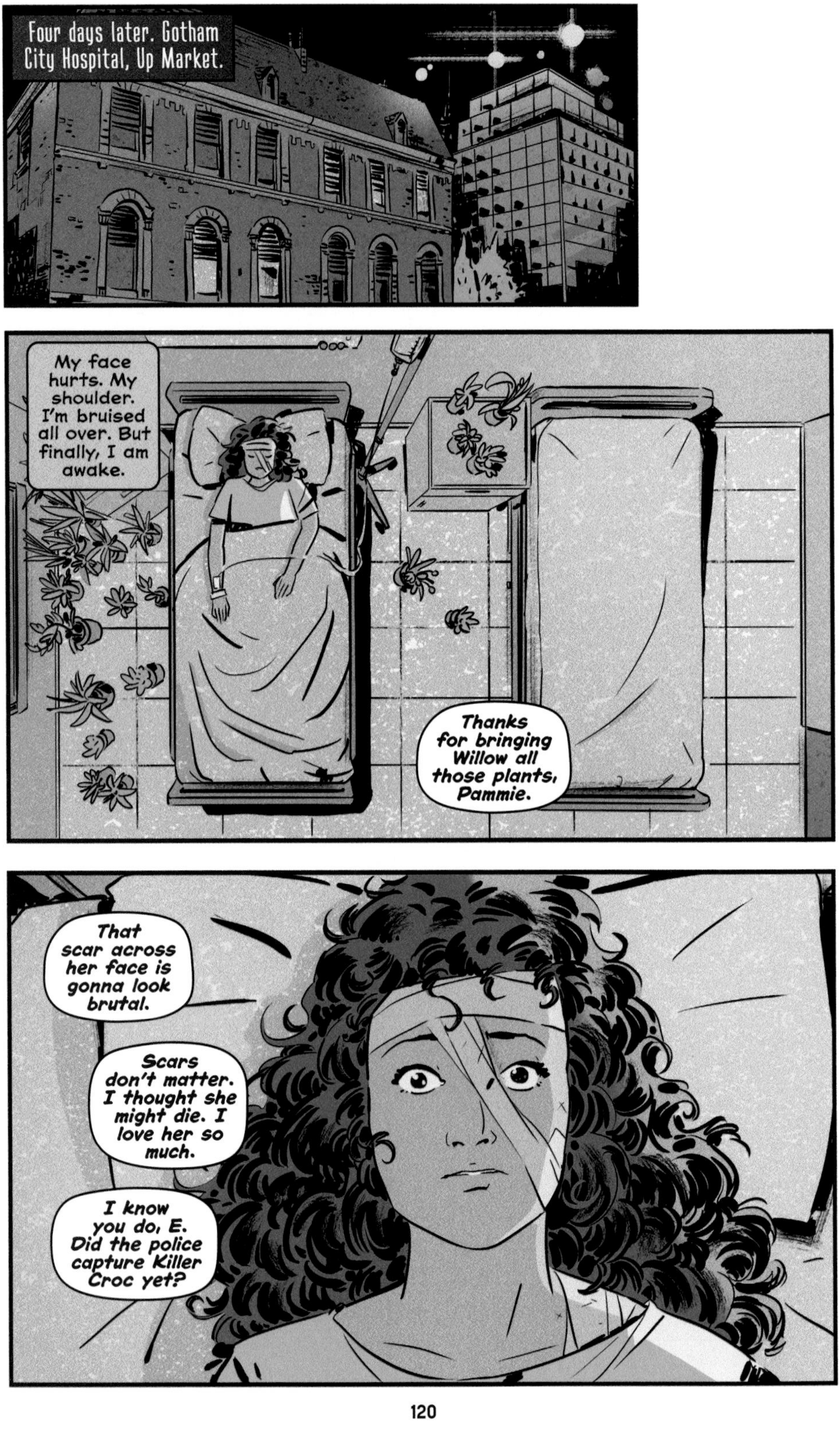
Four days later. Gotham City Hospital, Up Market.
My face hurts. My shoulder. I'm bruised all over. But finally, I am awake.
Thanks for bringing Willow all those plants, Pammie.
That scar across her face is gonna look brutal.
Scars don't matter. I thought she might die. I love her so much.
I know you do, E. Did the police capture Killer Croc yet?

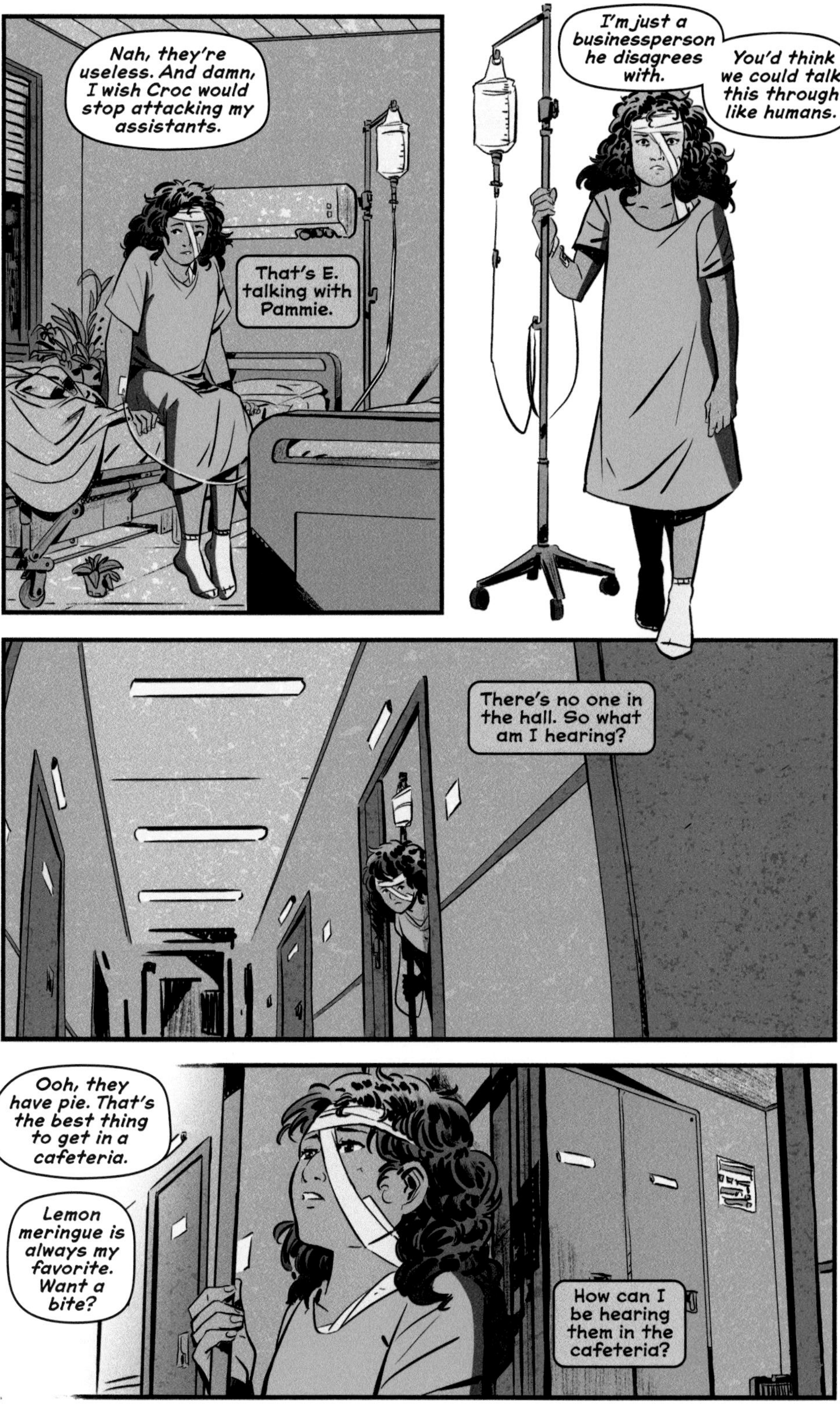
Nah, they're useless. And damn, I wish Croc would stop attacking my assistants.
That's E. talking with Pammie.
I'm just a businessperson he disagrees with.
You'd think we could talk this through like humans.
There's no one in the hall. So what am I hearing?
Ooh, they have pie. That's the best thing to get in a cafeteria.
Lemon meringue is always my favorite. Want a bite?
How can I be hearing them in the cafeteria?

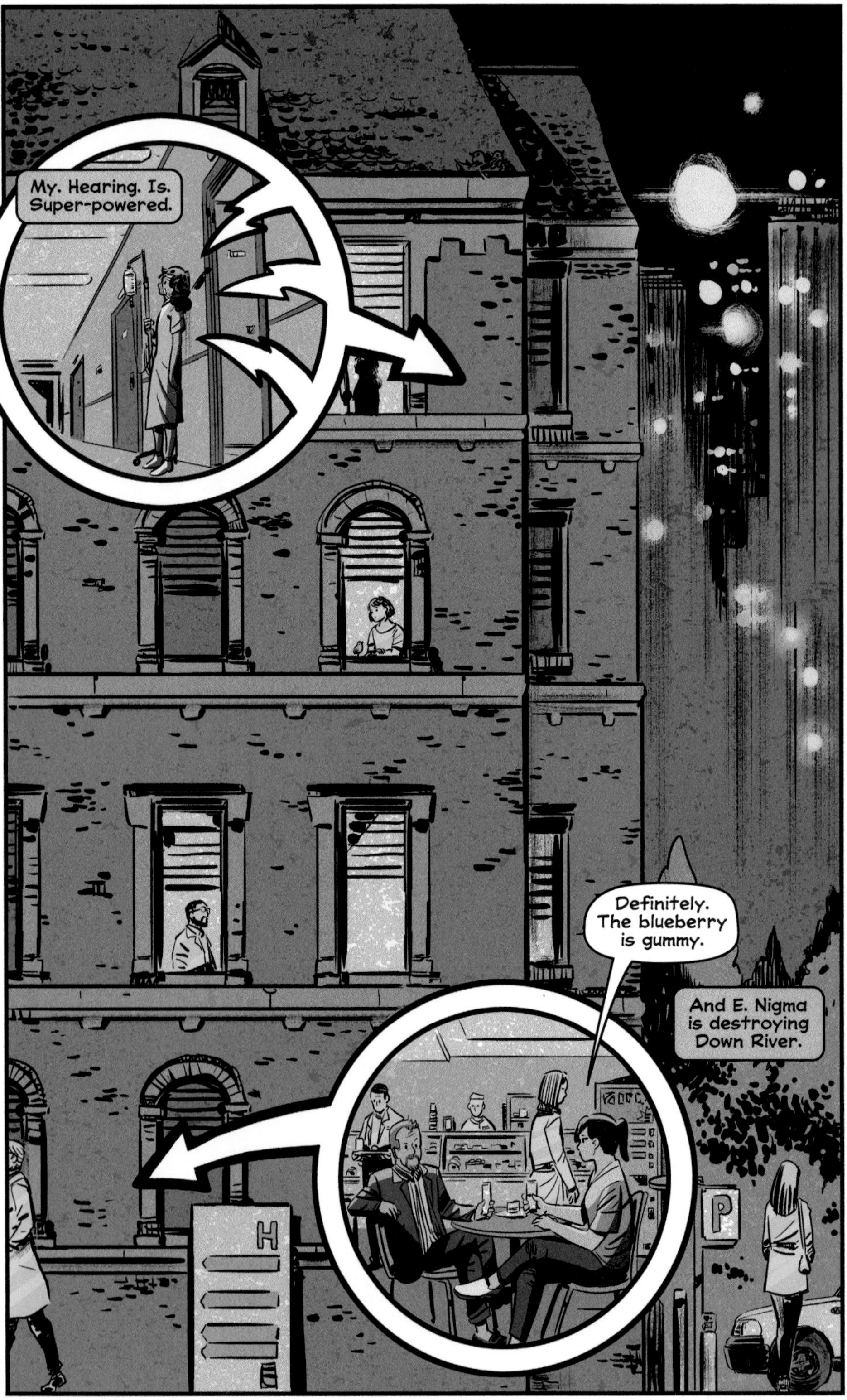
My. Hearing. Is. Super-powered.
Definitely. The blueberry is gummy.
And E. Nigma is destroying Down River.
H
P

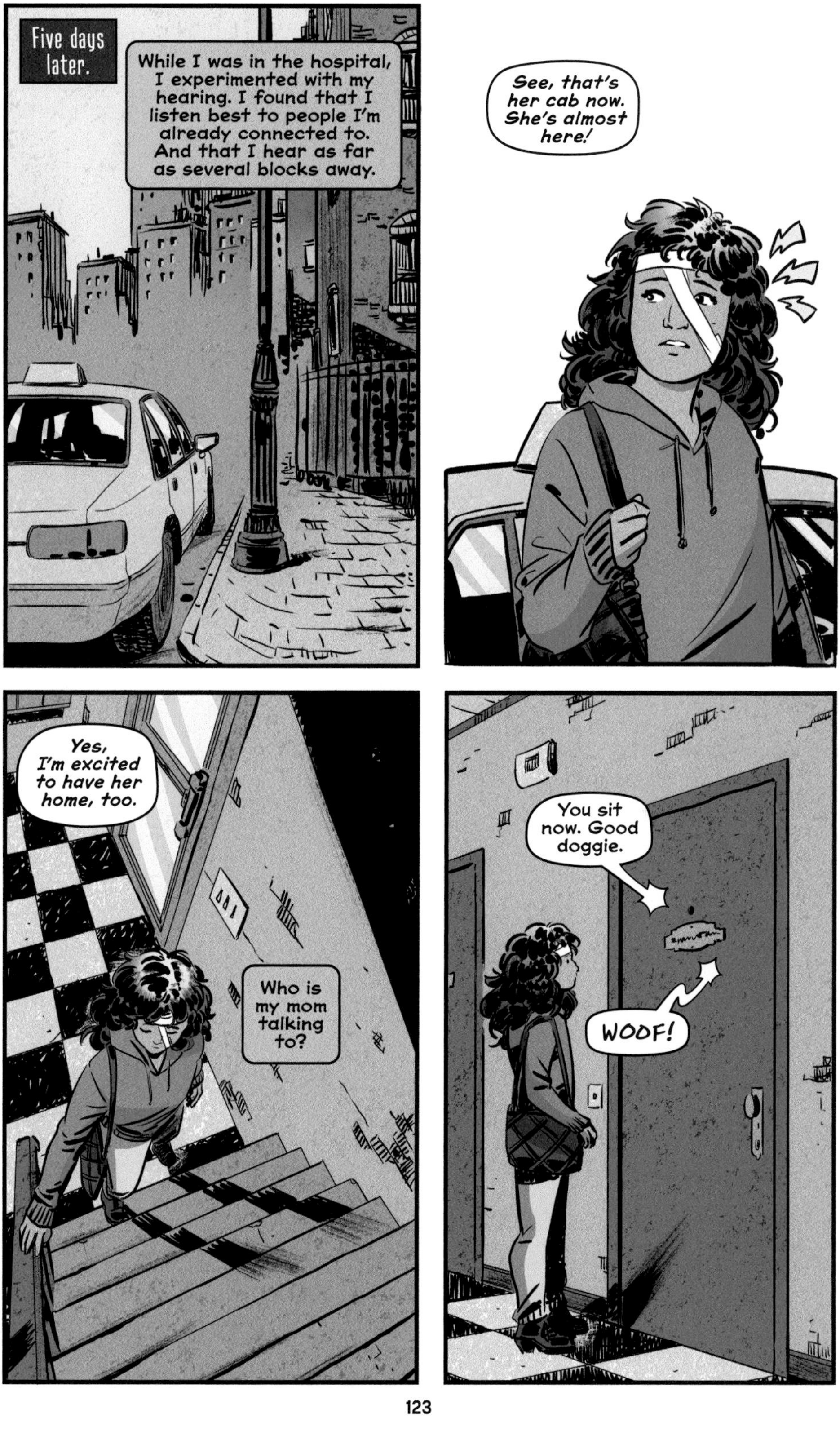
Five days later.
While I was in the hospital, I experimented with my hearing. I found that I listen best to people I'm already connected to. And that I hear as far as several blocks away.
See, that's her cab now. She's almost here!
Yes, I'm excited to have her home, too.
Who is my mom talking to?
You sit now. Good doggie.
WOOF!

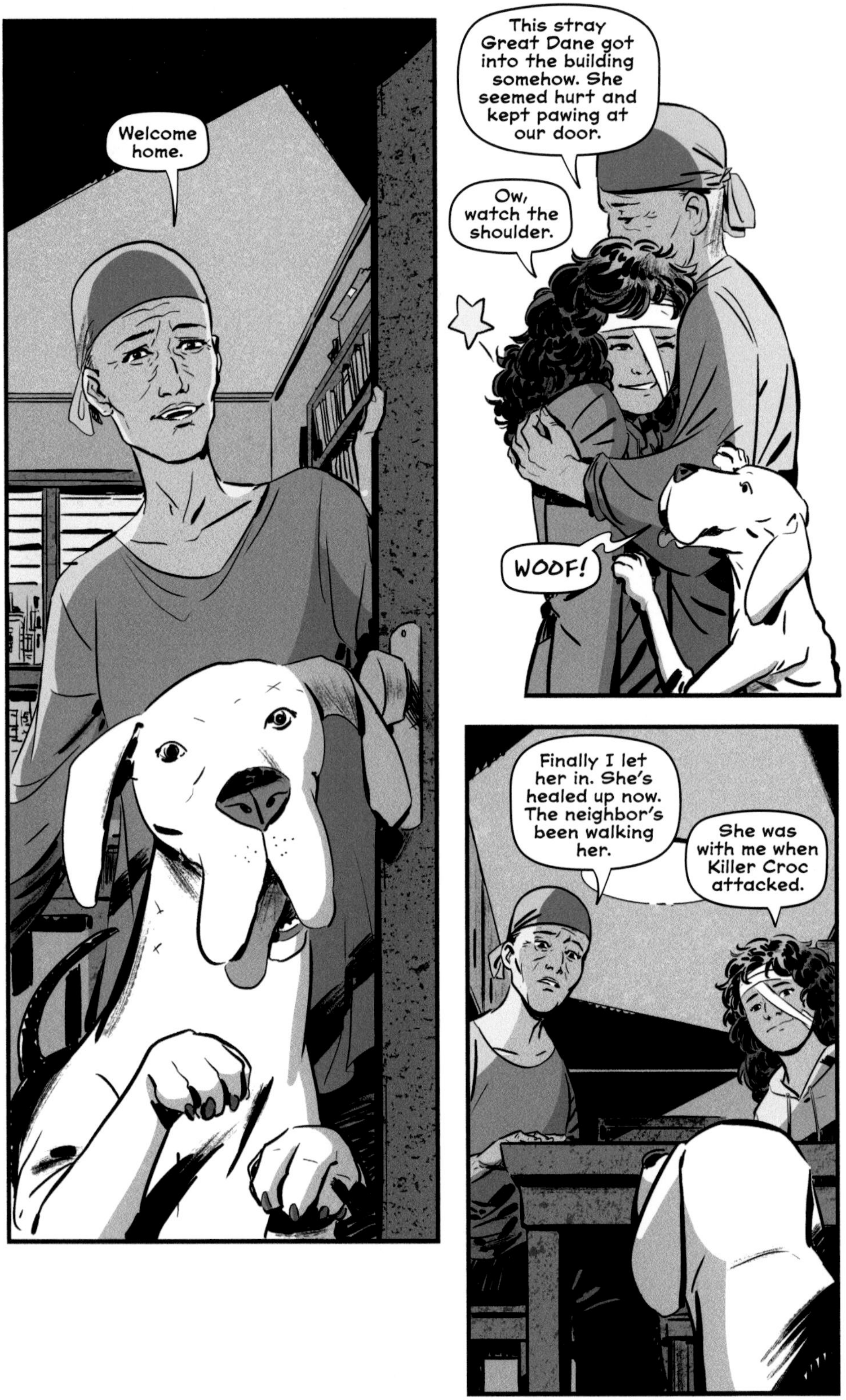
Welcome home.
This stray Great Dane got into the building somehow. She seemed hurt and kept pawing at our door.
Ow, watch the shoulder.
WOOF!
Finally I let her in. She's healed up now. The neighbor's been walking her.
She was with me when Killer Croc attacked.

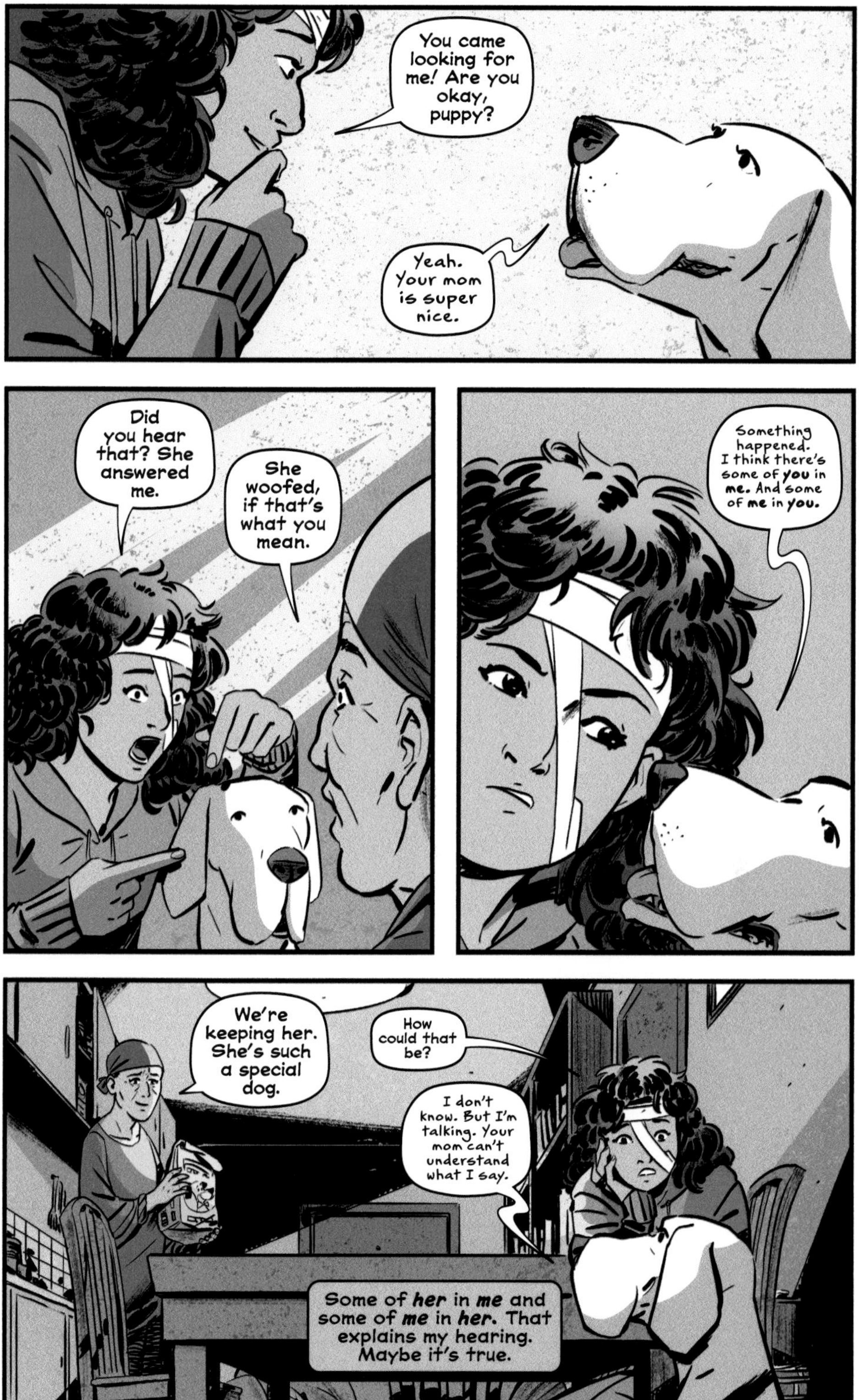
You came looking for me! Are you okay, puppy?
Yeah. Your mom is super nice.
Did you hear that? She answered me.
She woofed, if that's what you mean.
Something happened. I think there's some of **you** in **me**. And some of **me** in **you**.
We're keeping her. She's such a special dog.
How could that be?
I don't know. But I'm talking. Your mom can't understand what I say.
Some of *her* in *me* and some of *me* in *her*. That explains my hearing. Maybe it's true.

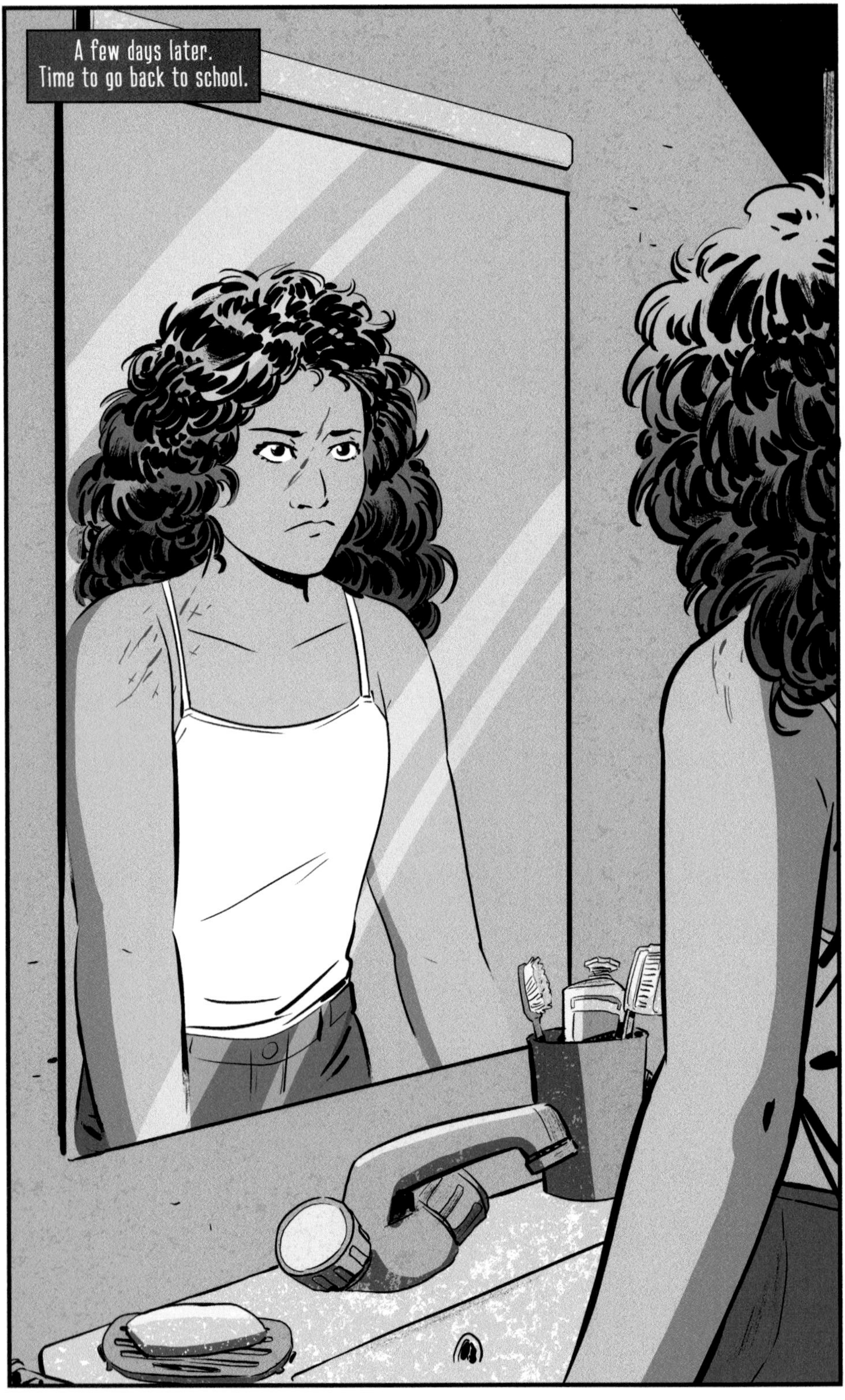
A few days later.
Time to go back to school.

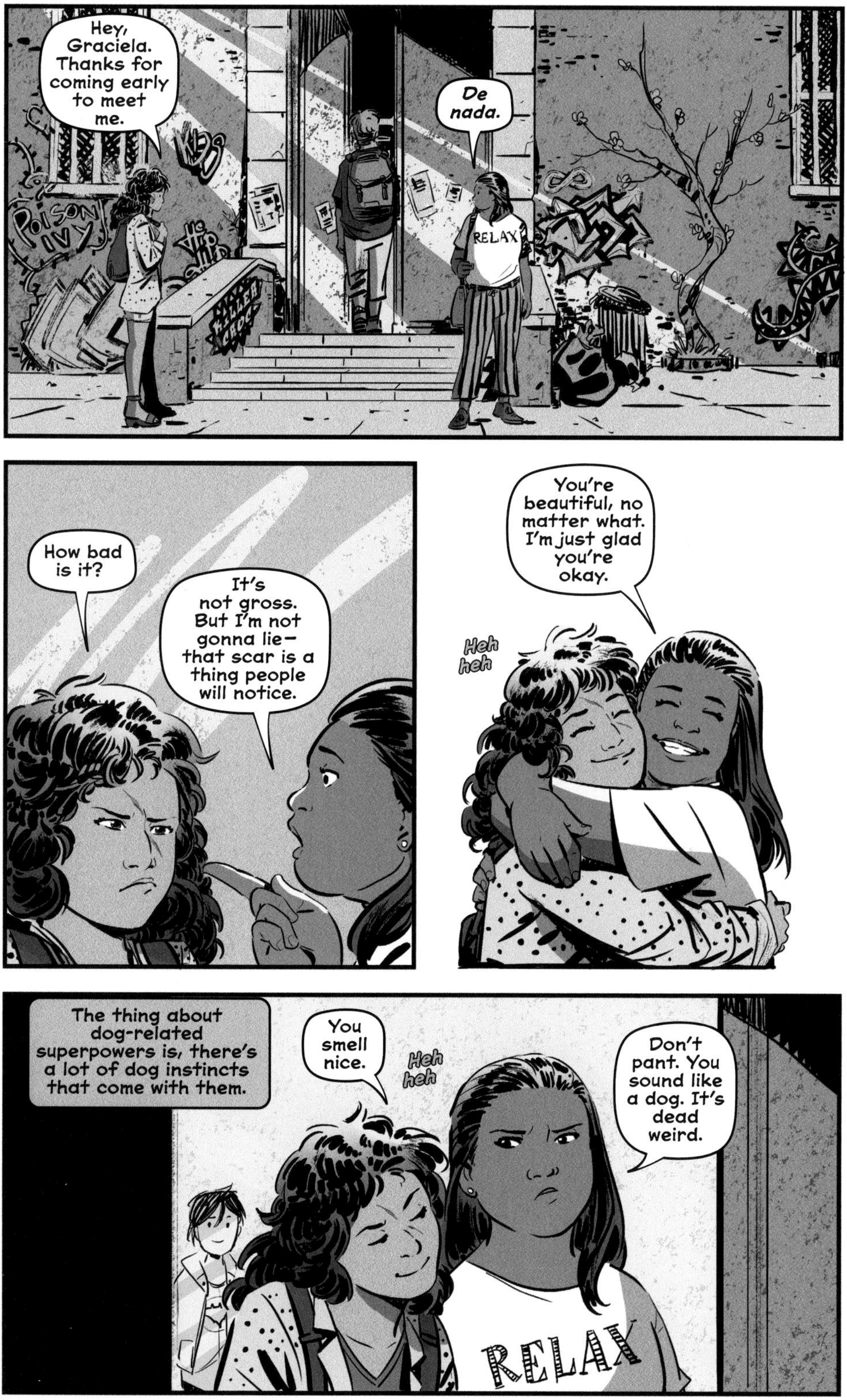
Hey, Graciela. Thanks for coming early to meet me.
De nada.
RELAX
How bad is it?
It's not gross. But I'm not gonna lie— that scar is a thing people will notice.
You're beautiful, no matter what. I'm just glad you're okay.
Heh heh
The thing about dog-related superpowers is, there's a lot of dog instincts that come with them.
You smell nice.
Heh heh
Don't pant. You sound like a dog. It's dead weird.
RELAX

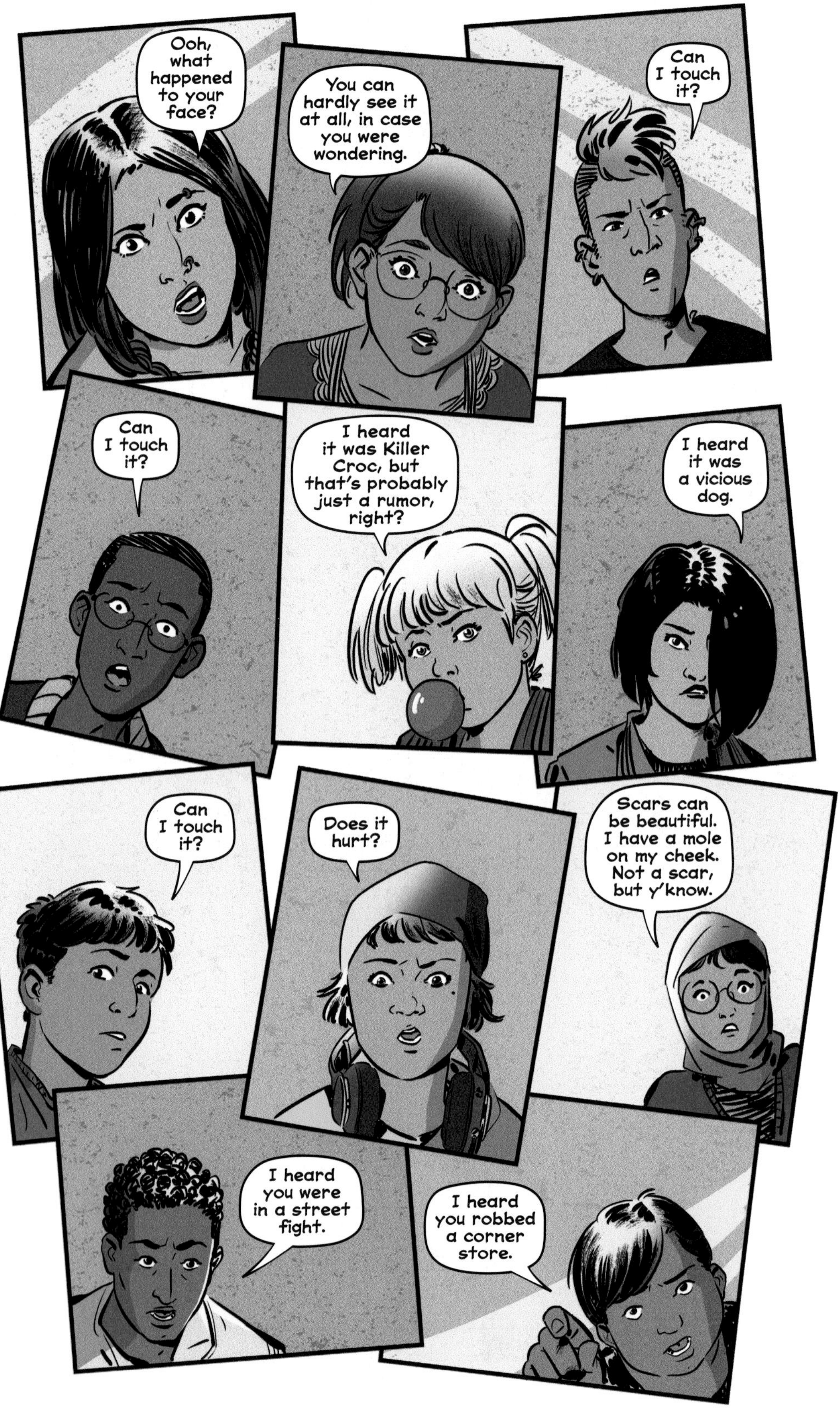
Ooh, what happened to your face?
You can hardly see it at all, in case you were wondering.
Can I touch it?
Can I touch it?
I heard it was Killer Croc, but that's probably just a rumor, right?
I heard it was a vicious dog.
Can I touch it?
Does it hurt?
Scars can be beautiful. I have a mole on my cheek. Not a scar, but y'know.
I heard you were in a street fight.
I heard you robbed a corner store.

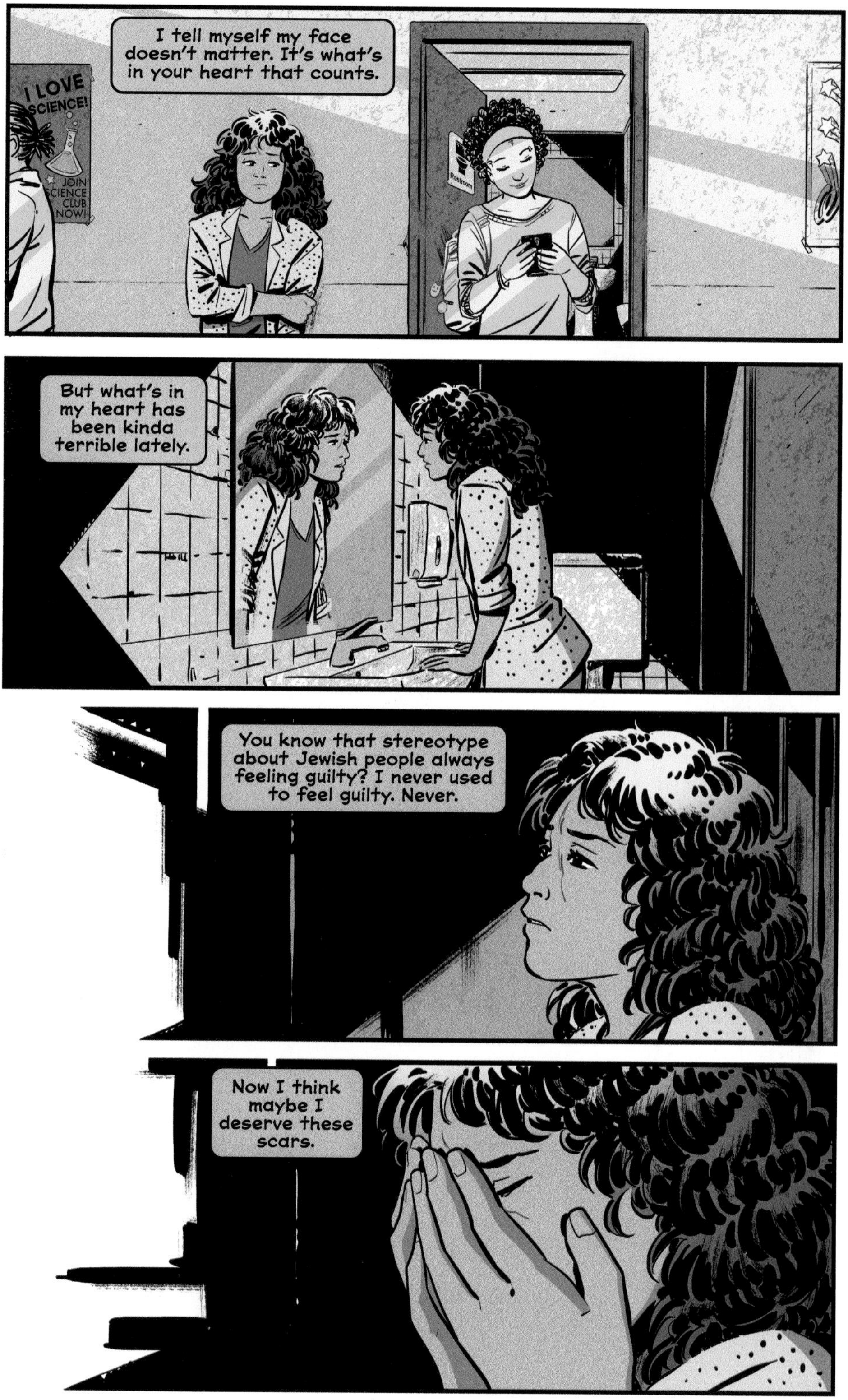
I tell myself my face doesn't matter. It's what's in your heart that counts.
I LOVE SCIENCE!
JOIN SCIENCE CLUB NOW!
Restroom
But what's in my heart has been kinda terrible lately.
You know that stereotype about Jewish people always feeling guilty? I never used to feel guilty. Never.
Now I think maybe I deserve these scars.

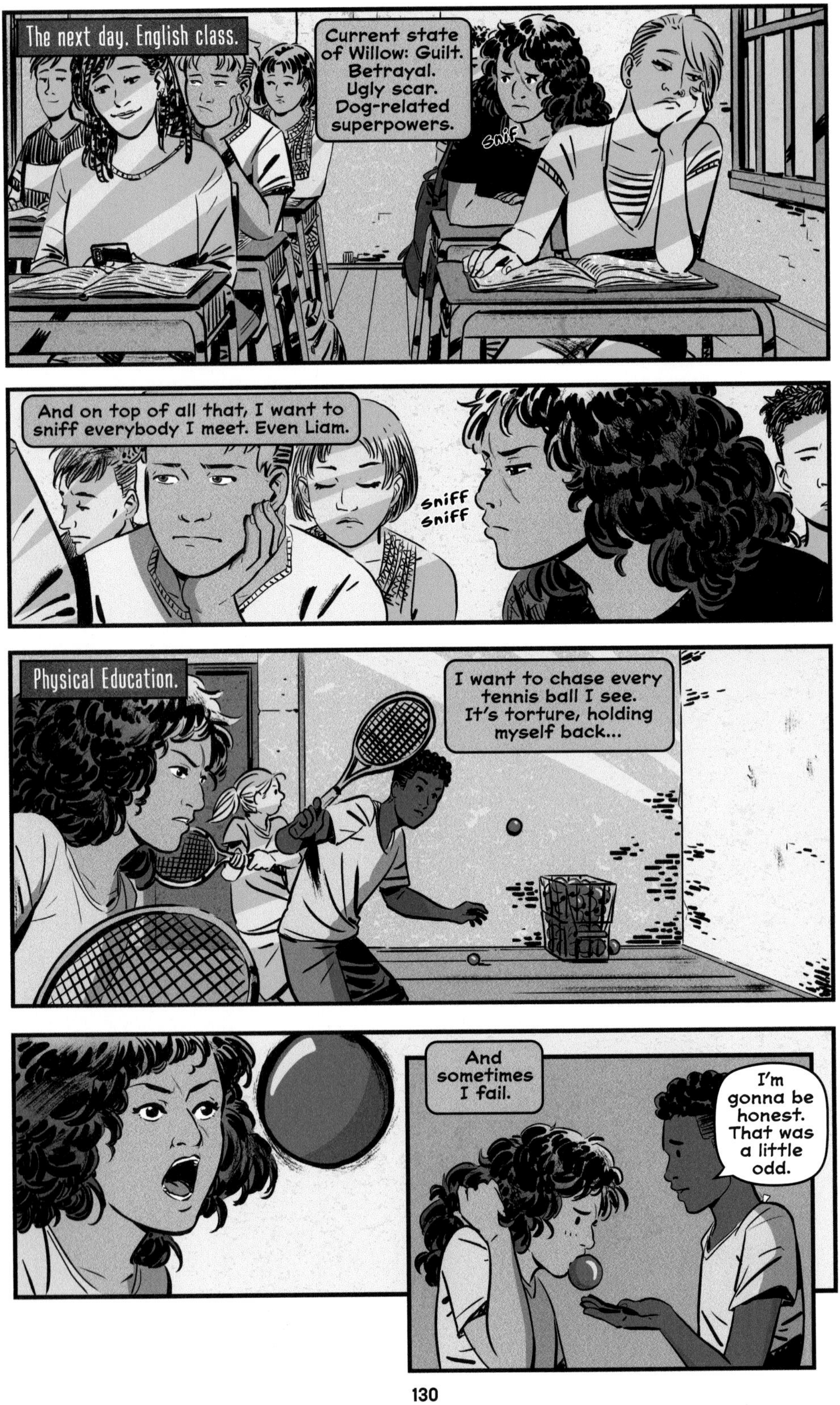
The next day. English class.
Current state of Willow: Guilt. Betrayal. Ugly scar. Dog-related superpowers.
SNIF
And on top of all that, I want to sniff everybody I meet. Even Liam.
SNIFF SNIFF
Physical Education.
I want to chase every tennis ball I see. It's torture, holding myself back...
And sometimes I fail.
I'm gonna be honest. That was a little odd.

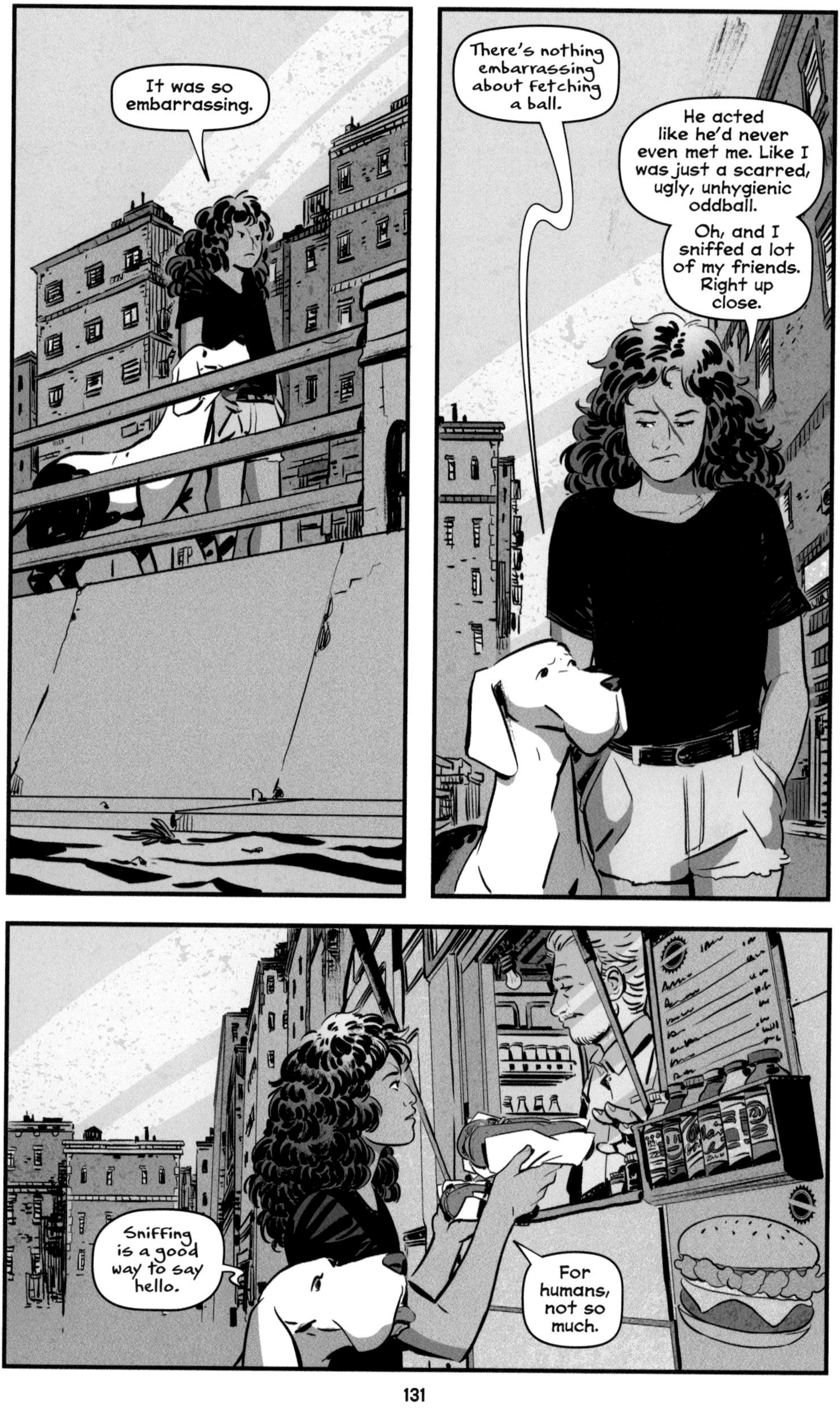
It was so embarrassing.
There's nothing embarrassing about fetching a ball.
He acted like he'd never even met me. Like I was just a scarred, ugly, unhygienic oddball.
Oh, and I sniffed a lot of my friends. Right up close.
Sniffing is a good way to say hello.
For humans, not so much.

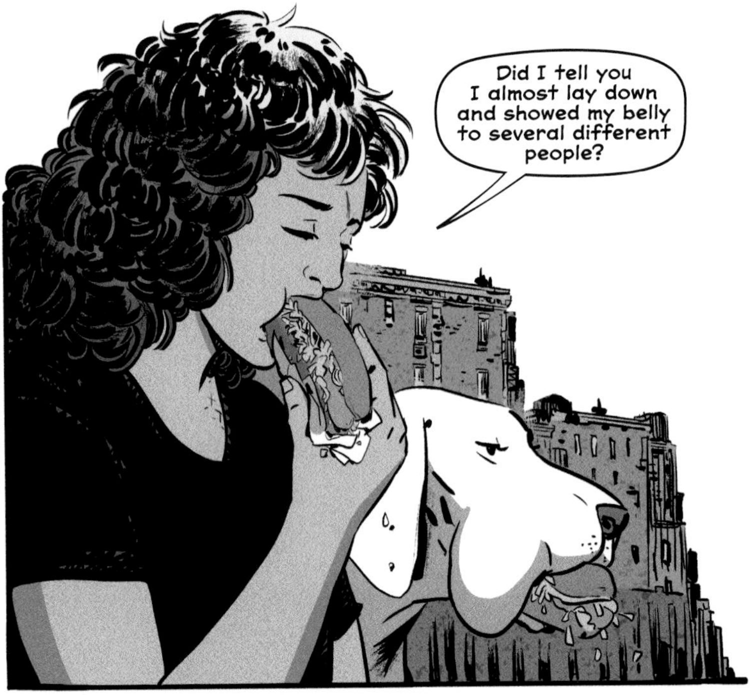
Did I tell you I almost lay down and showed my belly to several different people?

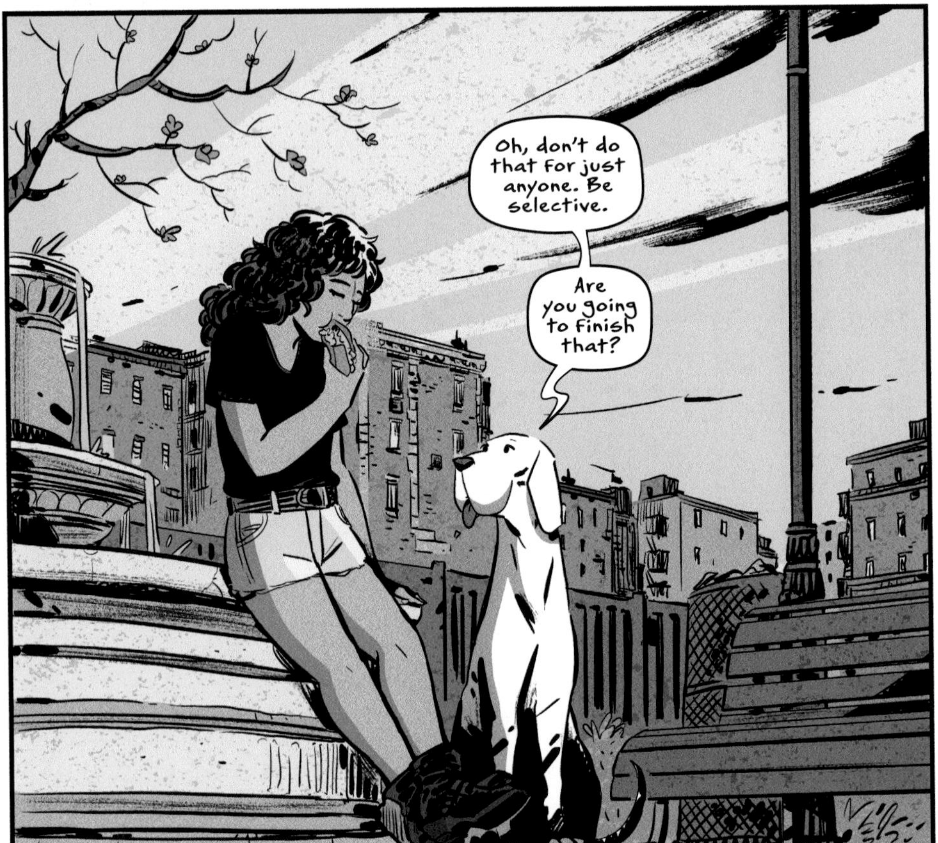
Oh, don't do that for just anyone. Be selective.
Are you going to finish that?

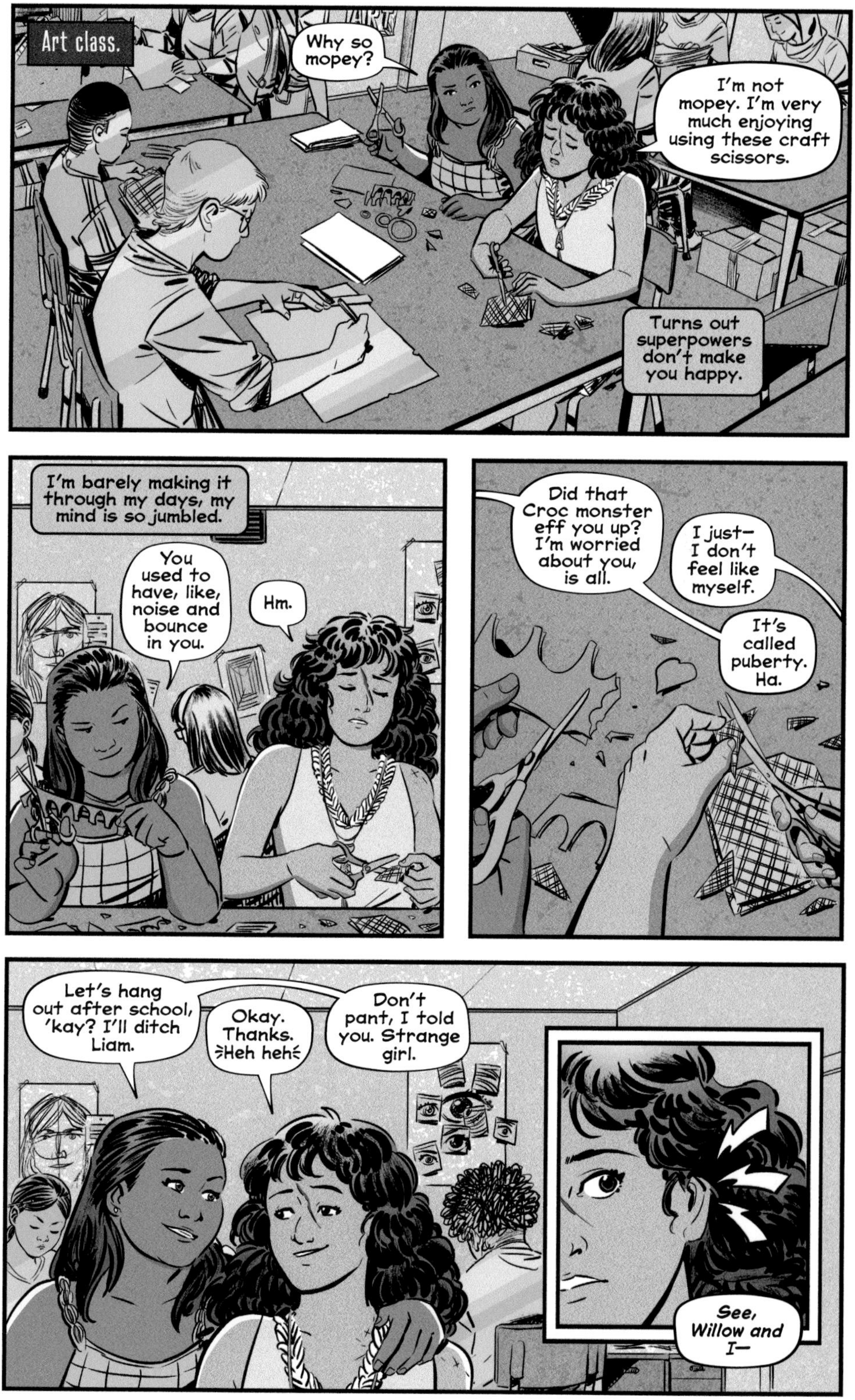

Art class.
Why so mopey?
I'm not mopey. I'm very much enjoying using these craft scissors.
Turns out superpowers don't make you happy.
I'm barely making it through my days, my mind is so jumbled.
You used to have, like, noise and bounce in you.
Hm.
Did that Croc monster eff you up? I'm worried about you, is all.
I just— I don't feel like myself.
It's called puberty. Ha.
Let's hang out after school, 'kay? I'll ditch Liam.
Okay. Thanks. Heh heh
Don't pant, I told you. Strange girl.
See, Willow and I—

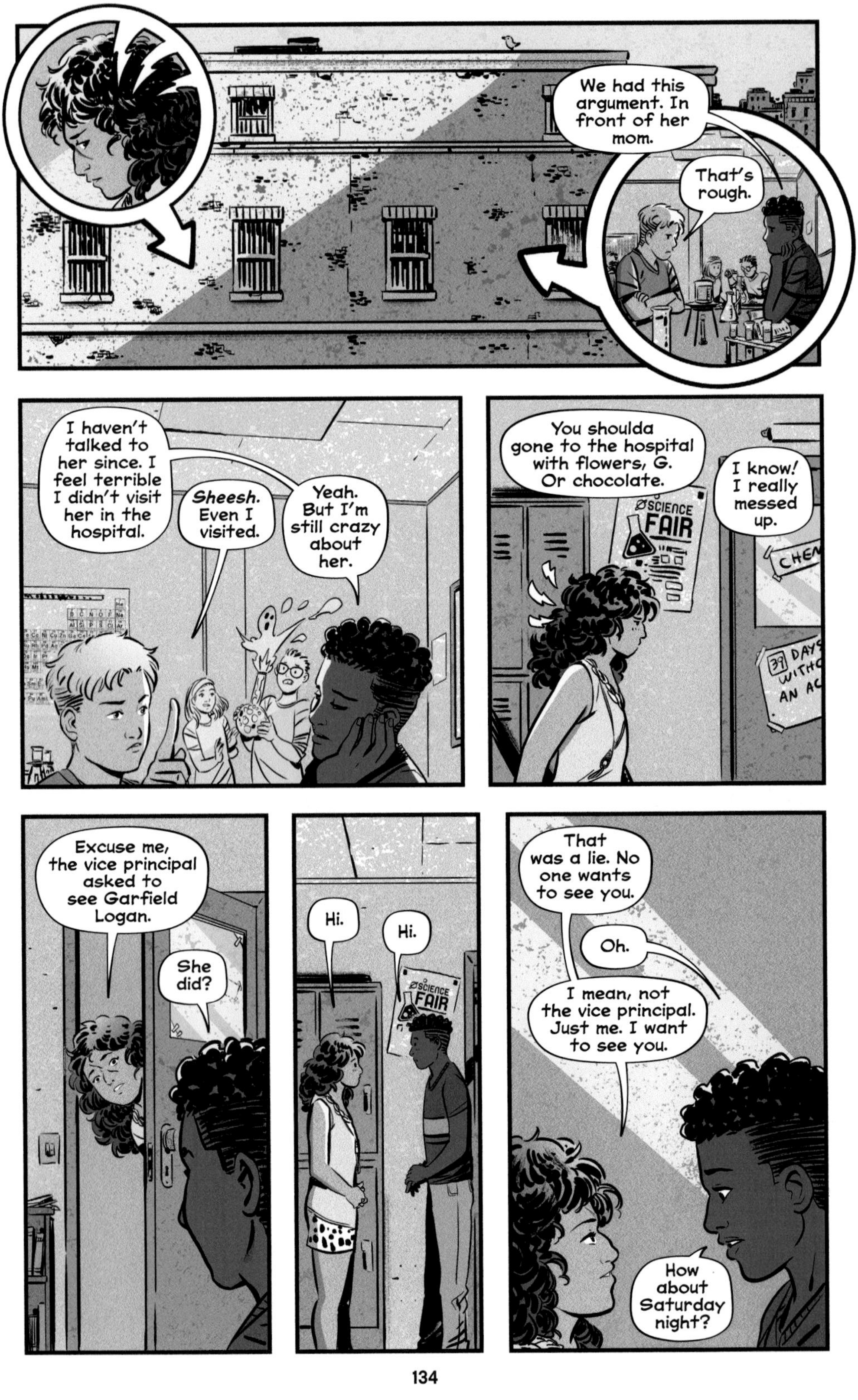
We had this argument. In front of her mom.
That's rough.
I haven't talked to her since. I feel terrible I didn't visit her in the hospital.
Sheesh. Even I visited.
Yeah. But I'm still crazy about her.
You shoulda gone to the hospital with flowers, G. Or chocolate.
SCIENCE FAIR
I know! I really messed up.
CHEM
37 DAYS WITHO AN AC
Excuse me, the vice principal asked to see Garfield Logan.
She did?
Hi.
Hi.
SCIENCE FAIR
That was a lie. No one wants to see you.
Oh.
I mean, not the vice principal. Just me. I want to see you.
How about Saturday night?

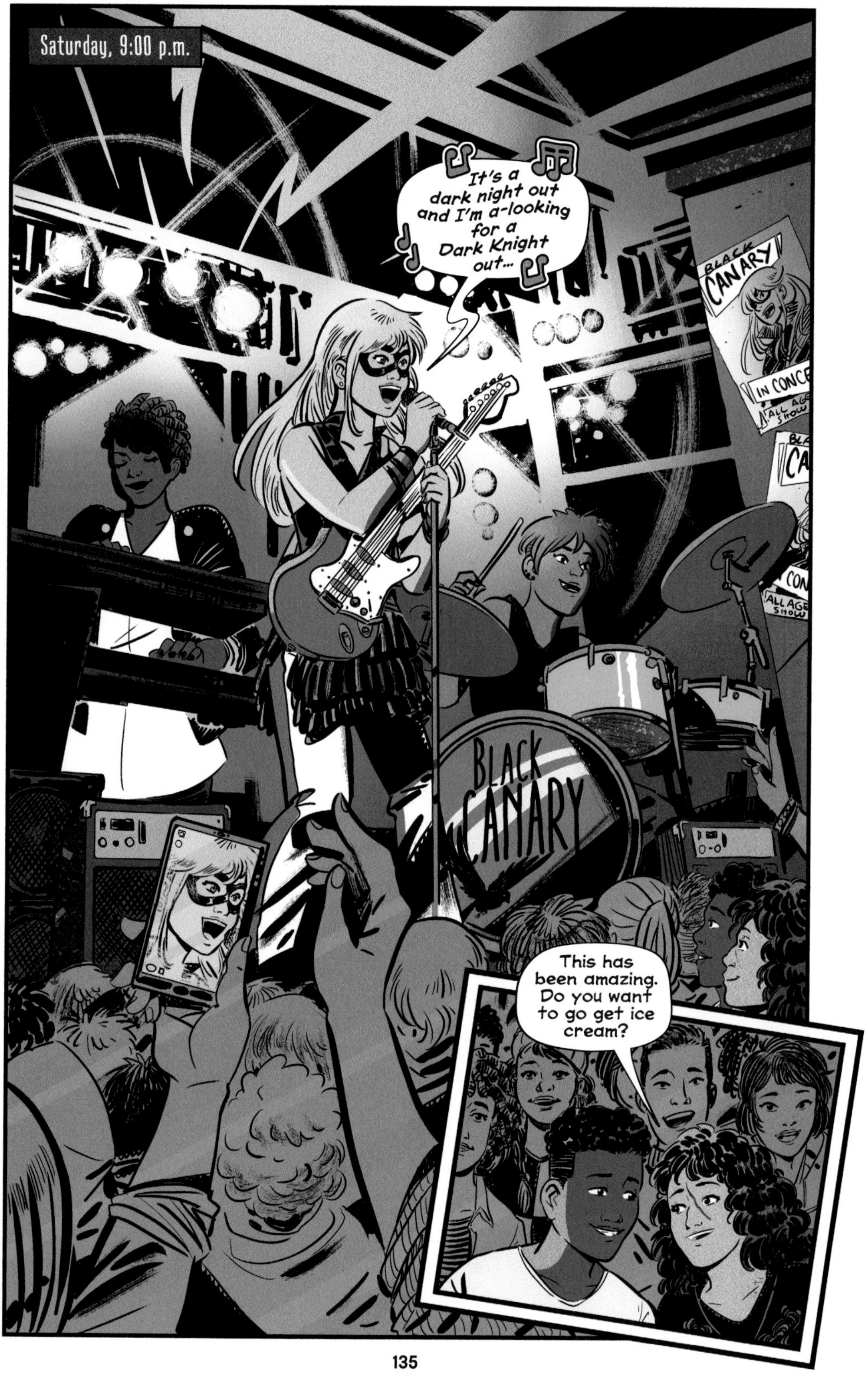

Saturday, 9:00 p.m.
It's a dark night out and I'm a-looking for a Dark Knight out...
BLACK CANARY
IN CONCERT
ALL AGES SHOW
BLACK CANARY
This has been amazing. Do you want to go get ice cream?

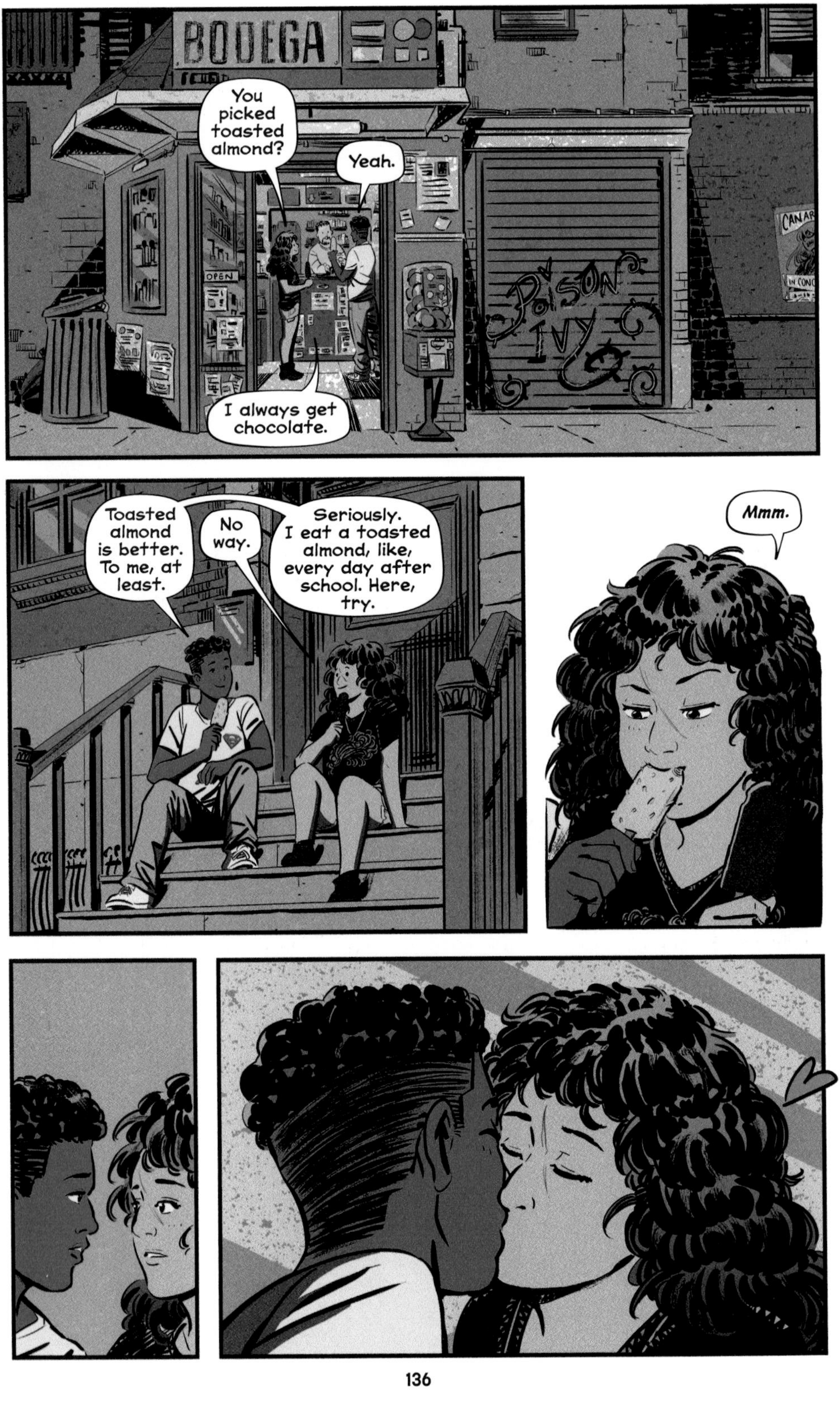
BODEGA
You picked toasted almond?
Yeah.
I always get chocolate.
OPEN
POISON IVY
Toasted almond is better. To me, at least.
No way.
Seriously. I eat a toasted almond, like, every day after school. Here, try.
Mmm.

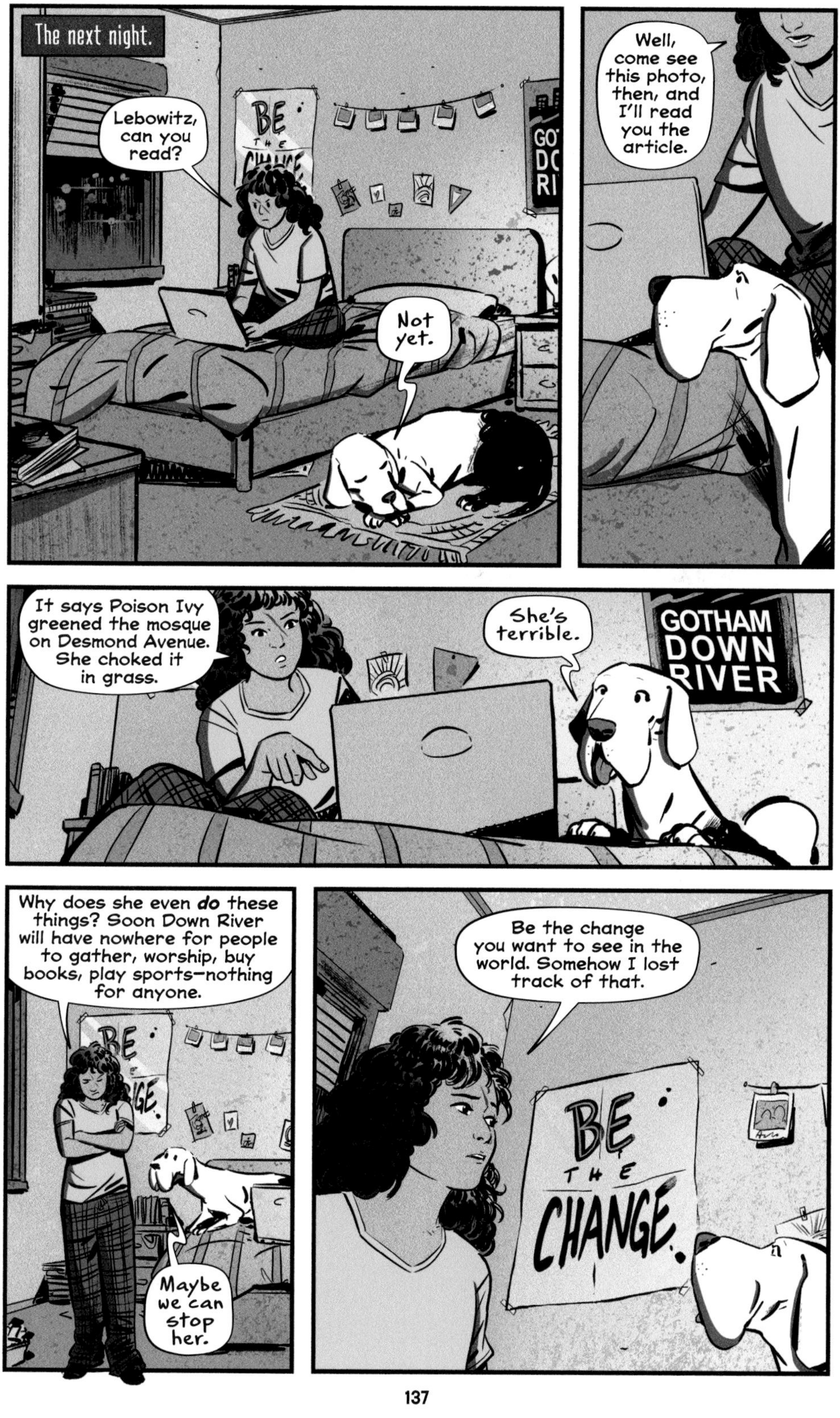
The next night.
Lebowitz, can you read?
Not yet.
BE THE CHANGE
GOTHAM DOWN RIVER
Well, come see this photo, then, and I'll read you the article.
It says Poison Ivy greened the mosque on Desmond Avenue. She choked it in grass.
She's terrible.
Why does she even **do** these things? Soon Down River will have nowhere for people to gather, worship, buy books, play sports—nothing for anyone.
Maybe we can stop her.
Be the change you want to see in the world. Somehow I lost track of that.

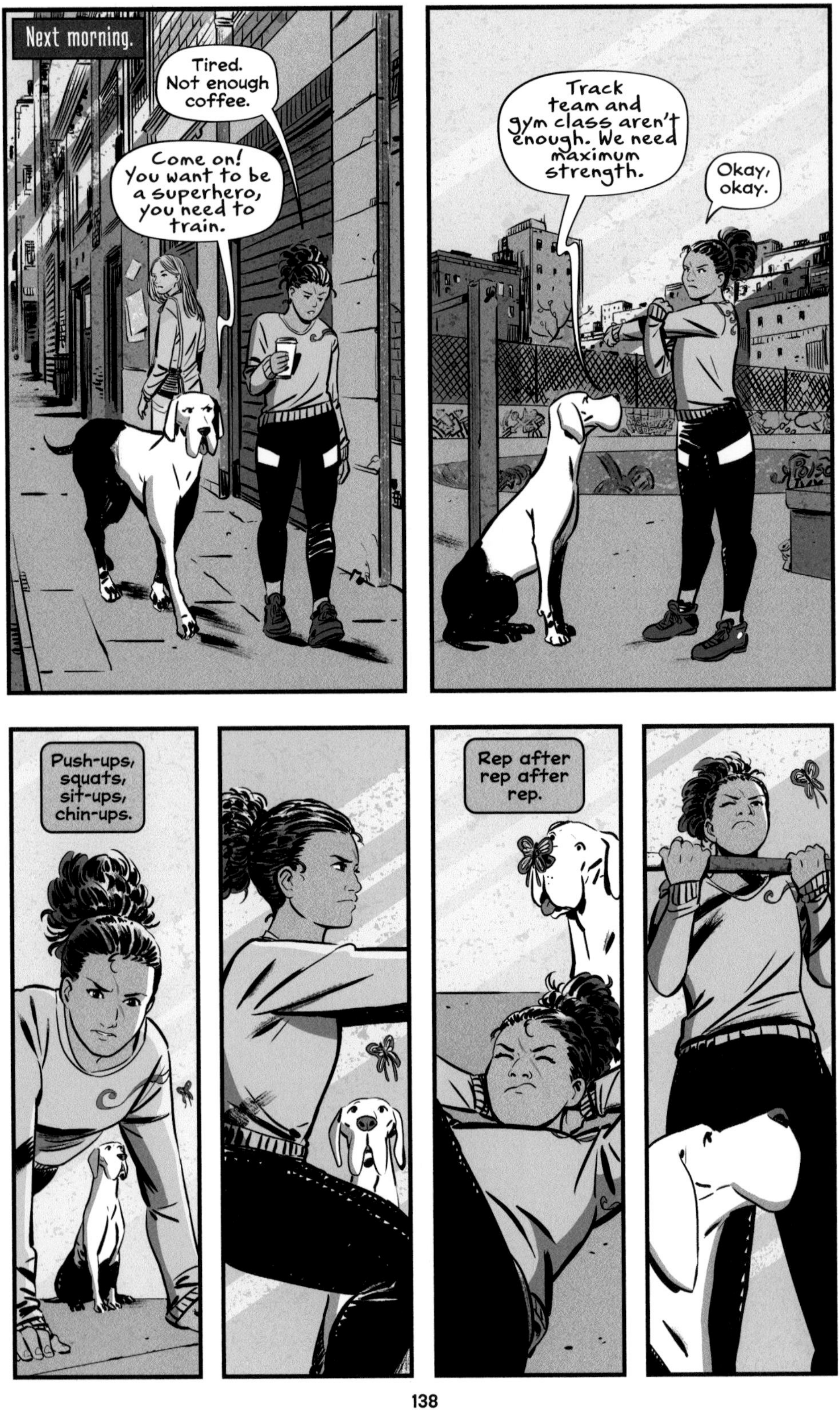
Next morning.
Tired. Not enough coffee.
Come on! You want to be a superhero, you need to train.
Track team and gym class aren't enough. We need maximum strength.
Okay, okay.
Push-ups, squats, sit-ups, chin-ups.
Rep after rep after rep.

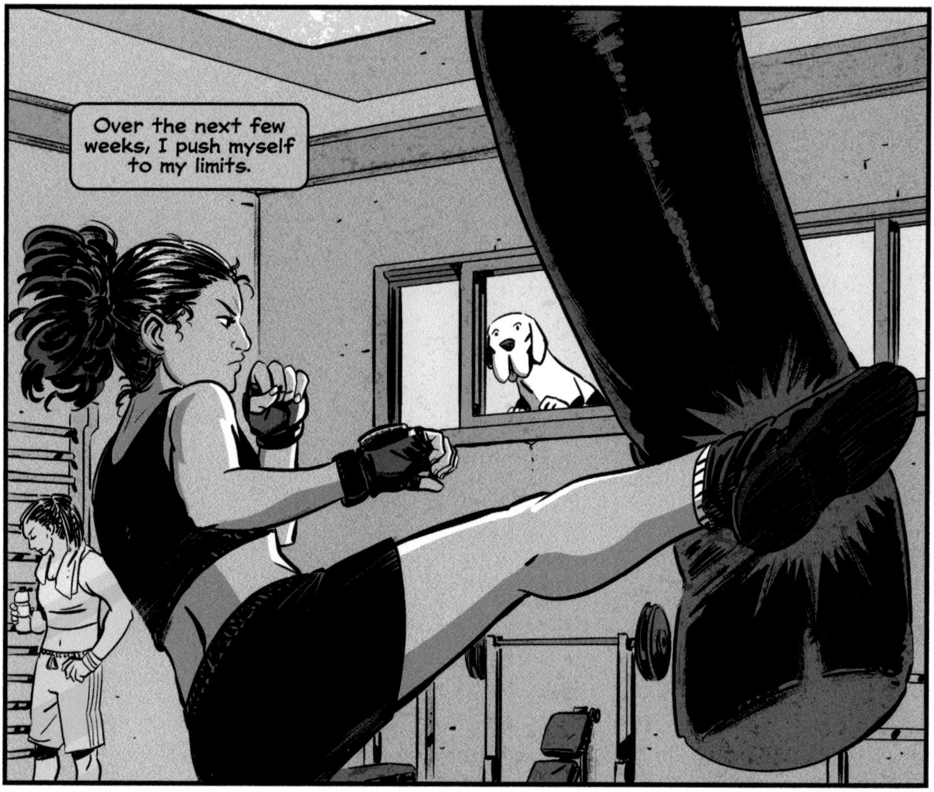
Over the next few weeks, I push myself to my limits.

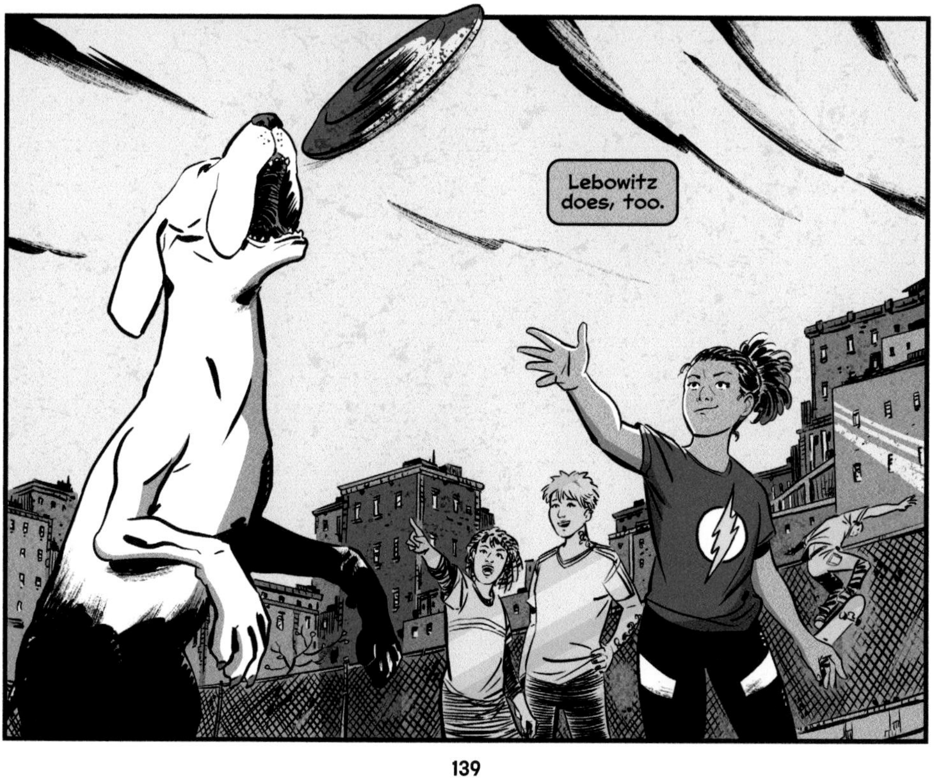
Lebowitz does, too.

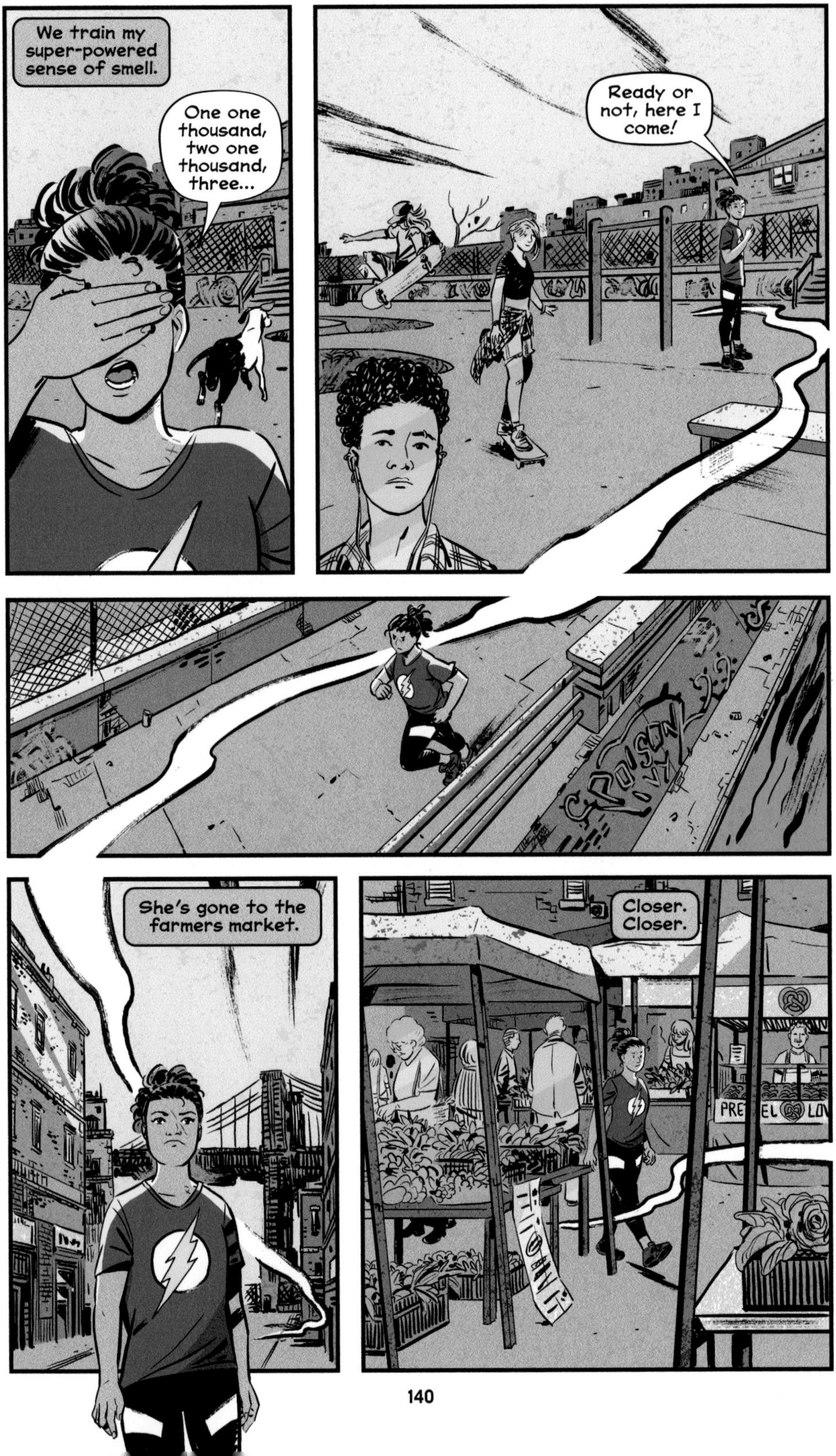
We train my super-powered sense of smell.
One one thousand, two one thousand, three...
Ready or not, here I come!
She's gone to the farmers market.
Closer. Closer.

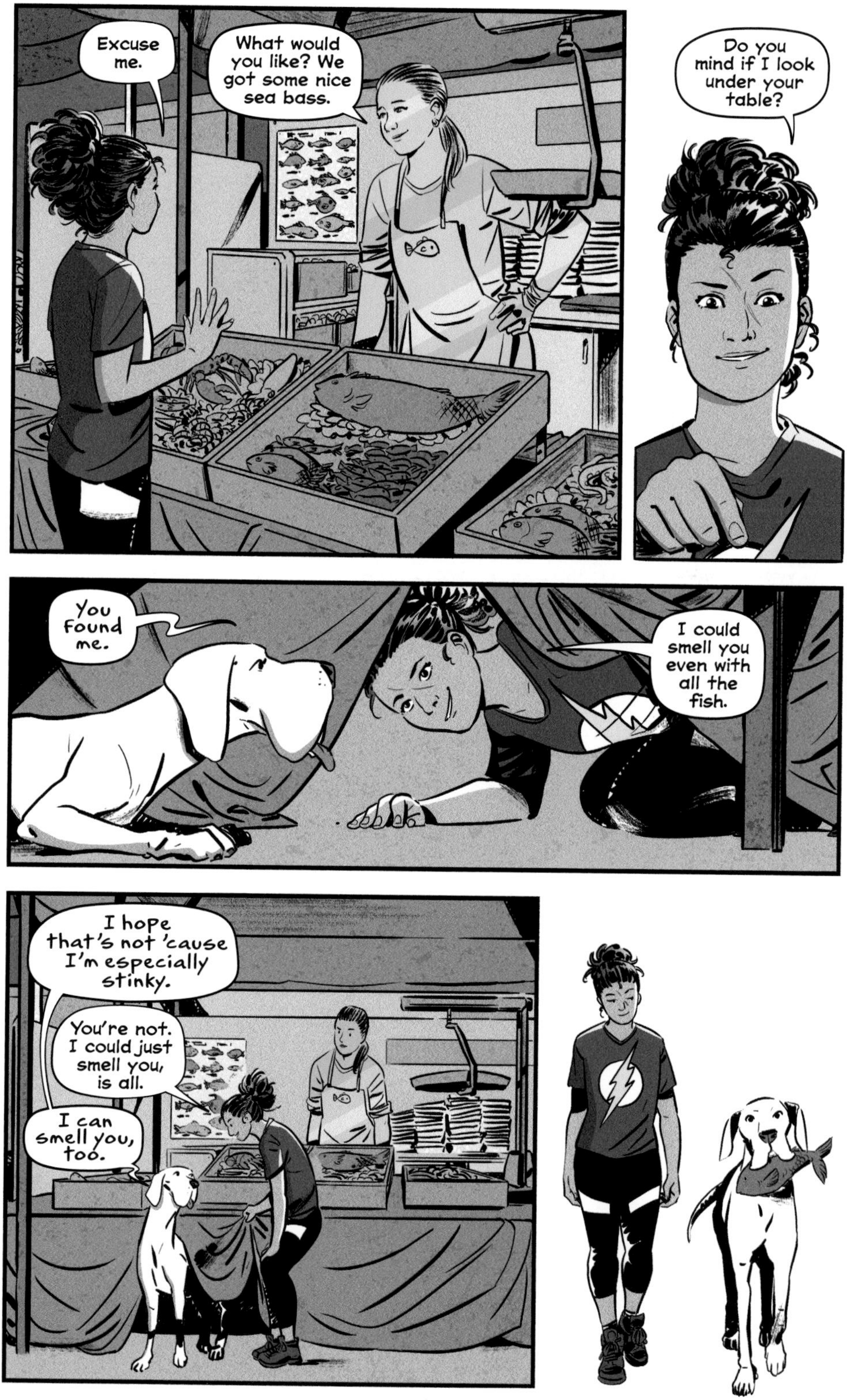
Excuse me.
What would you like? We got some nice sea bass.
Do you mind if I look under your table?
You found me.
I could smell you even with all the fish.
I hope that's not 'cause I'm especially stinky.
You're not. I could just smell you, is all.
I can smell you, too.

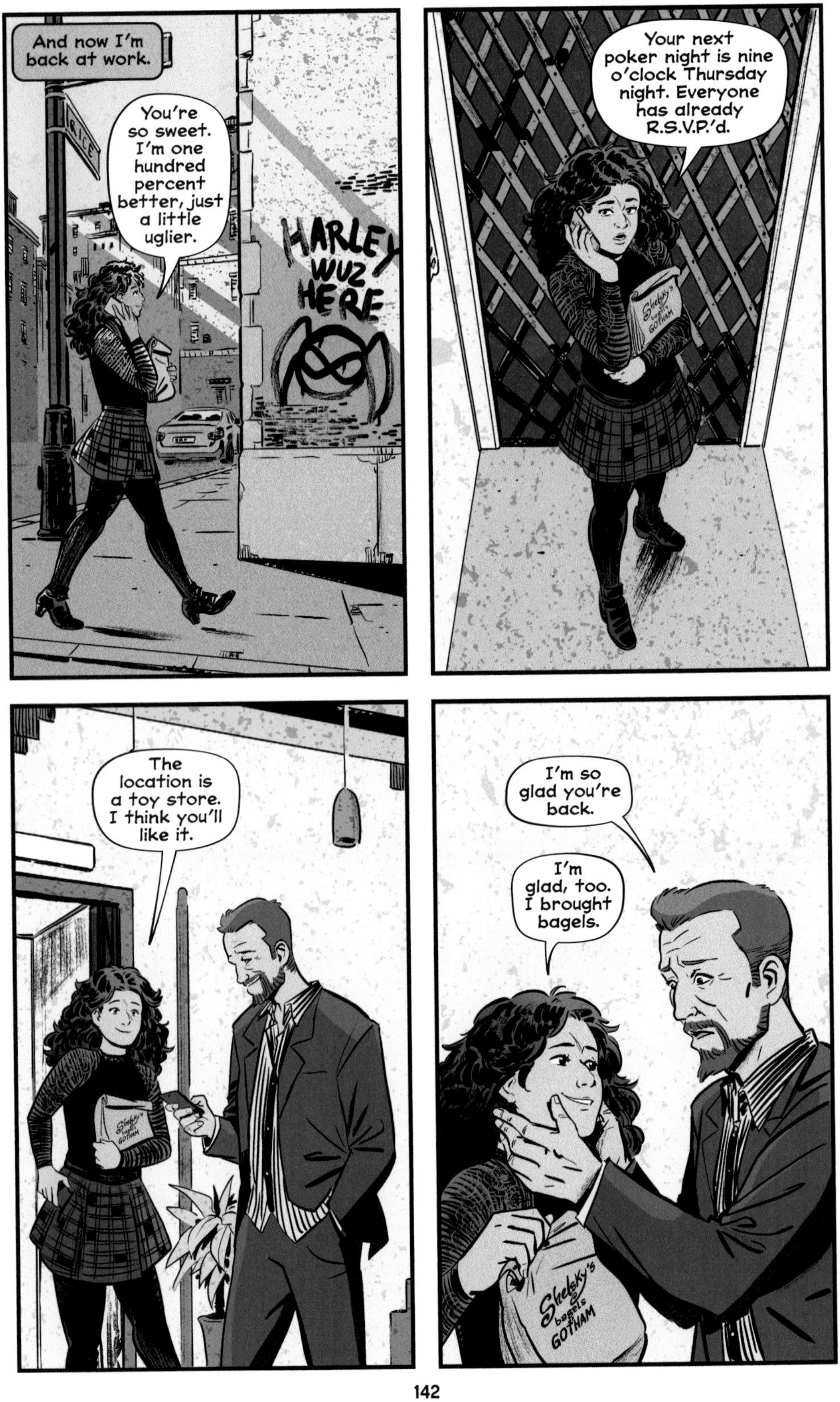
And now I'm back at work.
RICE
You're so sweet. I'm one hundred percent better, just a little uglier.
HARLEY WUZ HERE
Your next poker night is nine o'clock Thursday night. Everyone has already R.S.V.P.'d.
Shelsky's bagels GOTHAM
The location is a toy store. I think you'll like it.
Shelsky's bagels GOTHAM
I'm so glad you're back.
I'm glad, too. I brought bagels.
Shelsky's bagels GOTHAM

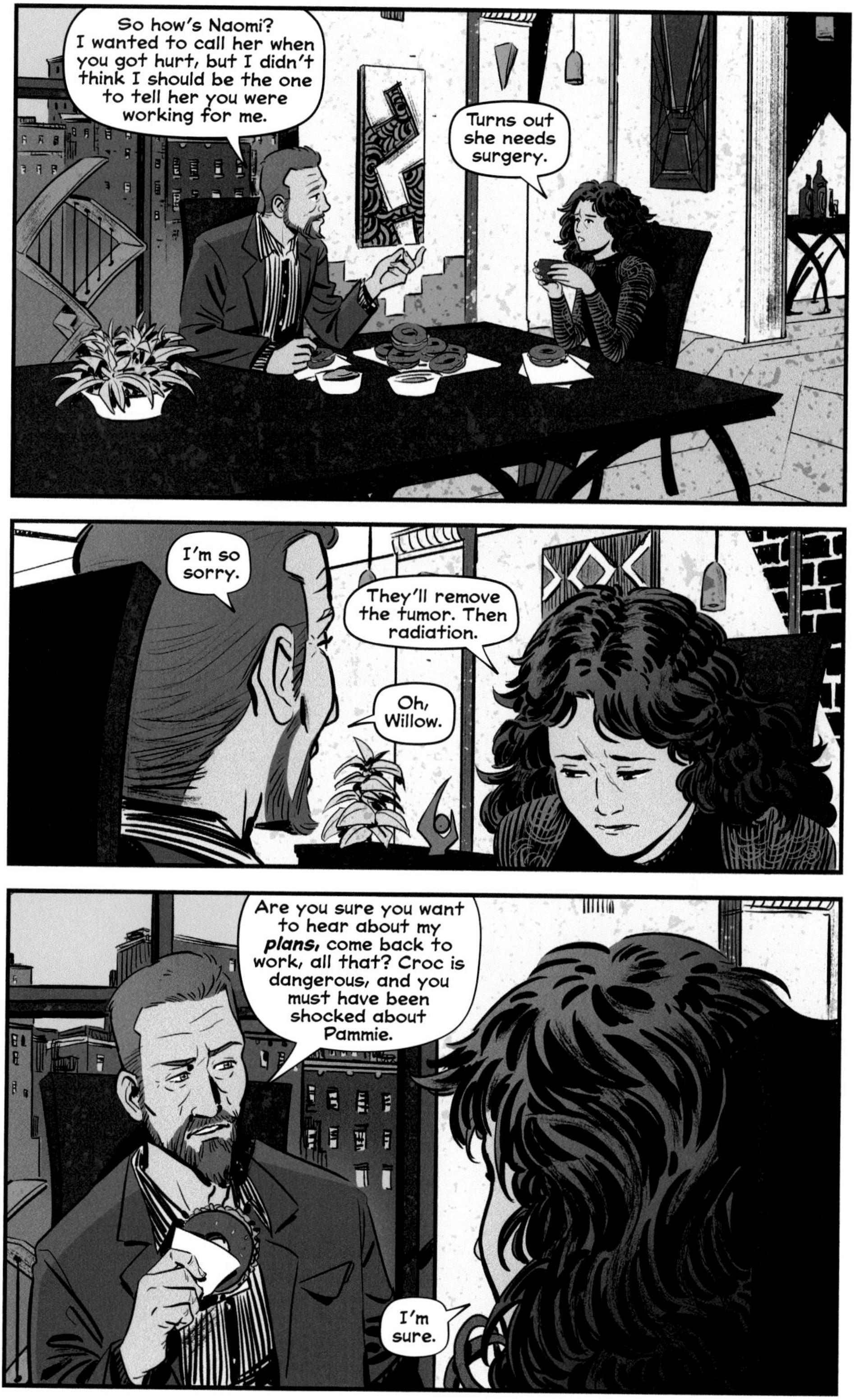
So how's Naomi? I wanted to call her when you got hurt, but I didn't think I should be the one to tell her you were working for me.
Turns out she needs surgery.
I'm so sorry.
They'll remove the tumor. Then radiation.
Oh, Willow.
Are you sure you want to hear about my *plans*, come back to work, all that? Croc is dangerous, and you must have been shocked about Pammie.
I'm sure.

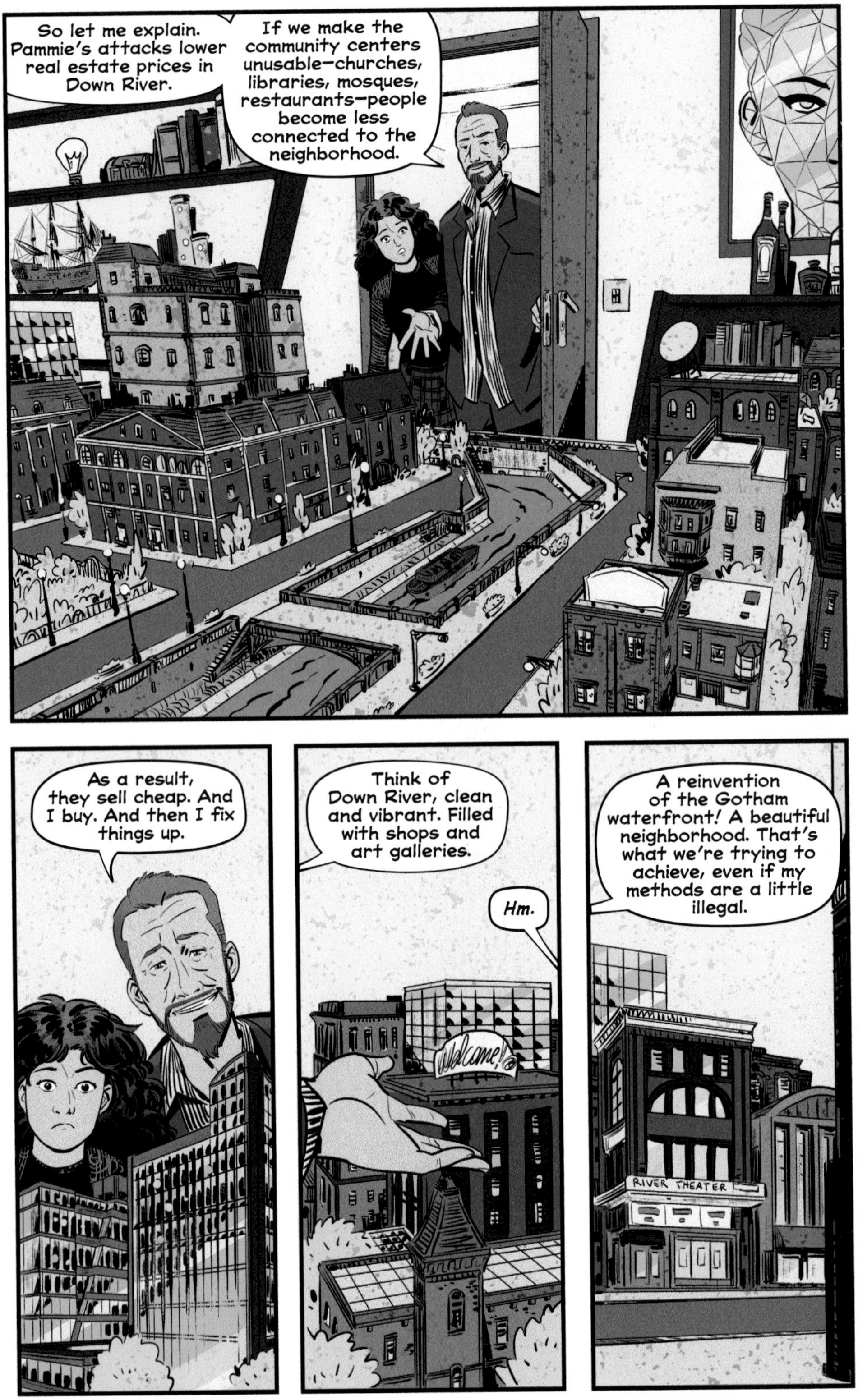
So let me explain. Pammie's attacks lower real estate prices in Down River.
If we make the community centers unusable—churches, libraries, mosques, restaurants—people become less connected to the neighborhood.
As a result, they sell cheap. And I buy. And then I fix things up.
Think of Down River, clean and vibrant. Filled with shops and art galleries.
Welcome!
Hm.
A reinvention of the Gotham waterfront! A beautiful neighborhood. That's what we're trying to achieve, even if my methods are a little illegal.
RIVER THEATER

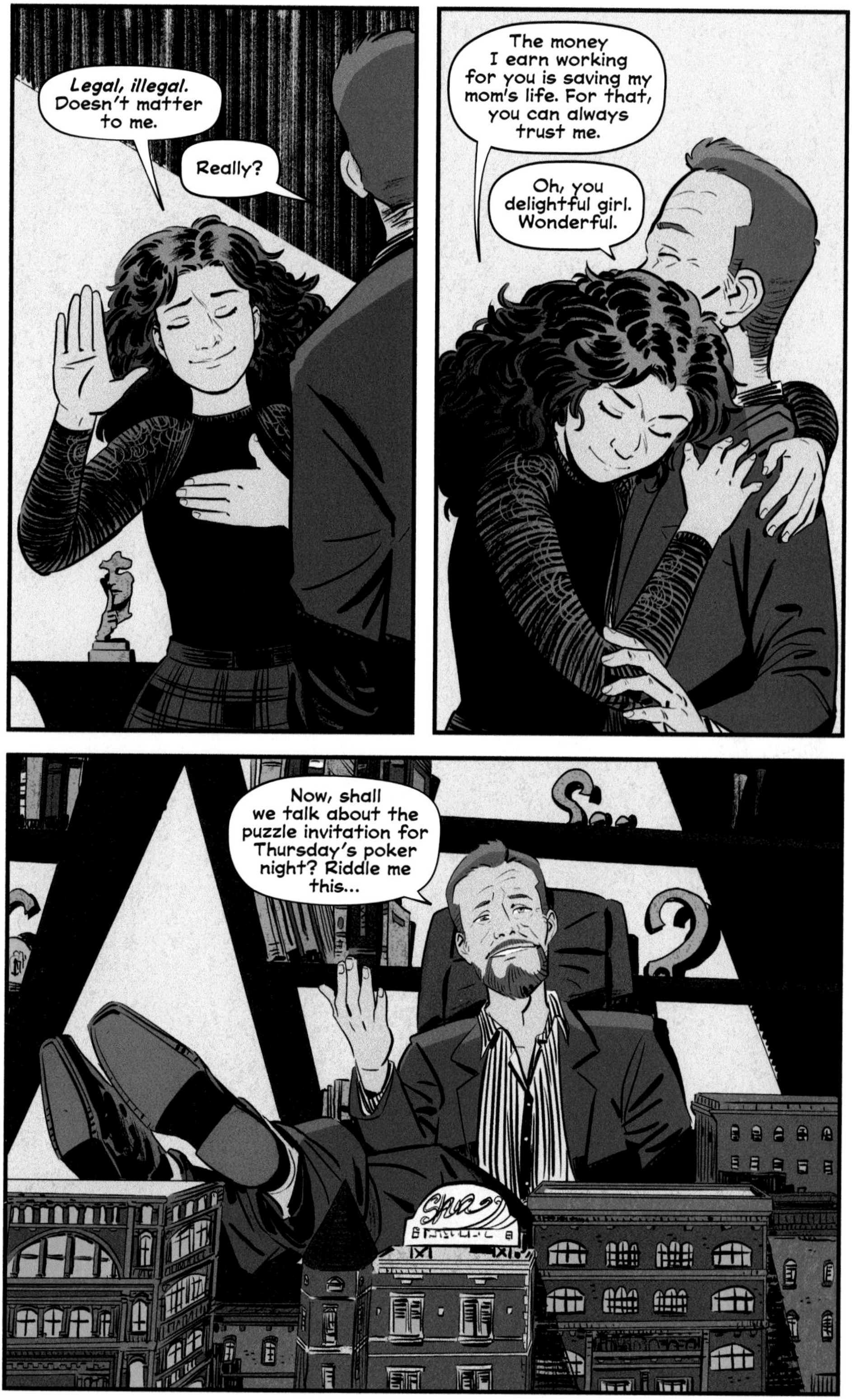
Legal, illegal. Doesn't matter to me.
Really?
The money I earn working for you is saving my mom's life. For that, you can always trust me.
Oh, you delightful girl. Wonderful.
Now, shall we talk about the puzzle invitation for Thursday's poker night? Riddle me this...

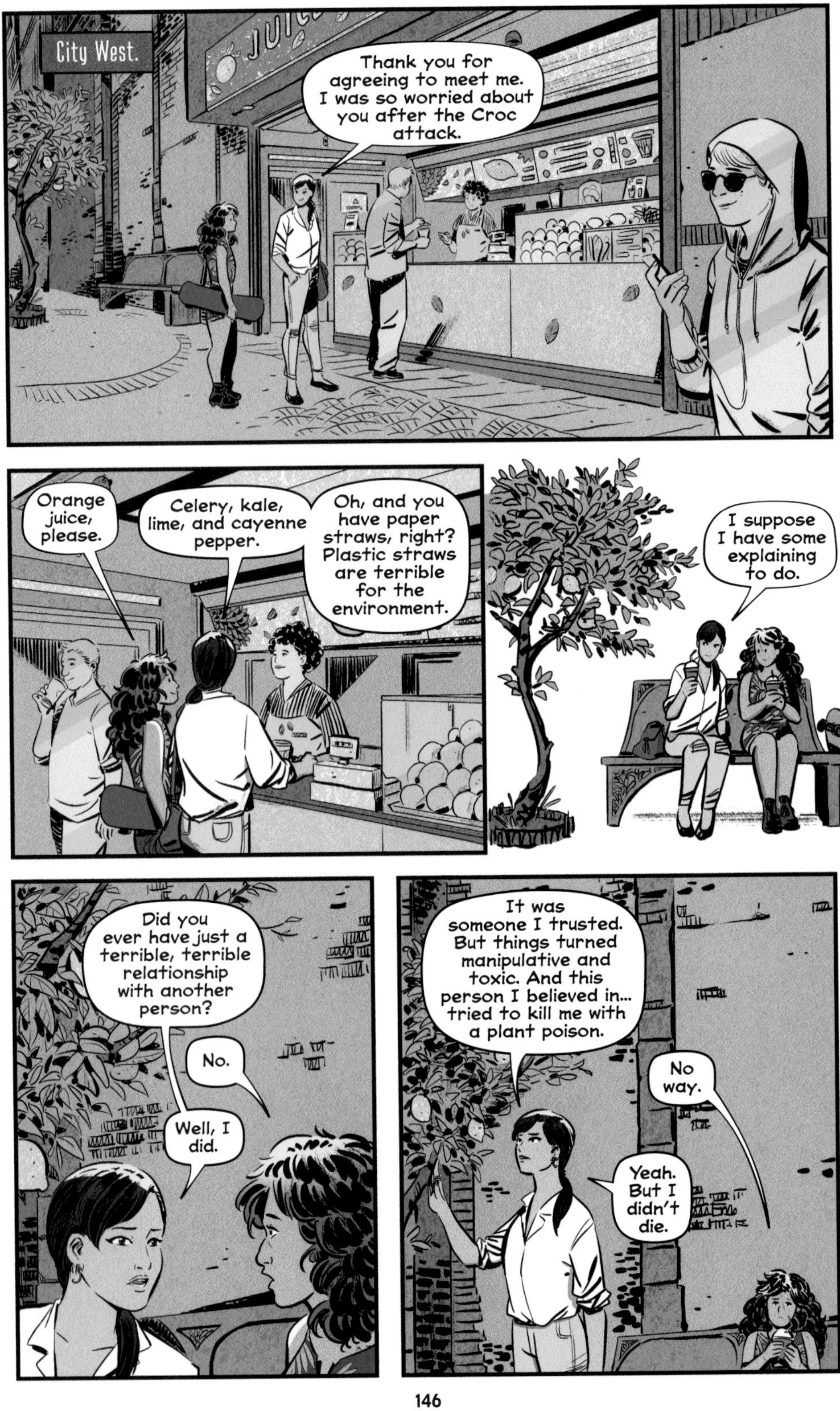

City West.
Thank you for agreeing to meet me. I was so worried about you after the Croc attack.
Orange juice, please.
Celery, kale, lime, and cayenne pepper.
Oh, and you have paper straws, right? Plastic straws are terrible for the environment.
I suppose I have some explaining to do.
Did you ever have just a terrible, terrible relationship with another person?
No.
Well, I did.
It was someone I trusted. But things turned manipulative and toxic. And this person I believed in... tried to kill me with a plant poison.
No way.
Yeah. But I didn't die.

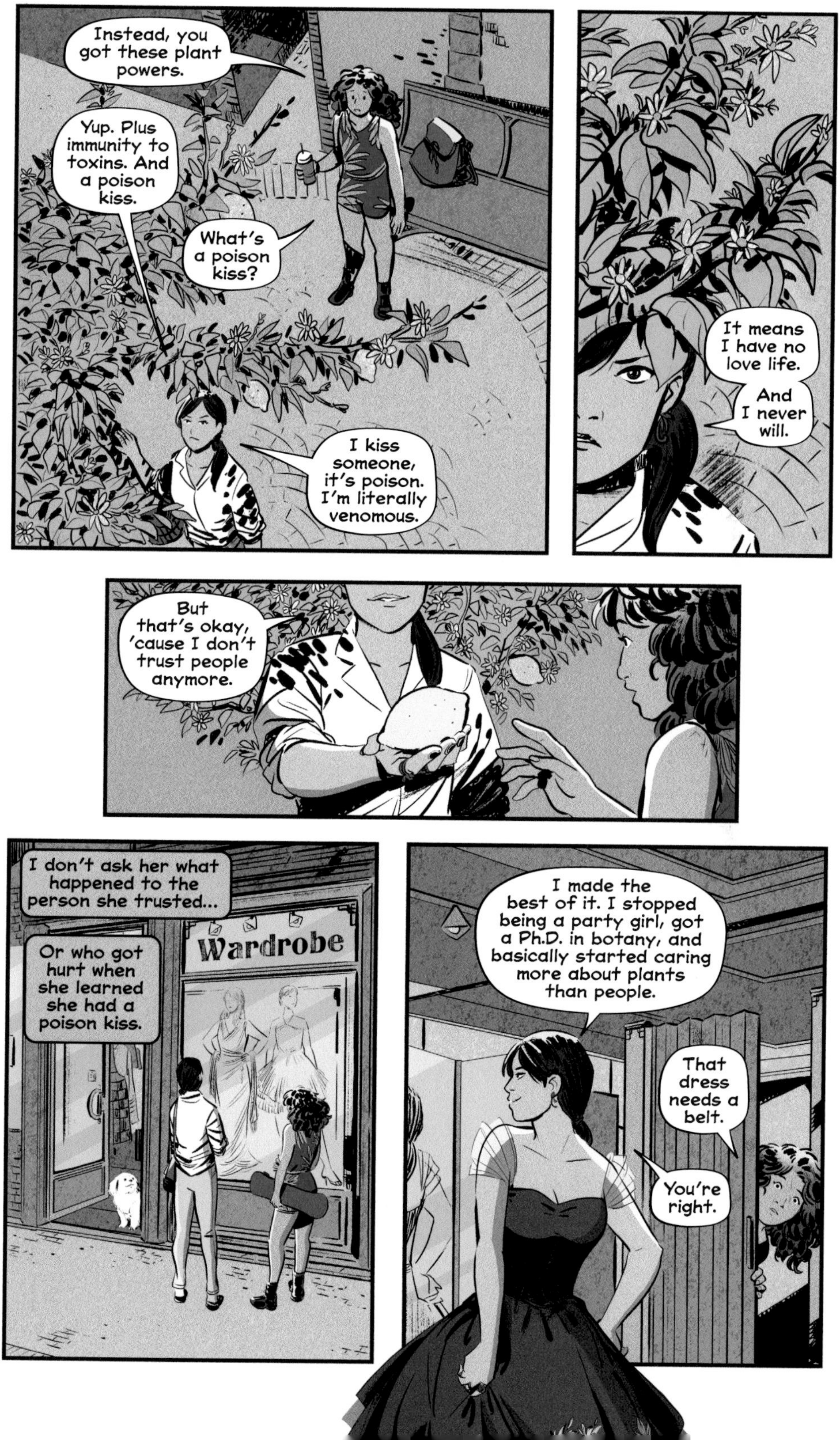
Instead, you got these plant powers.
Yup. Plus immunity to toxins. And a poison kiss.
What's a poison kiss?
I kiss someone, it's poison. I'm literally venomous.
It means I have no love life.
And I never will.
But that's okay, 'cause I don't trust people anymore.
I don't ask her what happened to the person she trusted...
Or who got hurt when she learned she had a poison kiss.
Wardrobe
I made the best of it. I stopped being a party girl, got a Ph.D. in botany, and basically started caring more about plants than people.
That dress needs a belt.
You're right.

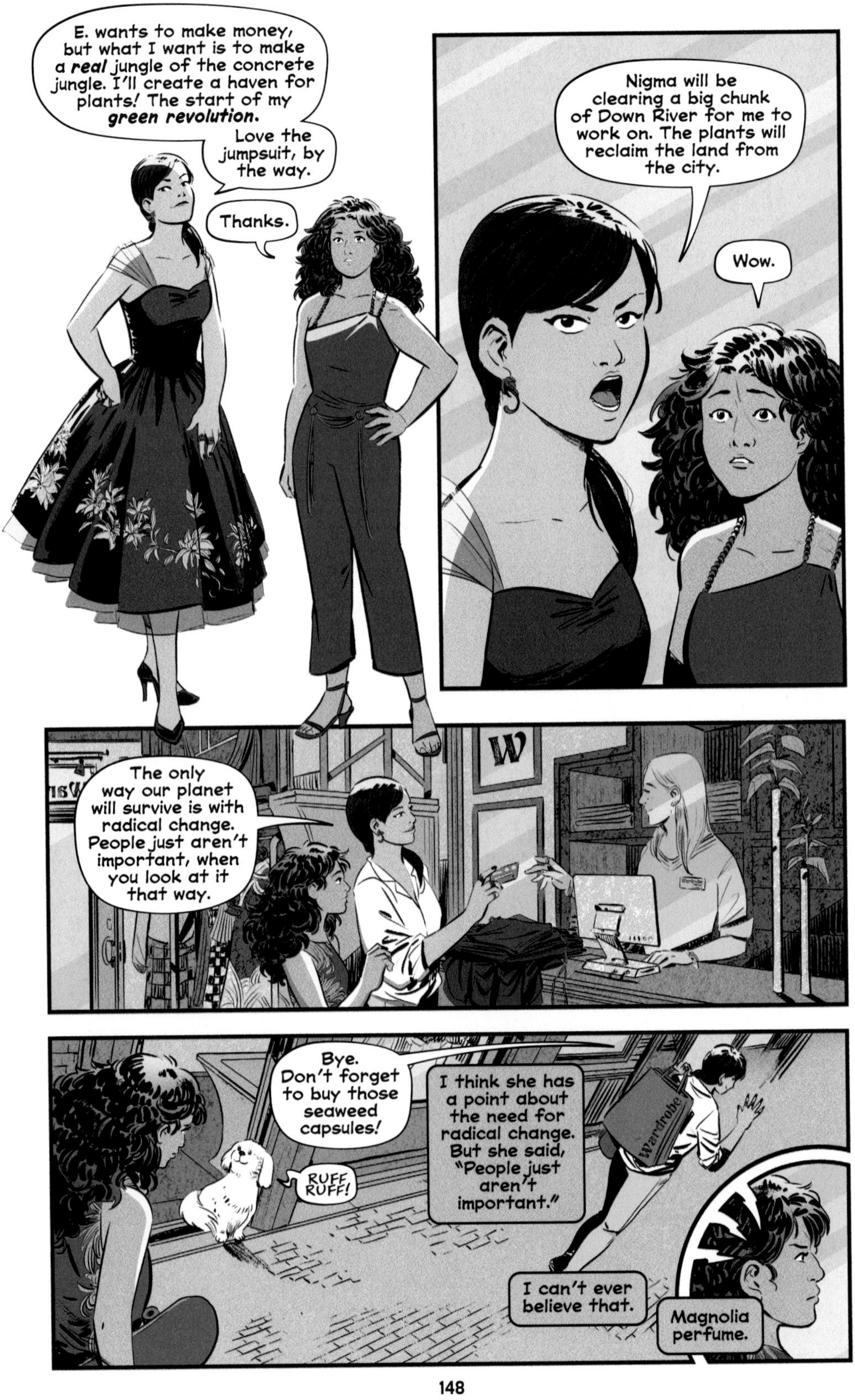
E. wants to make money, but what I want is to make a *real* jungle of the concrete jungle. I'll create a haven for plants! The start of my ***green revolution.***
Love the jumpsuit, by the way.
Thanks.
Nigma will be clearing a big chunk of Down River for me to work on. The plants will reclaim the land from the city.
Wow.
W
The only way our planet will survive is with radical change. People just aren't important, when you look at it that way.
Bye. Don't forget to buy those seaweed capsules!
RUFF RUFF!
Wardrobe
I think she has a point about the need for radical change. But she said, "People just aren't important."
I can't ever believe that.
Magnolia perfume.

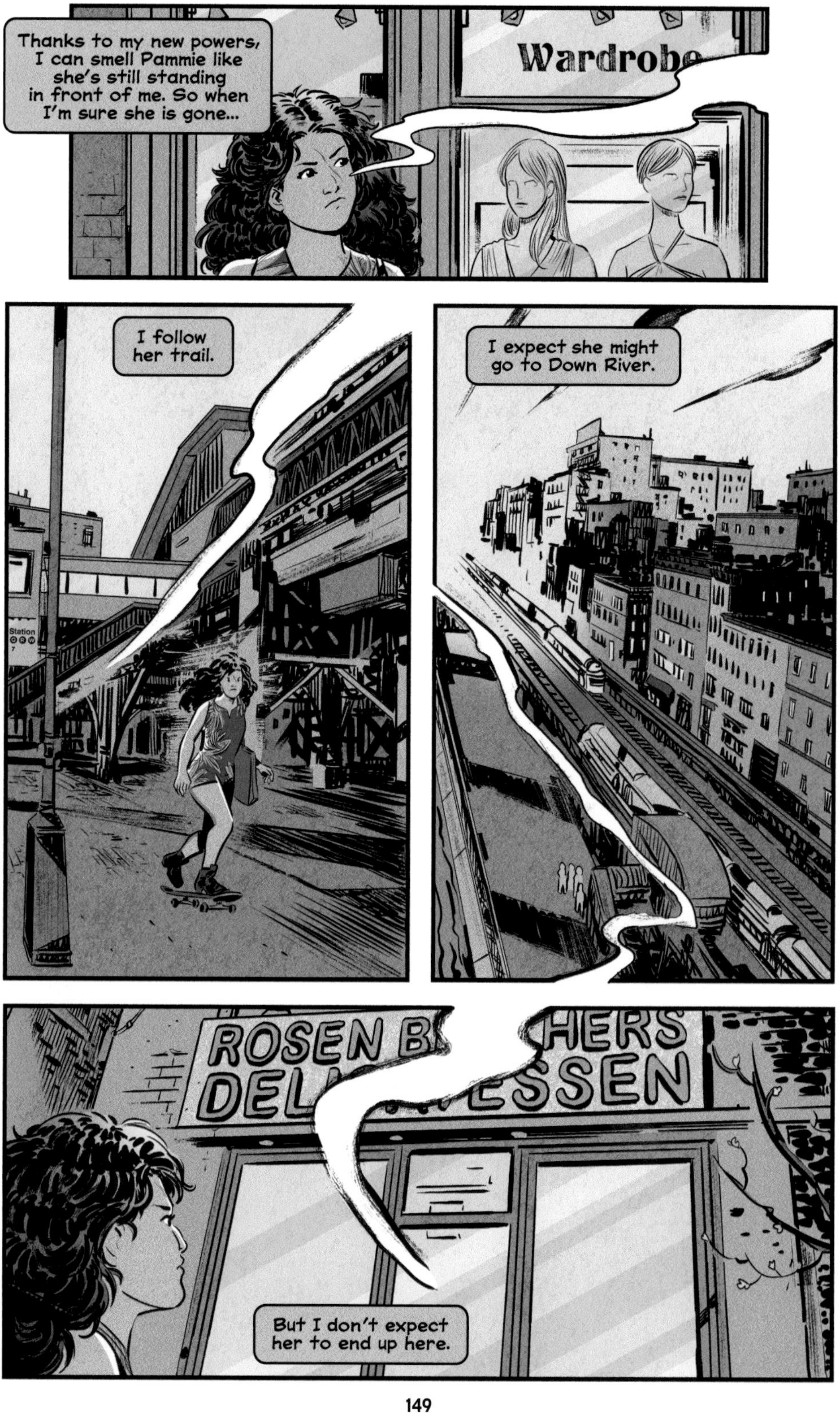
Thanks to my new powers, I can smell Pammie like she's still standing in front of me. So when I'm sure she is gone...
Wardrob
I follow her trail.
Station
I expect she might go to Down River.
ROSEN B HERS
DEL ESSEN
But I don't expect her to end up here.

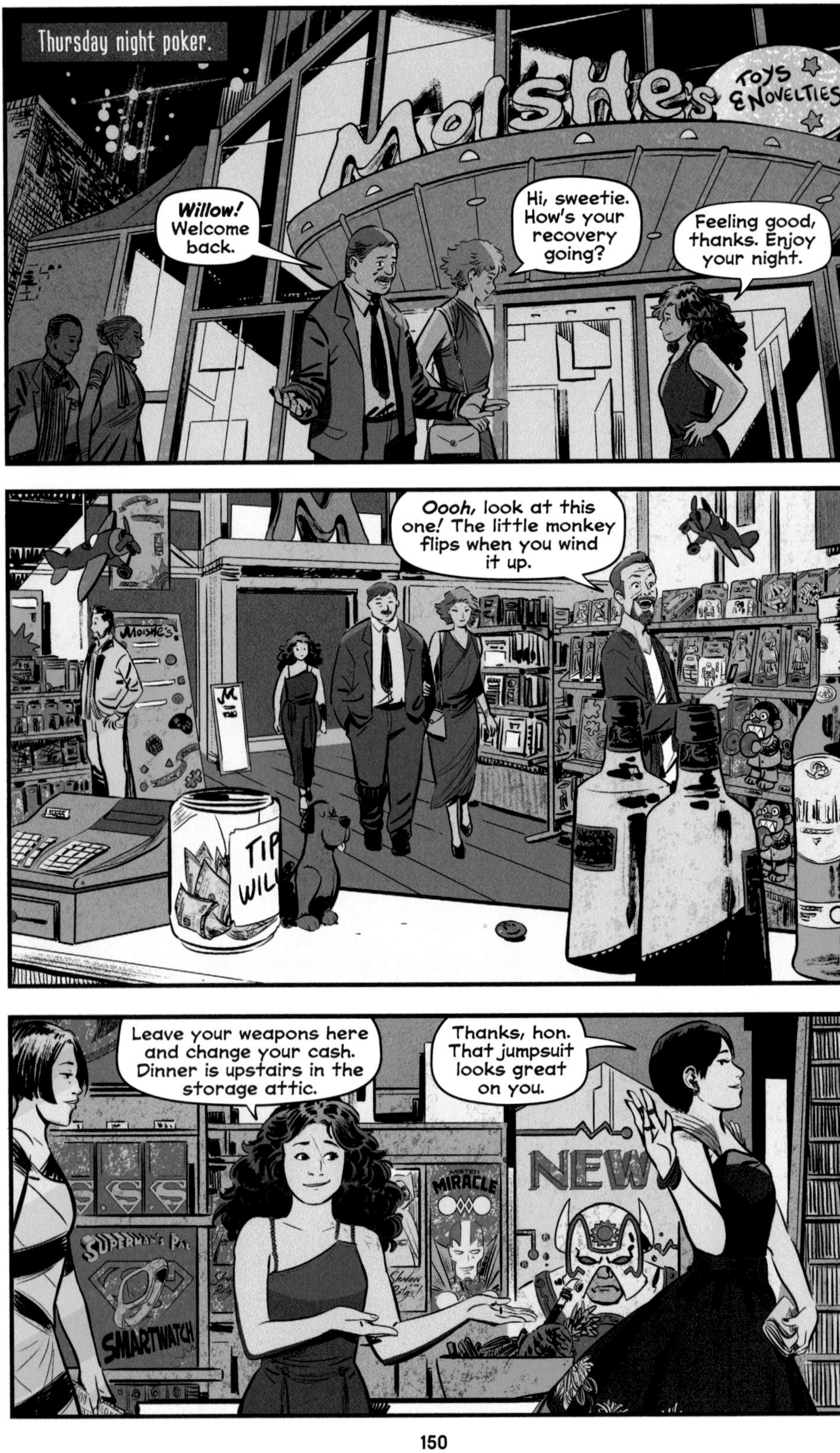
Thursday night poker.
MOISHE'S
TOYS & NOVELTIES
Willow! Welcome back.
Hi, sweetie. How's your recovery going?
Feeling good, thanks. Enjoy your night.
Moishe's
Oooh, look at this one! The little monkey flips when you wind it up.
Leave your weapons here and change your cash. Dinner is upstairs in the storage attic.
Thanks, hon. That jumpsuit looks great on you.
SUPERMAN'S PAL
SMARTWATCH
MISTER MIRACLE
NEW

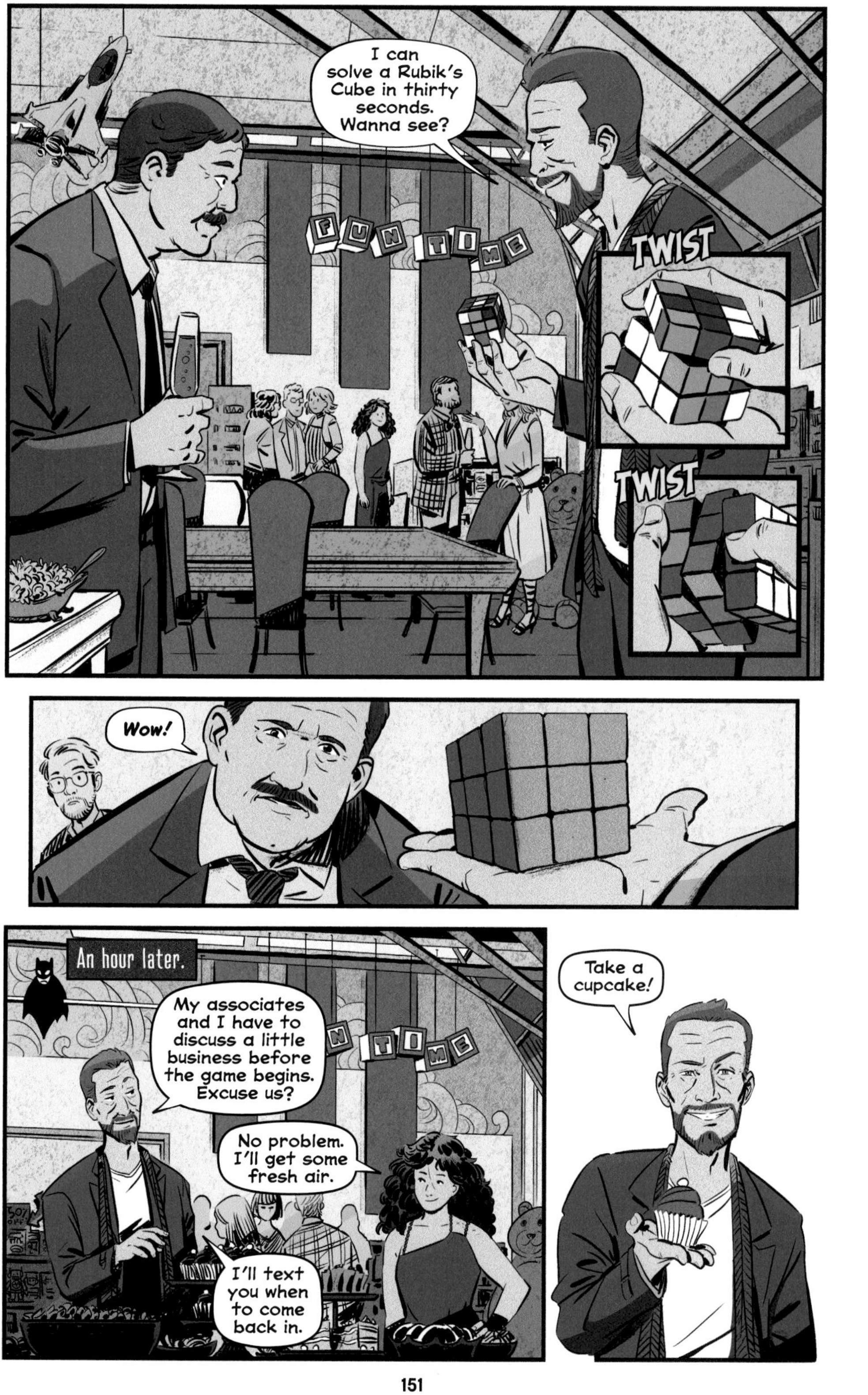
I can solve a Rubik's Cube in thirty seconds. Wanna see?
FUN TIME
TWIST
TWIST
Wow!
An hour later.
My associates and I have to discuss a little business before the game begins. Excuse us?
No problem. I'll get some fresh air.
I'll text you when to come back in.
Take a cupcake!

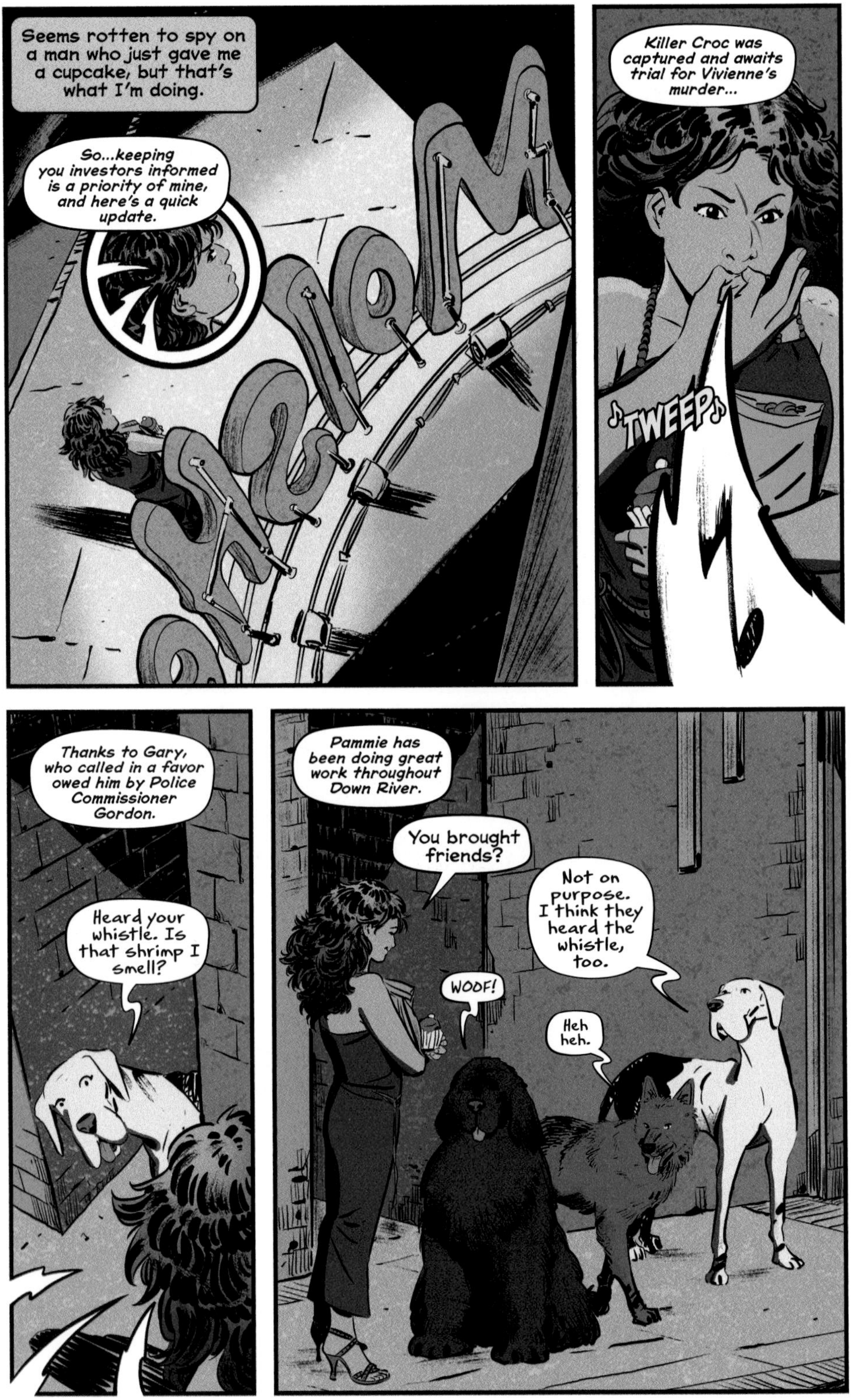
Seems rotten to spy on a man who just gave me a cupcake, but that's what I'm doing.
So...keeping you investors informed is a priority of mine, and here's a quick update.
Killer Croc was captured and awaits trial for Vivienne's murder...
TWEEP
Thanks to Gary, who called in a favor owed him by Police Commissioner Gordon.
Heard your whistle. Is that shrimp I smell?
Pammie has been doing great work throughout Down River.
You brought friends?
Not on purpose. I think they heard the whistle, too.
WOOF!
Heh heh.

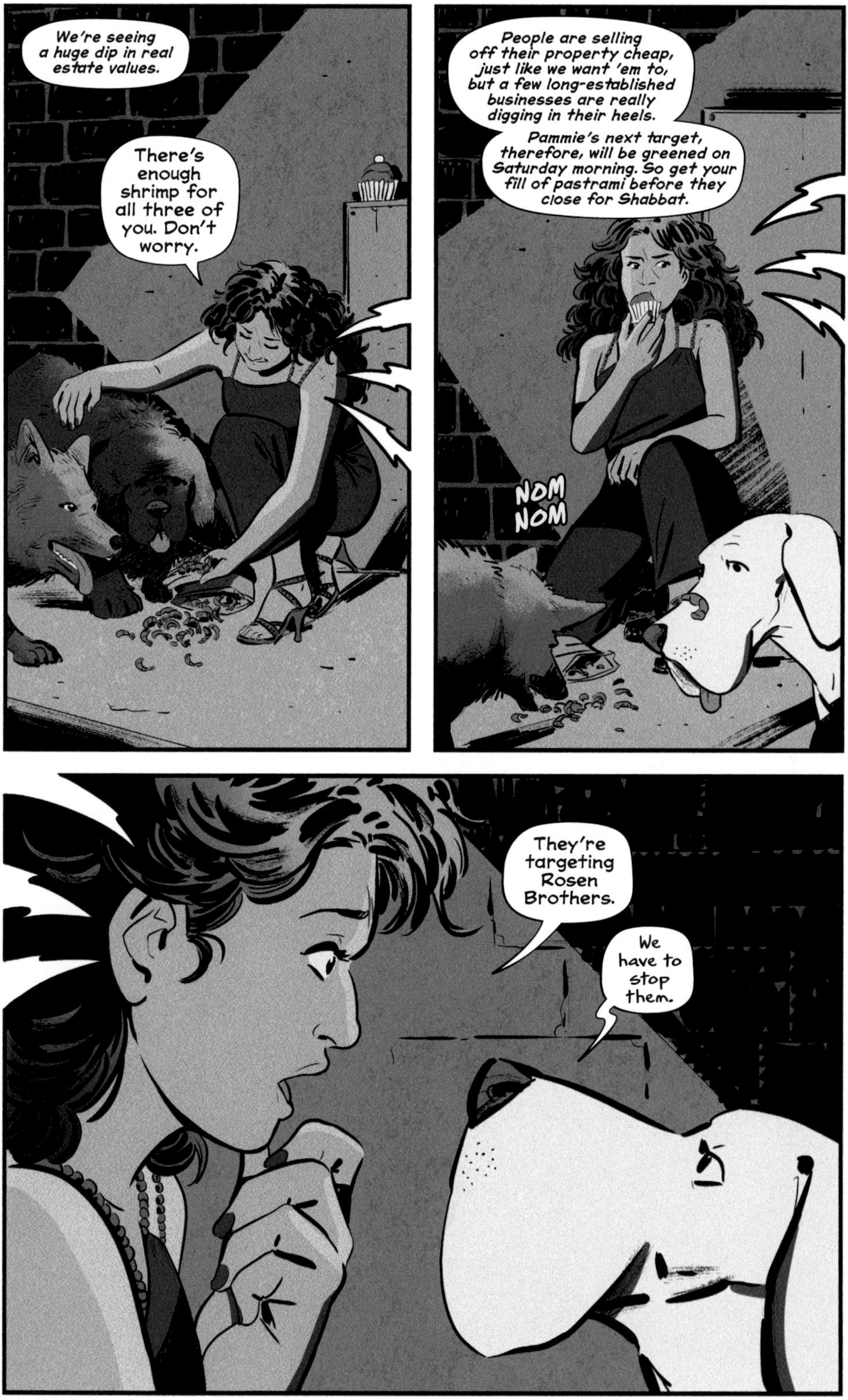
We're seeing a huge dip in real estate values.
There's enough shrimp for all three of you. Don't worry.
People are selling off their property cheap, just like we want 'em to, but a few long-established businesses are really digging in their heels.
Pammie's next target, therefore, will be greened on Saturday morning. So get your fill of pastrami before they close for Shabbat.
NOM NOM
They're targeting Rosen Brothers.
We have to stop them.

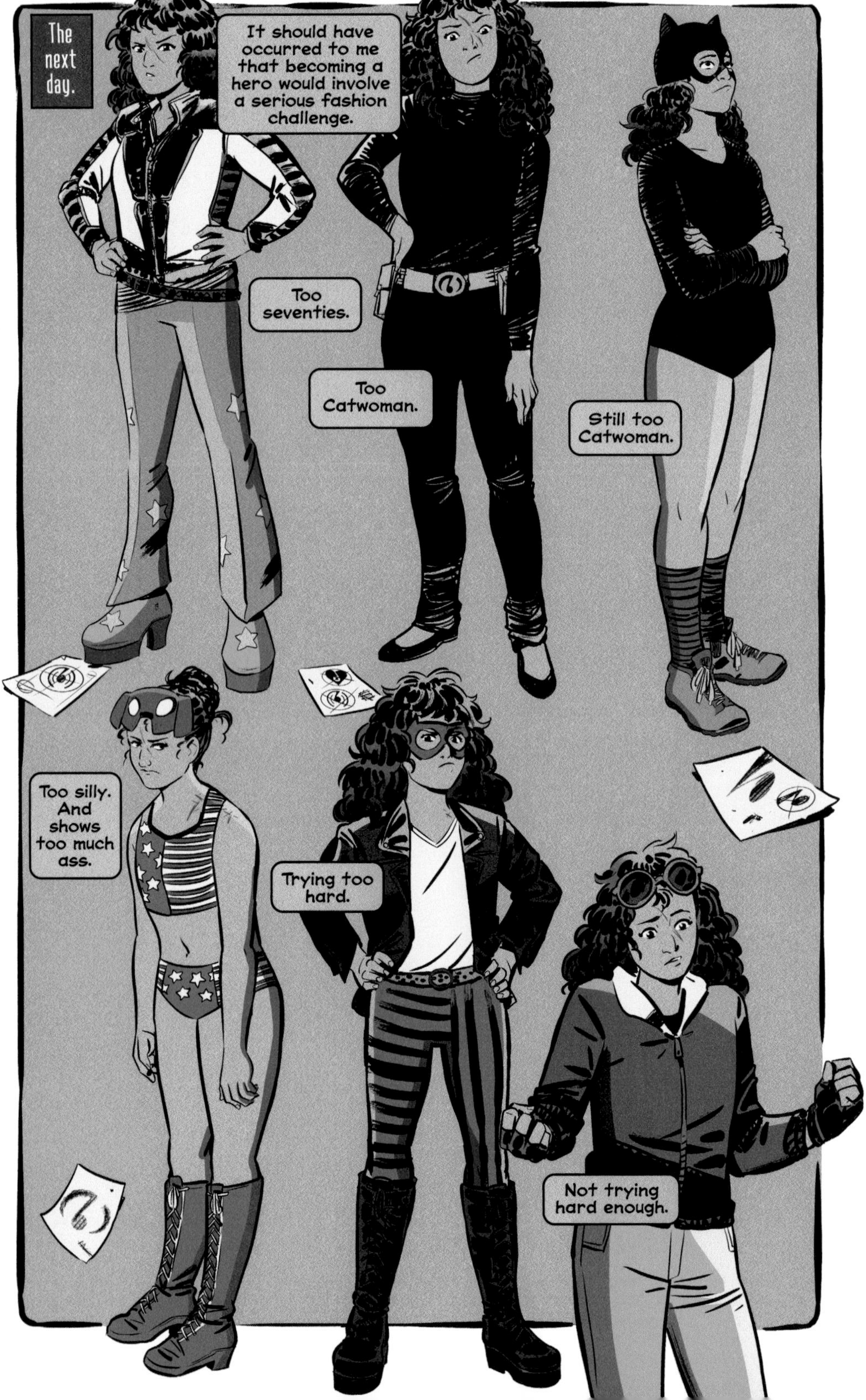
The next day.
It should have occurred to me that becoming a hero would involve a serious fashion challenge.
Too seventies.
Too Catwoman.
Still too Catwoman.
Too silly. And shows too much ass.
Trying too hard.
Not trying hard enough.

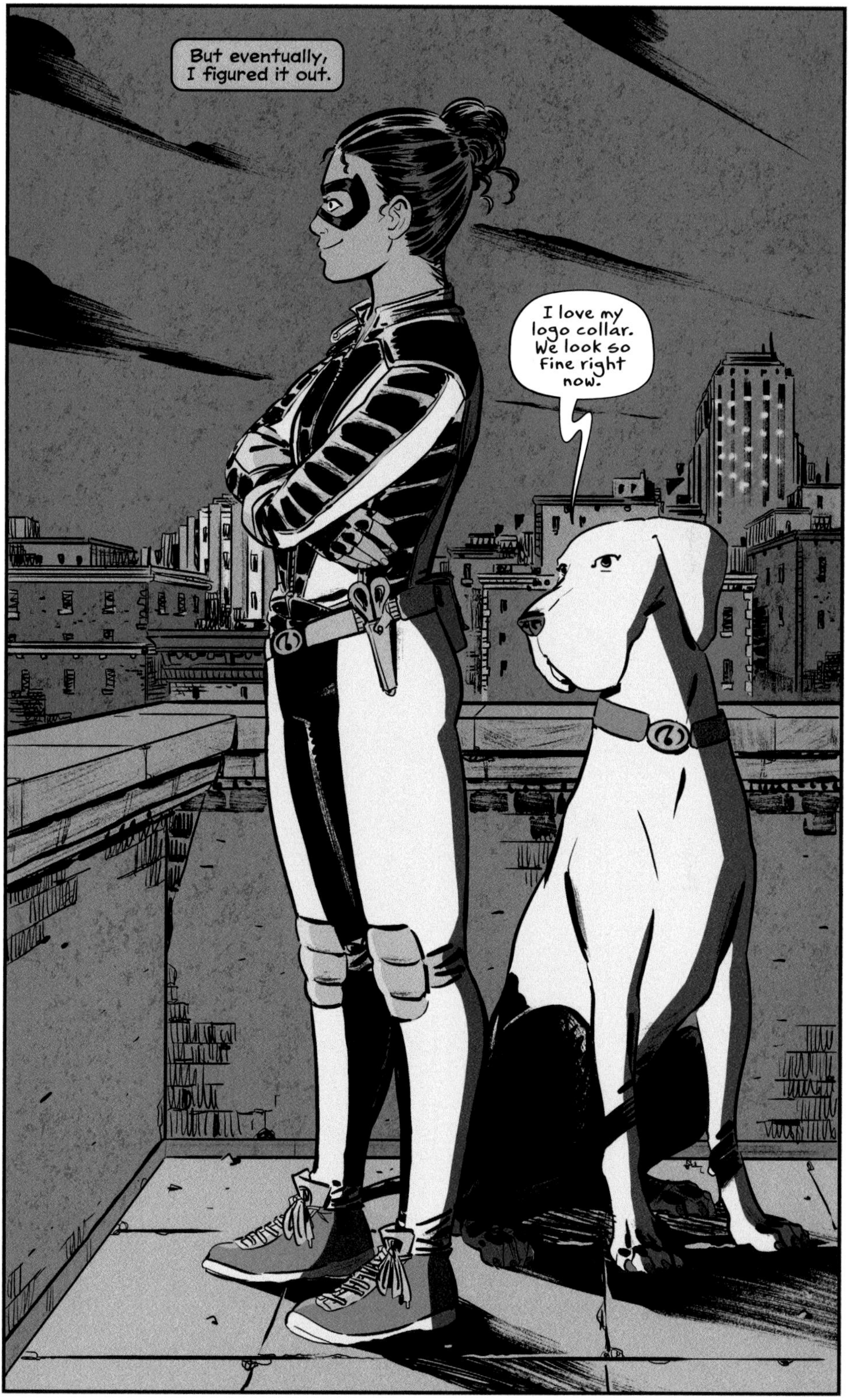
But eventually, I figured it out.
I love my logo collar. We look so fine right now.

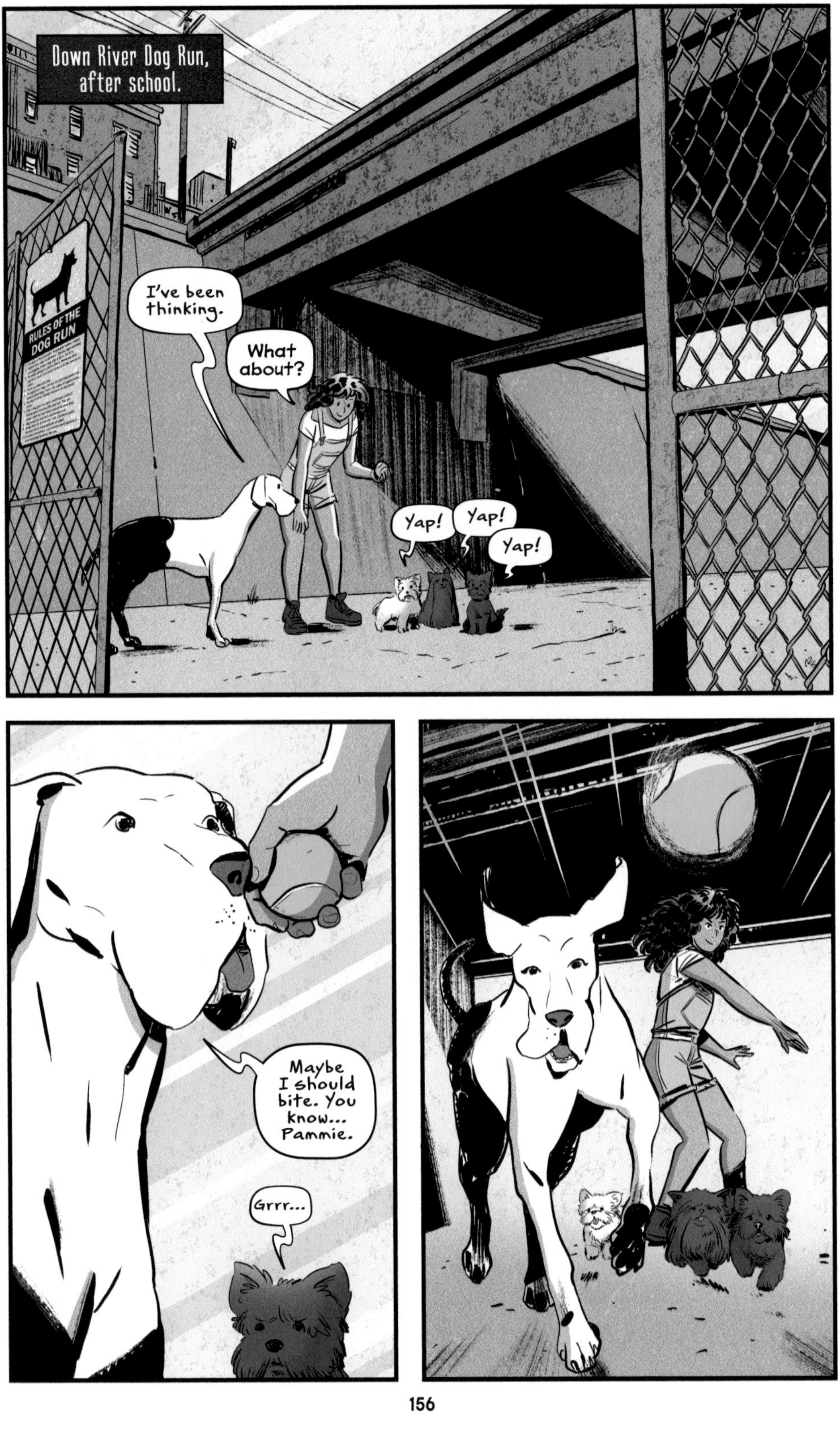
Down River Dog Run, after school.
RULES OF THE DOG RUN
I've been thinking.
What about?
Yap!
Yap!
Yap!
Maybe I should bite. You know... Pammie.
Grrr...

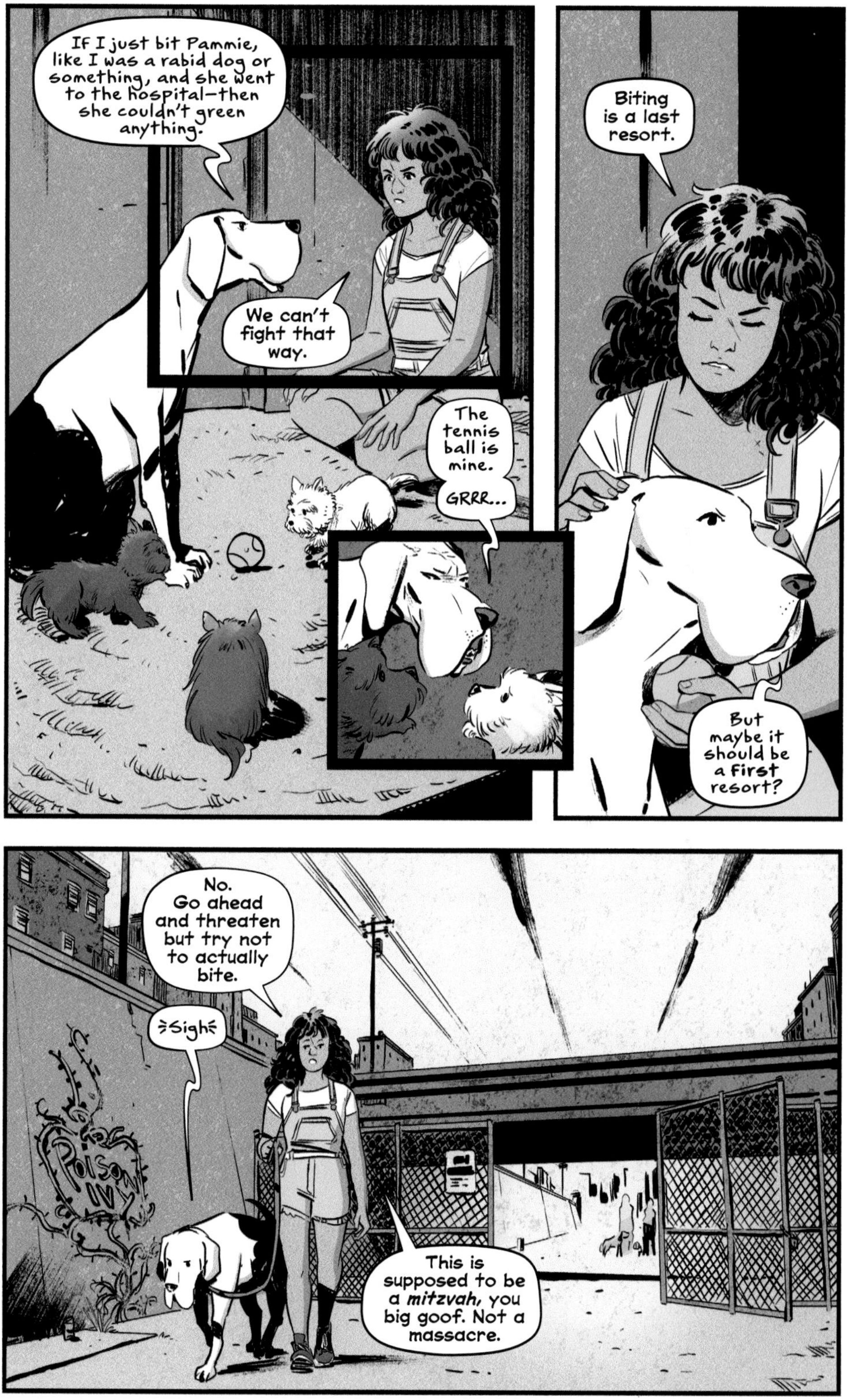
If I just bit Pammie, like I was a rabid dog or something, and she went to the hospital—then she couldn't green anything.
We can't fight that way.
The tennis ball is mine.
GRRR...
Biting is a last resort.
But maybe it should be a first resort?
No. Go ahead and threaten but try not to actually bite.
Sigh
POISON IVY
This is supposed to be a *mitzvah,* you big goof. Not a massacre.

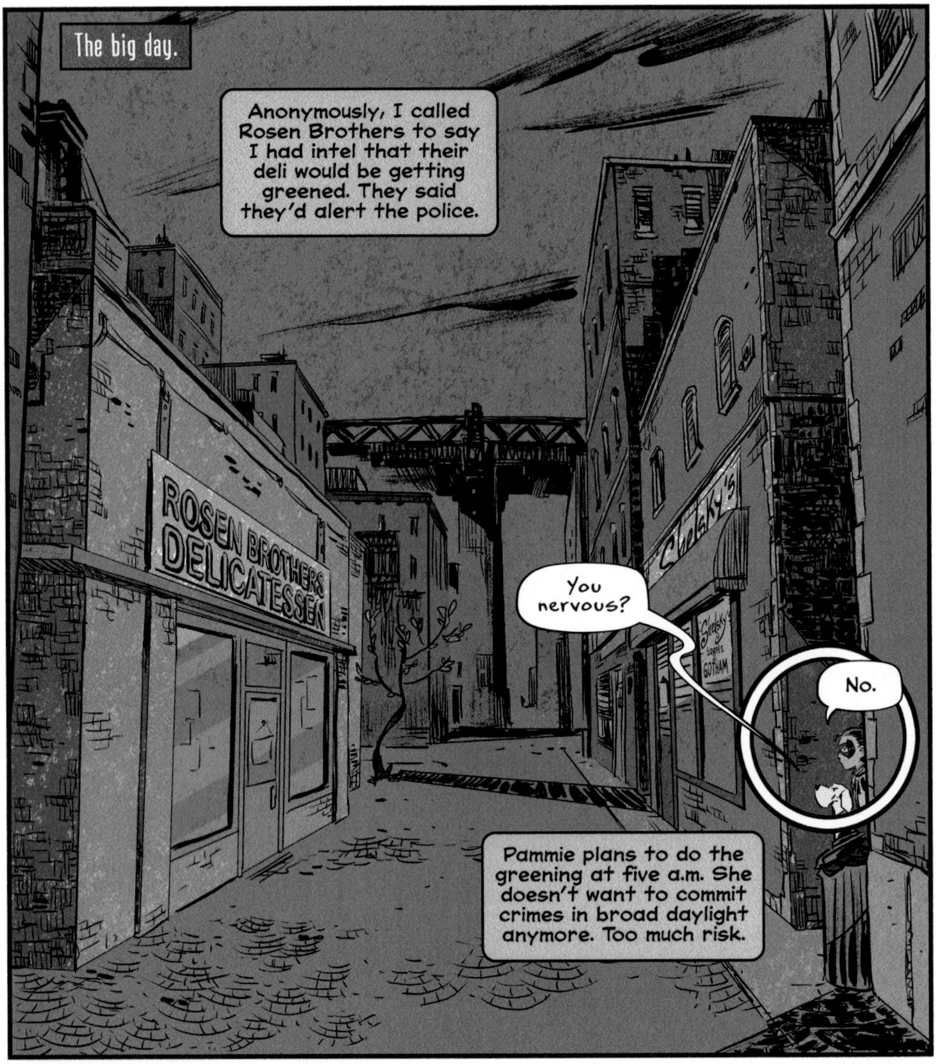
The big day.
Anonymously, I called Rosen Brothers to say I had intel that their deli would be getting greened. They said they'd alert the police.
ROSEN BROTHERS DELICATESSEN
You nervous?
No.
Pammie plans to do the greening at five a.m. She doesn't want to commit crimes in broad daylight anymore. Too much risk.

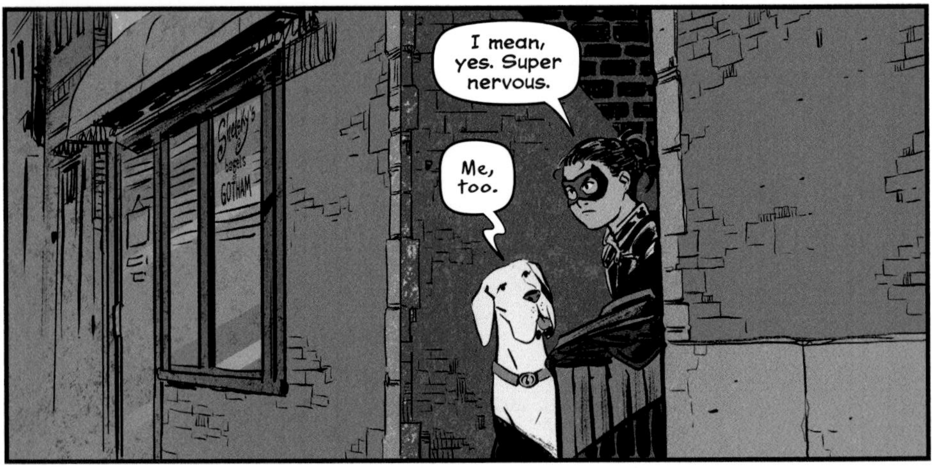
I mean, yes. Super nervous.
Me, too.

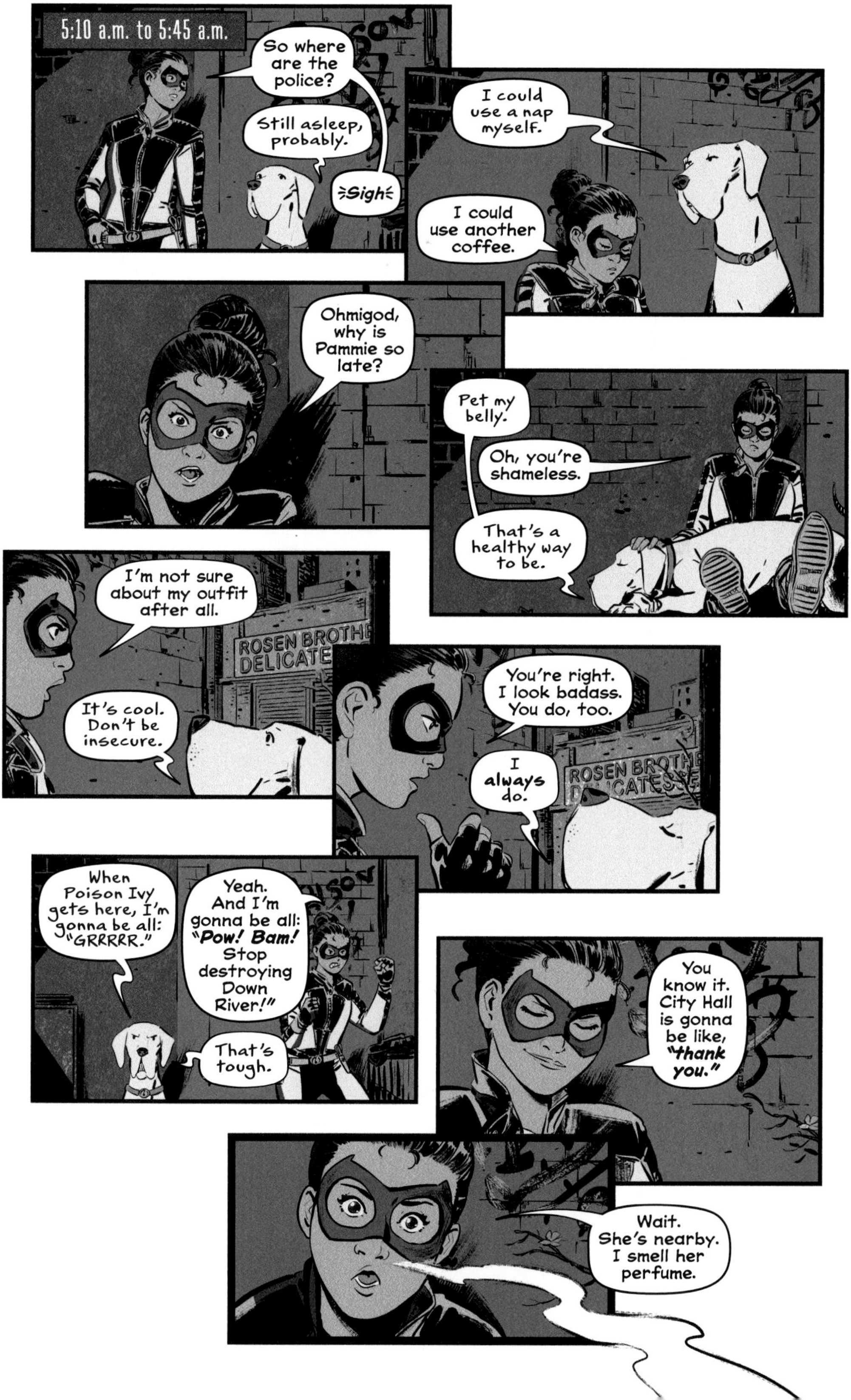
5:10 a.m. to 5:45 a.m.
So where are the police?
Still asleep, probably.
Sigh
I could use a nap myself.
I could use another coffee.
Ohmigod, why is Pammie so late?
Pet my belly.
Oh, you're shameless.
That's a healthy way to be.
I'm not sure about my outfit after all.
ROSEN BROTHE DELICATE
It's cool. Don't be insecure.
You're right. I look badass. You do, too.
I always do.
When Poison Ivy gets here, I'm gonna be all: "GRRRRR."
Yeah. And I'm gonna be all: "Pow! Bam! Stop destroying Down River!"
That's tough.
You know it. City Hall is gonna be like, "thank you."
Wait. She's nearby. I smell her perfume.

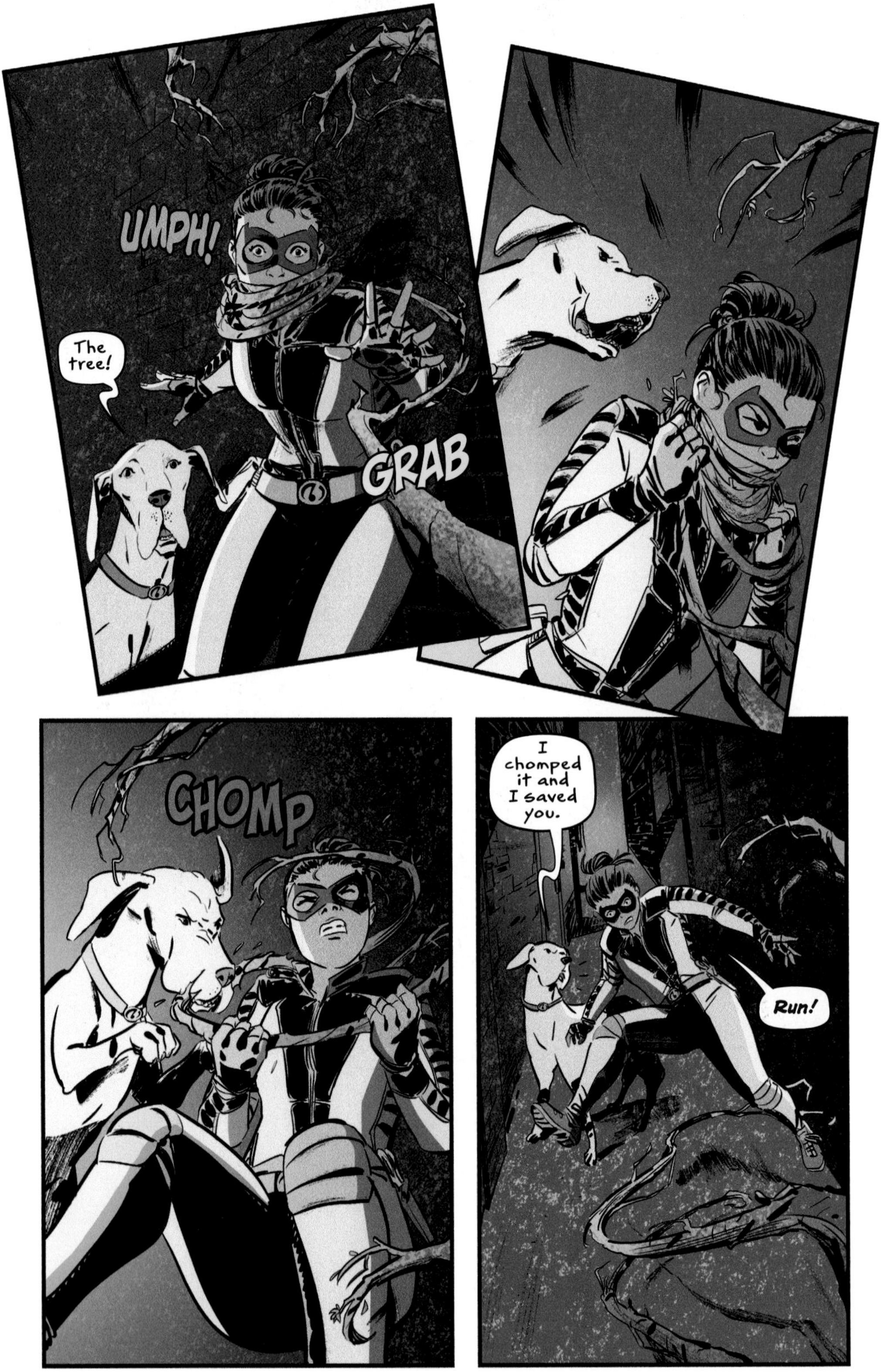
UMPH!
The tree!
GRAB
CHOMP
I chomped it and I saved you.
Run!

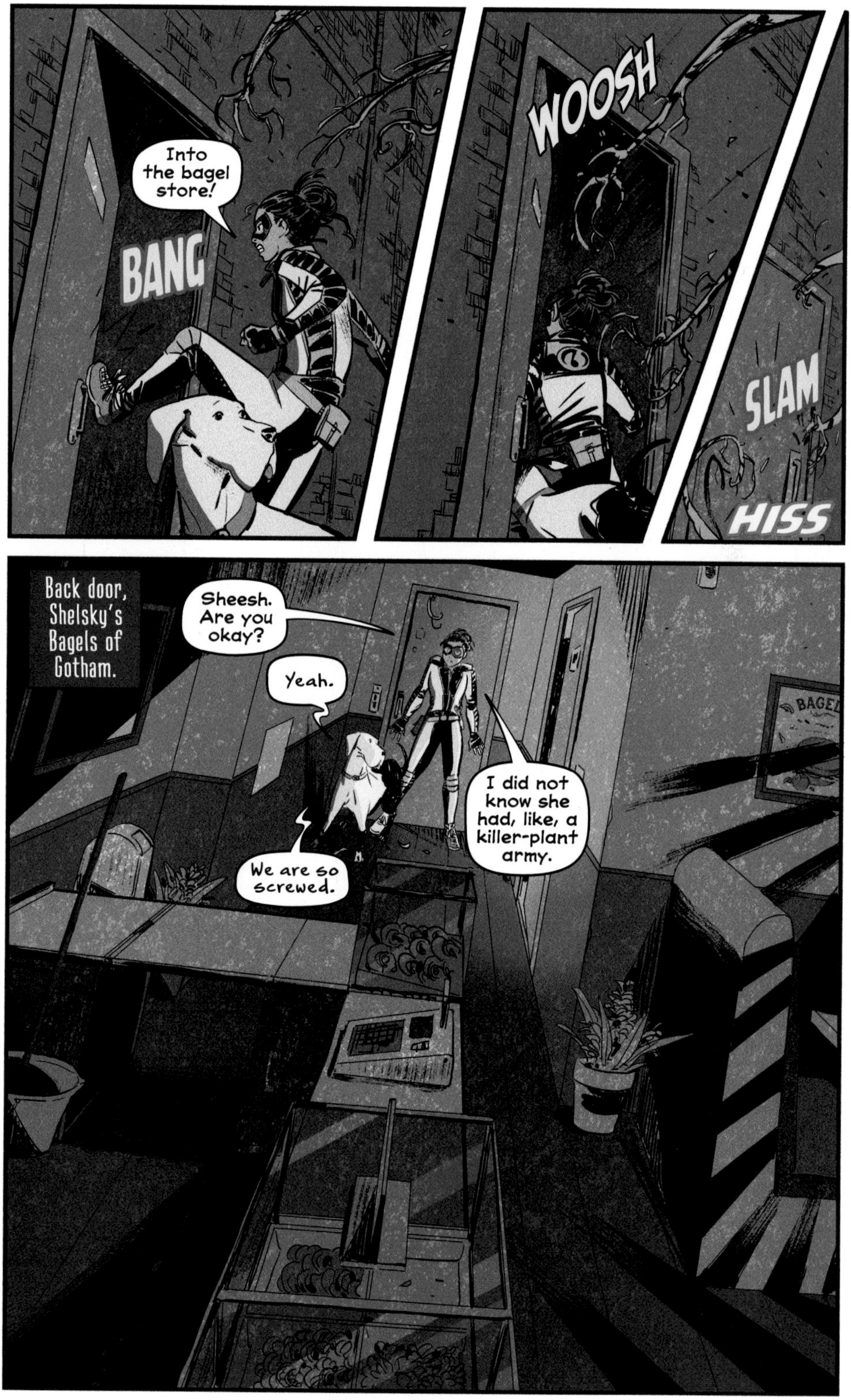
Into the bagel store!
BANG
WOOSH
SLAM
HISS
Back door, Shelsky's Bagels of Gotham.
Sheesh. Are you okay?
Yeah.
I did not know she had, like, a killer-plant army.
We are so screwed.

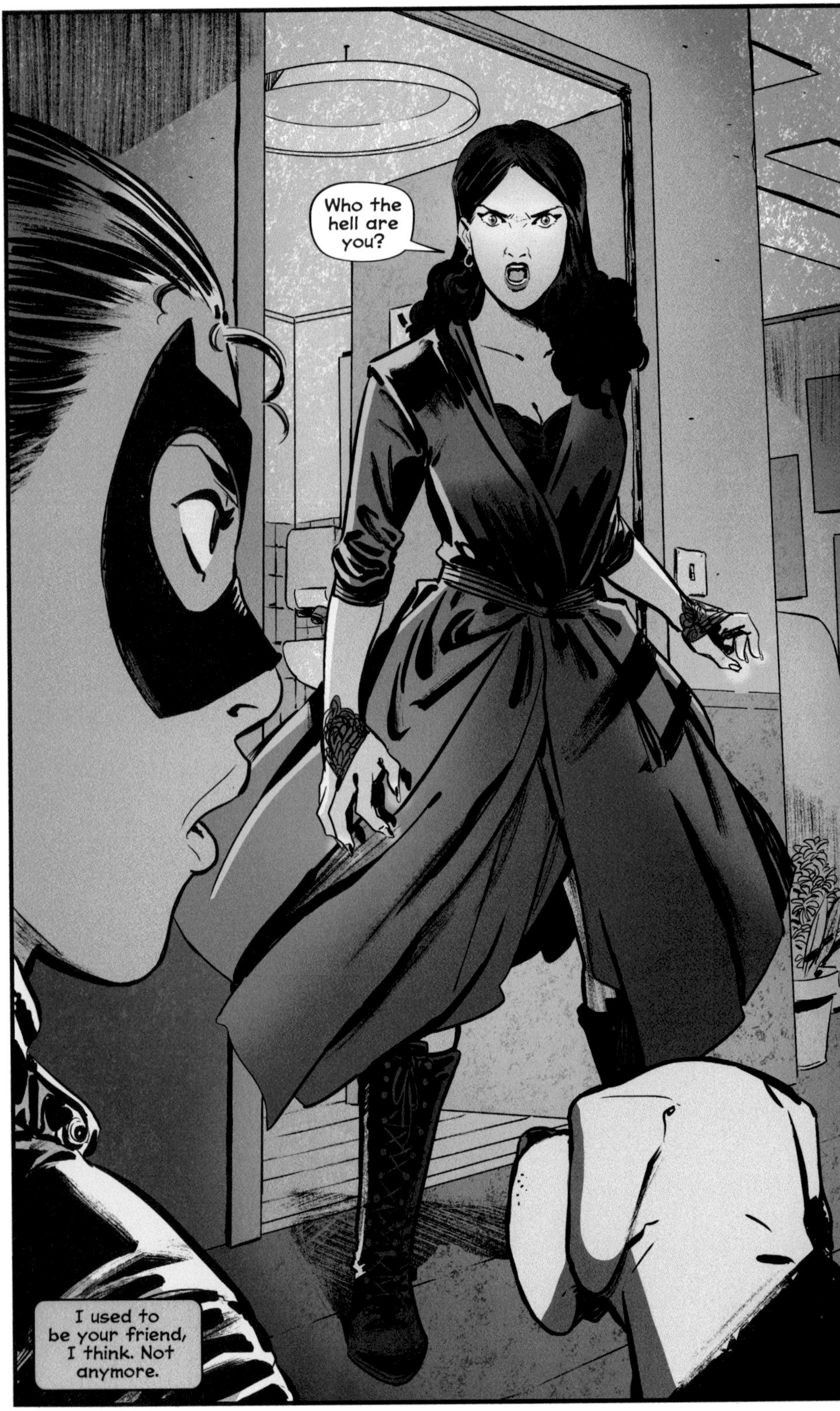
Who the hell are you?
I used to be your friend, I think. Not anymore.

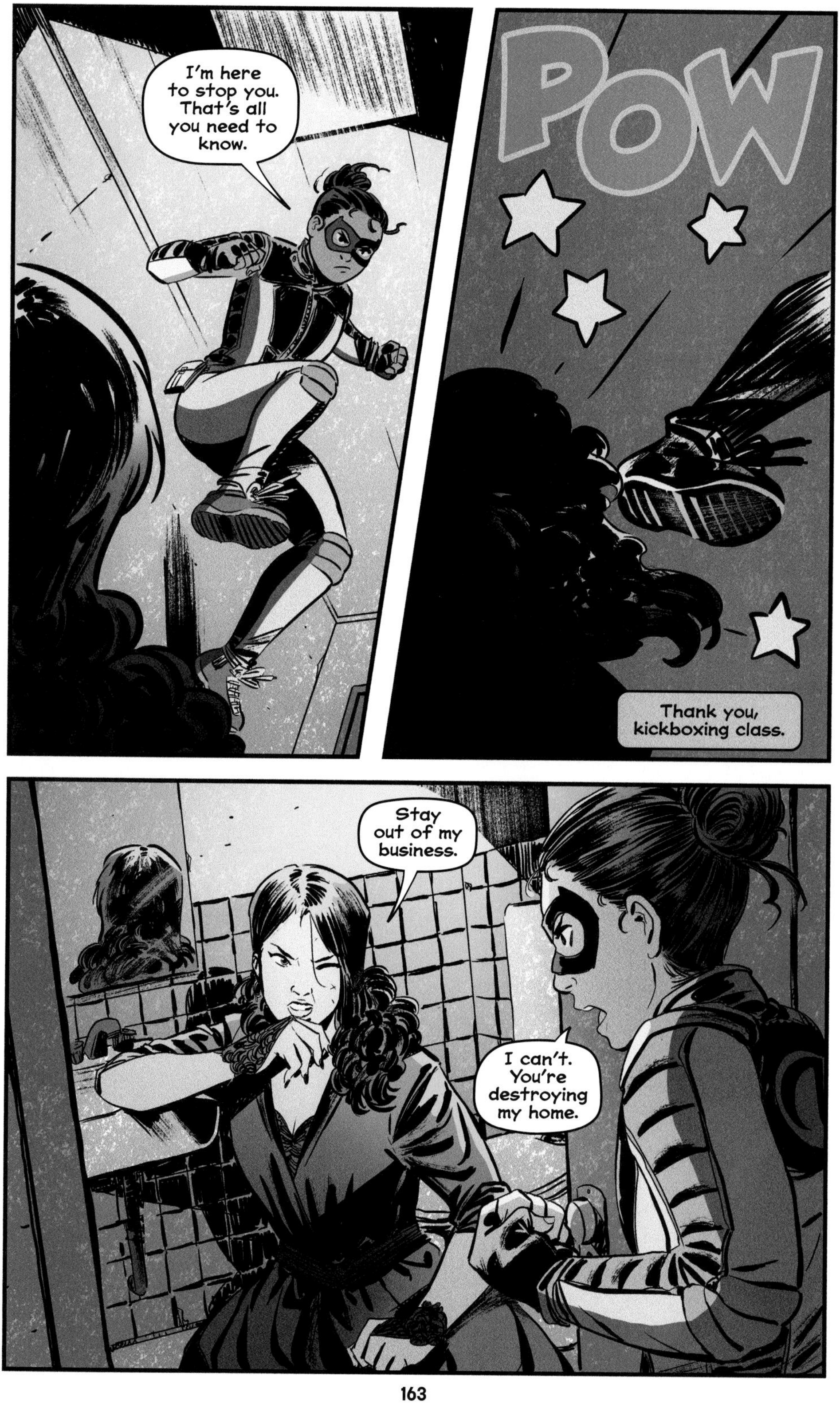
I'm here to stop you. That's all you need to know.
POW
Thank you, kickboxing class.
Stay out of my business.
I can't. You're destroying my home.

PUSH

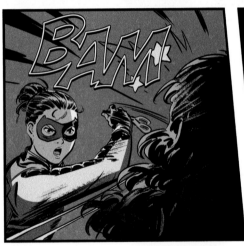

BAM

You can't hurt Down River like this. People are suffering.

Plants are the rightful inhabitants of Gotham. It's the *Earth* that's suffering.

There are no plants to call on in here. My scissors are at your throat. So listen to me.

Silly girl. There's always a plant somewhere. And they're just like dogs...

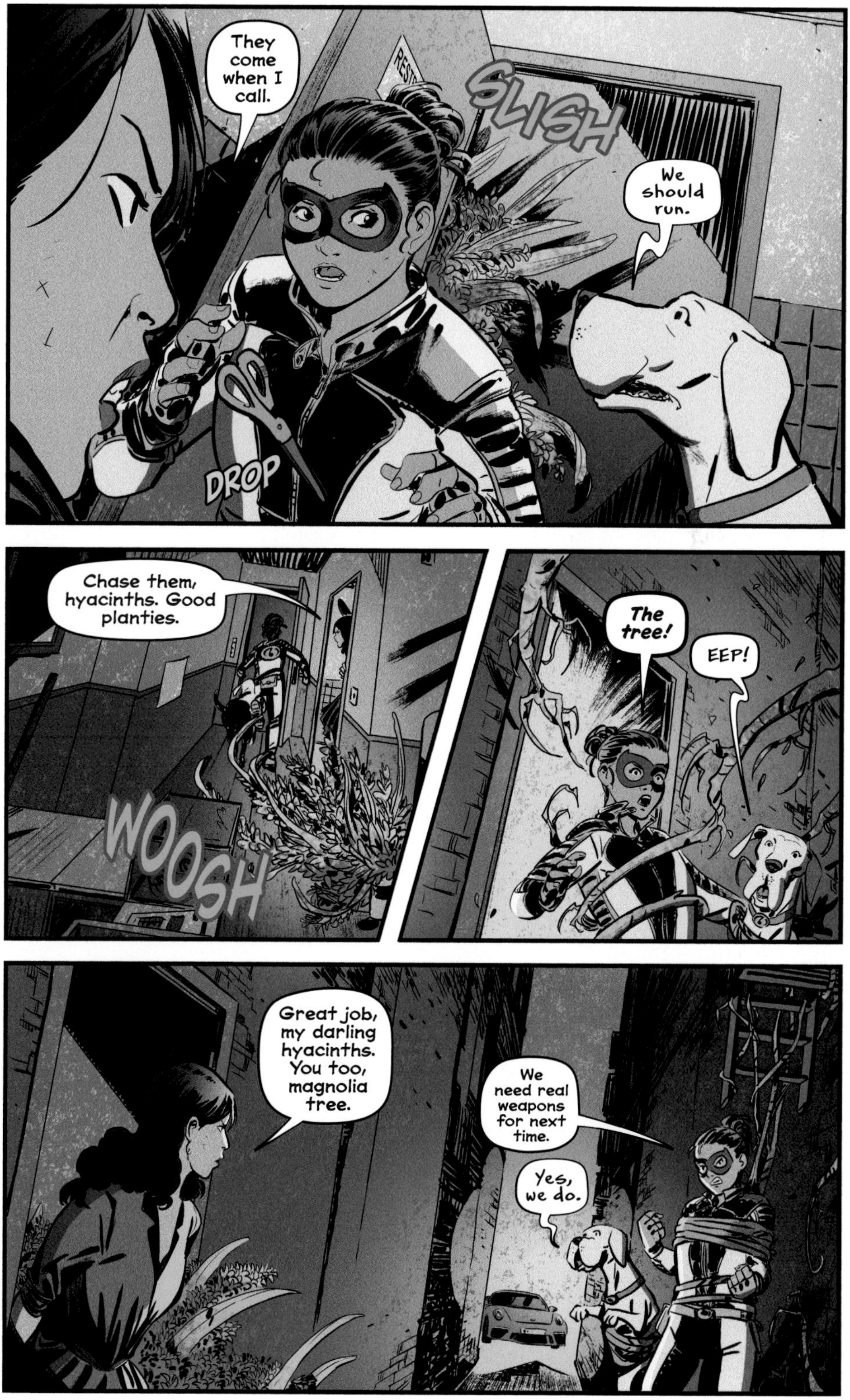
They come when I call.
SLISH
We should run.
DROP
Chase them, hyacinths. Good planties.
WOOSH
The tree!
EEP!
Great job, my darling hyacinths. You too, magnolia tree.
We need real weapons for next time.
Yes, we do.

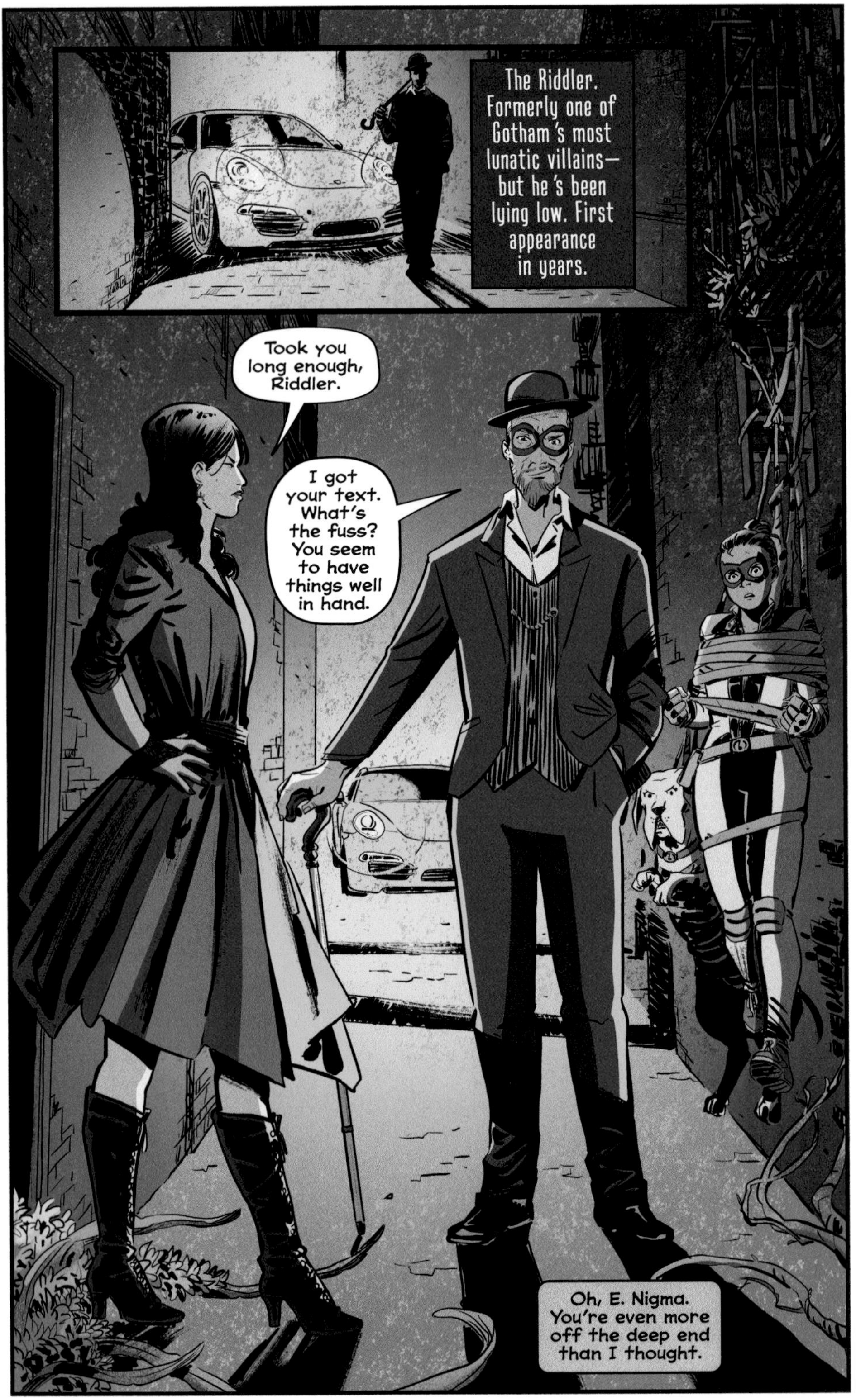
The Riddler. Formerly one of Gotham's most lunatic villains— but he's been lying low. First appearance in years.
Took you long enough, Riddler.
I got your text. What's the fuss? You seem to have things well in hand.
Oh, E. Nigma. You're even more off the deep end than I thought.

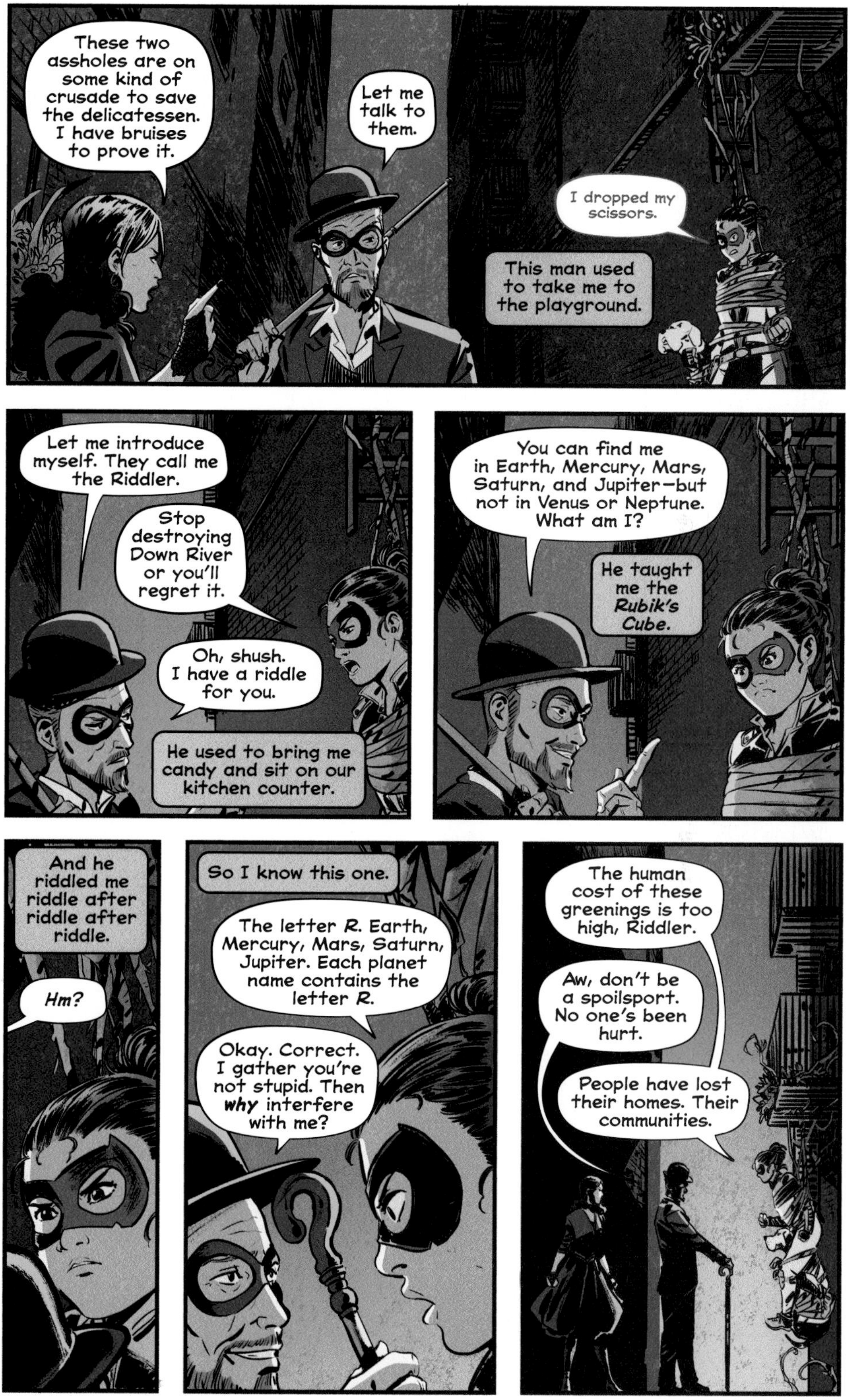
These two assholes are on some kind of crusade to save the delicatessen. I have bruises to prove it.
Let me talk to them.
I dropped my scissors.
This man used to take me to the playground.
Let me introduce myself. They call me the Riddler.
Stop destroying Down River or you'll regret it.
Oh, shush. I have a riddle for you.
He used to bring me candy and sit on our kitchen counter.
You can find me in Earth, Mercury, Mars, Saturn, and Jupiter—but not in Venus or Neptune. What am I?
He taught me the *Rubik's Cube.*
And he riddled me riddle after riddle after riddle.
Hm?
So I know this one.
The letter *R.* Earth, Mercury, Mars, Saturn, Jupiter. Each planet name contains the letter *R.*
Okay. Correct. I gather you're not stupid. Then ***why*** interfere with me?
The human cost of these greenings is too high, Riddler.
Aw, don't be a spoilsport. No one's been hurt.
People have lost their homes. Their communities.

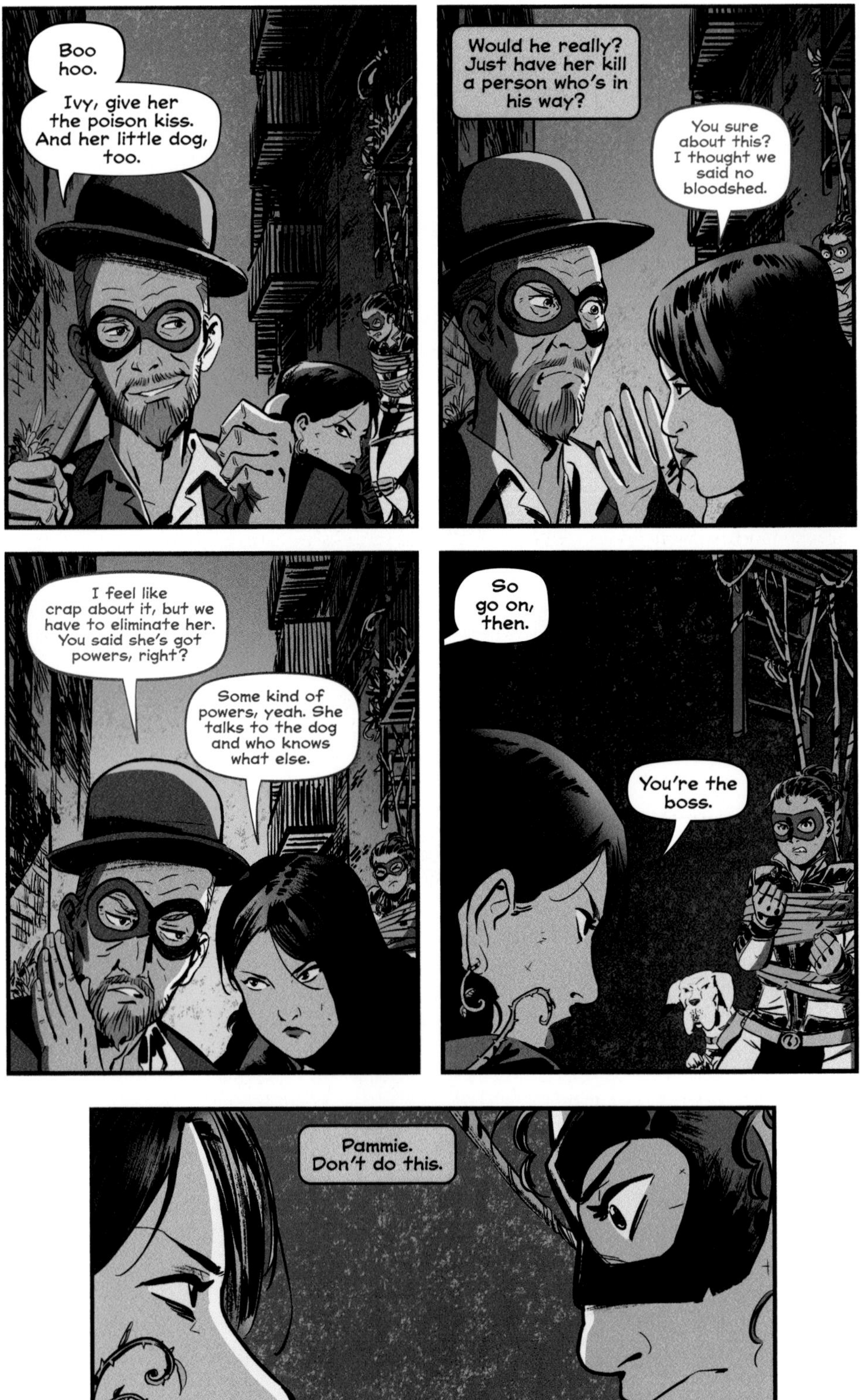
Boo hoo.
Ivy, give her the poison kiss. And her little dog, too.
Would he really? Just have her kill a person who's in his way?
You sure about this? I thought we said no bloodshed.
I feel like crap about it, but we have to eliminate her. You said she's got powers, right?
Some kind of powers, yeah. She talks to the dog and who knows what else.
So go on, then.
You're the boss.
Pammie. Don't do this.

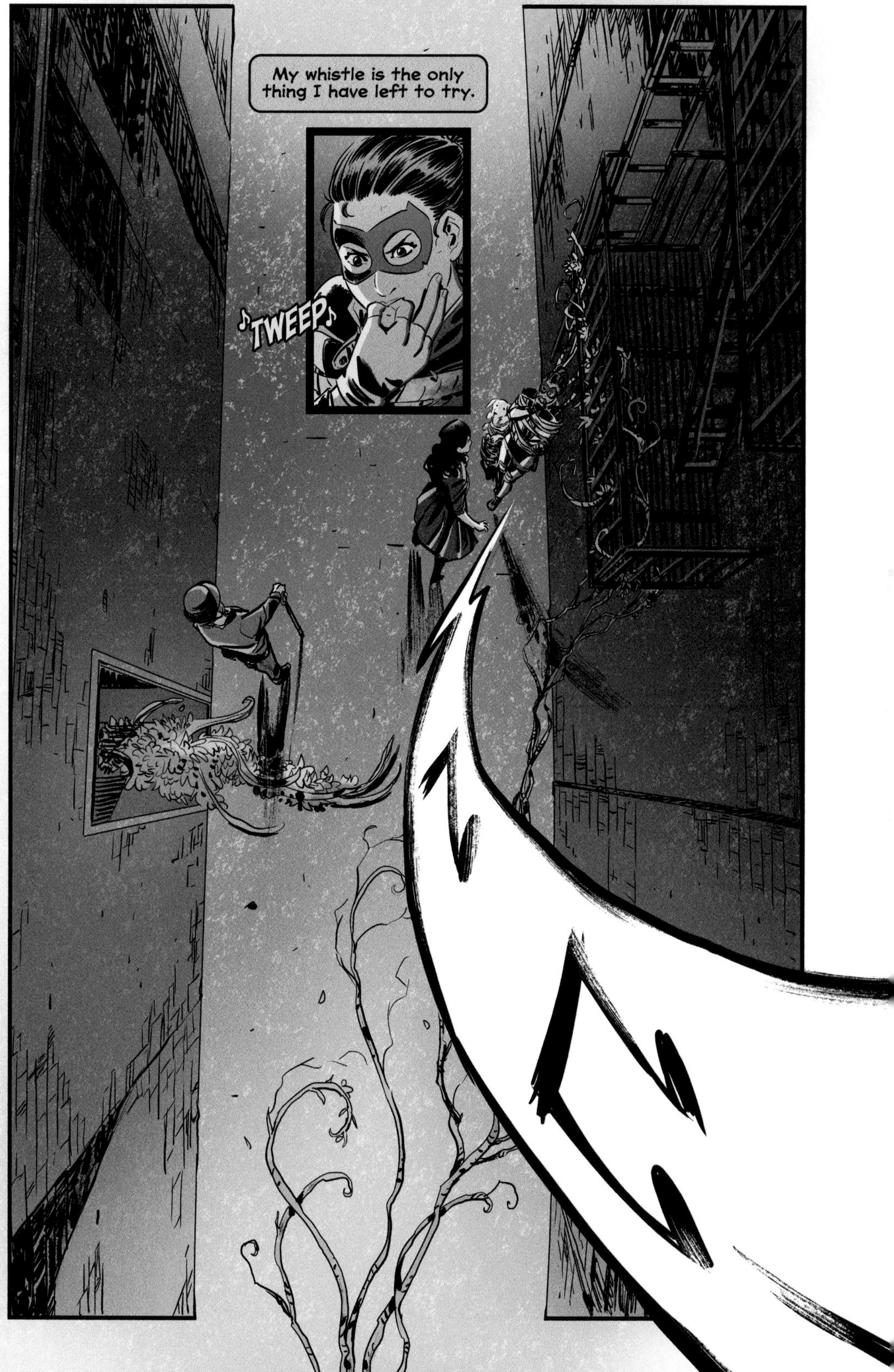
My whistle is the only thing I have left to try.
TWEEP

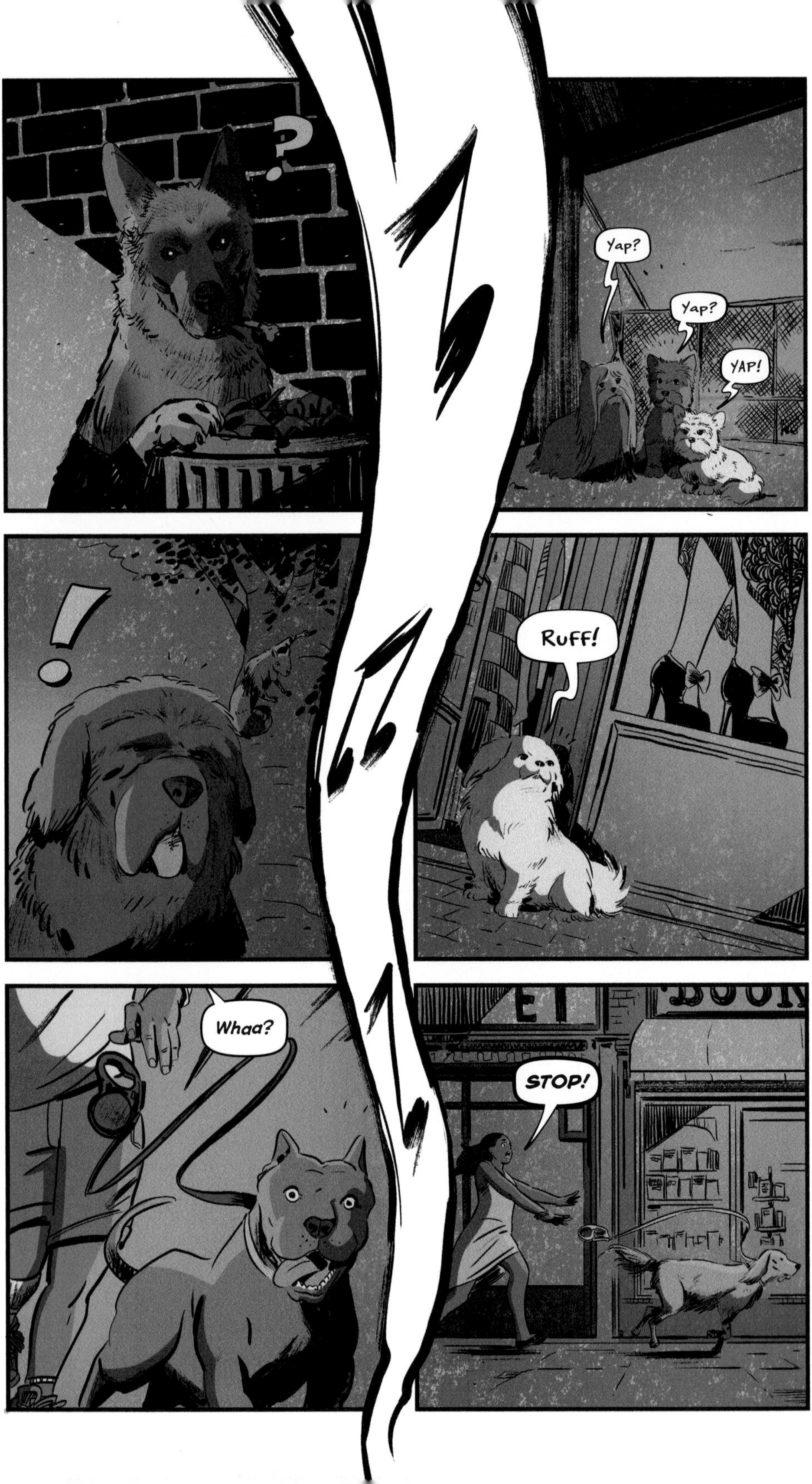
?
Yap?
Yap?
YAP!
!
RUFF!
Whaa?
STOP!

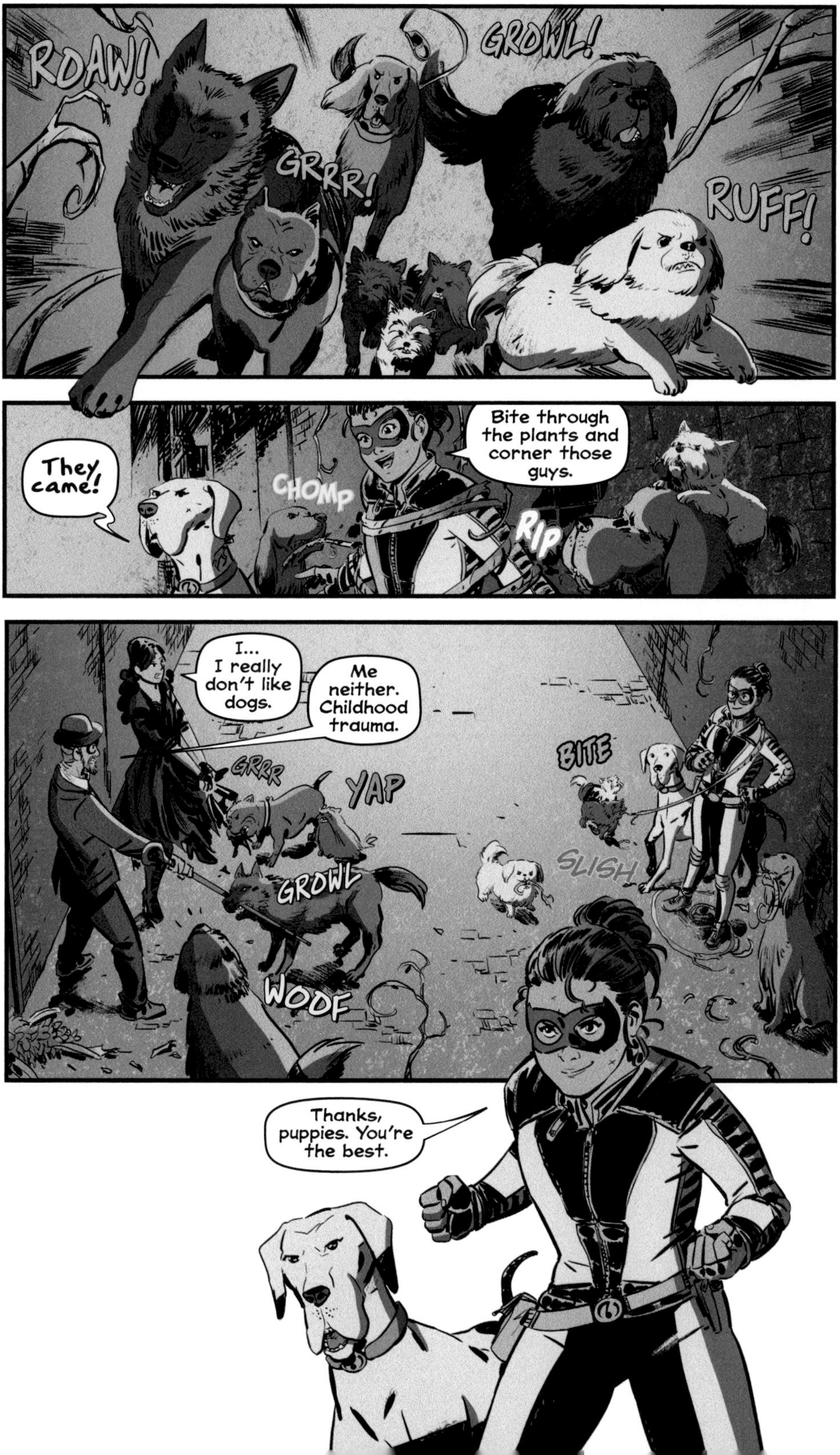

ROAW!
GROWL!
GRRRR!
RUFF!
They came!
CHOMP
Bite through the plants and corner those guys.
RIP
I... I really don't like dogs.
Me neither. Childhood trauma.
GRRR
YAP
BITE
SLISH
GROWL
WOOF
Thanks, puppies. You're the best.

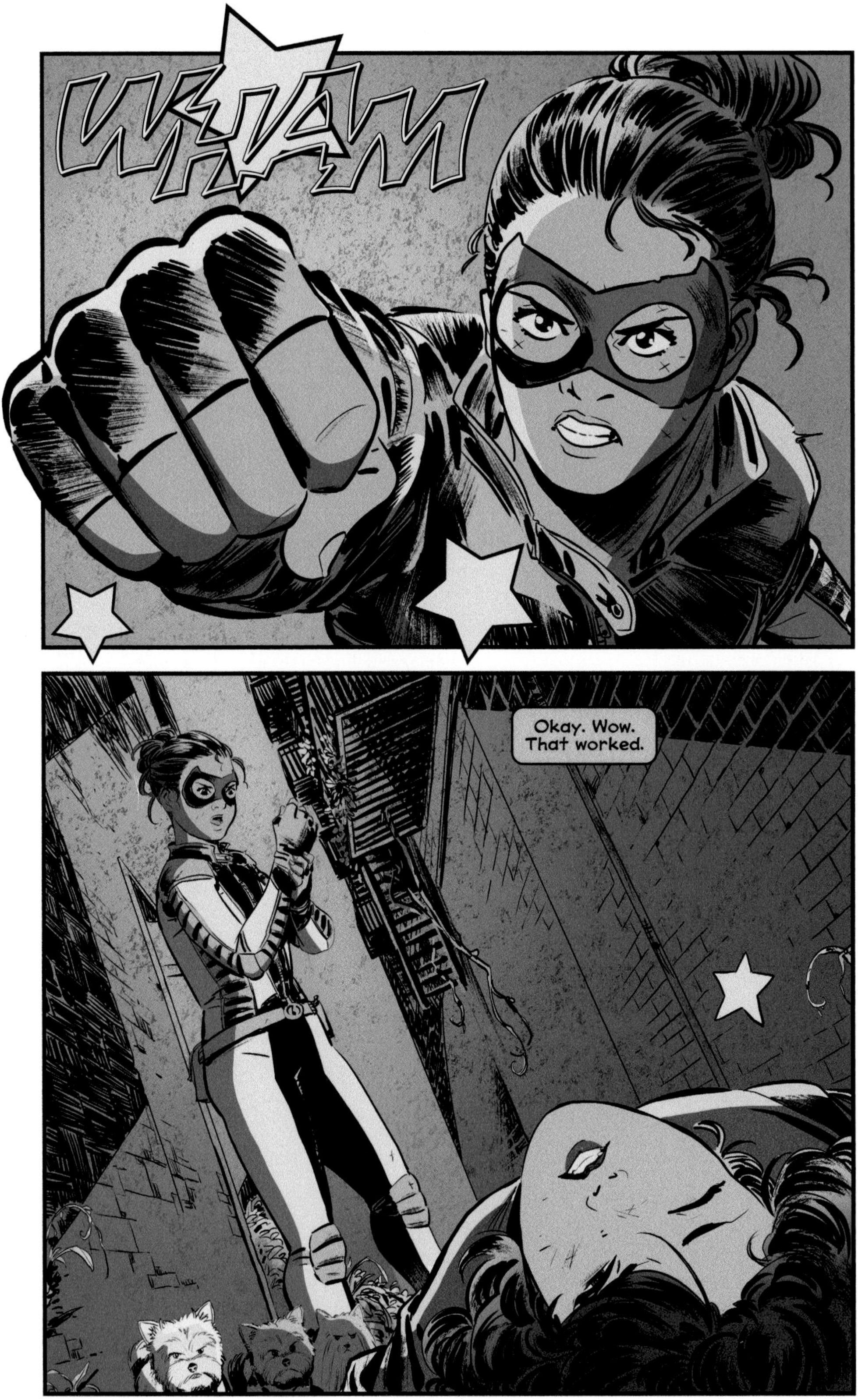
WHAM
Okay. Wow.
That worked.

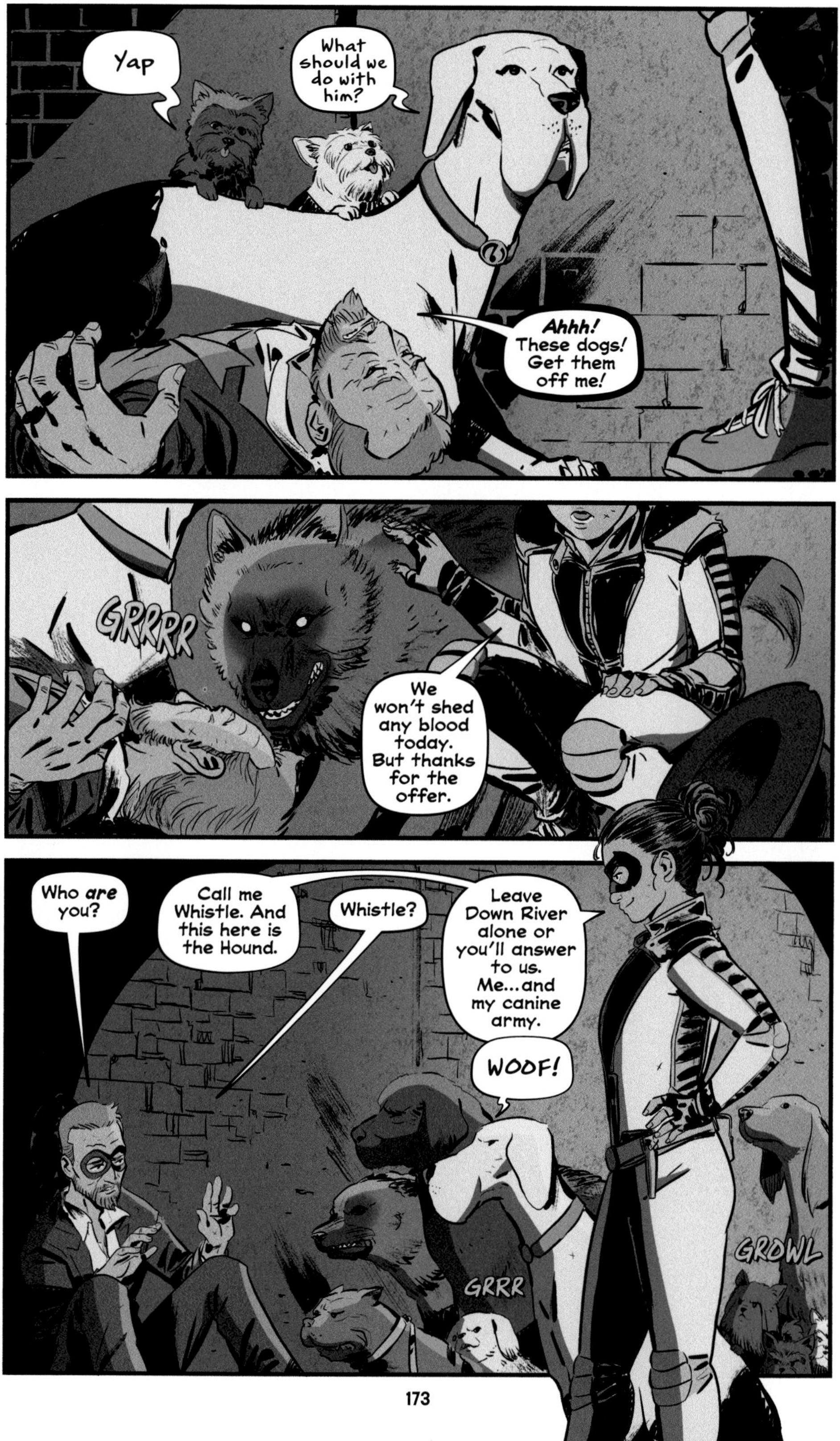
Yap
What should we do with him?
Ahhh! These dogs! Get them off me!
GRRRR
We won't shed any blood today. But thanks for the offer.
Who are you?
Call me Whistle. And this here is the Hound.
Whistle?
Leave Down River alone or you'll answer to us. Me...and my canine army.
WOOF!
GRRR
GROWL

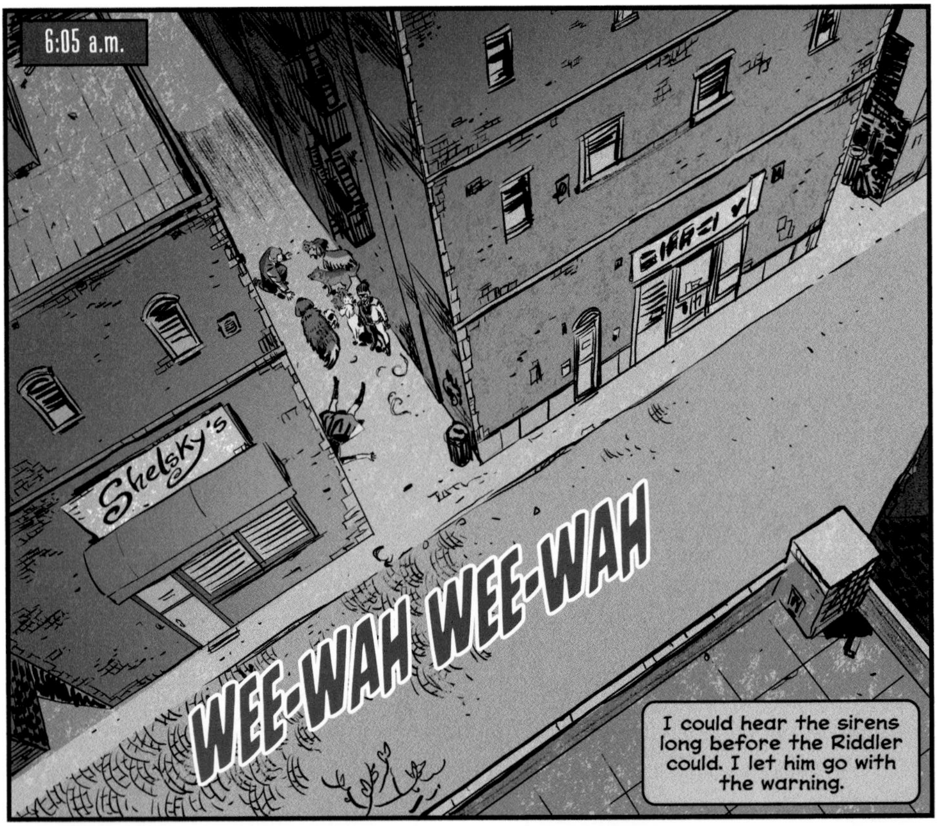
6:05 a.m.
Shelsky's
WEE-WAH WEE-WAH
I could hear the sirens long before the Riddler could. I let him go with the warning.

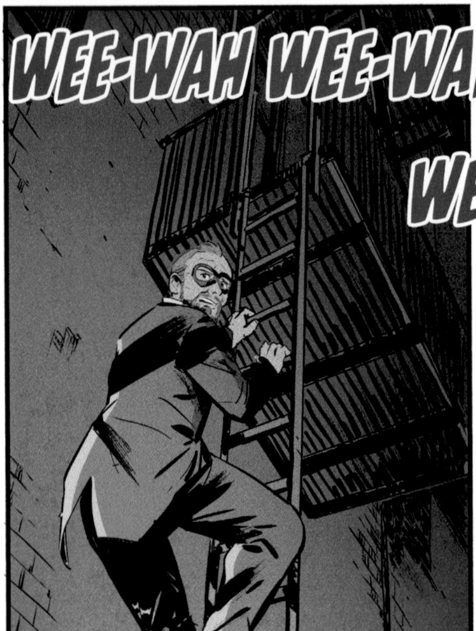
WEE-WAH WEE-WAH

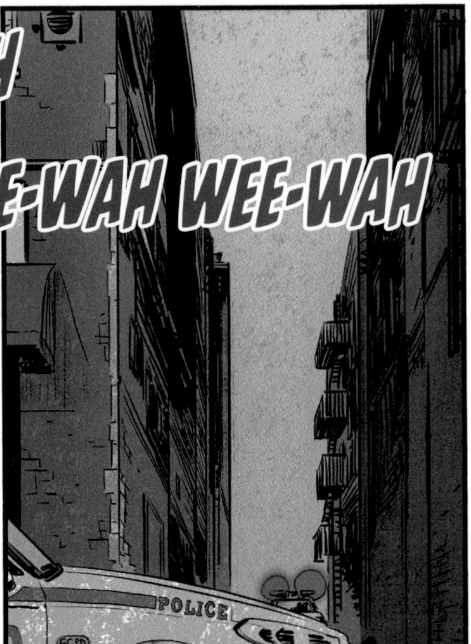
WEE-WAH WEE-WAH
POLICE

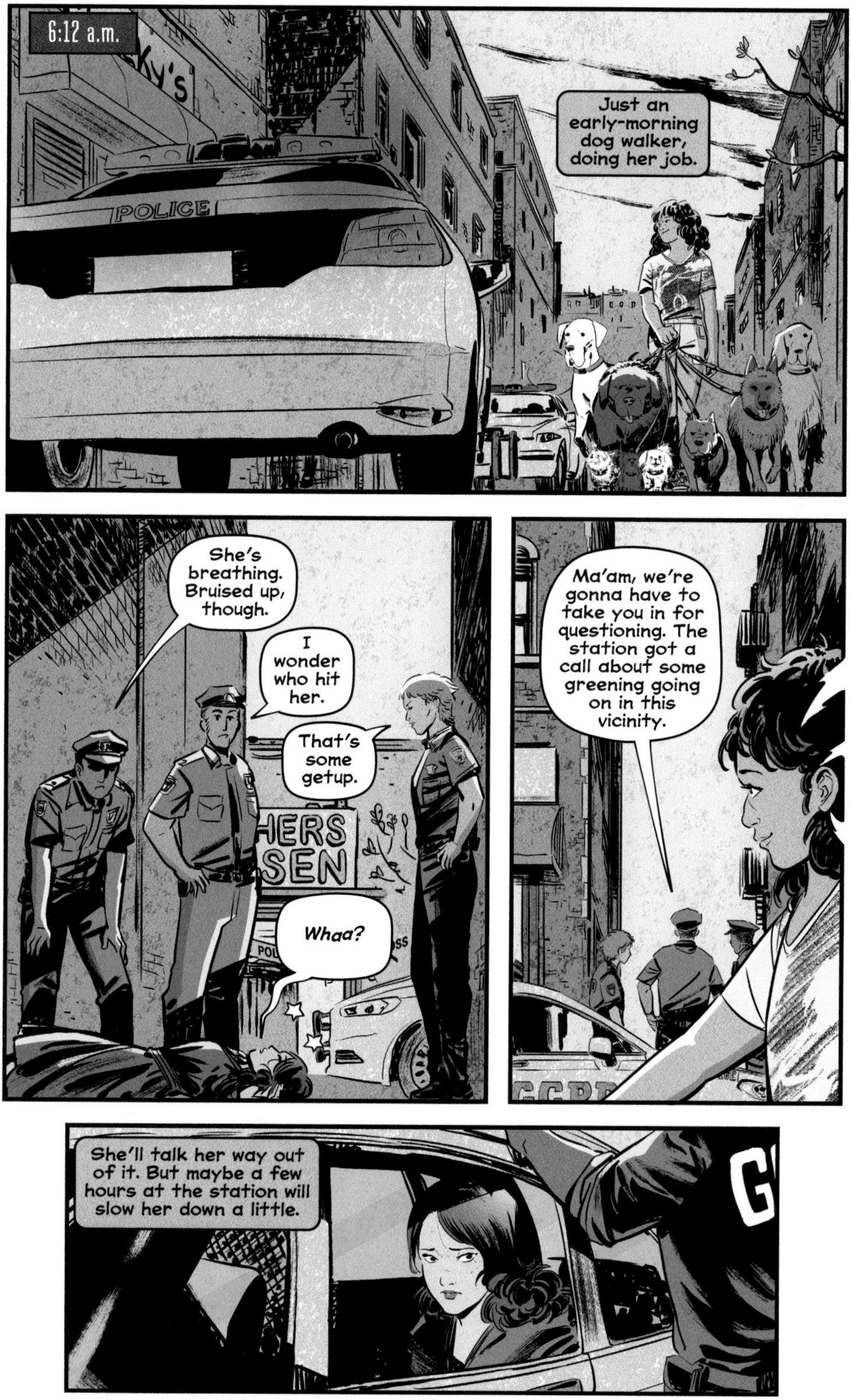
6:12 a.m.
Just an early-morning dog walker, doing her job.
POLICE
She's breathing. Bruised up, though.
I wonder who hit her.
That's some getup.
Whaa?
Ma'am, we're gonna have to take you in for questioning. The station got a call about some greening going on in this vicinity.
She'll talk her way out of it. But maybe a few hours at the station will slow her down a little.

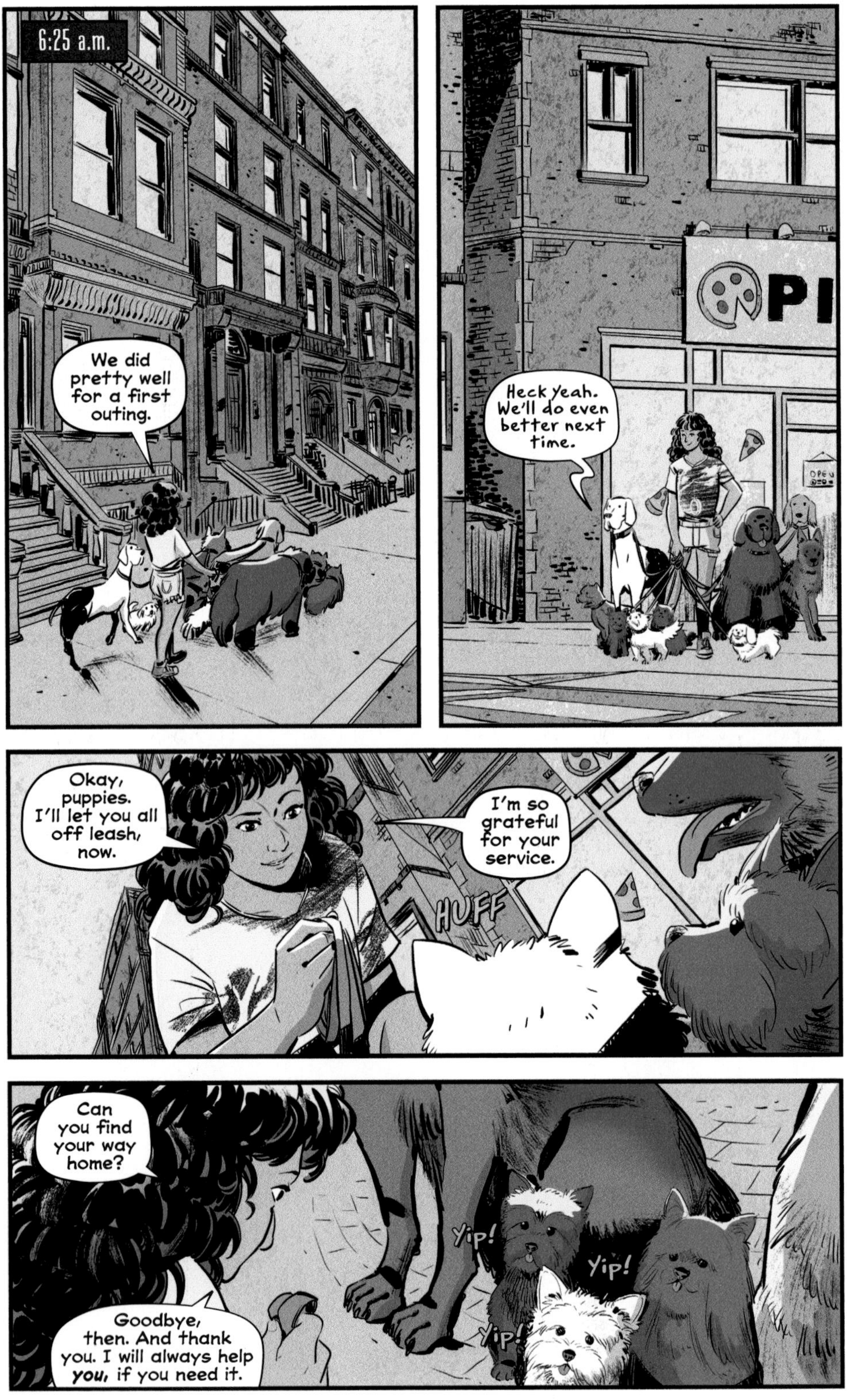
6:25 a.m.
We did pretty well for a first outing.
Heck yeah. We'll do even better next time.
PI
OPEN
Okay, puppies. I'll let you all off leash, now.
I'm so grateful for your service.
HUFF
Can you find your way home?
Yip!
Yip!
Yip!
Goodbye, then. And thank you. I will always help *you,* if you need it.

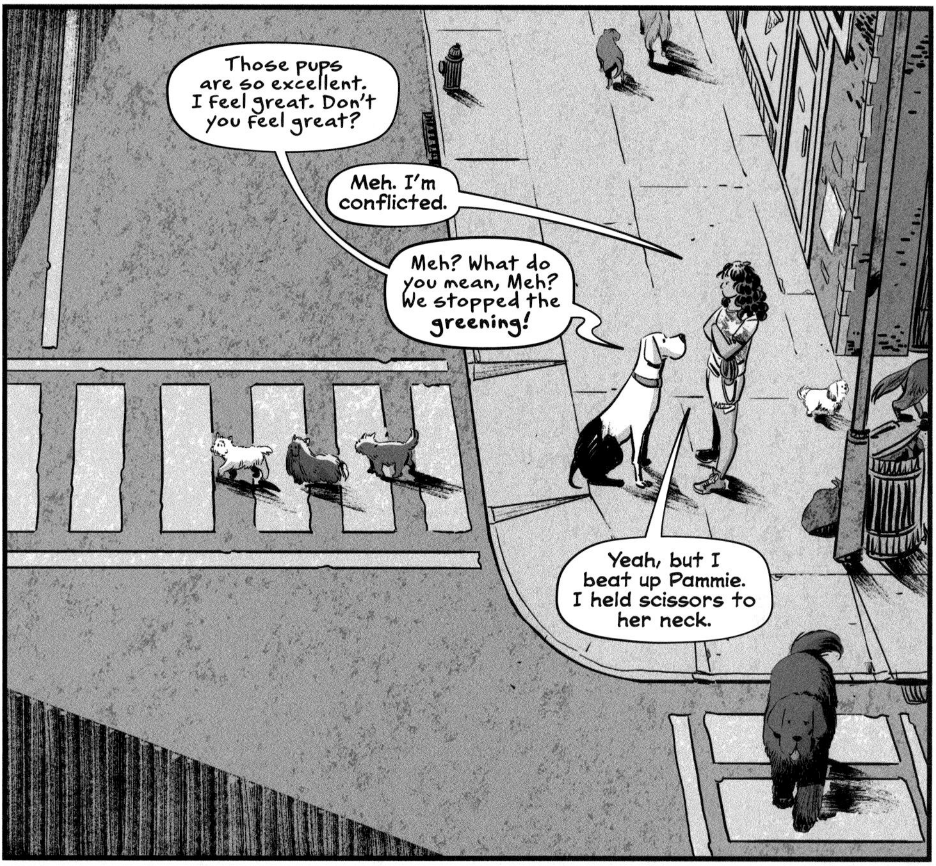

Those pups are so excellent. I feel great. Don't you feel great?
Meh. I'm conflicted.
Meh? What do you mean, Meh? We stopped the **greening!**
Yeah, but I beat up Pammie. I held scissors to her neck.

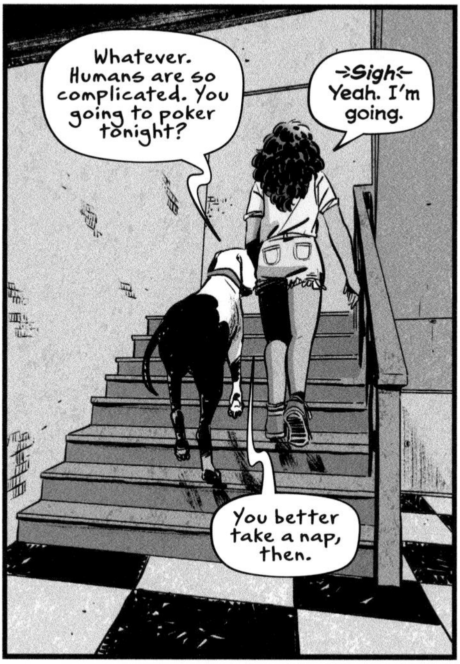

Whatever. Humans are so complicated. You going to poker tonight?
Sigh Yeah. I'm going.
You better take a nap, then.

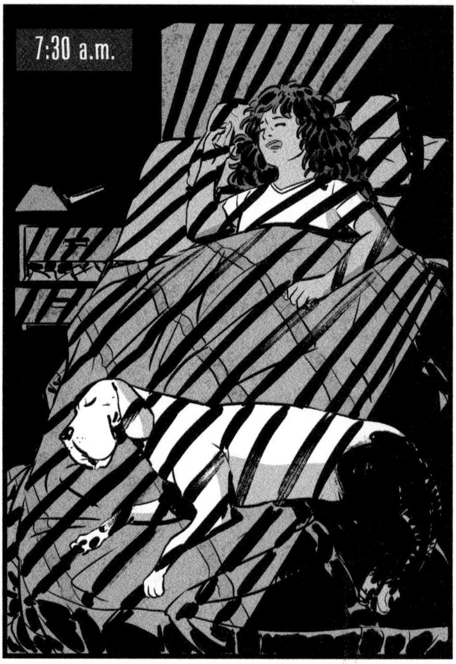

7:30 a.m.

part five: **new normal**

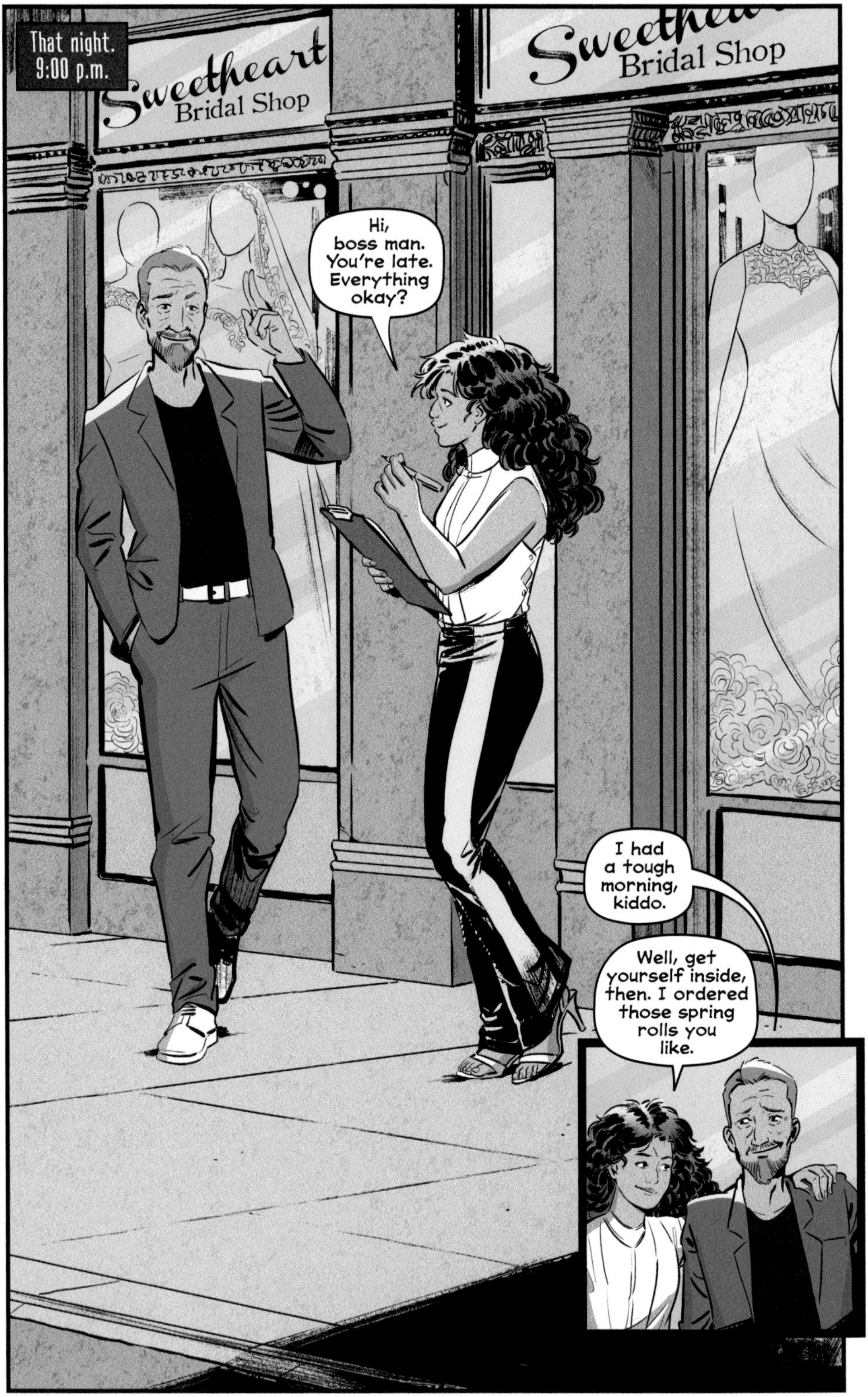
That night.
9:00 p.m.
Sweetheart Bridal Shop
Sweetheart Bridal Shop
Hi, boss man. You're late. Everything okay?
I had a tough morning, kiddo.
Well, get yourself inside, then. I ordered those spring rolls you like.

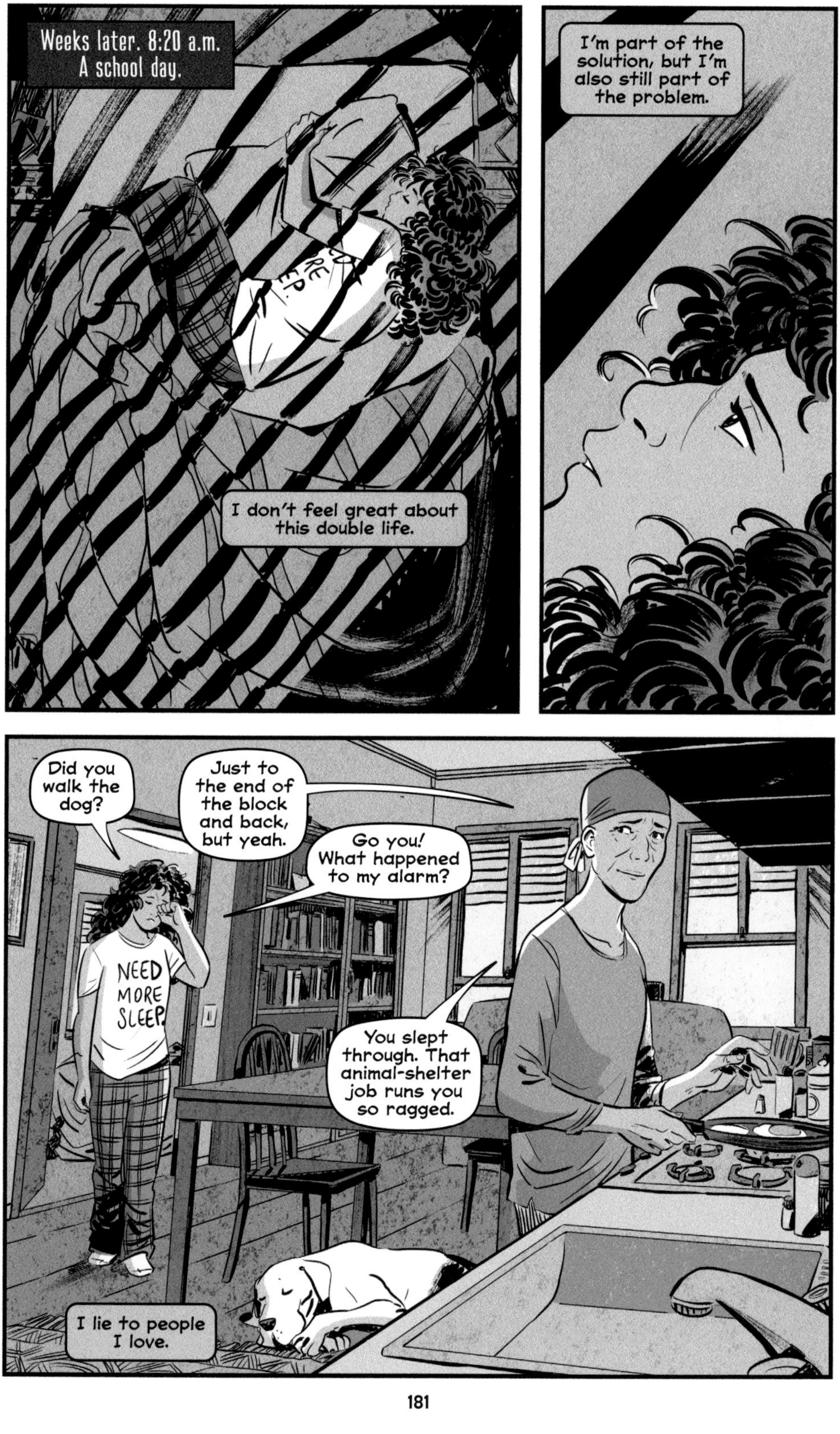
Weeks later. 8:20 a.m. A school day.
I don't feel great about this double life.
I'm part of the solution, but I'm also still part of the problem.
Did you walk the dog?
Just to the end of the block and back, but yeah.
Go you! What happened to my alarm?
NEED MORE SLEEP
You slept through. That animal-shelter job runs you so ragged.
I lie to people I love.

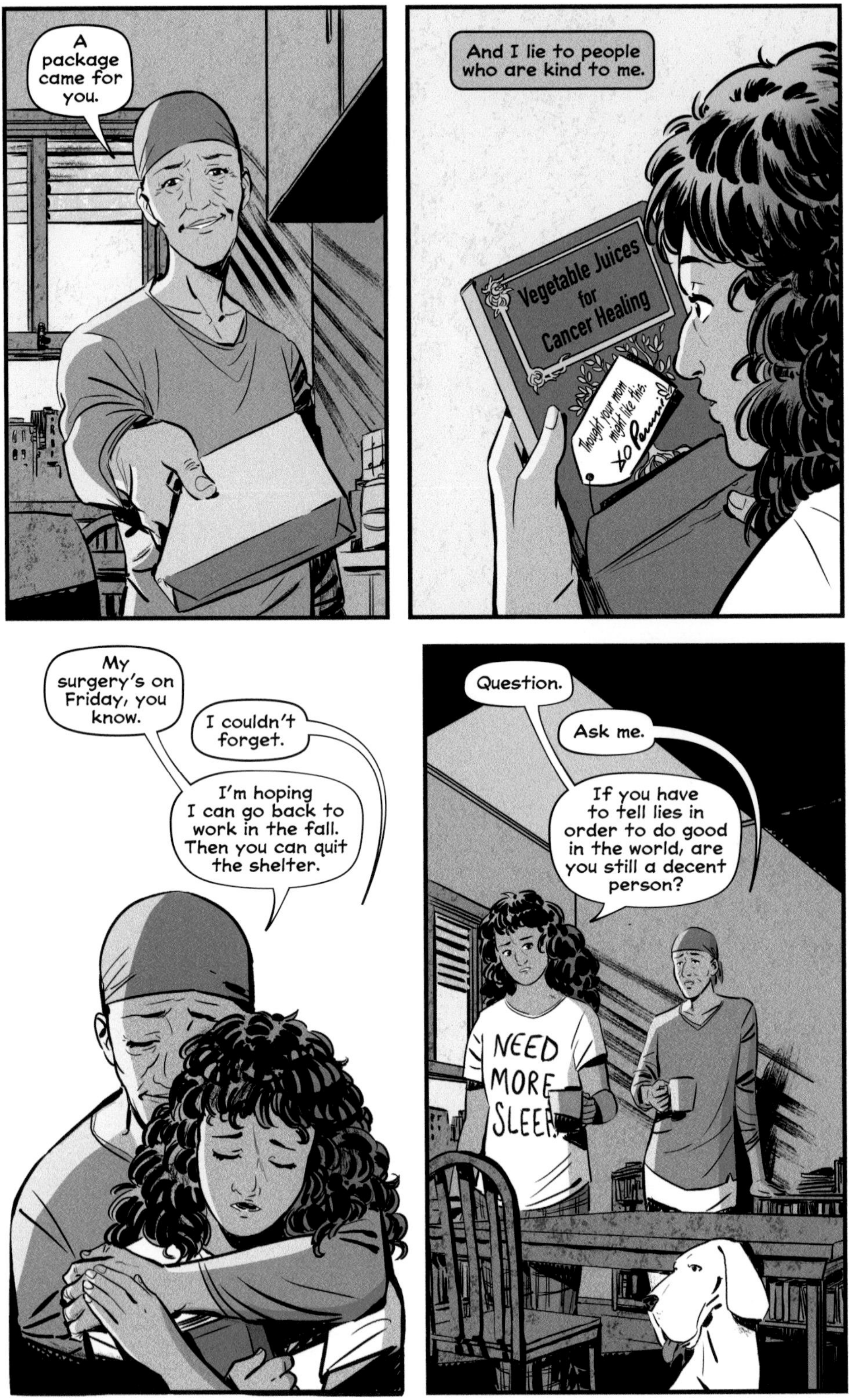
A package came for you.
And I lie to people who are kind to me.
Vegetable Juices for Cancer Healing
Thought your mom might like this.
My surgery's on Friday, you know.
I couldn't forget.
I'm hoping I can go back to work in the fall. Then you can quit the shelter.
Question.
Ask me.
If you have to tell lies in order to do good in the world, are you still a decent person?
NEED MORE SLEEP

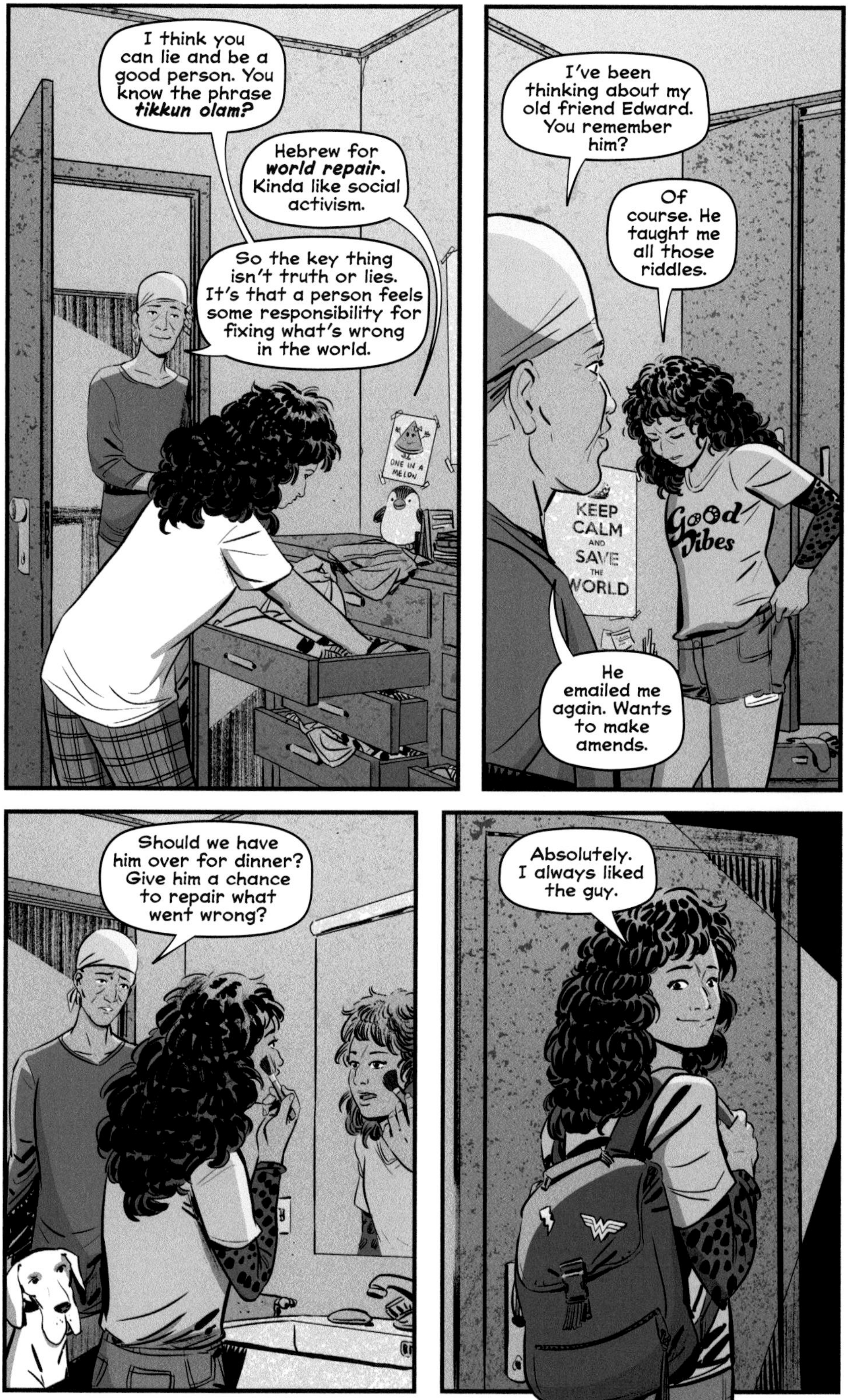
I think you can lie and be a good person. You know the phrase ***tikkun olam?***
Hebrew for ***world repair.*** Kinda like social activism.
So the key thing isn't truth or lies. It's that a person feels some responsibility for fixing what's wrong in the world.
ONE IN A MELON
I've been thinking about my old friend Edward. You remember him?
Of course. He taught me all those riddles.
KEEP CALM AND SAVE THE WORLD
Good Vibes
He emailed me again. Wants to make amends.
Should we have him over for dinner? Give him a chance to repair what went wrong?
Absolutely. I always liked the guy.

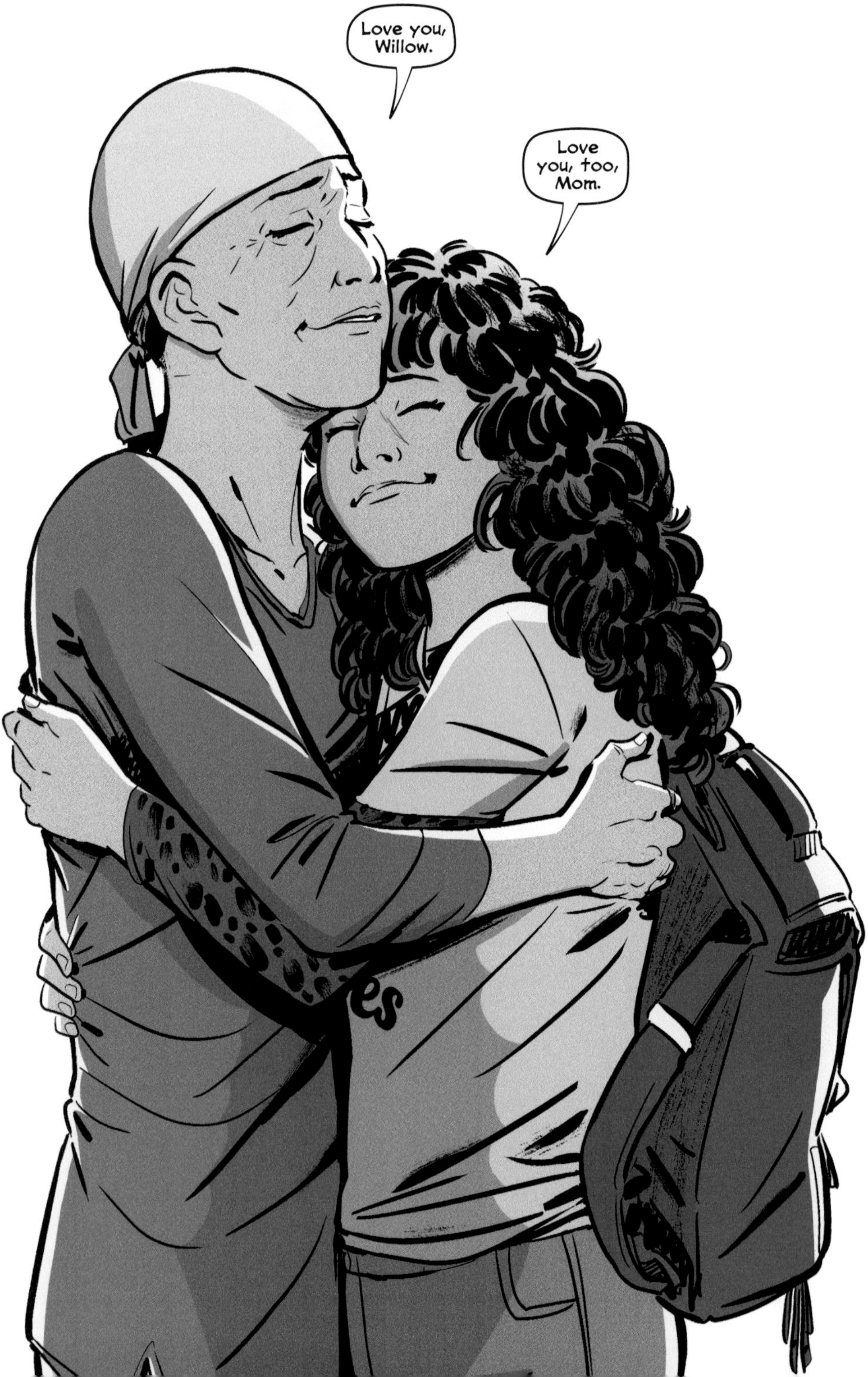
Love you, Willow.
Love you, too, Mom.

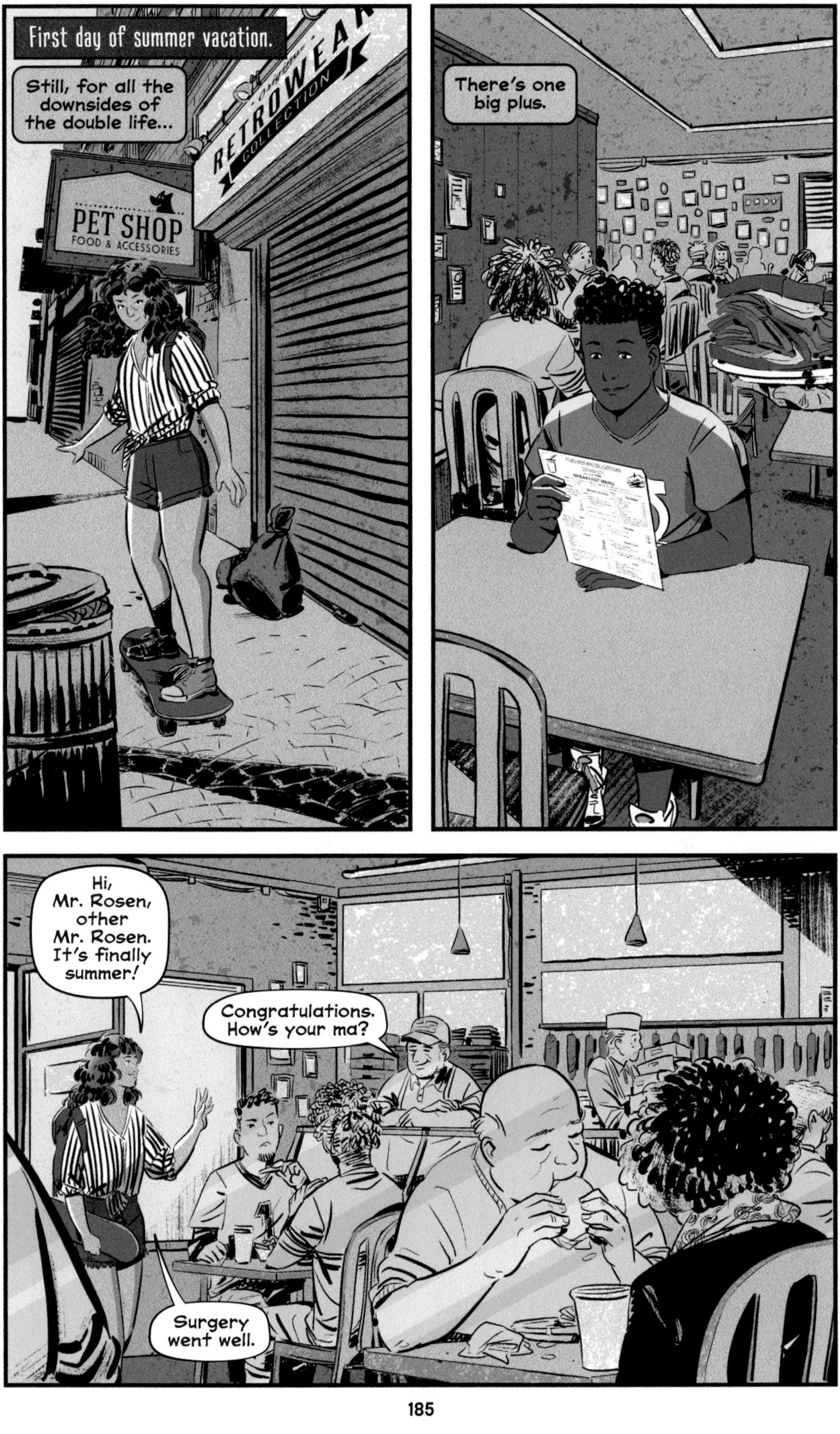
First day of summer vacation.
Still, for all the downsides of the double life...
RETROWEAR COLLECTION
PET SHOP
FOOD & ACCESSORIES
There's one big plus.
Hi, Mr. Rosen, other Mr. Rosen. It's finally summer!
Congratulations. How's your ma?
Surgery went well.

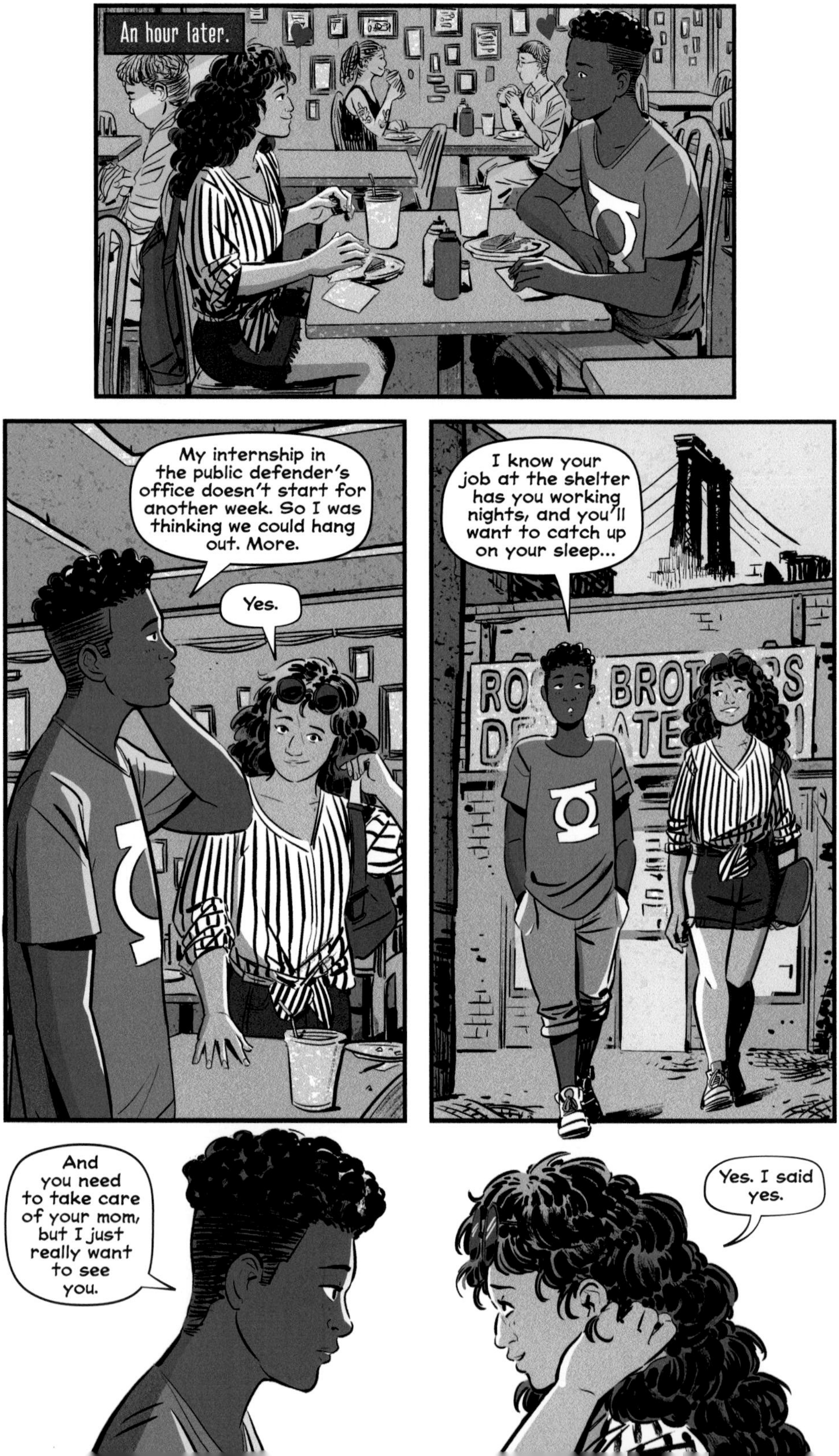

An hour later.
My internship in the public defender's office doesn't start for another week. So I was thinking we could hang out. More.
Yes.
I know your job at the shelter has you working nights, and you'll want to catch up on your sleep...
And you need to take care of your mom, but I just really want to see you.
Yes. I said yes.

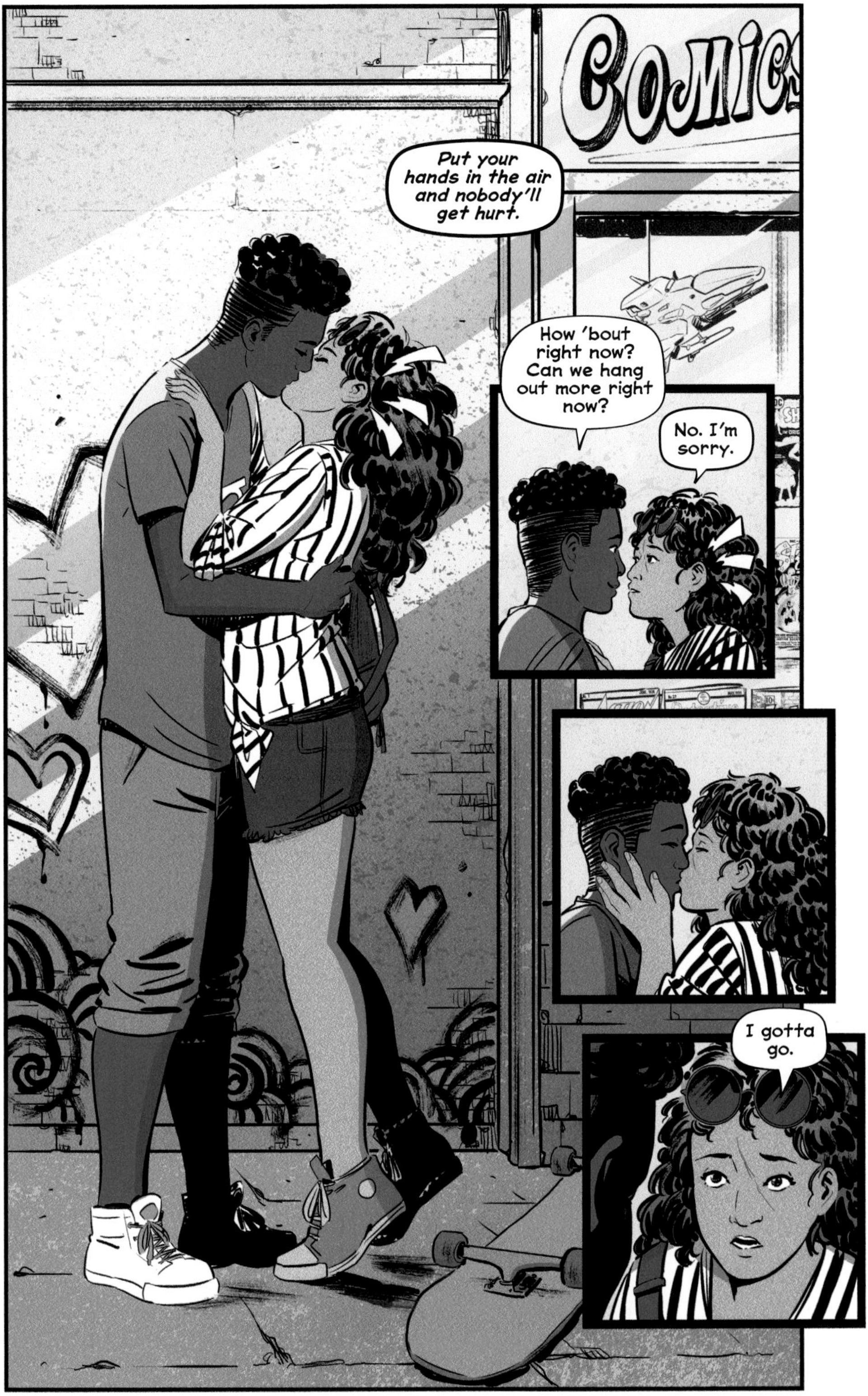
COMICS
Put your hands in the air and nobody'll get hurt.
How 'bout right now? Can we hang out more right now?
No. I'm sorry.
I gotta go.

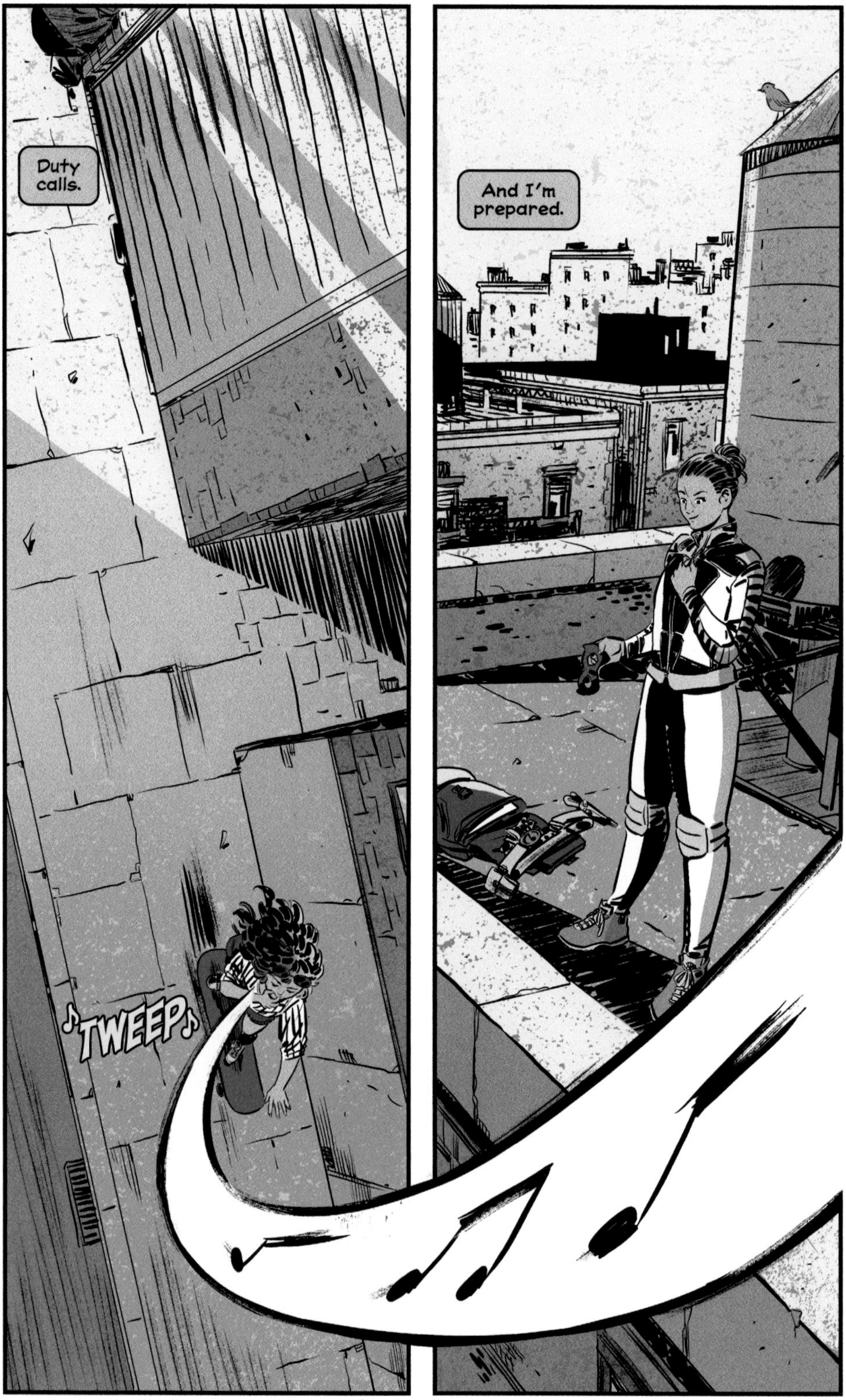
Duty calls.
TWEEP
And I'm prepared.

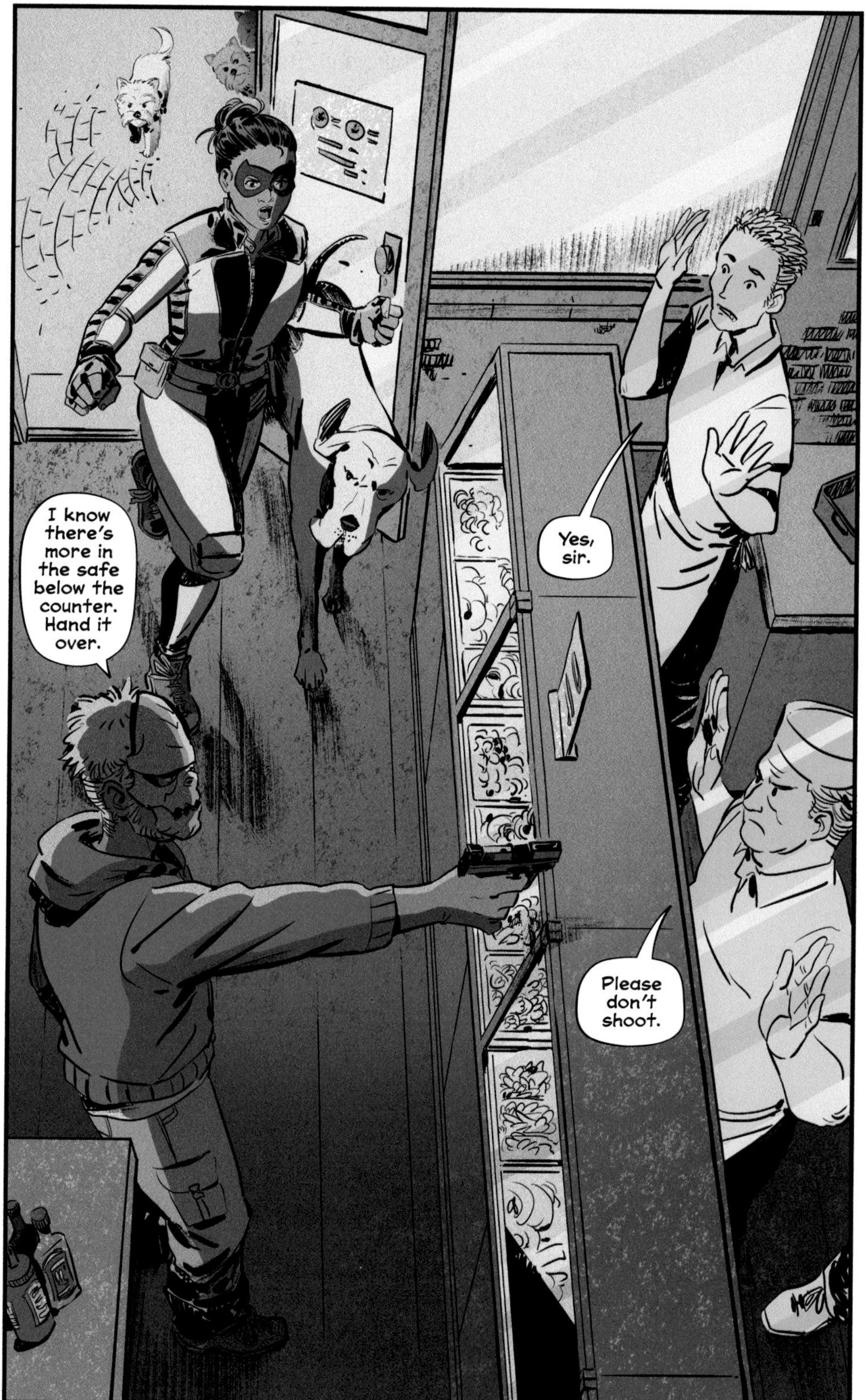
I know there's more in the safe below the counter. Hand it over.
Yes, sir.
Please don't shoot.

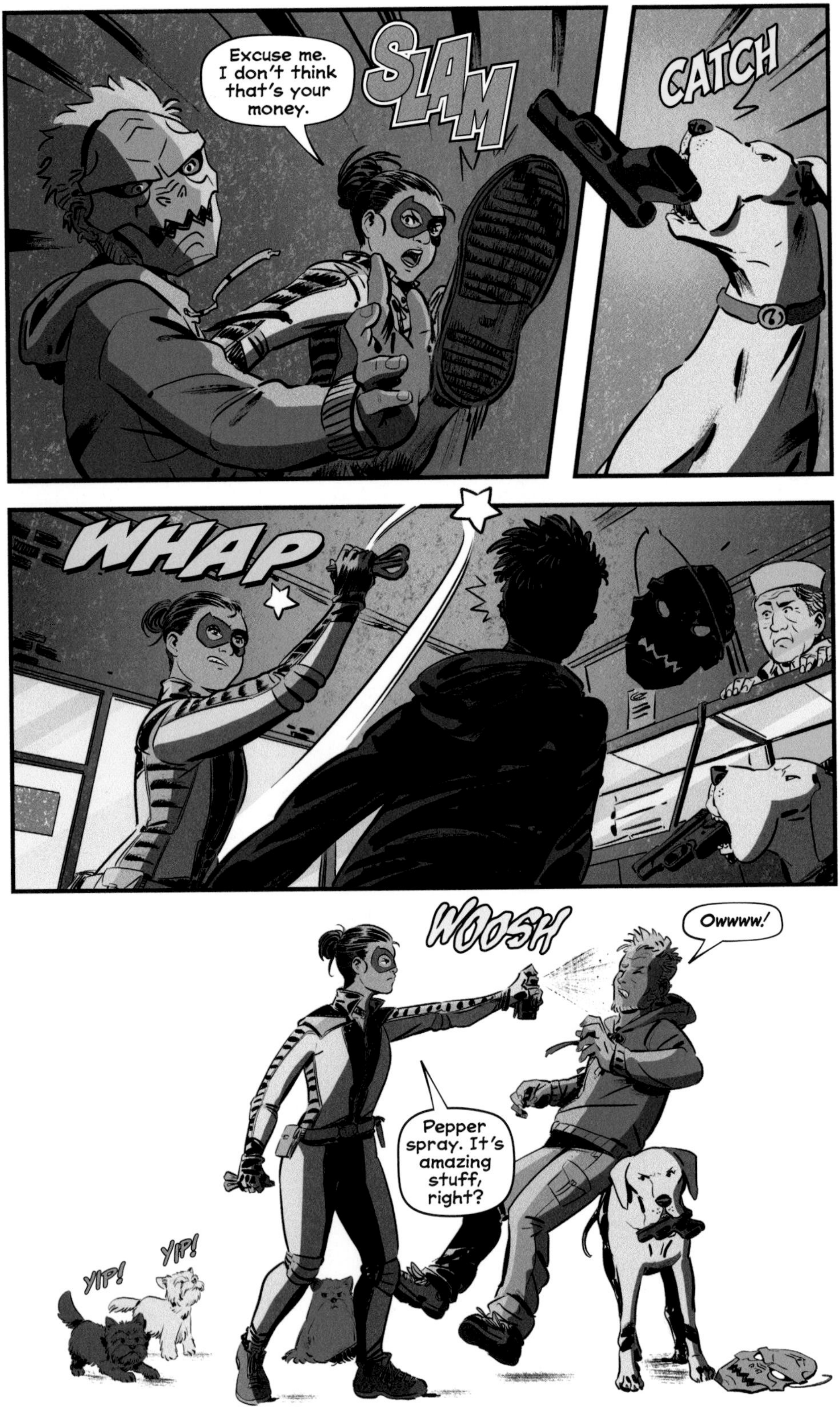
Excuse me. I don't think that's your money.
SLAM
CATCH
WHAP
WOOSH
Owwww!
Pepper spray. It's amazing stuff, right?
YIP!
YIP!

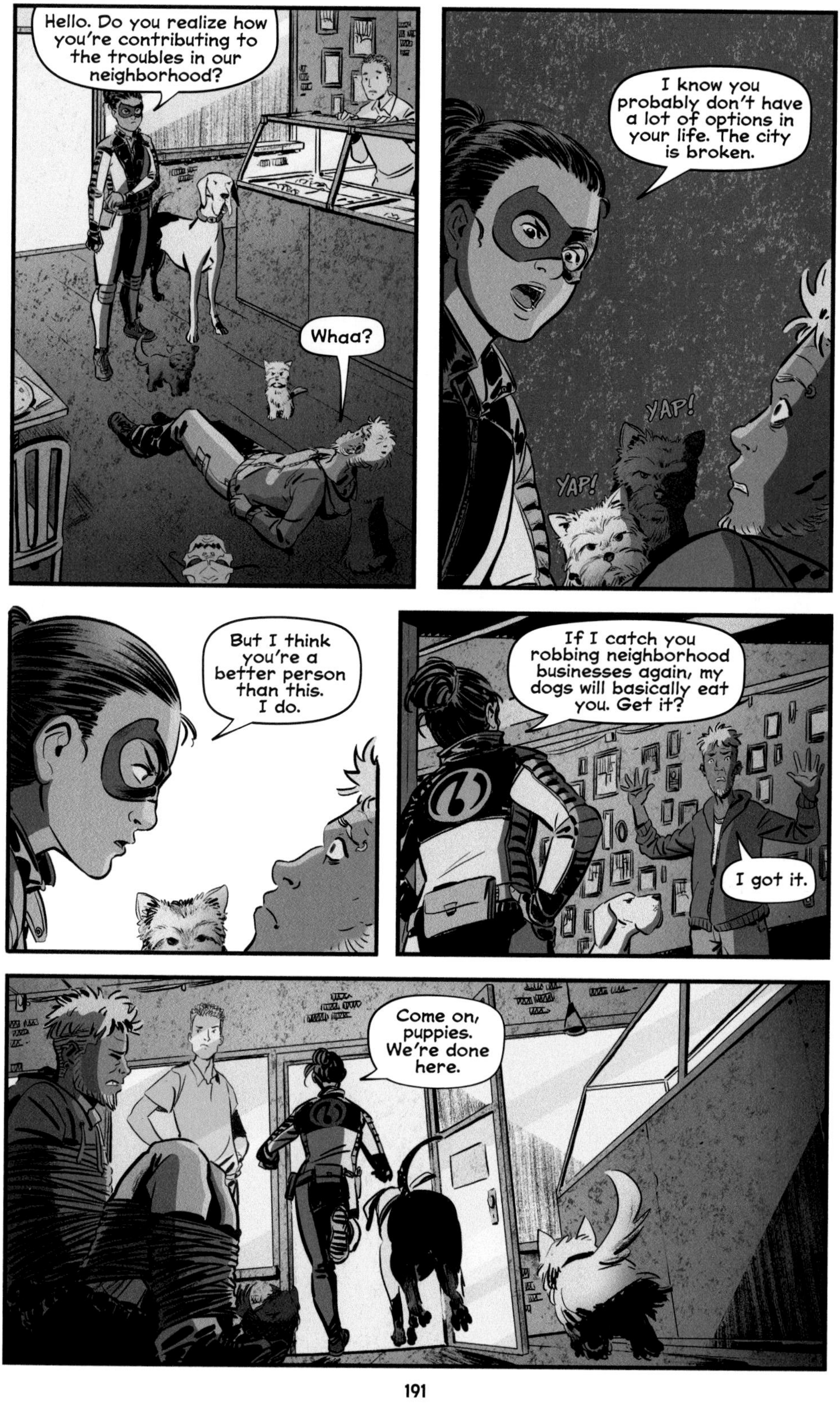
Hello. Do you realize how you're contributing to the troubles in our neighborhood?
Whaa?
I know you probably don't have a lot of options in your life. The city is broken.
YAP!
YAP!
But I think you're a better person than this. I do.
If I catch you robbing neighborhood businesses again, my dogs will basically eat you. Get it?
I got it.
Come on, puppies. We're done here.

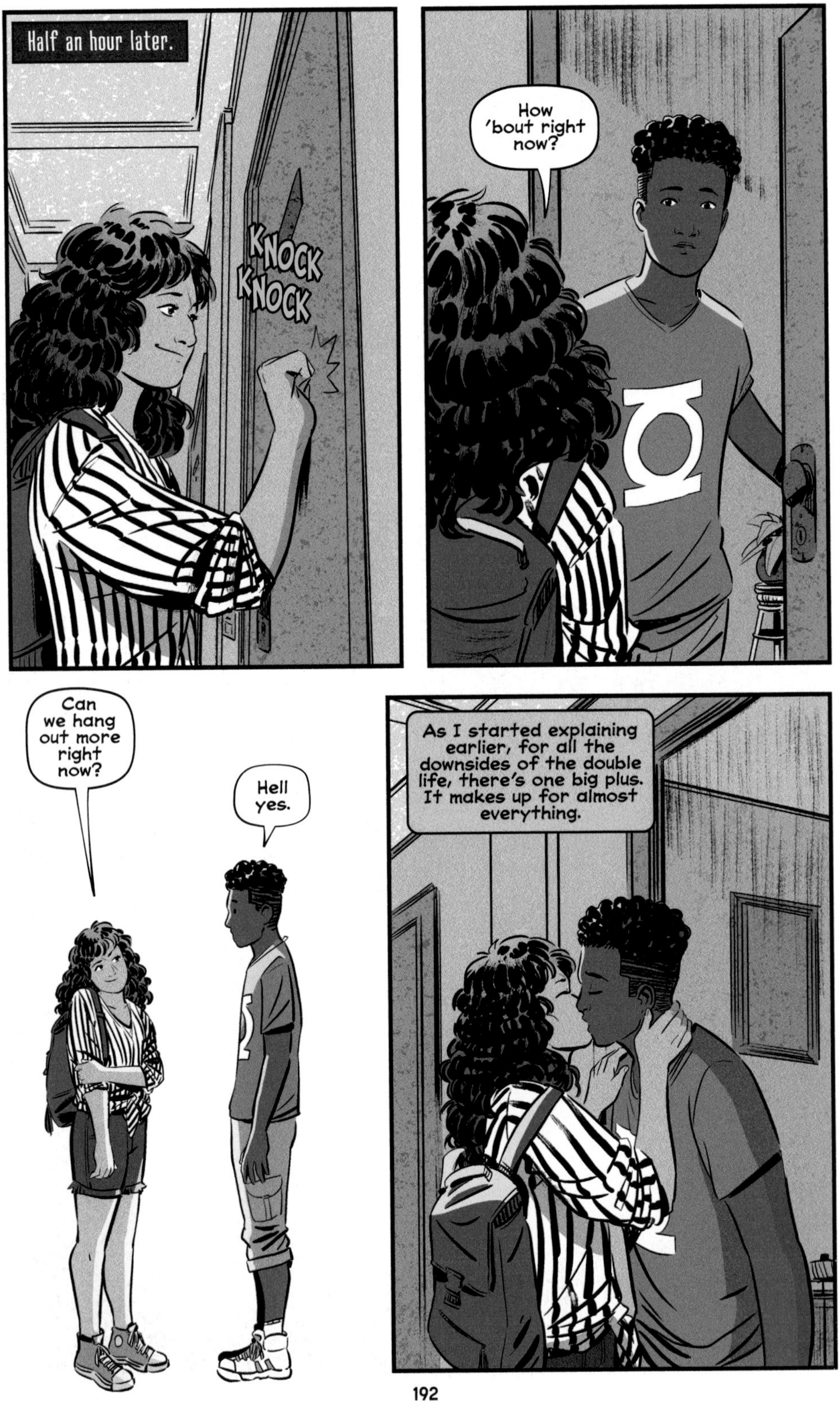
Half an hour later.
KNOCK KNOCK
How 'bout right now?
Can we hang out more right now?
Hell yes.
As I started explaining earlier, for all the downsides of the double life, there's one big plus. It makes up for almost everything.

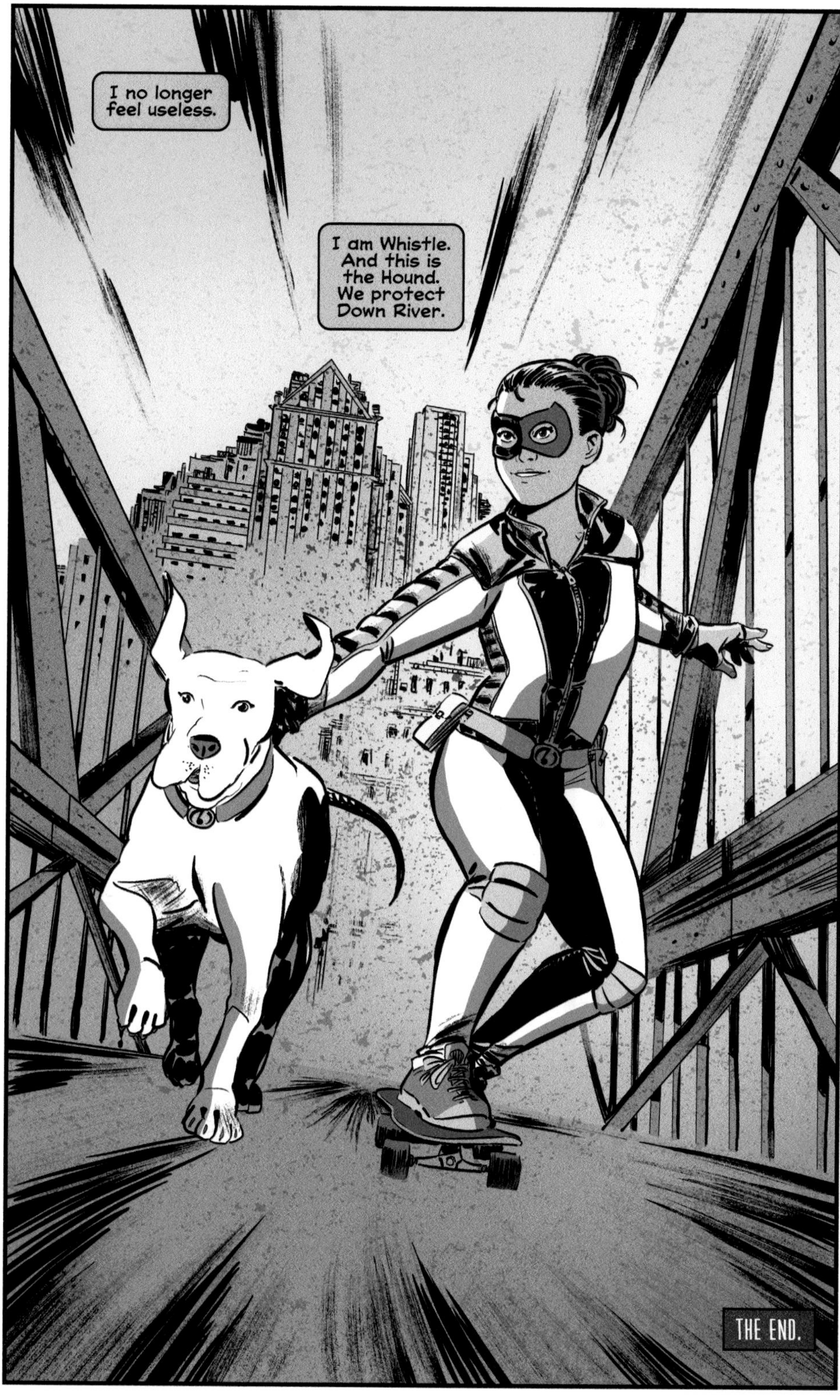
I no longer feel useless.
I am Whistle. And this is the Hound. We protect Down River.
THE END.

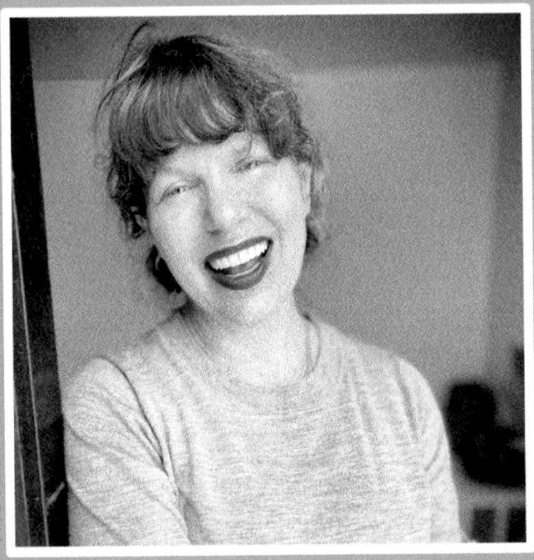

PHOTO BY HEATHER WESTON

e. lockhart

is the author of the *New York Times* bestsellers *Genuine Fraud* and *We Were Liars*. Her latest novel is *Again Again*. Other books include *The Disreputable History of Frankie Landau-Banks*, which was a National Book Award finalist and a Printz honor book. Twitter: @elockhart. Instagram: @elockhartbooks.

manuel preitano

is an Italian illustrator and graphic
designer, the co-creator of
the Destiny, NY series, and
illustrator of *The Oracle Code*,
written by Marieke Nijkamp and
published by DC Coimcs. He has
worked on a wide range of toy
designs, book covers, illustrations,
and comic books, both in the U.S.
and in Italy. He resides in Italy
with his comic book collection
and his beloved drawing tablet.
Instagram: @manuelcomicart.

Acclaimed author **Lilliam Rivera** and
artist **Steph C.** reimagine one of DC's
greatest Green Lanterns, Jessica Cruz,
to tell a story about immigration, family,
and overcoming fear to inspire hope.

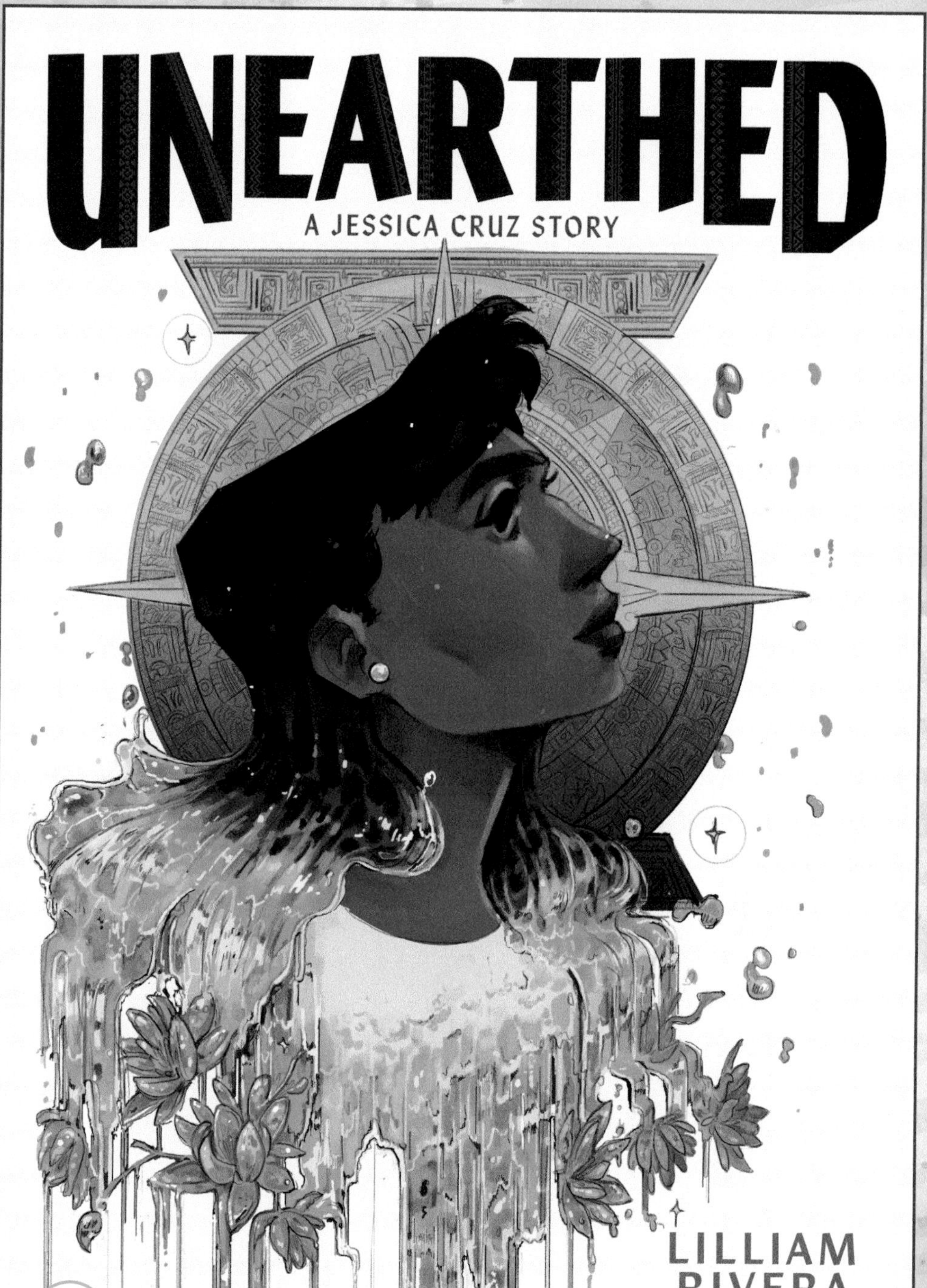
UNEARTHED
A JESSICA CRUZ STORY
LILLIAM RIVERA
STEPH C.

Turn the page for a sneak peek!

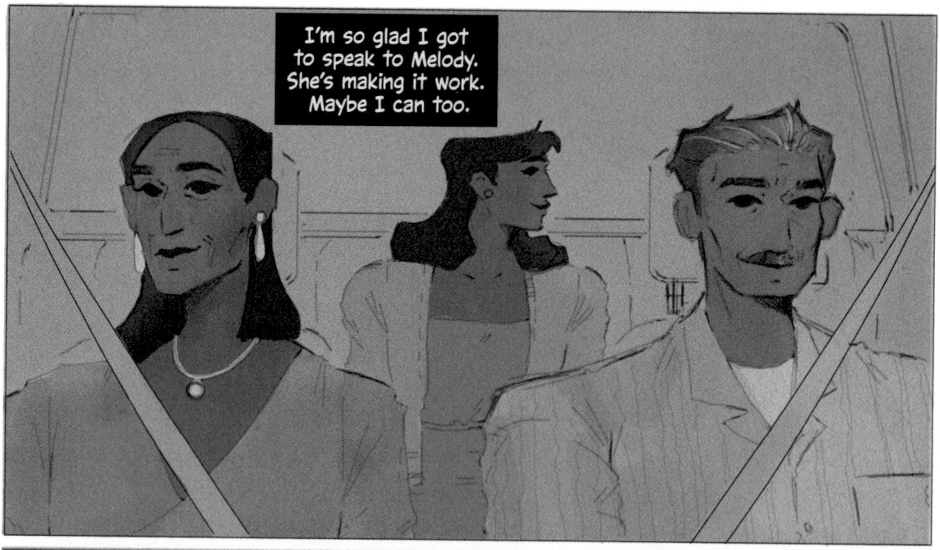
I'm so glad I got to speak to Melody. She's making it work. Maybe I can too.
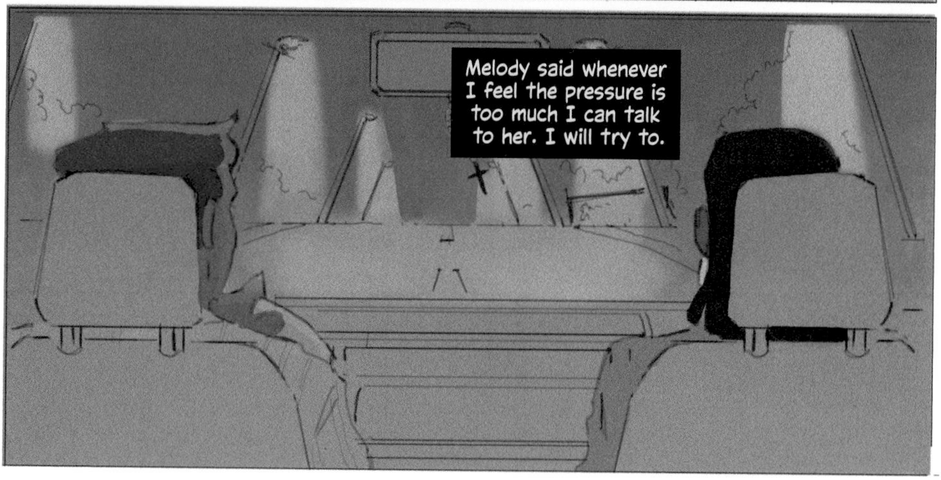
Melody said whenever I feel the pressure is too much I can talk to her. I will try to.
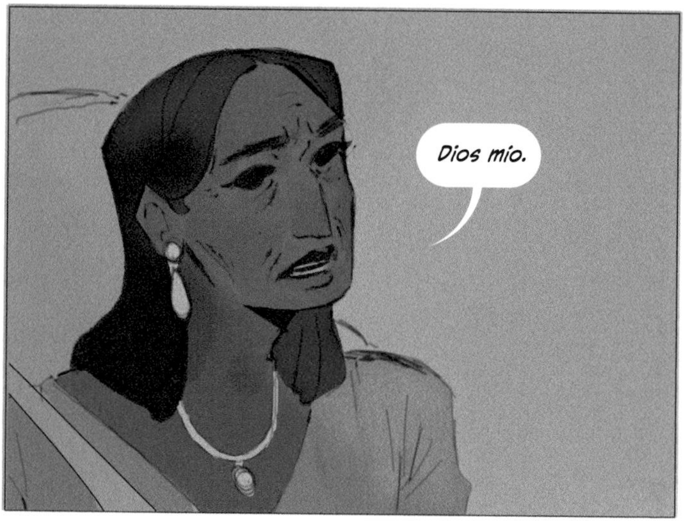
Dios mio.

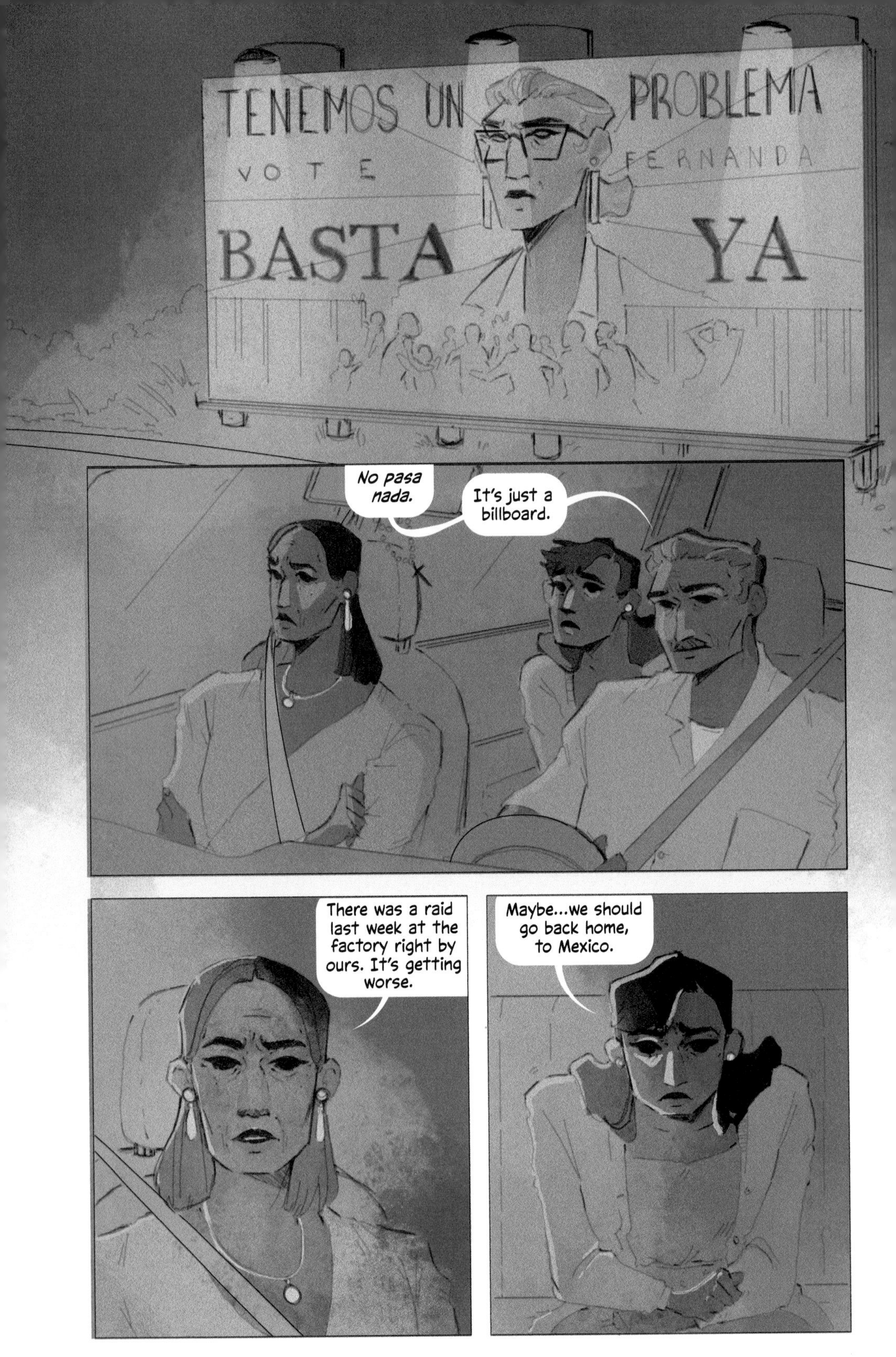
TENEMOS UN PROBLEMA
VOTE FERNANDA
BASTA YA
No pasa nada.
It's just a billboard.
There was a raid last week at the factory right by ours. It's getting worse.
Maybe...we should go back home, to Mexico.

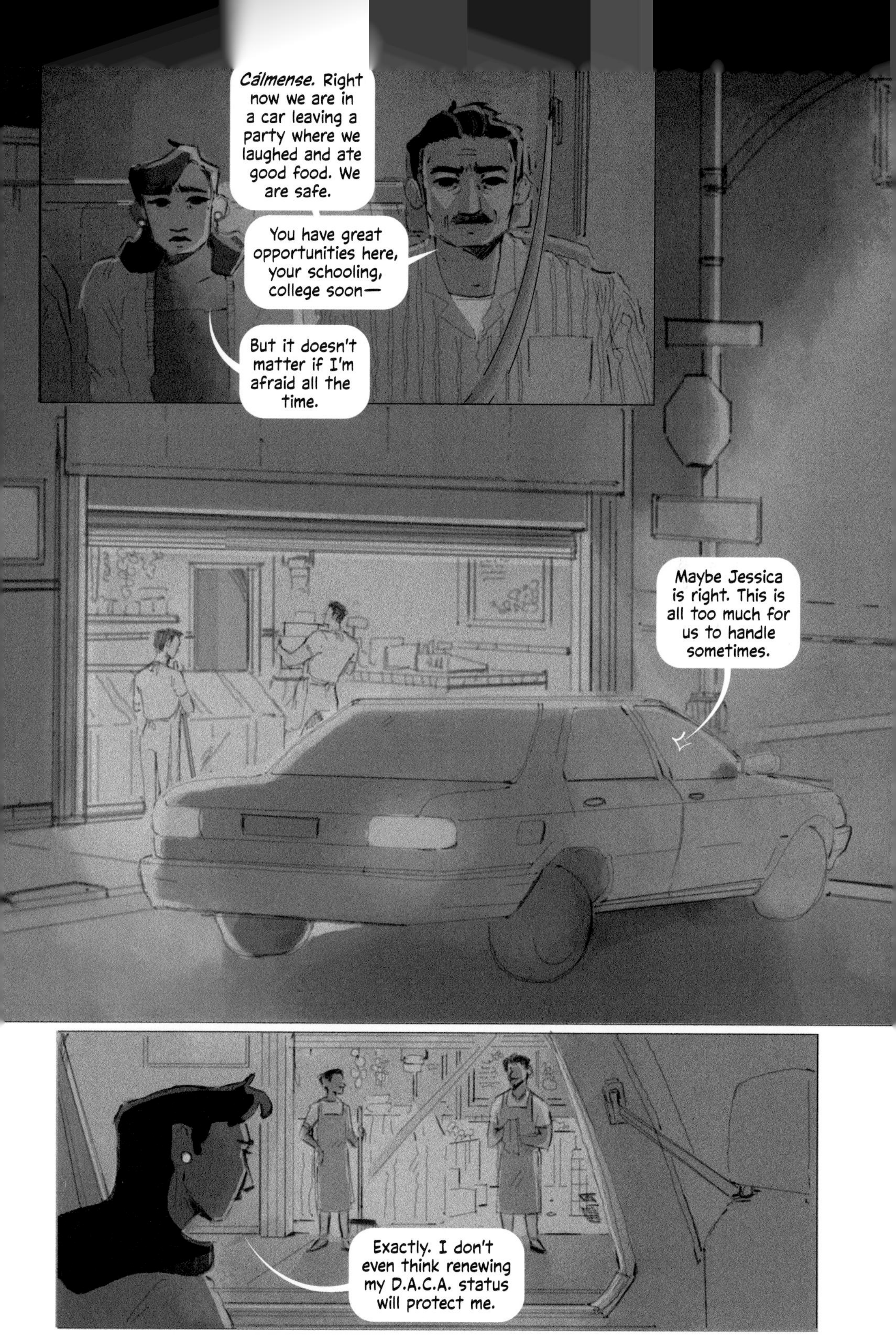
Cálmense. Right now we are in a car leaving a party where we laughed and ate good food. We are safe.
You have great opportunities here, your schooling, college soon—
But it doesn't matter if I'm afraid all the time.
Maybe Jessica is right. This is all too much for us to handle sometimes.
Exactly. I don't even think renewing my D.A.C.A. status will protect me.

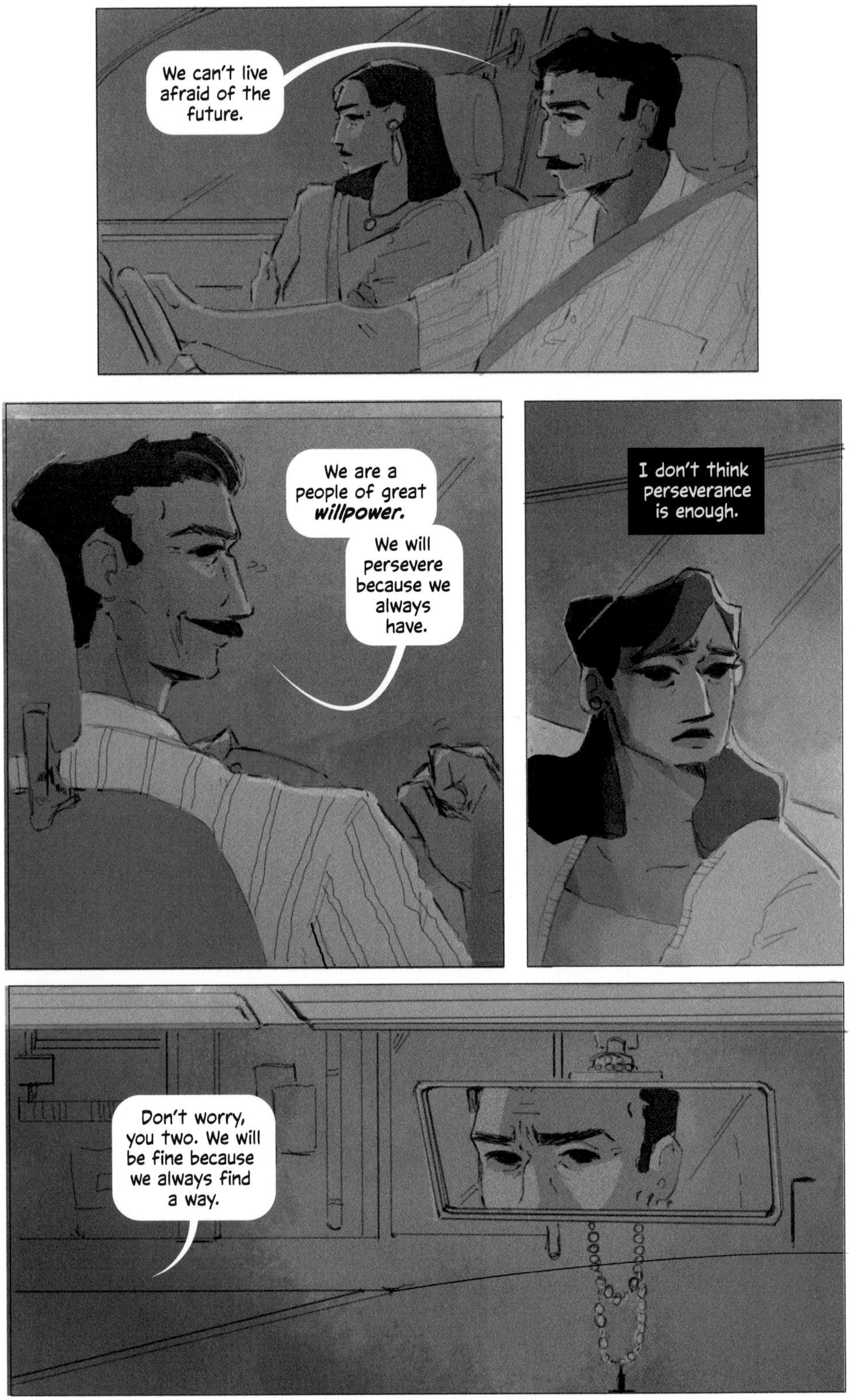
We can't live afraid of the future.
We are a people of great *willpower.*
We will persevere because we always have.
I don't think perseverance is enough.
Don't worry, you two. We will be fine because we always find a way.

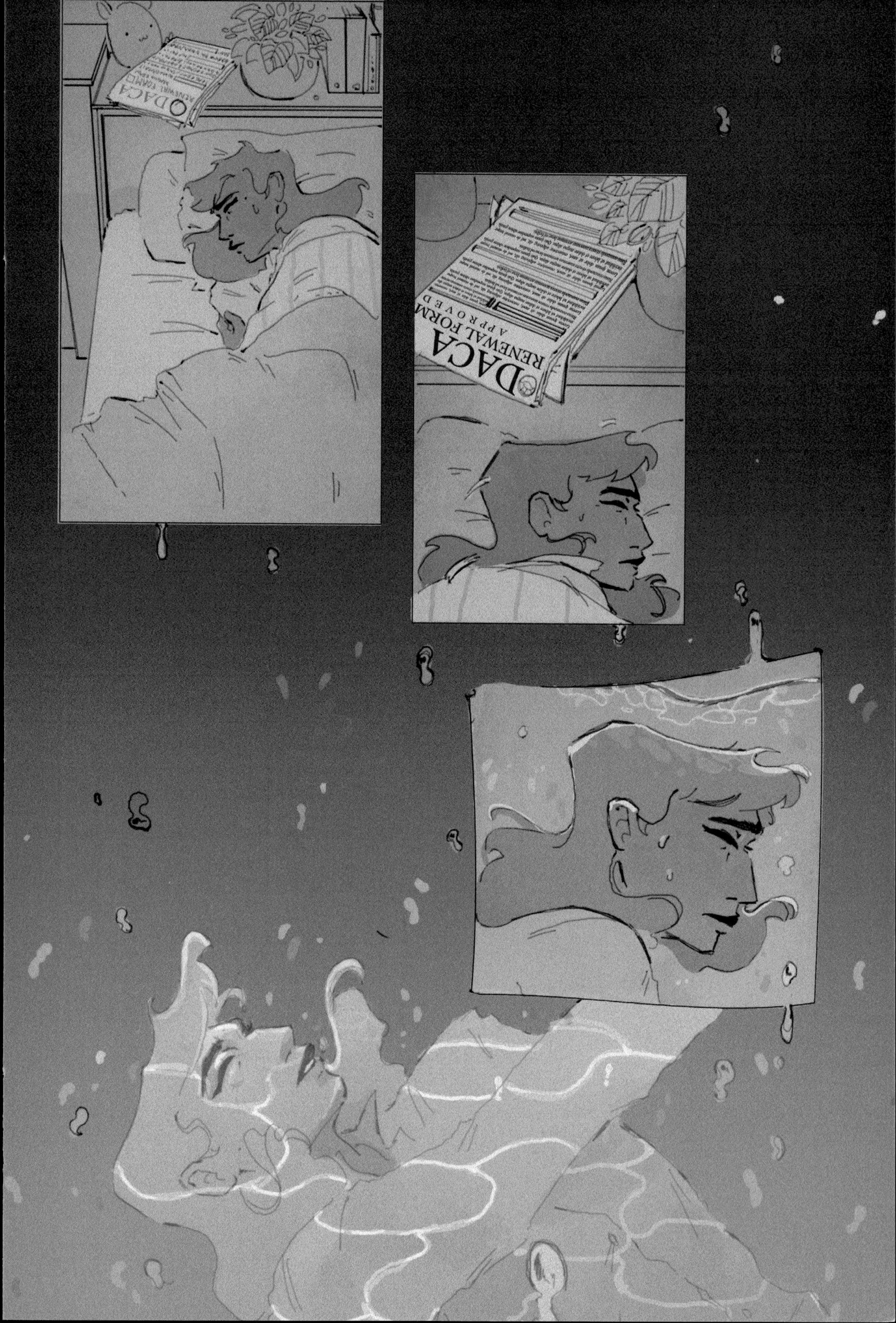

DACA
RENEWAL FORM
DACA
RENEWAL FORM
APPROVED

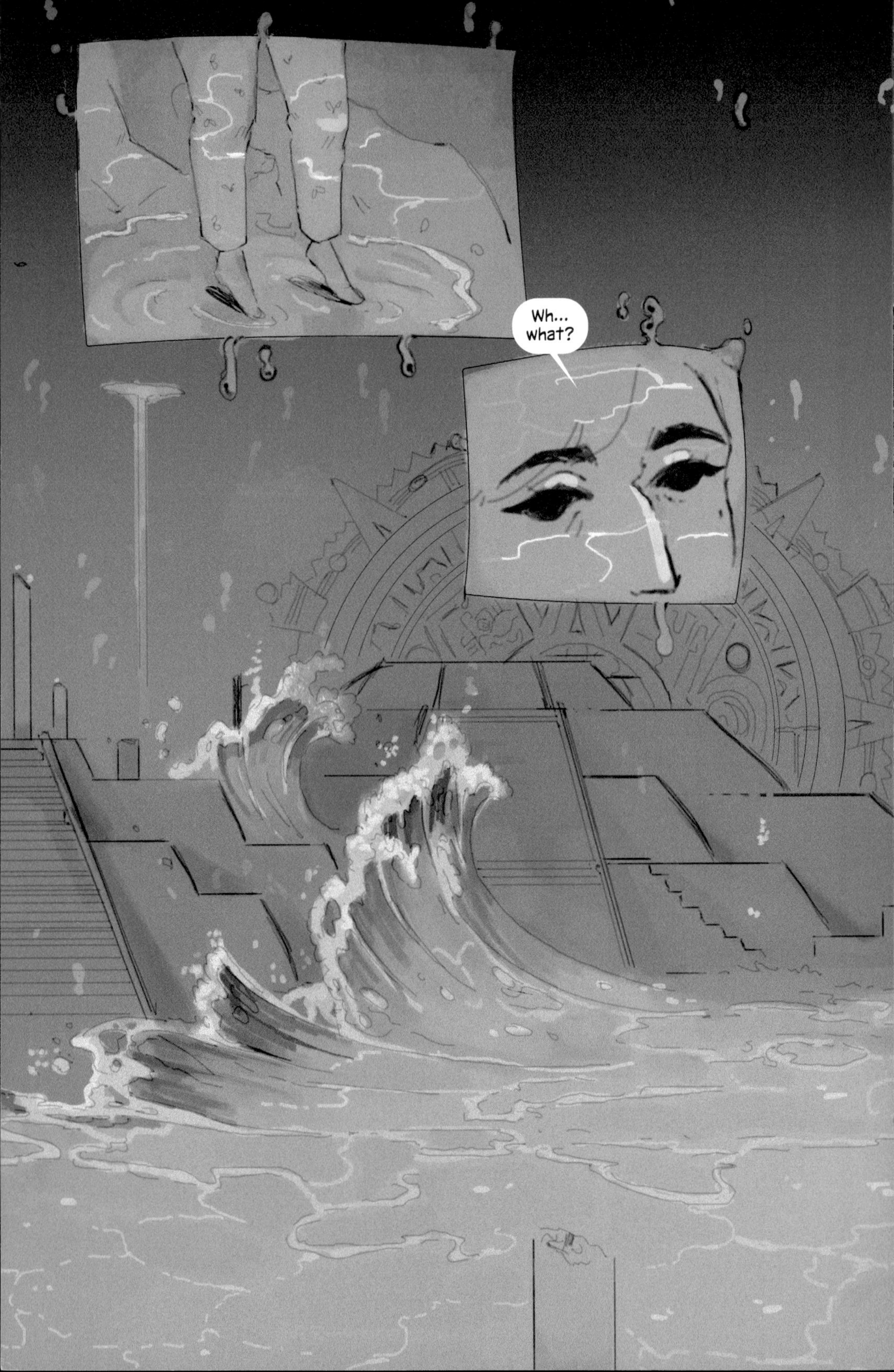
Wh... what?

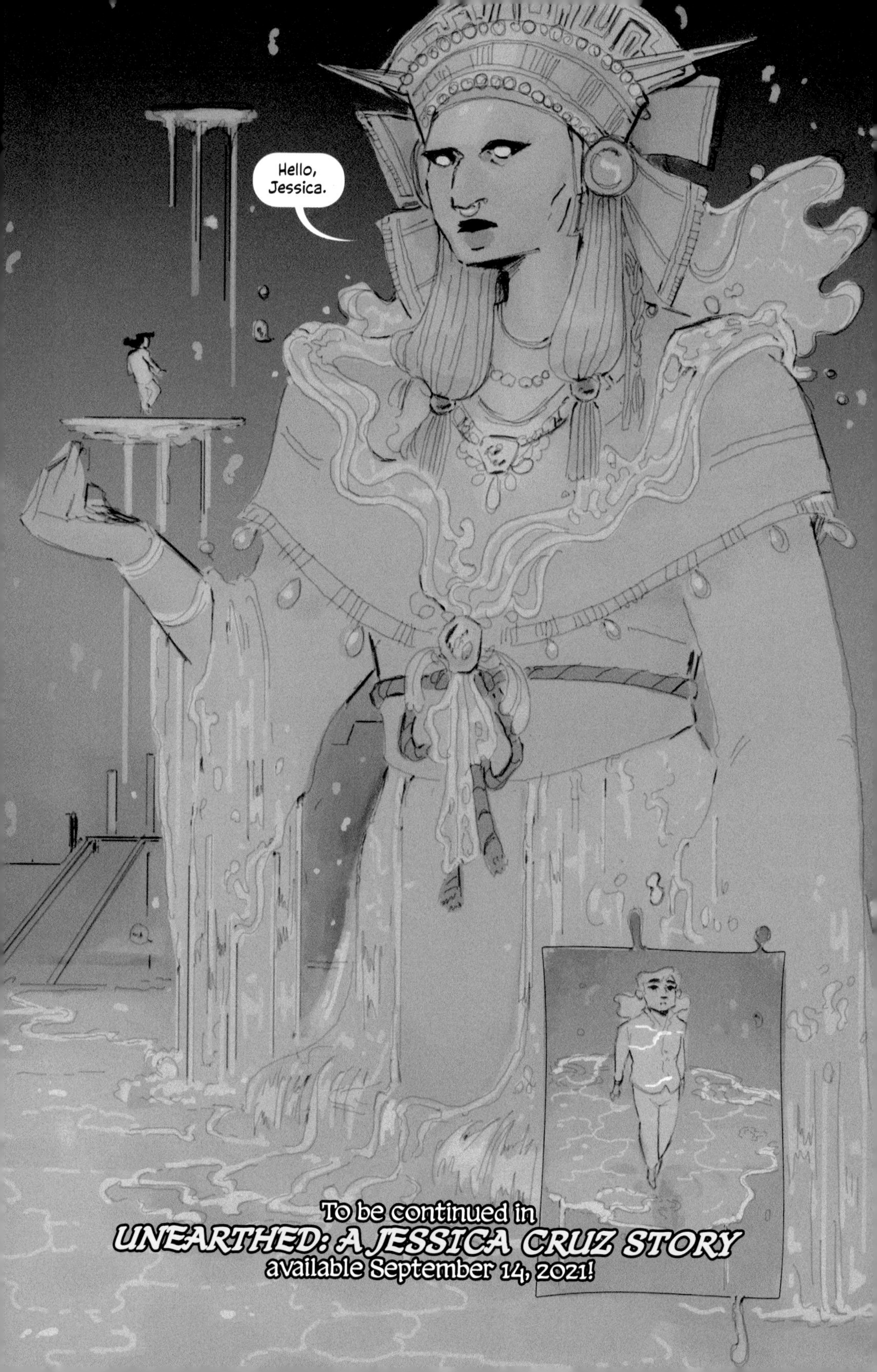
Hello, Jessica.
To be continued in
UNEARTHED: A JESSICA CRUZ STORY
available September 14, 2021!

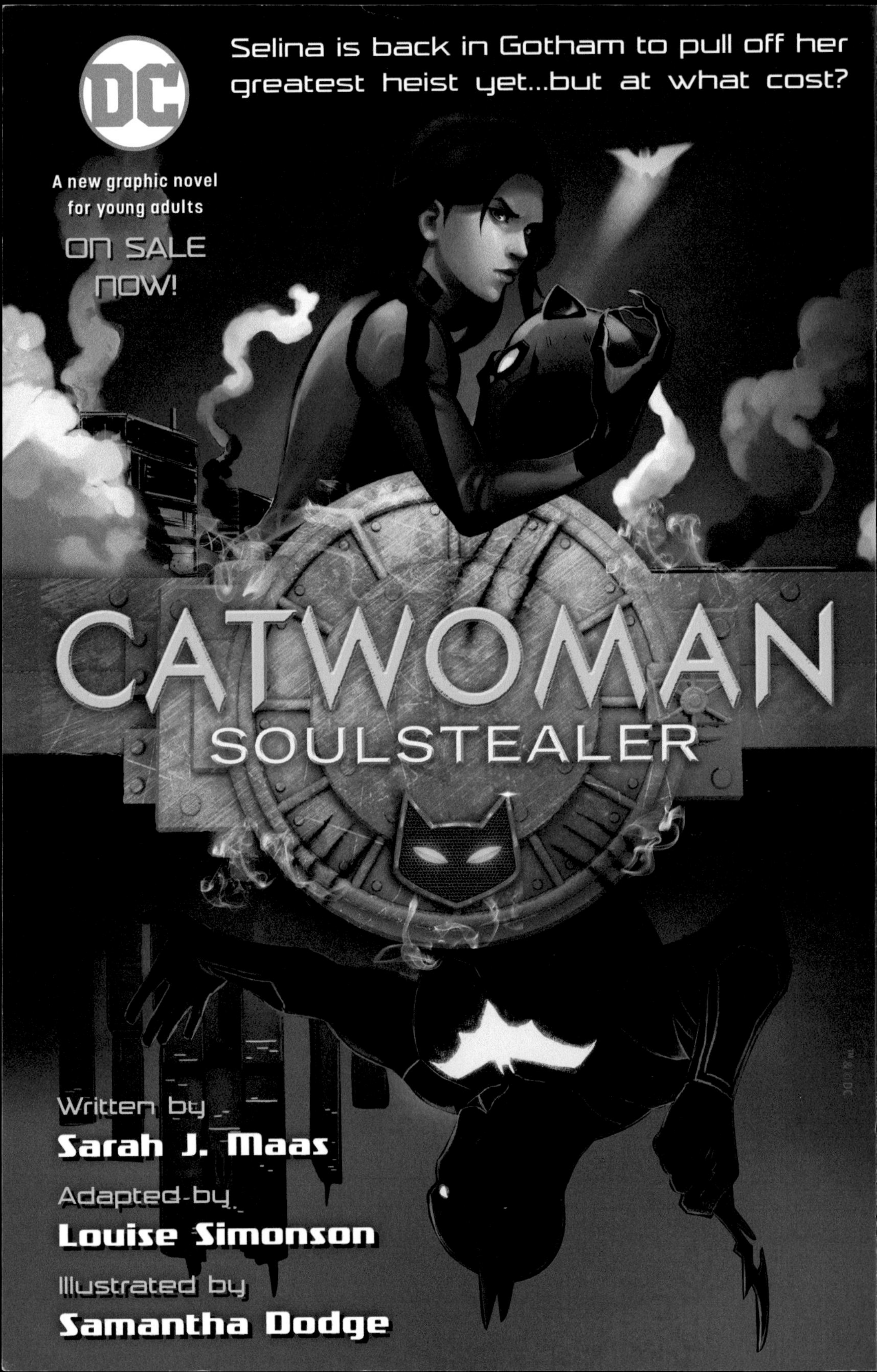

Selina is back in Gotham to pull off her greatest heist yet...but at what cost?

CATWOMAN
SOULSTEALER

Written by
Sarah J. Maas

Adapted by
Louise Simonson

Illustrated by
Samantha Dodge

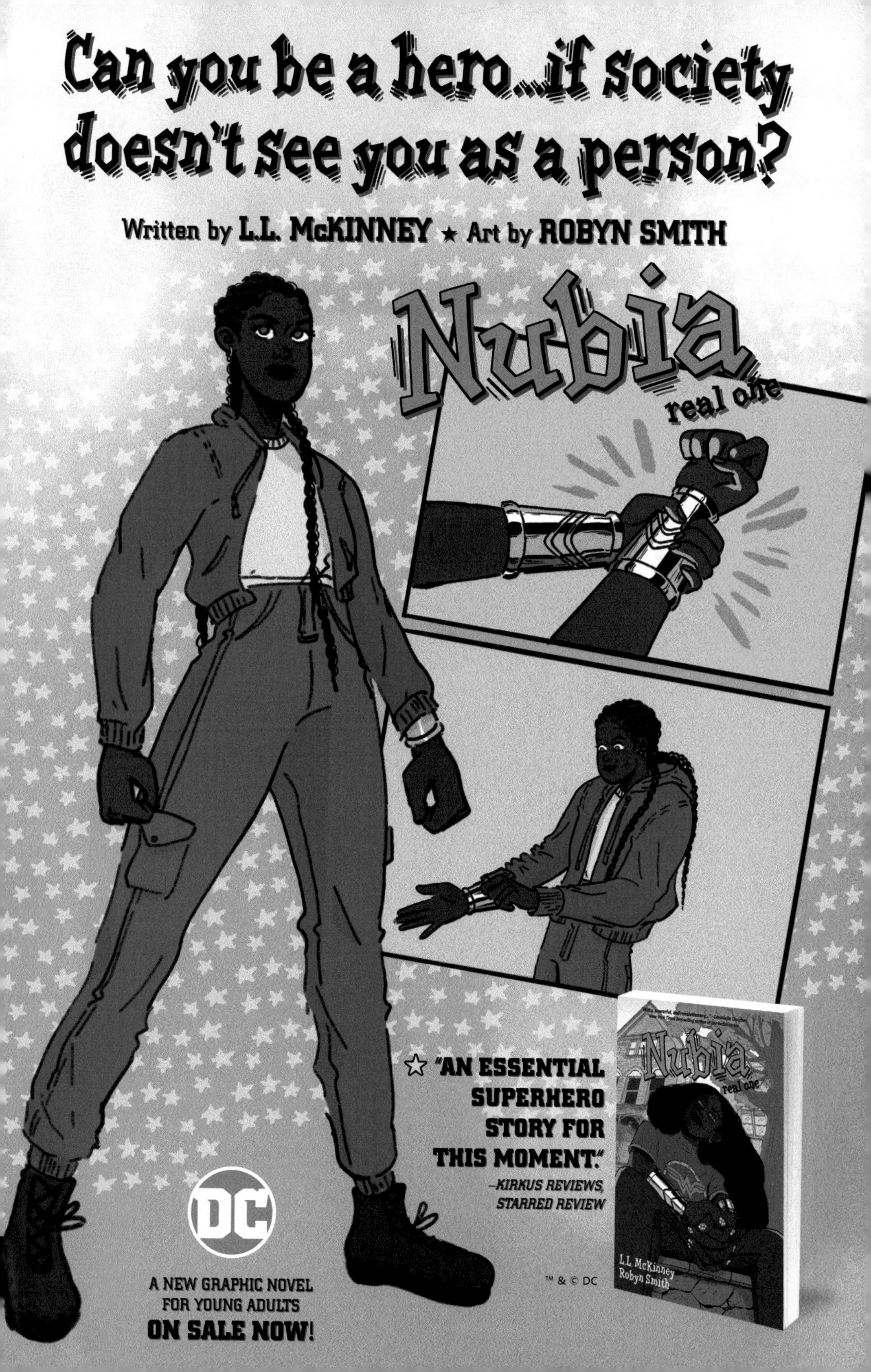

Can you be a hero...if society doesn't see you as a person?
Written by L.L. McKINNEY ★ Art by ROBYN SMITH
Nubia
real one
☆ "AN ESSENTIAL SUPERHERO STORY FOR THIS MOMENT."
–KIRKUS REVIEWS, STARRED REVIEW
Nubia
real one
L.L. McKinney
Robyn Smith
DC
A NEW GRAPHIC NOVEL FOR YOUNG ADULTS
ON SALE NOW!
™ & © DC

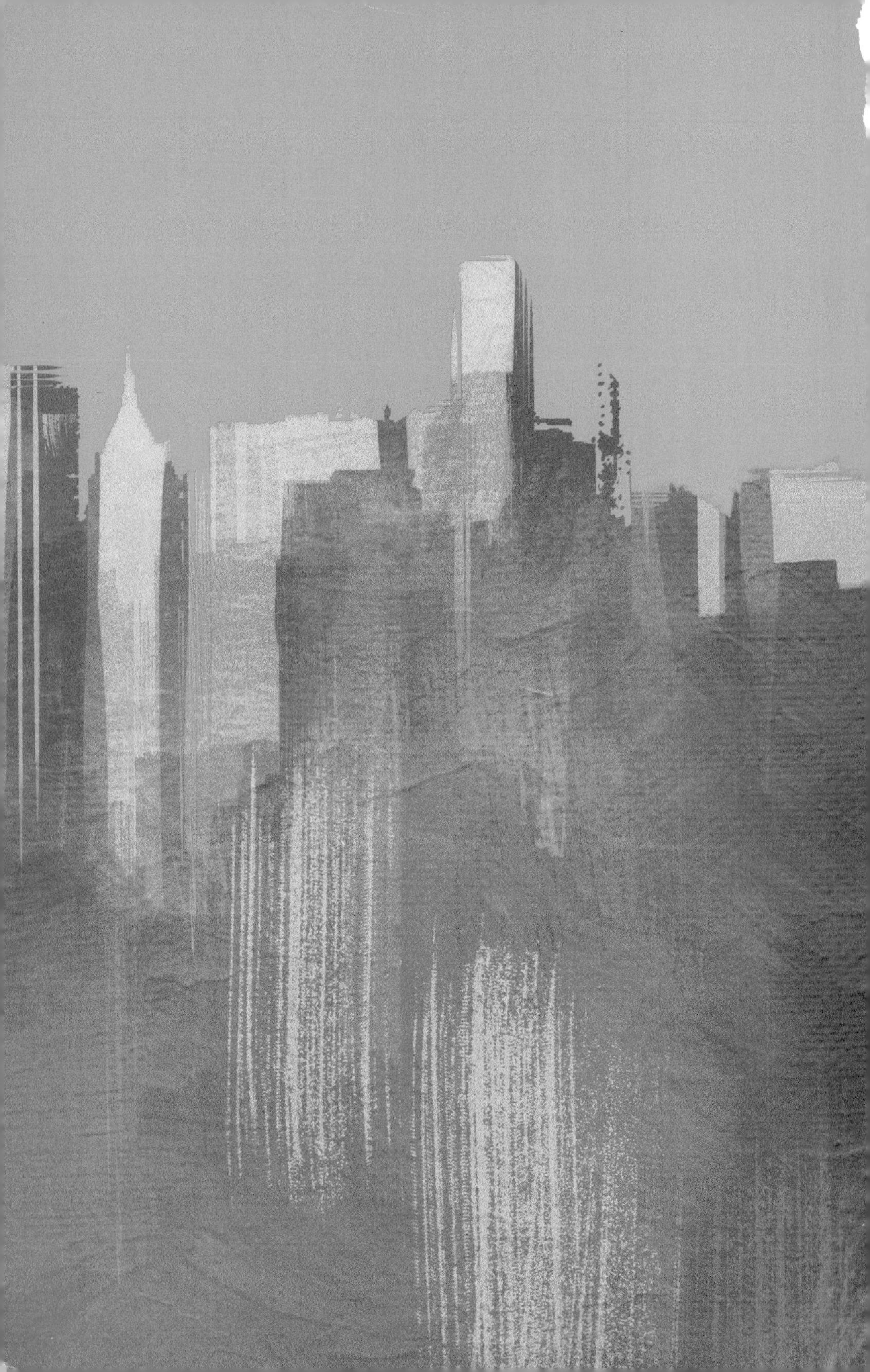